Praise for USA TODAY bestselling author

KASEY MICHAELS

"Kasey Michaels aims for the heart and never misses."
—*New York Times* bestselling author Nora Roberts

"The historical elements…imbue the novel with powerful realism that will keep readers coming back."
—*Publishers Weekly* on *A Midsummer Night's Sin*

"A poignant and highly satisfying read…
filled with simmering sensuality, subtle touches of repartee, a hero out for revenge and a heroine ripe for adventure.
You'll enjoy the ride."
—*RT Book Reviews* on *How to Tame a Lady*

"Michaels' new Regency miniseries is a joy.… You will laugh and even shed a tear over this touching romance."
—*RT Book Reviews* on *How to Tempt a Duke*

"Michaels has done it again….
Witty dialogue peppers a plot full of delectable details exposing the foibles and follies of the age."
—*Publishers Weekly* on *The Butler Did It* (starred review)

"Michaels can write everything from a lighthearted romp to a far more serious-themed romance.
[She] has outdone herself."
—*RT Book Reviews* on *A Gentleman by Any Other Name* (Top Pick)

"[A] hilarious spoof of society wedding rituals wrapped around a sensual romance filled with crackling dialogue reminiscent of *The Philadelphia Story*."
—*Publishers Weekly* on *Everything's Coming Up Rosie*

Also available from Kasey Michaels and Harlequin HQN

**Coming soon, the next sparkling novel
in the Redgraves series**

What a Lady Needs

What an
Earl
Wants

KASEY MICHAELS

HARLEQUIN®
entertain, enrich, inspire™

Recycling programs
for this product may
not exist in your area.

ISBN-13: 978-0-373-77676-4

WHAT AN EARL WANTS

Copyright © 2012 by Kathryn Seidick

Printed in U.S.A.

Dear Reader,

For this series of four books, I've stepped back in time to the year just before the Regency officially began in February of 1811.

Hellfire clubs have always interested me, as has the politics surrounding the years of the Napoleonic Wars. The thing is, however, when I read histories I immediately begin weaving plots and peopling those plots with characters who make the whole business of history more alive to me.

You could say that's the reason for all historical romances, I suppose. A love of the era you're reading about, and an interest in the well-being and happily-ever-afters of the characters the author has plunked down in the middle of all of it.

I hope you enjoy *What An Earl Wants,* and then move on to read the stories of the earl's three siblings, the headstrong Lady Katherine, the frankly adorable Valentine, and the (he believes) love-resistant Maximillian.

Happy reading...and please visit me online if you have a chance!

Kasey Michaels

With affection, to Debi Allen,
lovely lady *extraordinaire!*

What an
Earl
Wants

PROLOGUE

Kent, England
1789

THE GROUND SEEMED SUITABLE enough for the purpose. Nearly a tunnel of well-scythed lawn on the Saltwood estate, the carefully planted double row of trees serving as a rather romantical canopy overhead. Or it would have, were it summer, which it was not. In fact, it was the dead of winter and, in the false light before dawn, cold as a witch's teat.

But, then again, no colder than the heart of the man now surveying the scene, no matter how appearances would prompt the casual onlooker to dismiss him as a mindless dandy.

"I say, Burke, shouldn't there be a mist curling about our legs? Yes, I'm convinced of it. All the best early morning duels feature wispy tendrils of curling mist. I would have thought it mandatory. You'll hold my cape, of course?"

The seventeenth Earl of Saltwood, one Barry Redgrave by name, lifted his arms and negligently shrugged out of his sable-lined cape, then laughed as his horrified valet sprang forward in a panic to rescue the magnificent thing before it could hit the ground.

"Ah, well executed, Burke. My compliments." Relieved of the concealing cape, the earl was revealed to be not only a well set-up gentleman but also an exceedingly handsome man, or would be, were it not for a certain indescribable hardness about his dark blue eyes. His humor never quite seemed to reach them.

"You've drunk half the night away, my lord. You really must reconsider your timing," Burke pleaded, now struggling with both the cape and the heavy rosewood box containing the Saltwood dueling pistols.

"I must, Burke?" The earl removed his tricornered hat with the lilac plume, placed it on Burke's head at a jaunty angle, and then discreetly adjusted his snow-white periwig. "Why? Because of the lack of a mist? God's teeth, man, it's actually in the rules?"

"I don't believe so, my lord, no. I meant only that you might be a mite…foxed, my lord," the valet said, sighing.

"More than a mite, Burke," the earl acknowledged, suddenly seeming amazingly sober. "I do my best shooting when three parts drunk. But if it calms you, I promise if I see three of him I'll prudently aim for the one in the middle. However, if the unthinkable were to occur, you know what to do."

"Yes, my lord," Burke said, visibly trembling. "Everything goes to the Keeper, who also knows what to do."

"Make me pretty, Burke, and well attended by handmaidens, or I shall come back to haunt you," his lordship warned, and then laughed at his valet's horrified expression. "I'm not about to *die,* you old woman. I'll never die. Satan protects his own. Now, how does our importune Frenchman look to you? Quavering in his boots I should hope, as my reputation must surely precede me."

Burke hazarded a look toward the plain black coach and the surgeon just now conversing with the very tall man and his second. "I don't think so, no, sir. Rather, I should say, he appears *determined.* I should be remiss if I failed to mention that the duty of a second is to dissuade you from dueling, sir, and to broker a peace with the opponent's second, one that will be acceptable to both sides."

"A waste of breath best employed to cool your porridge once we're finished here, Burke. There can be no acceptable solution other than that already decided upon. The man has been poking my lady wife."

"Many have, sir," Burke said, sighing once more. "Begging your pardon, my lord, and no offense meant."

"None taken, my good man," the earl said, flourishing a snowy linen handkerchief unearthed from his magnificent lace cuff before delicately pressing it to the right corner of his mouth, so as to not disturb the small star-shaped black patch he wore at the left. "Maribel has seen more cocks than any three generations of hens. With my express encouragement, although I should point out she defied me with this one. In any event, her perfidy serves only as a convenient excuse."

"Sir?"

"Ah, my apologies. I wasn't clear enough for you, Burke? It has become apparent to me for reasons I won't bore you with at the moment that my opponent must cease drawing breath in the next quarter hour at most." The earl replaced the handkerchief and shot his cuffs before smoothing down the lilac velvet of his frock coat, putting out his right foot to admire the dull sheen of his satin breeches in the waning moonlight. "Too much, do you think, Burke? This rig-out, I mean. I didn't wish to appear shabby, although I might make a richer target in this cursed moonlight than previously considered. Well, no matter. Shall we be on with it?"

"If there is no other way?"

The earl's jawline went hard as he touched a hand to the small golden pin in the shape of a rose in full bloom stuck into the foaming lace of his cravat. "There probably exist a veritable plethora of other ways, but I have chosen this one, magnanimously granting the dishonorable creature an honorable death. Civilized murder, if you will, with man-made rules. And, of course, a lesson quite literally brought home to my lady wife, hmm, when I bring his bloodied body to her bedchamber, to fling it at her feet? Please allow my fornicating opponent first choice of weapons."

Burke did as he was told, and much too short a time later he was huddled alongside the surgeon and the other second, watching the combatants stand back-to-back, pistols raised to their shoulders, the duel about to commence. The earl appeared to be at his ease, a smile on his handsome face. The Frenchman, his chin held high, was pale-cheeked yet determined, as if knowing he was probably about to die.

Yes, Burke thought, civilized murder. All but an execution.

The earl himself began counting out the paces before they would stop, turn and shoot. "…eight…nine…*ten*."

Burke closed his eyes, only opening them again when the sound of a single shot ripped the morning silence, jolting nesting birds into startled flight. The two men now faced each other across the expanse of winter dead grass, their right arms extended, their pistols aimed at each other. Rather like statues, frozen in place.

But then the earl turned about rather stiffly, as if hunting something, and Burke looked to the opposite line of trees and the cloaked figure standing there, head and shoulders wreathed in blue smoke.

"Now there's something I hadn't expected..." the Earl of Saltwood said at last, just before he dropped to his knees and pitched forward onto the ground, dead.

CHAPTER ONE

London, England
1810

THE EIGHTEENTH EARL of Saltwood, one Gideon Redgrave by name, struck a pose just inside the entrance
of the narrow house in Jermyn Street, looking for all
the world a sketch from the *Journal des Dames et des
Modes* come to life. Not by so much as a flicker of an
eyelid did he give away the fact that he'd no idea he'd
knocked on the door of number forty-seven only to
be ushered into a gaming house. His man of business
would answer for that omission when next he saw him;
the earl didn't care for surprises.

He allowed a curtsying maid of indeterminate years
to relieve him of his hat, gloves and cane, and then
shrugged off his evening cloak, watching as the woman
folded it lovingly over her arm. A gold coin appeared
from his pocket, and he held it in front of her wide-
open blue eyes. A copper coin would do for most, but
Gideon Redgrave believed the gold coin to be an invest-
ment, one that would pay dividends when his belongings came back to him in the same pristine condition
in which they'd been handed over, rather than having
suffered the unfortunate accident of walking out the
door in his absence.

"Yours if my possessions are safely returned when I leave," he told her, and the maid bobbed her head enthusiastically before scurrying away.

He resumed his pose, meant to have all eyes come to him and their owners too busy being either envious or impressed to think up mischief while he surreptitiously acclimated himself to his surroundings. And the eighteenth Earl of Saltwood's appearance was, without fail, nothing short of enviably impressive.

The superb tailoring of his darkest blue cut-away tailcoat accentuated the snowy perfection of his silk brocade waistcoat, but not so much as it displayed the earl's astonishingly fit physique, broad shoulders, flat stomach and narrow waist. Pantaloons of formfitting buff doeskin clung lovingly to long, muscular lower limbs, ending just at the calf, above silk stockings and low-heeled black patent evening shoes.

His only ornamentation, other than the thin black grosgrain ribbon hanging about his neck and attached to the quizzing glass tucked into a small pocket of his waistcoat, was the small golden rose depicted in full bloom and no more than a single inch in circumference, nestled in the folds of his intricately tied cravat. This latter bit of fancy was a recent affectation, one that had caused comment in some circles, but to date, no one had dared speak of it to his lordship.

Thick, longish hair the color of midnight tumbled over his smooth forehead in natural curls that sent other gentlemen to their valets and the crimping iron to duplicate. Hints of his Spanish mother could be seen in the strong, aquiline nose that saved him from too much beauty, the unexpected fullness of his mouth, the sensual smolder in his dark eyes. There was an earthiness about the man not completely disguised by the trappings of fine clothes, a sense of dangerous energy tightly leashed yet always simmering just below the sophisticated surface.

In a word, the eighteenth Earl of Saltwood was intimidating. In two, if applying to the female population, he was marvelously irresistible.

When he was noticed, and he was always noticed, several of the men who recognized him for what he was, if not who he was, prudently realized they had pressing business elsewhere and quit the room in some haste. Conversations broke off abruptly. Hands stilled in the act of shuffling cards or pulling in chips. The more daring among the players turned their chairs about for a better view of what was sure to be an interesting few minutes, at the least.

One of the hostesses, the term surely taken quite as loosely as the morals of any female in the hall, ran her moist tongue around her lips rather hungrily. She gave her smiling approval of the impossible-to-disguise manly muscle between the gentleman's thighs and took two steps forward, tugging down on the already low neckline of her cherry-red gown before she was grabbed at the elbow and hastily pulled back.

"For Lord's sake, Mildred, control yourself. He's not here for that."

Gideon Redgrave extracted his chased-gold quizzing glass, raising it to one eye, and slowly surveyed the surprisingly well-lit and clean yet faintly down-at-the-heels room before allowing his gaze to halt and hold on the woman who had just spoken.

She advanced on him with some purpose, the light of confrontation in her sherry-brown eyes, her fairly remarkable chin tilted up as if she had somehow raised the battle flag and was announcing her intention to unleash a broadside. But then she stopped, smiled and dropped into a mocking curtsy.

"Lord Saltwood," she intoned quietly, her voice slightly husky, as if she might be whispering risqué endearments in the privacy of a candlelit boudoir, "I've been expecting you. Do you prefer a public airing of our differences, or would you care to retire to my apartments for our chat?"

She was...magnificent. Gideon could think of no other description. Taller than most women, slim almost to the point of thinness, yet subtly curved. Hair the color of flame against the severity of her high-necked black gown, skin the color of finest ivory. The eyes, mocking, the mouth, full and wide...and *knowing*. No sane man could look at her without imagining his fingers tangling in that mass of warm curls tumbling around her shoulders, sinking himself deep between her thighs, plunging into the promised fire as she wrapped long legs up high around him.

Which, of course, would be total madness.

Gideon's eyes widened fractionally, just enough to dislodge the glass, and he deftly caught it by its ribbon and replaced it in his pocket. "You've the advantage of me, madam. You are—?"

"Exactly who you think I am, my lord," she returned, her wide smile frosting only slightly about the edges. "And now that you and your glowering face have

served to quite ruin what had promised to be a profitable evening, you will please follow me."

She turned sharply, the scent of sweet lavender tick-
ling his nostrils as her fiery mane, seeming much too
heavy for her slim neck, swung about as if in a belated
attempt to catch up with her. Her modest gown, a stiff,
unyielding taffeta so in contrast to the riot of tumbling
curls, rustled as she walked.

"Here now, where do you think you're—?"

She raised her hand to the faintly rotund, gray-haired
man who had stepped out from behind the faro table,
his eyes on the earl as if measuring his chances of
knocking him down. Though he clearly found them
miniscule, he straightened his shoulders, no doubt prepared to give his best if asked. "Simply carry on, Richard, if you please. I'm fine."

"Yes, you do that, Richard," Gideon drawled as
he and the woman easily made their way through the
throng of patrons who had all stepped back to afford
them a pathway. He was painfully aware he somehow
had been put in the ignoble position of potential de-
spoiler of virgins, which was above everything ludicrous. "Your employer's virtue is safe with me."

A young man, looking fresh from the country and
obviously a fellow with more hair than wit, dared to
chuckle at this remark. "There's virtue here? Stap me, I
wouldn't have come if it was *virtue* I was looking for."

"Stubble it, Figgins," the man next to him warned,
saving Gideon the trouble of having to turn back and
waste a dark stare on the impudent puppy. "Don't you
know who that is? The fella's a Redgrave, for God's
sakes. He spits bigger'n you."

Gideon suppressed a smile. He hadn't heard that one before. But how convenient that his reputation preceded him; it made life so much easier.

He stepped forward as he realized the woman had stopped in front of a baize door, clearly waiting on him to open it for her. Liked to play at the lady, it would seem, straight down to the prim black gown and the erect nature of her posture. Pity for her that her hair and eyes and mouth—and that voice—hadn't been informed of this preferred pretense.

"Oh, please, allow me," he drawled sarcastically, bowing her ahead of him as he depressed the latch, before following her up a long, steep flight of stairs surprisingly located just on the other side of the door. The stairs were between two walls and just well lit enough for him to be able to enjoy the sway of her bottom as she climbed ahead of him, holding up her stiff skirts, affording him a tantalizing glimpse of slim ankles, as well. Ah, and a hint of calf. Lovely.

The woman was contradiction after contradiction. Buttoned nearly to her chin, yet her slippers were silver-heeled black satin. He could imagine himself kissing them from her feet and then rolling down her hose, just so far, because he enjoyed the feel of silk-encased legs on his back....

He was forced to hold the banister as she stopped, extracting a key from a pocket in her gown and slipping it into the lock. He'd wondered about that, the easy access to the staircase, and how many times in the course of an evening this route might be traveled by patrons and the women.

As if to assure him, she stepped inside the apartments, motioning for him to close the door behind him as she said, "No one is allowed here. We won't be disturbed. Would you care for wine, or would you rather simply be on with it?"

"That's direct, in any case. Be on with what, madam? I had thought I was calling at a private residence, the object conversation. Seeing the nature of this house, the possibilities have become almost limitless. Not that I'm not tempted."

She lit a taper and gracefully moved about the room, lighting candles. "You flatter yourself, my lord, and insult me. I'm not in such dire need of funds. We turn cards here, nothing else."

Gideon sat himself down on a nearby chair, deciding she could remain standing if she so wished, but he was going to make himself comfortable. Redgraves always made themselves comfortable; and the more comfortable they looked, the more on guard any sane person in their midst became. "You might explain that to— Mildred, was it?" he suggested amicably.

He did his best not to blink as she toed off the silver-heeled shoes and kicked them beneath a table as if happy to be rid of them. "I cannot presume to control the world, my lord, only the small portion of it beneath this roof. Mildred and the others make their own arrangements as to what they do outside this establishment."

"That's…civilized. So, a gaming hell, but no brothel. A fine line between disreputable and despicable. Am I to perhaps applaud?"

She looked at him, long and hard, and then reached up both hands and deftly twisted the heavy mass of curls into a knot atop her head before walking over to a small drinks table holding a single decanter of wine. "I don't particularly care what you do, my lord," she said as she poured some of the light amber liquid into a single glass before turning to face him. "As long as you relinquish guardianship of my brother to me."

"Oh, yes, Miss Collier, the demand presented to me via your solicitor. I can readily see the eminent sense in that. Clearly a fit place for the boy."

"The name is Linden, my lord. *Mrs*. Linden. I'm a widow."

Gideon could not suppress his smile this time. "Of course you are. How very proper. My apologies."

"You can take your apologies, my lord, and stuff them in your...ear," she said, and then turned her back to him as she lifted the glass to her lips. She didn't sip; she drank. He could see that her hand trembled slightly as she lowered the empty glass to the tabletop. The wine was for courage, clearly. He almost felt sorry for her.

Almost.

But then she turned back to him, her eyes shining in the light of the candles. "We've begun badly, haven't we? Are you certain you don't care for a glass of wine?"

"A lady shouldn't drink alone, I suppose. Very well." Gideon got to his feet and availed himself of the decanter. The wine, when he tasted it, was unexpectedly good, when he'd assumed it would be cheap and bitter. "Do you have a first name, madam?"

The question seemed to surprise her. "Why would you— Yes. Yes, I do. Jessica."

"Preferable to either Linden or Collier. Very well.

My condolences on your recent loss, *Jessica*. I was remiss in not stating that at the outset."

"My father's death means nothing to me, my lord, as we'd been estranged for several years. But, thank you. I only wish to become reacquainted with my brother."

"Half brother," Gideon corrected. "The son of your father and your stepmother, also sadly deceased. You have no questions about that sad event?"

Jessica shrugged her shoulders. "No. Should I? When I read about their deaths in the *Times,* an accident with their coach was mentioned. I'm only glad Adam was away at school, and not in the coach with them."

"All right," Gideon said, looking at her carefully. "There's still the matter of a rather large fortune, not to mention the Sussex estate. All of it in trust for your half brother, who was not estranged from his parents."

"That's also of no concern to me. I support myself."

"Clearly," Gideon said, casting his gaze around the sparsely furnished room. "Bilking raw youths in town on a spree profitable, is it?"

"We don't *bilk* anyone, my lord. We don't allow it. If we see some fool gaming too deep, he's sent on his way."

"Vowing to sin no more, I'll assume, his ears still ringing from the stern lecture you've administered."

Jessica looked at him unblinkingly, her brown eyes raking him from head to toe before seemingly settling on his chest; perhaps she wouldn't be so brave if she looked into his eyes. "I don't like you. *Gideon.*"

"I can't imagine why not. Another man wouldn't have answered your summons. I'll admit to curiosity being my motive for obliging you, but please don't hold that against me."

"And it only took you a month, and then you arrived on my doorstep at this ungodly hour of the night, clearly as an afterthought. Or perhaps your planned evening turned out to be a bore, leaving you at loose ends? I'm sorry, I suppose I should be flattered."

She turned her back to him once more, bending her neck forward. "You may as well be of some use. If you could help with these buttons? Doreen is still busy at the front door, and I'm near to choking."

Gideon raised one well-defined eyebrow as he weighed the invitation, considering its benefits, its pitfalls…her motives. "Very well," he said, placing his wineglass next to hers. "I've played at lady's maid a time or two."

"I'm certain you have played at many things. Tonight, however, you'll have to content yourself with a very limited role."

"You're a very trusting woman, Jessica," he said as he deftly—he did everything deftly—slipped the first half-dozen buttons from their moorings. With the release of every button, he made sure his knuckles came in contact with each new inch of ivory skin revealed to him. Even in the candlelight he could see where the gown had chafed that soft skin; no wonder she longed to be shed of it.

Still, he took his time with the buttons until, the gown now falling open almost entirely to her waist, she stepped away from him just as he considered the merits of running his fingertips down the graceful line of her spine.

"Thank you. If you'll excuse me for a moment while I rid myself of this scratchy monstrosity?"

"I'll excuse you for any number of things, my dear, as long as you're not gone above a minute. You wear no chemise?"

"As you're already aware," she answered, throwing the words at him over her shoulder, bare now as her gown began to slip slightly. "I loathe encumbrances."

She disappeared into another room, leaving Gideon to wonder why a woman who so disliked encumbrances had buttoned herself up into a black taffeta prison. Did she think the gown made her look dowdy? Untouchable? Perhaps even matronly? If so, she had missed the mark on every point.

A widow. He hadn't expected less from her than that obvious clunker; there wasn't a madam in all of London who wasn't the impecunious widow of some soldier hero, making her way in the world as best she could.

And, if he was lucky yet tonight—he would be inevitably, in any case—she was about to *make her way* with him, in hopes of her charms rendering him imbecilic to the point of granting her request to take over the guardianship of her half brother.

Or, more to the point, guardianship of her half brother's considerable fortune.

A month ago he had roundly cursed Turner Collier for having lacked the good common sense to have altered his decades-old will, leaving guardianship of his progeny to his old chum, the Earl of Saltwood. Perhaps Collier had thought himself immortal, which should hardly have been the case, considering what had happened to his old chum.

But there'd been nothing else for it, not according to Gideon's solicitor, who had notified him that he had gratefully ended his guardianship of Alana Wallingford upon her recent marriage, just to be saddled with yet another ward a few months later.

At least this time there would be no worries over fortune hunters or midnight elopements or any such nonsense. No, this time his worries would be for reckless starts, idiotic wagers, juvenile hijinks and hauling the boy out of bear-baitings, cockfights and gaming hells such as the one owned by the youth's own half sister.

All while the whispers went on behind his back. There'd been anonymous wagers penned in the betting book at White's on the odds of Gideon forcing Alana into marriage with him in order to gain her fortune. Whispered hints Alana's father, Gideon's very good friend, had been murdered within months of naming Gideon as his only child's guardian. There definitely had been suggestions as to whom that murderer might be.

Now there had been a second "unfortunate coaching accident" directly impacting the Earl of Saltwood. And another wealthy orphan placed into his care immediately after that "accident." Coincidence? Many didn't think so.

After all, Gideon was a Redgrave. And everybody knew about those Redgraves. Wild, arrogant, dangerous, if always somewhat delicious. Why, look at the father, the mother; there was a scandal no amount of time could fade from the consciousness of God-fearing people. Even the dowager countess remained both a force to be reckoned with and a constant source of whispered mischief and shocking behavior. Nothing was beneath them, even as they believed nothing and no one above them....

"Shall we return to the wars, Gideon?"

He blinked away his thoughts and turned to look at Jessica Linden, who had somehow reappeared without his notice. She was clad now in a dark maroon silk banyan with a black shawl collar and quilted cuffs that fell below her fingertips. The hem of the thing puddled around her bare feet. Once again her curls tumbled past her shoulders, a perfect frame for her fine, enchanting features. For a tall woman, she suddenly seemed small, delicate, even fragile.

Clearly an illusion.

"My late husband's. I keep it as a reminder," she said, raising her arms enough that the cuffs fell back to expose her slim wrists. "Shall we sit? My feet persist in feeling the pinch of those dreadful shoes."

He gestured to the overstuffed couch to his left, and she all but collapsed into it, immediately drawing her legs up beside her to begin rubbing at one narrow bare foot. The collar of the banyan gaped for an enticing moment, gifting him with a tantalizing glimpse of small, perfect breasts. Clearly she was naked beneath the silk.

The woman was as innocent as a viper.

"How is Adam?" she asked before he could think of a damn thing to say that didn't include an invitation to return to her bedchamber, this time in his company. "I haven't seen him in more than five years. He was just about to be sent off to school, as I recall the moment. What was he? Twelve? Yes, that was it, as I was all of eighteen. He cried so, to leave me."

Gideon began doing quick mental arithmetic. "Making you a woman of three and twenty? A young widow."

"Ah, but positively ancient in experience, and closer to four and twenty in reality. And you? Edging in on a hundred, I would think, if we're to speak of experience. You've quite the reputation, Gideon."

"Only partially earned, I assure you," he told her as he retook his chair and crossed one leg over the other, looking very much at his ease while his mind raced. "But to answer your question, your half brother is well and safe and here in London. I've hired a keeper for him rather than return him to school before next term."

Jessica nodded. "That's only fitting. He's in mourning."

"He is? Perhaps someone ought to explain that to him. All I hear, secondhand through said keeper, is how fatigued he is with twiddling his thumbs while the entire world goes merrily along just outside the door, without him."

She smiled at that, and Gideon knew himself to be grateful he was already sitting down, for she had a wide, unaffected smile that could knock a man straight off his feet.

"A handful, is he? Good. As our father's son, it could have gone either way. I'm gratified to learn his spirit wasn't crushed."

Now this was interesting. "I barely knew the man, as he was a contemporary of my father's. He was a demanding parent?"

"We'll speak with the gloves off, as I see no sense in dissembling. After all, I've heard the rumors about your own father, and the two men were friends. James

Linden, fairly ancient, more than a little mean when in his cups, and a lazy waste of talent, was the lesser of two evils, and here I am. Disowned, widowed, but self-sufficient. Perfectly capable of taking on the guardianship of my brother until he reaches his majority. The last place I want him is anywhere our father wanted him, under the control of anyone he thought *fitting*." She directed a disconcerting glare toward his cravat. "Do you understand now, *Gideon?*"

He touched his hand to the golden rose in his cravat before he realized what he'd done and quickly got to his feet. "You had my pity, Jessica, until the end. I'm many things, but I am not my father."

"No, I suppose you aren't. You haven't yet tried to seduce me, and after all my clumsy efforts to the contrary. Geld you, did he? No, I don't think so. You want me, that's obvious enough."

At last, Gideon understood the whole of it. He waved his hand in front of him, indicating her pose, the banyan, even her nakedness beneath the silk, the glass of wine that had been raised to her lips by a trembling hand; a drink for courage. "You've got a weapon somewhere about you, don't you?"

"Not the complete fool, are you? Very well. Only a very small pistol, holding but a single shot, but deadly, if it became necessary. I can use it to much more advantage than James ever could, even though he taught me. And before you ask, yes, I was willing to trade my body for your agreement to relinquish your guardianship of Adam, within limits, of course." She stood up, chin high, sherry-brown eyes locked with his, her hands going to the silk tie at her waist. "I still am."

He decided it would be safer to be insulted. "And I repeat, madam, I am not my father."

She tilted her head to one side. "You aren't? Your stickpin says differently. That particular rose, by any other name, Gideon, sends out the same stink."

Gideon's jaw set tightly. What in bloody hell was going on here? "You know about that?"

"I know about the Society, yes," she repeated, the light of battle leaving her eyes, to be replaced by a sadness that was nearly palpable. "Among my late husband's many failings was a tendency to run his mouth when he was in his cups. The mark of membership in a most exclusive group of rascals. A flower, in point of fact a golden rose, to commemorate a deflowering, plucking the bud as it were, bringing it into full bloom. But you wear it, you know what it is, what you did to *earn* it."

"The pin was my father's. The rest was rumor or, more probably, bravado," Gideon heard himself saying, even as he hoped he was speaking truth. "It was nothing like that. Only drunken fools and their games, thinking themselves some damned hellfire club. It was all cloaks and oaths of secrecy and more drunkenness and willing prostitutes than anything else. Simply grandiose talk, and all a long time ago."

Her smile was sad, almost as if she pitied him. "So you say. Thanks to James, I never learned for certain. Your father had been long dead by then, your family estate no longer their gathering place. But whatever the Society was, it didn't end with him. You truly profess to not know that? It went on five years ago, it may still go on. If I recall correctly, my father was not too many years above sixty when he died. James was not much younger when we married, and still…capable."

One more mention of James Linden, and Gideon believed he might go dig up the man, just so he could bash in his skull with the shovel.

"No. You're wrong. Everything ended with my father's death. This is something else."

"*This,* Gideon? Are we speaking at cross purposes? What is *this?*"

Gideon was seldom the loser in any verbal exchange, but the more he said, the more control of their conversation he seemed to be ceding to her. He didn't much care for the feeling.

"I'll have my town carriage sent for you tomorrow at eleven, to bring you to Portman Square to see your brother. Kindly outfit yourself accordingly."

At last he seemed to shock her, put her off her stride. But not for long. "Would that include wearing a dark veil to conceal my face, or will the carriage be driven directly around to the mews, and the servants' entrance?"

Not before time, he realized, Gideon decided he'd had enough.

He closed the distance between them in two short steps, taking hold of her right wrist before she could successfully reach into the slightly drooping pocket that had given away the location of her pistol.

With his free hand he delved into the pocket and withdrew a small silver pistol, indeed a favorite of cardsharps. He forcefully turned her hand over and pressed the thing in her palm.

"Go on, you idiot woman. I'm about to *ravish* you. Shoot me."

She made no move to close her fingers around the weapon. "You don't mean that."

"Don't I? Are you sure? I can have anything I want from you, Jessica Linden, any time I want it. Most men could. Get rid of that toy before somebody turns it on you. I don't know what all this James Linden of yours taught you over and above honing that sharp tongue of yours, but he should have pointed out that you can't bluff worth a damn."

He saw the tears standing in her magnificent eyes but chose to ignore them. God save him from fools, most especially well-intentioned martyrs who always seemed to think right was on their side and justice would prevail. He turned and walked away from her, exposing his back to her, not stopping until his hand was on the latch of the door leading to the stairs.

"At eleven, Jessica. And if you dare insult me by wearing that black monstrosity or anything like it, I'll tear it off you myself. Understood?"

He'd barely closed the door behind him when the sound of what he presumed to be the derringer hitting the wood brought a smile to his face. He rather doubted James Linden taught her how to do that. No, that was a purely female reaction, and if there was one thing Jessica Linden was, it was female.

CHAPTER TWO

As she watched Richard's meticulous recounting of the previous night's profits, Jessica was twice forced to cover a yawn with her hand, both times earning a reproving look from her friend and business partner.

"Forgive me, Richard," she said as he finished at last. "I didn't sleep well last night, I'm afraid."

"He was upstairs here for some time, Jess. He upset you."

"He didn't make me happy, I'll agree to that," she said as she locked the satisfyingly full strongbox. "This isn't going to be easy."

"It shouldn't *be* at all. Surely the boy is old enough to mind himself? I was out on my own before I was ten, just a kiddie, making my own way."

"Indeed you were," Jessica agreed, having heard the story of Richard's past more than a few times, in more than a few versions, with probably none of them completely true. "But when you have money, the law sees things differently. Adam doesn't reach his legal majority for another three years, and for all I know won't receive control over his inheritance even then. It all depends on the terms of our father's will."

"And in the meantime, he's stuck with those queer buggers, the Redgraves. Nasty piece of work, that fellow last night, for all his fine clothes. I've seen eyes like that before. Slice your throat for you as soon as look at you. Just uses a clean knife."

Jessica laughed softly as she returned the strongbox to its hidey-hole beneath the floorboards. She disliked keeping so much money in the house, but they had to be prepared for losses as well as profit.

She stood back as Richard rolled the rug down over the floorboards. "We were right to finally come here to London. So many foolish young men eager to be rid of their quarterly allowance. Our profits astound even me. Only a few more months, Richard, and we can have our inn. Are you still set on Cambridge? Of late I've been thinking of someplace more to the south, nearer the Channel. Perhaps even a port city?"

"With that Bonaparte scum running amok and crowing as how he's coming here any day? No, Jess, no ports for the likes of me. Waking up one morning with a bunch of Froggies parading through the town? I don't think so. It's good English joints of beef we'll be serving up from our kitchen, not slimy snails slipping and sliding off the plate."

"Bonaparte isn't going to invade, Richard. He's much too busy with his new Austrian wife. She'll bring him low one day, you know. You'd think the man would be a better student of history. Women are always the downfall of powerful men, one way or another." She sent him a wide smile. "It's what we do."

Richard stood up, preparing to go downstairs to his small room at the back of the house they'd rented only a few short months previously. "And is that what you're planning to do with the Earl of Saltwood? I'd go easy with any such notion, I would. The man's no fool. I saw it in—"

"In his eyes. Yes, I remember. I'm not saying I'm out to destroy him, for goodness' sake. All he has to do is give me my brother. He couldn't want him."

"Nor his inheritance," Richard told her. "Man's rich as that Croesus fellow. But if it's some gauntlet you threw down to the earl, and knowing you it was, you've put his back up, so's now he wouldn't give you a crust of bread, just because he knows you want it. Better to ply some wiles or some such thing, not that I'm saying you should."

Jessica averted her head, sure her cheeks were flaming, damn her fair coloring. "He's got a mistress set up at the bottom of Mount Street."

"And another tucked into a bang-up to the echo flat in Curzon Street, some Covent Garden warbler. Then there's his other lady birds, the widow Orford and Lady Dunmore, or so I heard it told just last night, while the two of you were up here and the gossip was flying about downstairs like shuttlecocks in a high wind. Sets them up like dominos, tips them over when he's done with them, leaving them their fond memories, since not a one of them ever had a bad word to say about him, not any of the dozens of them. Dozens, Jessica. So, never mind what I said about wiles. You want this one to do your bidding, don't do his. That's what I'm thinking."

"You know I've never—"

"After Jamie Linden, who would?" Richard said, sighing. "But I know you, and you *dangled,* didn't you? Made promises you'd no intention of keeping, thinking yourself smarter than any man. Dangerous business, that, with one like Saltwood. Better to walk away now. The boy'll come to no harm. Saltwood's no fool. He has to know everyone's watching him."

"Because he's a Redgrave."

"Because he's his father's son, yes. You know what they say."

Jessica walked over to the pier glass and inspected her reflection. "His father was a rake and a libertine, and when he called out his wife's lover in a duel, she hid herself nearby and shot him in the back before she and her lover fled to the continent, leaving her children behind as if they didn't matter to her. Not that she was any better than he was in any event, having had more lovers than most of us have fingers and toes. Yes, I've heard it all. I would suppose it was either Saltwood buries himself in the cellars on his estate to hide his shame or he becomes what he's clearly become."

"An arrogant, to-hell-with-you bastard only an idiot with more hair than wit would ever dare to say any of that to, in case you haven't considered that."

"I don't have to say it, Richard. The man knows his own family history. He should likewise understand I want my brother away from him. Gideon Redgrave may not be his father, as he claims he's not, but he's still that arrogant, to-hell-with-you bastard who clearly cares for no one save himself. Heartless, Richard, there's no question. Adam was always such a quiet boy. Gentle, almost painfully shy. I left him once, having no choice, and it broke my heart. But now that I have a second chance, I can't simply walk away. The Earl of Saltwood will have him for breakfast, otherwise."

"And you for lunch?"

Jessica pulled a face at him and then turned to Doreen, who had just entered from the stairway. "You're looking more than usually harassed. Is something wrong?"

"There was a knock at the door, ma'am. A pounding, more like. So I went down and answered it so as whoever it was wouldn't break the door down, because it sounded as if the wood was already splintering, it did, and there he was, ma'am, and there he stays until I can talk to you, because that's what I told him after he was done telling me what he told me."

Richard bent his head and rubbed at his temples. "We don't need to know it all, Doreen, as I keep telling you. Just the pertinent bits."

"Yes, sir, Mr. Borders, sir. I'm just saying I didn't invite the fellow inside, but it was either stand aside or get myself bowled over, sort of. I told him the house was closed to callers until eight of the clock, but he paid that no nevermind at all, saying as how he's here to stay and where's his room. I told him, I said, there's no room here for the likes of you—rough-looking fellow he is, you know—but he's still standing there. Right where he was standing when he first stepped inside as I was telling him to stay out."

"And me out of headache powders," Richard grumbled, getting to his feet. "Very well, lead me to him."

Jessica snatched up her bonnet, pelisse and gloves. "I'll go down with you. The Saltwood coach will be here shortly, if the man meant what he said, and I don't think he wastes his words on lies unless they'd be of some benefit to him, which my presence in Portman Square is not."

"That was nearly as convoluted as Doreen, my dear. I'd be careful of that," Richard warned, holding open the door so that Jessica could precede him down the narrow staircase.

Jessica was still smiling as she reached the first floor and entered the gaming room, wrinkling her nose at the stale smell of tobacco. Other than the tables, covered each day with white cloths to keep off the dust, the room was empty…if she didn't count the near mountain of a young man standing just inside the main door, turning a large-brimmed hat in his hamlike hands.

"And you are…?" she asked, not certain she wished to approach any closer.

"Seth, ma'am," he said, lifting his huge bowed head, directing an innocent wide-eyed blue stare at her. "His lordship sent me."

Jessica relaxed for a moment, until it registered with her that the lad—for he seemed quite young— was dressed like a common laborer. "Oh, for pity's sake. *You're* the Saltwood coachman? He sent a dray wagon, did he? Well, you can just go back to his lordship and tell him thank you very much, but I can find my own way to Portman Square, as his insult may delay my arrival but it did not dissuade me."

"Ma'am?"

Richard had already gone to one of the front windows and looked down onto the street. "There's no coach out there, Jessica. Or dray wagon." Allowing the heavy curtain to drop once more, he tapped Seth on his shoulder, or as near to it as Richard could reach, as Seth was as tall as he was wide. "Why did his lordship send you, my good fellow?"

The boy flushed to the roots of his red hair. "To protect the lady, sir. In case of any rum coves making a fuss over losing their blunt or getting frisky or drunk or such like. His lordship will pay my wages, and that he's already done, ma'am. All you need do, his lordship says, is feed me and give me somewheres to sleep. His lordship says that you got the bad end of it, ma'am," he said, hanging his head once more. "I suppose I do eats a bit."

"Entire small villages just for breakfast, I should think," Richard said, smiling at Jessica as he walked over to her. "Now here's a turn-up for the books, isn't it? The earl has sent you...protection. Puzzling."

Jessica was livid. "Maddening, not puzzling. He's insulting me. Telling me I can't protect myself."

"And how would he know that, Jess? No, answer me this instead. How do *you* know that's why he sent the boy?" Richard asked, looking at her closely. "What did happen up there last night?"

The jingle of harness followed by the sound of the knocker saved Jessica from answering. "That has to be the coach. Richard, if you'll get Seth settled?"

"We could bed him down in the stables. If we had stables. So we're keeping him?"

Jessica shot a quick look at Seth, who reminded her of a woodcut she'd once had, that of a gentle-eyed dragon spreading its wings to protect a group of children lost in the woods. "I don't suppose we really have a choice, do we? And it will add to my arguments to have Adam here, if we've got a...protector. It's a wonder his lordship didn't think of that."

"I doubt there's much his lordship doesn't think of,"

Richard said, escorting her out to the street. "It's not too late to reconsider, Jess. Don't do this. I know he's your brother, but you haven't lived in his world for a long time. He could break your heart."

"I've told you, my heart broke long ago. It can't break again. But having Adam with me might help mend it." She patted Richard's plump cheek as a liveried footman opened the coach door and put down the steps. "Think good thoughts while I'm gone, and don't let Seth loose in the kitchens unless it's to help Doreen pare vegetables."

"We're really going to keep him? I thought you were just being nice until you can think up an excuse to send him on his way."

Jessica had one foot on the coach step when she turned to her business partner. "I'm being amenable. I will continue to be amenable until Adam is residing under my roof. Besides, it might be a good idea to have a bit of enormous muscle to point to if anyone becomes a problem."

"Pointing would be probably be enough," Richard agreed as he stepped forward and shut the coach door behind her. "I know it would be enough for me. But until we see if he's anything more than big, I'll keep my wooden club beneath the table, if you don't mind. It has served me well so far."

Jessica smiled until the coach moved off, but then allowed her true feelings come to the surface.

Gideon Redgrave had sent her *protection,* had he? From everyone but him, considering Seth was in his employ. Perhaps the youth's true purpose was to spy, which would make perfect sense to her...and if it made perfect sense to her, his lordship undoubtedly had already thought of it.

But, mostly, Seth was an insult, a reminder that she might have James's pistol, she might consider herself quite a good shot, but she had not been able to bring herself to do more than threaten with it.

Well, of course she hadn't shot him!

She would have been hanged in any event, as blowing a hole in an earl was frowned upon by the courts. She wouldn't have been able to rescue Adam from the man, because she'd be locked up and then executed. Too many people had seen him climb the stairs with her; it wasn't as if she and Richard could have hidden the body somewhere and then hauled it to some alleyway and left it there.

She'd thought of all those things in the few seconds she'd had to reach into her pocket and close her hand around the pistol before the earl had swooped down and taken the weapon from her. A pity she hadn't thought of them *before* she'd so blatantly offered herself to him. It simply had seemed prudent to have it in her pocket, that's all. The weapon had given her courage, she supposed. *Too bad it hasn't given me brains,* she thought, pulling a face.

It was seeing that damned golden rose in his cravat. She'd seen it, and something had seemed to go *snap* in her brain.

She still didn't know how she felt about his refusal. Relieved, definitely. Not that she wasn't willing to make any sacrifice in order to gain custody of Adam; although the gesture had been rather melodramatic, hadn't it? *My body for my brother.* She'd been offering the man a bite of candy when he already had bought up half the stores of sweets throughout London.

And yet, ashamed as she was now, in the clear light of day, she felt insulted, as well. He hadn't even seemed *interested.* If anything, he'd seemed amused.

She'd been too blatant. Even now, she felt hot color racing into her cheeks as she thought of how she'd behaved. Misbehaved. Her body for her brother? How stupid! The man could have any woman he wanted just by cricking a finger in her direction.

And, according to Richard, he already did.

Two mistresses? And a pair of *ton* ladies to boot? That seemed excessive. The man was more his father's son than he might wish people to think. And again— he wore the golden rose.

"I *have* to get Adam out of there, no matter what I must do to best the man!" she exclaimed aloud, punching her gloved fist into her palm, refusing to consider she might be sounding very much like some overwrought and probably hare-witted heroine in a melodrama.

Still, her determination lasted throughout the quarter-hour journey to Portman Square through the heavy midmorning traffic. But when the coach halted, and she was helped down to the flagway in front of the imposing facade of the Redgrave mansion, a tiny voice in the back of her head whispered less confidently, "How do you propose to do that, exactly?"

Shaking off the question, she reminded herself her brother was behind that large black door with the lion's head knocker. She put out her chin as a mental battering ram and headed inside as if she was accustomed to being welcomed in the finest London houses.

"Mrs. Linden, to see his lordship," she said imperiously as she stripped off her gloves and untied her bonnet, even as she belatedly realized Doreen should be standing just behind her to take possession of the things. Stupid! How could she have forgotten she was to be chaperoned at all times? This was what living her catch-as-catch-can life for the past five years had done to her; she kept forgetting she wasn't supposed to be able to fend for herself. She should have brought Seth, that's what she should have done. Protection, indeed! She'd never needed more than Richard and his heavy club at the gaming house. Here in Portman Square, an entire regiment of Seths probably wouldn't come amiss!

She shoved both bonnet and gloves at the footman. "His lordship, young man. See to it."

"If you was to wait here, ma'am," the fairly astonished-looking footman said, indicating the open door to what had to be the ground-floor room reserved for tradesmen and those petitioners seeking interviews.

Her fingers still at her throat, as she'd been about to untie the closing of her pelisse, Jessica looked through a dull red haze of anger to the curving staircase that led to the first floor, and then to the small room. "Oh, I think not. I've reconsidered my visit. Kindly inform his lordship I have been and gone."

So saying, she retrieved her bonnet and gloves from the clearly relieved footman, and quit the house. She stood on the top step of the portico as she retied her bonnet and pulled on her gloves, realizing that the coach was now slowly circling the square, so that the horses should not be forced to stand while she was inside.

Well, that presented a problem, didn't it? Not to mention putting quite the crimp in her grand exit. She wasn't about to go running after it, crying *yoo-hoo*, waving it down. Besides, she'd had just about enough of his lordship's *courtesy* for one morning. She had two feet, and she knew how to use them.

She looked to her left, and then to her right. Two feet, yes. Now if only she knew what direction in which to point them....

"Ma'am?"

Jessica turned about slowly, to see that the footman had opened the door behind her, probably to warn her to take herself off, as loitering on his lordship's door-step was not allowed.

"I'm going," she said tightly. "You don't have to apply the boot."

"Oh, but, ma'am, you're to come inside. Please."

She whirled about in her anger, skewering the footman with a look meant to set him back a step, which it did. "I am, am I? You'd be wrong there. I don't have to go anywhere. That might be something you could tell his lordship. I'm not his to command."

"No, ma'am. That is to say, ma'am, it was me what thought to put you in the...that is to say, his lordship is awaiting your pleasure in the drawing room. Ma'am?"

All the anger in Jessica drained away. The footman had made a valid assumption. She wasn't dressed in the first stare, Lord knew. She'd arrived unaccompanied. What else was the man to think but that she'd been summoned, perhaps to interview for some domestic position? Ha! If the earl were to do the interviewing, a *position* would definitely be involved!

"Very well." She reentered the mansion, feeling slightly abashed, which was enough to bring back her anger. She'd no idea she was so prickly; she'd always believed herself to be a pleasant person at the heart of the thing. "What is your name?" she asked the footman kindly as, yet again, she handed over her belongings.

"Waters, ma'am," the youth said, bowing as he laid her pelisse over his arm. "I'll be taking you upstairs now and turning you over to, that is to say, where Mr. Thorndyke will announce you to his lordship. And thank you again, ma'am."

"You did as you were trained, I'm sure," Jessica told him, handing over a coin. "The error was mine. Was his lordship that rough on you?"

Waters bowed again, not quite fast enough to hide his relieved smile. "His lordship could blister paint with that tongue of his, ma'am. But not on me, ma'am. Not this time. It was Mr. Thorndyke what explained how I was wrong. He's not half bad."

Jessica shot a look up the staircase, to where she could see a tall, gray-haired man, most probably Thorndyke, waiting for her. She was being passed along to the Upper Reaches. How fortunate she was.

"Really? In other words, Waters, he'll be escorting me into the lion's den. Lucky for me, then, I'm no lamb."

"Ma'am?" the footman all but squeaked, looking nervous once more.

"I'll make my own way up the stairs," she told him.

"Just don't put my things too far away, as I might be needing them again quite shortly."

So saying, she lifted her hem a fraction and her chin a fraction more before heading up the staircase, her gaze already locked with that of the butler, or majordomo, or whatever the man considered himself, and by the look of him he considered himself at least two social levels above that of his lordship's visitor.

And all for the lack of a maid, or a maiden aunt, or some paid companion. Really, society was a set of ridiculous rules. She was well out of it. Were she a man, none of this would apply, and she'd already be sitting in the drawing room with one leg draped over the other, sipping wine instead of the tea she'd be offered, if she was offered anything at all.

And from the looks of Thorndyke, she wouldn't be.

"Mrs. Linden to see his lordship, who already knows I'm here, so that we'd all three of us be wasting our time pretending he doesn't," she announced before Waters, who had quickly divested himself of her belongings and was hurrying up the stairs after her, could open his mouth. "Just point me in the right direction and you can go back to polishing the silver, or stealing it, whichever pleases you."

The butler opened and closed his mouth a time or two before drawing himself up even straighter than before and motioning to the pair of closed doors to the left of the wide hallway.

"Good. At least we're done with foolishness," Jessica declared, her head positively spinning, and knowing she was being ridiculous. But as ridiculousness seemed to be the order of the day, why should she attempt to put a stop to it now?

Of course, that left her with either throwing open the double doors in some dramatic gesture of defiance or knocking on one of them and waiting to be admitted. She probably should have thought of that. She probably should give some thought to the embarrassing realization that she hadn't been thinking at all since first encountering the Earl of Saltwood, devil take his hide.

CHAPTER THREE

"ALLOW ME, MA'AM," Thorndyke said, stepping ahead of Jessica. He opened a single door and stepped inside. "My lord? I'm happy to say, sir, Waters caught her for you." He then stepped back out and bowed her in, his smile and rather knowing wink nearly causing her to trip over her own feet as she entered the drawing room, only to be stopped again, this time by a pair of sniffing, tumbling dogs.

"Brutus! Cleo! Withdraw!"

The dogs, large puppies, really, and of some indeterminate breed, immediately turned their backs on her, to take up positions on either side of the Earl of Saltwood, who was standing in the very center of the enormous room, looking for all the world as if he'd only lately crawled out of bed.

Gone was the impeccable attire of the previous evening; this was a gentleman at home, and making himself very much at home, indeed. Clad only in buckskins and a white lawn shirt, and minus waistcoat, jacket and cravat, his hair a tumble of dark curls, he held a glass of wine in one hand and something rather limp and filthy in the other.

"I was led to believe I was expected," Jessica said, staring at the limp and filthy thing. "Is that dead?"

Gideon held up the object in question, which proved

to be a crude cloth replica of a rabbit, half its stuffing gone. Both dogs, still sitting up smartly, began to whimper piteously, one of them wagging its tail so violently its entire back end shook. "This? I'm merely training these two young miscreants to avoid temptation."

Jessica eyed the back-end-wriggling dog. "I see. It's always good to avoid temptation. And how is that going?"

"It could be better." He tossed the rabbit in the general direction of the windows as two canine heads whipped about to follow its arc of flight. The whimpering increased. The dog on the left, the back-end wriggler, began to inch across the carpet on its rump. "Brutus! Stay!"

The dog looked to its master, its brown eyes eloquent with pleading, before scooting sideways another inch.

"St-ay," Gideon warned again, dragging out the word.

"It's late for a wager, I know, but a fiver the male gives in and the bitch stays put."

"Your blunt really just on Cleo, as that idiot Brutus probably won't last more than another ten seconds," Gideon said, nodding.

"Less. Ten seconds is an eternity. And the bitch resists. That's the wager."

The earl nodded. "All right. Done."

Brutus tried, he really did. His agony was palpable, his need immense. He actually made it for another four seconds (Jessica counted them off aloud), before he gave in to temptation and pounced on the rabbit.

Cleo watched, yawned widely and then turned in a circle before settling herself in front of the fireplace.

Jessica approached his lordship, her hand extended, palm up. "That's five pounds you owe me, my lord. Men always give in to temptation, and for the most part, sooner rather than later."

His smile had something clenching deep in her belly. "With women more apt to follow orders. Obey."

She rallied at this suggestion, clenching belly ignored. "Hardly. She's merely waiting for a better offer, one she doesn't have to share."

"And now we're not speaking of dogs," Gideon said, waving her to the nearest sofa. "Please, be seated."

She waited for him to say something about his attire, some sort of offhand apology for appearing without jacket or waistcoat, at the least. But he looked so at his ease she didn't really expect it. Rather, it was as if he was saying, *This is my home and I do what I want, when I want, where I want, up to and including tossing filthy cloth rabbits in this splendidly appointed drawing room.*

"Comfortable, Gideon?" she finally asked as, still holding his wineglass, he took up a seat on the facing sofa.

Once again he smiled, and once again, that certain clenching feeling took hold in her belly. "I was wondering how long it would take until you had to say something. All I can answer is to quote you, I suppose. I dislike encumbrances."

"Loathe. I believe I said *loathe*."

He shrugged. "A female word. In either case, let it be said we both enjoy being comfortable. There's a reason gentlemen stand so tall in their finery, you know. Mostly it's because we can't bend, or even remove our own jackets, and risk slicing off our earlobes with our shirt-points if we turn our necks independently of our head and shoulders."

He's trying to make me like him, Jessica thought angrily. He's saying without words: *Look at me, I'm a simple man. I may be Earl of Saltwood, but at the heart of things I'm only a man, one who loves his dogs and his comforts. I'm not who you think I am, your brother is safe with me.*

Either that, or he was returning her favor of last night, already half stripped and ready for seduction. There was also that. Was that what Thorndyke's wink had been all about? Did the servants think she'd been *sent* for, only surprised when she'd shown up at the front door? The thought had already occurred to her downstairs. Good God, yes, that was it! He was about to take her up on her offer. Here. Right here. Probably on the floor, just to double the insult. After all, he was a Redgrave, and above nothing. And she'd come here today like a dog called to heel. She'd *obeyed*.

She had to know. She felt horribly certain she was right, but she had to know.

"My brother, Gideon. He's here? He's not, is he? You've sent him away. You haven't even so much as told him about me."

Brutus had finished with the rabbit, that hadn't put up much of a fight in any case, and was now sitting beside Gideon, his head on the man's knee. The earl scratched him behind the ears, clearly all forgiven.

"Hmm?" he said, redirecting his gaze to her. "I'm sorry?"

"No, you aren't," Jessica said, getting to her feet. "I don't know what sort of mean game you're about, my Lord Saltwood, but I am not playing it. My brother, sir. Or else I'll find my way to the door."

The dark eyes, moments earlier open and amused, narrowed to dark slits. The friendliness was gone, leaving only the man. The menace. The reputation.

"Not if I don't want you to," he said, rising, as well. "You do perceive the difference between now and last night, I'm sure. That is what you're thinking of, isn't it? You, without a chaperone, clearly a *knowing* woman, appearing as requested at a bachelor establishment— worse, at the domicile of one of those rascally reprobate Redgraves. Even that lunkhead of a footman saw the way of things. But, please, continue this belated show of astonishment if you must. I'm amenable either way, actually, although I would prefer you don't prolong the pretense until it becomes tiresome. In other words, I'll play, but I will not lower myself to halfheartedly chasing you around the furniture. It might upset the dogs."

Oh, God. He was big. He was so big. Handsome into the bargain, yes, but mostly, he was so big. She couldn't outrun him. His servants would be of no help to her. He was right. She'd come here of her own free will. She ran a gaming house. She was no lady, disowned by her own father. She was nothing, nobody, not anymore. No one would care....

"You wouldn't dare," she said even as she backed up a step, shot her gaze toward the doors. The closed doors.

"I wouldn't? Very well, I did agree to play. I'll oblige you, if that's how you like it. Let's see, how shall I say this? I suppose I'll simply say the expected."

He took another sanity-destroying step toward her. "Ah, Mrs. Linden, as you very well know, there is little I wouldn't dare. And, out of your own mouth, little you wouldn't offer. I've considered that offer rather pleasantly overnight, deciding a month of your services to be sufficient to my needs, six weeks at the outside, before you bore me. But in the cold light of day I realized I would be remiss if I were to agree to such a bargain without first tasting the wares. For all I know, you might not be very good at pleasuring a man of my peculiar tastes."

She grabbed at the fragile straw that he was only trying to frighten her, pay her some of her own back for the pistol, if nothing else. The odds weren't in her favor, but she had no options, none. She'd have to stand her ground. *Bluff,* knowing she held the inferior hand.

He took another step toward her and reached out, trailing his index finger from the base of her neck to the modest bodice of her gown, hooking that finger inside the fabric and tugging on it. "Is that red hair a promise, or a tease? Is your willing body lying beneath mine a proposition worth my consideration? Tell me, Jessica. *Are* you any good? Convince me."

"I've only to scream for help." Her voice shook with the fear she was trying so hard to conceal.

"Be my guest. But remember, my staff is loyal to me. And, being a Redgrave staff, they are doubtless used to all sorts of noises, including feminine shrieks."

Then she was nudged from the side, nearly losing

her balance before looking down to see Cleo had roused herself from her nap and somehow insinuated her body between them. The bitch had the rabbit between her jaws and was nudging at Jessica as if asking her to come away and play with her.

Or was the dog attempting to save her? It was a highly unlikely yet lovely thought.

"Does she attack on command?" Jessica said, putting her hand atop Gideon's and pointedly removing it from her bodice. "If she were to feel I were under some sort of duress, you understand?"

Gideon looked down at the hopeful dog and smiled, shook his head. All the dark menace was gone, replaced by that insufferable smile. "A good question. You're a cool one, aren't you, Jessica? Although Cleo here apparently sniffs something amiss. Fear, perhaps? That would be disturbing and quite puts a crimp in my assumptions, doesn't it? No matter what, it would appear you've been granted a reprieve. You wanted to see your brother. I'll have Thorndyke fetch him."

"What?" All that talk, those threats and then…nothing? *Damn him.*

She watched in astonished relief as he walked over to the bell pull, blindly stepping back until the backs of her legs came in contact with the edge of the sofa, at which point she sat down with a thump. Cleo deposited the fairly damp rabbit in her lap and then lay down, her head on Jessica's feet.

Jessica bent down to rub behind the dog's ears. "He may have been all bluster and having some of his own back, you know. Males are like that, always wanting the upper hand, or at least to make sure we females think they've got it," she whispered to the animal. "He only did what I would have expected from him. Yes, that's it. I don't believe he actually would have done anything… possibly. Perhaps. But thank you."

Thorndyke entered the room a few moments later, doing a fine job of pretending he wasn't looking at Jessica, and then retired with a bow after being ordered to produce young master Collier, who had been last seen by his lordship slopping up eggs in the breakfast room.

Jessica considered this. Did a man, even a Redgrave, seduce a woman while that woman's brother was in the same house? No, he did not. He'd merely, meanly, meant to frighten her, give her some of her own back (sans pistol, thank goodness, not that the man wasn't a weapon unto himself). And he'd succeeded, admirably. Again, *damn the man!*

"Then you did tell him I would be here this morning?" she asked as Gideon picked up his wineglass once more and retook his seat.

"I warned him to get his backside out of bed before two, which is not his custom. I doubt he'll be pleased to meet anyone less than a scantily clad harem girl wishing to have him recline against her lap whilst she fed him sugared figs."

"Don't measure others by your own yardstick, Gideon," Jessica warned tightly. "He's not a Redgrave."

Gideon chuckled softly. "Oh, yes, we Redgraves are mightily high on sugared figs."

Jessica glared at him. "That wasn't the part of your description I was alluding to, my lord. It's a well-known fact the Redgraves are prone to excesses of a…of a…" She was at a loss as to how to finish that statement.

"You're prone to excesses," she finally ended, lamely. After all, if she had ended with "of a carnal nature," he would most probably have laughed so hard he would have fallen off the sofa. She believed she was beginning to get a sort of figurative *handle* on the man now, understand him better. In short, he was a menace!

"Really? We're that bad? I had no idea. Although, clearly, you seemed to have been lapping up tales of the infamous Redgravian debauchery. You should have seen your eyes, Jessica. You believed every word I said."

He had her there. It wasn't as if she'd any certain knowledge of *Redgravian debauchery.* She'd certainly heard about his lordship's light's-o-love. *Four* mistresses? That seemed excessive and spoke of an unhealthy appetite, in her opinion. She knew he was a neck-or-nothing rider who often wagered on himself in races and had yet to lose. She knew he had knocked down Gentleman Jackson not once, but twice, until the renowned pugilist had declared he wouldn't step in the ring with him again. She knew he won all the top prizes driving with the Four-in-Hand Club. She knew he gambled deep but never wildly. She knew he had no enemies because even the most foolish of London gentlemen perceived the wisdom of calling him friend.

She had, in short, made a study of the man, indeed his entire family, these past weeks. But, really, when she got right down to it, she didn't know anything about the current crop of Redgraves but what she'd heard.

He had two younger brothers, Maximillien and Valentine, and a single sister, Katherine. Maximillen had sailed as one of the Royal Navy's youngest coxswains, and Valentine had been classically educated in Paris and Toulon, managing to remain there even as Bonaparte conducted his on-again, off-again war on England, only returning home a few months ago.

Katherine had come to Mayfair for her Season last spring but hadn't really *taken,* seeing as how she was unfashionably tall and dark-haired, and favored her infamous Spanish mother in her looks in a year where petite blondes were considered all the go. Her suitors had hoped for the mother's morals, as well, and their mamas had cringed at the thought of "foreign-looking" grandchildren. But it had been Katherine herself who had answered an impertinent question about her brother the earl, voiced in the center of the dance floor at Almack's, with a stunning punch to the questioner's nose, breaking it quite nicely, word had it. She hadn't come to town this Season, which to Jessica's mind made more of a statement about Lady Katherine's disdain for society than any possible fear of it or shame over her actions.

Jessica felt she most probably could like Lady Katherine. Lords Maximillien and Valentine were of no real concern to her, although she imagined they were no better or worse than their brother. As to their grandmother, the dowager countess? All Jessica had heard about the woman was that she knew every secret of every man and woman and even royal, and there wasn't a single person in all the *ton* who wasn't scared spitless by her.

Jessica felt she most probably could like Lady Saltwood, as well.

She did not like Gideon Redgrave, however. Not his

reputation, not the man who had just very clearly made a complete fool out of her. *Damn him.*

"Before your brother deigns to join us," he said now, presumably having had his fill of looking at her as if she might be a bug under a microscope. "We're quits of this ridiculous offer of yours? You insulted me with your patently insincere offer, not to mention that idiocy with the pistol. In short, as a seductress, Jessica, you are an abysmal failure. I, on the other hand, succeeded admirably in pointing out I am not to be insulted, not without consequences. And, much as you may believe yourself irresistible, I am more than confident I can stumble along through the remainder of my days without learning, firsthand, and, needless to say, most intimately, whether or not you are a true redhead. In short, I am willing to accept your apology and move on."

She was certain she now looked as if her eyes would simply pop out of her head. "You…you…*how dare you!*"

He sighed and shook his head, as if saddened by her outburst. "Make up your mind, Jessica. Harlot or genteel widow fallen on hard times. Which is it to be? So far, I would have to say you've mastered neither role. But before you answer, let me make one thing clear to you. I choose my own women, and they come to me willingly or not at all. I've no desire to bed a martyr, no matter how lovely."

There was one part of Jessica, one very small, even infinitesimally tiny part of her that took in the words "no matter how lovely," and considered them a compliment. She shoved that infinitesimal part into a dark corner of her mind and locked the door on it, intending to take it out later and give it a good scold.

"You've made your point, Gideon. Several times, in a variety of unconscionably crude and insulting ways. In my defense, I can only point out that I was, am, desperate. I offered you the only thing I had—"

"Please don't tell me you're referring to your virtue. I don't believe that's been yours to bestow for quite some time. Unless the fabled Mr. Linden was a eunuch?"

"No," Jessica said quietly, "far from it." She took a steadying breath. "A month. You ignored my solicitor's communications for a month, and then you came to see me in person, looking just as I'd imagined you. Arrogant, overweening, for all the world as if you owned it. You weren't going to listen to reason. And you wear the golden rose. That told me all I needed to know. I...I offered you what interests you most. And damn you, Gideon Redgrave, I did it knowing who you are. *What* you are. If you had half a heart, which you don't, you would have realized what that cost me."

Gideon sat back on the sofa, rubbing a hand across his mouth as he looked at her. He looked at her for a long time.

"I'm sorry," he said at last.

"Excuse me?" She hadn't any idea what he was going to say, but what he said made no sense at all.

"I repeat, Jessica. I'm sorry. Tell me—sans the golden rose, would you have made your offer?"

Slowly, silently, she shook her head. "No."

Once again, he rubbed his hand across his mouth,

still looking at her closely. "And you believe it still goes on? The Society."

Jessica shifted uncomfortably on the cushions. "As of five years ago, yes. I can't say for certain about now. But you know this."

"No, Jessica, I don't," he said, getting to his feet, suddenly seeming decades older than his years. "I only know that in the past twelve months, four of my late father's cohorts in that damn *Society* of his have been murdered. Your father included. I wear the golden rose to signal that I know the hunting accident, the accidental drowning, the fall down the stairs, your father's coaching accident—they all were in fact murders."

He had to be spouting nonsense. "I don't understand. My father was *murdered?* He and his wife both? How can you know that?"

"Later," Gideon said, turning toward a small commotion in the hallway. "I believe I'm about to be gifted with the sight of a touching family reunion. Or not," he added, smiling, as a tall, rail-thin, ridiculously over-dressed and harassed-looking youth stomped into the room.

"Now what the bloody blue blazes do you want?" the youth demanded, clutching a large white linen serviette in one hand even as he took a healthy and quite rude bite out of the apple he carried with him. Speaking around the mouthful of fruit, he continued, "First you order me out of bed without a whisper of a reason, then you say I leave the house on penalty of death— as if that signifies, as I might already be dead for all the life you allow me. Then you send me off to stuff my face when Brummell himself swears no sane man breaks his fast before noon, and now you want me in here to— Well, hullo, ain't you the pretty one."

"Ad—*Adam?*" Jessica was on her feet, but none too steadily. This ridiculous popinjay couldn't be her brother. Adam was sweet and shy, and sat by her side as she read to him, and cried when their father insisted he learn to shoot, and sang with the voice of an angel.

The youth turned to her and gifted her with an elegant leg, marred only when he nearly toppled over as he swept his arm with a mite too much enthusiasm.

"Bacon-brained puppy," Gideon muttered quietly. "Your brother, Jessica. Behold."

She *beheld.* Adam Collier was clad very much in the style of many of the youths who, from time to time, were hastily escorted out of the gaming room as being too raw and young to be out on their own with more than a groat in their pocket, so eager were they to be separated from their purses. Unpowdered hair too long, curled over the iron so that it fell just so onto his forehead, darkened and stiff with pomade. Buckram padding in the shoulders of his wasp-waisted blue coat, a patterned waistcoat that was a jangle of lurid red-and-yellow stripes, no less than a half-dozen fobs hanging from gold chains, clocked stockings hugging his too-thin shanks. And was that a, dear Lord, it was—he had a star-shaped patch at the corner of his mouth.

"Adam?" she repeated, as if, having said the name often enough, she'd believe what her horrified eyes were telling her. She didn't want to believe it. Her brother hadn't grown up, he'd simply gotten taller, slathered his face with paint to hide his spots and turned into an idiot. His only submission to the formalities was the black satin mourning band pinned to his upper arm. And that was edged with black lace. He wasn't oppressed, he certainly wasn't heartbroken. He was his brainless twit of a mother, in breeches.

"I fear you have the advantage of me, madam," Adam drawled with a truly irritating and affected lisp as he approached, clearly intent on kissing her hand. His red heels made his progress somewhat risky, but he managed it, nearly coming to grief only when Brutus ran up to him, intent on sniffing his crotch. "Stupid cur. Do I look like a bitch in heat to you?"

"Don't blame the dog, you sapskull. You might instead want to rethink the brand of scent you bathe in. As it is, we're chewing on it," Gideon said, retiring to the mantel, but not before shooting Jessica an amused look. "Say hello to your half sister."

Adam stopped, searched among his many chains for a gilt quizzing glass on a stick, and lifted it to his eye. "M'sister? Jessica, was it? No, that's impossible," he said, shaking his head. "She's dead these past half-dozen years or more. Bad fish, something like that. Mama told me most distinctly." Then his mouth opened in shock, and he pointed the quizzing glass accusingly in her direction. "Imposter! Charlatan! The old reprobate cocks up his toes, and they come out of the woodwork, looking for his blunt. Fie and for shame, woman!"

Gideon rejoined Jessica in front of the sofas. "I've been thinking, Mrs. Linden. I may have been unduly hasty in denying your request for guardianship, and even thin-skinned. It must have been the pistol. Perhaps we can reopen negotiations," he suggested quietly.

At last Jessica regained use of her tongue, which

she'd been in some danger of swallowing. "I don't think so," she told him, still goggling at the creature in front of her. "You can have him. As to the other, I'll expect you in Jermyn Street tonight, at eleven." Then she clapped her hands to her mouth, realizing what she'd said. "The…the other being discussing this business of murders. Not…not *you know*."

"What? She's leaving? I've routed her, by God!" Adam clapped his hands in delight. "Yoicks! And away!"

"Oh, stubble it, you nincompoop," Jessica bit out as she brushed past him.

Gideon's delighted, infuriating laughter followed after her, all the way down the stairs.

CHAPTER FOUR

"YOU'RE LOOKING HARASSED," Lord Maximillien commented as he entered the study in Portman Square and perched himself on the corner of his brother's desk. "At least you'd look harassed if you were anyone else. The Earl of Saltwood is never harassed. He is a— Is there such a word as *harasser?*"

"What do you want, Max?" Gideon asked, putting down the letter opener he'd been balancing between his fingertips.

"Me? To bid you farewell, I suppose. I leave for Brighton in an hour, on orders from Trixie. There's some clever barque of frailty she's befriended, a bit o'muslin with a problem our grandmother thinks might rouse me from my boredom. In any case, she's been matchmaking. In a weak moment, I agreed to sign on as cohort. It's my adventurous spirit, you understand."

Gideon looked at his brother and shook his head in mock dismay. "You even look like an adventurer. Your shirt cuffs are unbuttoned and too long, that cravat's an insult, those smoked glasses a ridiculous affectation— and I may soon enlist Thorndyke to help hold you down while I scrape all that hair off your face."

Max bent his head and looked at his brother overtop the blue-smoked rimless glasses he'd discovered a few months earlier in a small shop on Bond Street. "All that hair? A simple mustache, a cunning patch beneath my bottom lip—hardly *all that hair*."

Gideon pointed up at him, twirling his finger. "And the rest of it? Looks to be the beginnings of a beard to me. I imagine even a whore with a problem won't tolerate a fellow who only allows himself to be shaved three times a week."

Max stabbed his fingers through the heavy thatch of dark brown hair he wore halfheartedly parted in the center of his head, its length covering his ears, the whole waving around his almost aesthetically beautiful face. Only his dark eyes, so like Gideon's, threw out the warning that this was no pretty fool; perhaps why Max had delighted in finding the smoked glasses. "Allow? I'm not so lazy. I shave myself, brother. Shave myself, dress myself, wash my own rump."

"And two of those tasks performed in the dark, apparently. Never mind," Gideon said, not about to admit his brother was one devilishly handsome creature, the sort who could cause small riots among the ladies if he put his mind to it. "What's the Cyprian's problem?"

"Other than being ambitious, penniless and of questionable morals? Transport. I'm simply to find a way to get clever girl and ardent swain to Gretna, wed over the anvil and all but publicly bedded so there can be no annulment, all accomplished ahead of any pursuit. You know Trixie. She's a romantic."

"She's a pernicious troublemaker, and that's in the best of times. Who's to be the gullible groom—and you'll notice hearing Trixie has cultivated a whore as bosom chum holds no shock. No, it's the groom who interests me."

Max grinned wickedly. "So you see it, too? I did a bit of checking. It's Wickham's only grandson. Geoffrey something-or-other. Second in line to the dukedom until his papa, cursed with a spotty liver and still sucking up gin morning till night, sticks his spoon in the wall. Which will probably happen any day now according to Trixie, as they've already laid straw outside the man's door in Grosvenor Square so the invalid isn't pestered on his sickbed by the noise of traffic, and called in the Autum bawlers for some final-ditch prayer vigil. He should be toes cocked up just in time for the new heir—that would be this Geoffrey fellow—to present his *fait accompli* bride to his grandfather, shocking the old fellow to the point of apoplexy."

"Two deaths? That's ambitious, even for our grandmother. She's counting on an even pair?"

"Apparently. She's already had me scribble a wager in the betting book at White's. *A certain interested party offers odds of eight-to-five a certain duke W-dot-dot-dot*—as if nobody would know it's old Wickham—*will depart this earthly coil on or before fifteen June of the current year.* Lord Alvanley's holding the stakes."

"Of course it's Alvanley. The man's always in need of funds, and I'm sure Trixie is paying him well. Plus, I think she once had him as a lover. So. Wickham. It took her long enough," Gideon said, nodding approvingly. "Damn near twenty years. I wouldn't wager against her, or attempt to stop her. Go with God, Max."

"I'll go with most anyone, as well you know. But first—what's this about twenty years? This isn't just her usual mischief? What did old Wickham do to set her off?"

Gideon leaned back in his chair, mulling the idea that his brother should be made aware of their grandmother's motive. After all, Max had already decided Trixie was up to something. "I suppose it's time you knew. Trixie has always felt she had some…scores to settle. One of them is that, hard on the heels of our family shame, Wickham suggested the Saltwood title and holdings be dissolved and returned to the Crown, due to the scandal. More than suggested. The petition grew legs and damn near got as far as to have an airing in Parliament before it could be squashed. We stood to lose everything."

"Bastard."

"He gives bastards a bad name. Self-righteous prig, that's what he was, casting stones while setting himself up as some holier-than-thou man of impeccable morals. And it wasn't only him. There were three others heading up the action, until they were shown to be not as moral as they purported themselves to be, and the petition was withdrawn."

"And Trixie was the one to point this out?"

"I never said that, but you can draw your own conclusions. One was discovered at a house party, in bed with the host's wife—he died in the inevitable duel. Only weeks later, the second was bankrupted over gaming debts suddenly being called in by the person who'd bought up his vouchers—he shot himself rather than face ruin. And the third was actually imprisoned and barely escaped hanging after it was learned he'd been diddling a family footman, the pot boy and, rumor has it, his own nephew, with or without their agreement. But as I said, all that was years ago."

"God, I adore that woman, much as she terrifies me," Max said in some admiration. "Why did she wait so long with Wickham?"

"Probably because she was diddling *him.* You've seen her diamond choker, that ruby bib she sets such store by? They're only a sampling. She's been bleeding the fool dry on and off for years. Oh, close your mouth. You know Trixie. She's a cat with a mouse, playing with it as long as it amuses her, and then, once bored, she pounces. I remember her telling me a few months ago that the man has developed what she termed a *disky heart,* making him of no further use to her. She's probably already ordered the gown she'll don as one of the chief mourners when they wall him up in the family mausoleum."

"And had the bill sent to Wickham?" Max added, pushing himself up from the desk. "'Frailty, thy name is woman.'"

"True enough. A true possessor of all the better vices, both moral and spiritual. We lesser mortals can only admire and aspire. But as she has ever pointed out, she isn't evil. She'd never strike just for the thrill of the thing. All her targets are deserving of her attention in one way or another, at least to her mind."

And then Gideon frowned.

"What? You're suddenly back to that same puss that greeted me when I came in here. Is it something to do with Trixie?"

Four men, dead in separate *accidents* in the past year. All four former members of the secret society founded by Trixie's son. Twenty years. Some would think that too long to wait for revenge, for some perverted sense of justice. But then how did he explain Wickham?

"No," Gideon said firmly, not liking his thoughts and definitely unwilling to share them. "Nothing to do with Trixie. I was simply searching my mind for a way to rid myself of that primping, posturing fool I've inherited."

"Adam?" Max said unnecessarily. "Aren't you going to toss him back to school next term?"

Gideon fingered the letter that had arrived in the morning post. "According to the headmaster, that's not possible. He was full of apologies, but it would seem he and a few of the instructors convened a meeting concerning young master Collier, and decided they would forego the pleasure of his company in future. I can't say I blame them. The headmaster went on at some length about my ward's sad lack of talent save a decided propensity for calamity. He actually set fire to his rooms when he employed a candle to burn loose threads from his waistcoat and the damn thing flamed, so that he screeched and tossed it in a cupboard, then went off to dinner. If not for a quick-thinking proctor, they could have lost the entire dormitory."

"I'd never say the boy doesn't rattle when he walks, so many loose screws in his brainbox. But there's other schools."

"Yes, there are. He's been asked to vacate several of them. If I buy him a commission the tongues will wag that I'm trying to have him killed in order to gain his inheritance, and if I send him to the estate Kate will have murdered him within the week. In other words, I've been sitting here this past hour or more cudgeling my brain to discover what sin it was I've committed I'm being punished for in the form of that paper-skulled twit."

"Some sin? Only one? If I weren't in such a hurry to be off, I could pen you a list. Not only that, but I don't think I can stand watching you this way, brother. Glum. Defeated. It's so unlike you. So much so, I find myself wondering if there's something you're not telling me, something much more disturbing than locating a deep well in which to deposit your latest ward."

Maximillien could play the fool with the best of them, but he was rarely *fooled*.

Gideon looked at his brother. "Go away, Max."

"Ah, then I'm right. I'll have to write Val and tell him. Where is our baby brother, by the way?"

"I was unaware Valentine still required a keeper."

"Another subject open to debate. But we should at least be aware of where he is, don't you think?"

"Not if we don't want to know," Gideon suggested, smiling in real amusement. "But, to ease your mind, the last I heard he was heading for some place in Lincolnshire, to lend support to a friend whose father had, to quote our brother, taken a turn for the worse."

"That's kind of him. So he's off to be a supporting prop at some deathbed?"

"Hardly. The bad turn was financial. His friend merely needed someone to put up the blunt for his trip home. Naturally, Valentine offered one of our coaches, and his company on the journey. And probably half his allowance for this quarter, knowing Val."

"He's a good friend. Or, as Kate often says, a numb-skull. She swears some day that soft heart of his will land him in the briars. Has he ever said no to an appeal? Then again, considering that ludicrous fribble we've got residing with us now, have you? It's your soft heart, both you and Val are stuck with soft hearts. Thankfully, Kate and I escaped the taint."

Gideon directed yet another cool, dispassionate stare at his brother. "Are we done here now?"

"Oh-ho, speaking of briars," Max said, putting up his hands in mocking defense. "How about I leave you to your troubles and be on my way?" He turned to quit the room, but at the last moment turned back to add, "Thorndyke told me of your rather unusual visitor this morning. Showed up all unaccompanied and left in some sort of huff. Spirited, that's the world Thorny used. Curious. But she's not the reason for that long puss, correct?"

"Goodbye, Max. Safe travels."

"I thought as much. Thorndyke said she's quite the looker. Red hair. I've always been partial to red hair on a woman. I don't even mind the freckles. She have freckles, Gideon? Even where the sun doesn't reach?"

When Gideon was really angry, he went quiet, the sort of quiet that could sound, to the object of his anger, much like a loud clashing of cymbals.

"Right," Max said, nodding. "Forgive me. Clearly the lady is not a subject open to discussion. I'm off to ease the path of true love, Val is off to be a supporting prop, Kate is steadfastly refusing to leave the estate, and you're—well, whatever it is you're doing, I suppose you'll let the rest of us know in your own good time."

Once his brother was gone, Gideon rested his chin in his hand for a full quarter hour, thinking, and then pushed back his chair, giving in to the inevitable. There was nothing else for it, he had to confront Trixie.

AN HOUR LATER HE WAS cooling his heels in his grand-mother's drawing room in Cavendish Square, staring down the pair of yellow pug dogs who were eying his highly polished Hessians as if they would take great pleasure in lifting their legs against them.

She'd named the beasts Gog and Magog, after the ancient carved wooden giants that stood just outside the Guildhall, perhaps because they were no more than ten inches from ears to paws, or perhaps because she was amused by the thought the giants were reportedly the product of a coupling of wicked Roman daughters and the demons then inhabiting Albion, one day to be Britain. To Trixie, that would explain quite a bit about her fellow citizens of the realm.

In any case, Gideon thoroughly detested the dogs and, in return, they didn't care a whit what he thought of them. It was rather lowering....

"Gideon, my pet, what terrible thing have I done that brings you to my door?"

Giving the dogs one last warning look, Gideon got to his feet to admire Lady Beatrix's entrance, accom-plished, as always, with a mixture of imperiousness and panache that was the envy of her detractors—all of them women.

She was no young girl, but the extraordinary beauty of her youth had for the most part stayed with her as she moved through the years, softening a bit about the edges, her blond hair lighter now that it was streaked with silver, her blue eyes alive and sparkling even as small laugh lines framed them. Her chin and swanlike neck remained those of a much younger woman, perhaps because of the queenly way she held her slim, fit body erect, perhaps because a crafty Mother Nature had decided a determined chin was the only warning a sane man should need.

There was, Gideon had decided long ago, a true dearth of sane men in England.

The Dowager Countess of Saltwood had been married to her late husband at sixteen, had borne her only child at seventeen, buried her husband at twenty-one and been terrorizing society ever since. First it was her son's guardian who had learned Beatrix Redgrave may not have been in control of her life for those twenty-one years, but she was in control of it now, even if she'd had to bed and then blackmail her son's guardian to do it until the underage earl reached his majority.

Marriage, to the widowed countess, was little more than a way for men to control women, beget heirs and have someone to satisfy their base desires when they were too lazy or cheese-paring to seek out a whore. Beatrix would not willingly put her head in the marital noose again, although she had rather elevated the discreet taking of lovers to a sort of art form. Reportedly, thanks either to her late husband's prowess or her own appetites, she was very good at what she did, but whether she truly enjoyed what she did was her secret. Her grandchildren rather thought she did, or she wouldn't *indulge* herself quite so much, although they were secretly appalled that she continued to indulge now and then as she drew ever closer to her seventieth birthday.

Mostly, with the marked exception of her grandsons, Trixie, Gideon believed, loathed men as a clearly inferior species.

Now, wafted along on dainty slippers and a soft cloud of the intoxicating scent that was her own special mix, she held out her arms to her oldest grandson, allowing him to capture and kiss her hands. He did take her hands in his, but only so that he could pull her closer, lean in and kiss both her artfully powdered cheeks.

She tilted her head and smiled archly. "Oh, so very *vaillant*. You must cut a wide swatch through the ladies with that little trick."

"I can only do my best."

"Yes, and I hear you do your best quite a lot, you naughty scamp. I can excuse Lady Malvern, I suppose, as she's passably attractive, save for those unfortunate ears. They're not her fault, and she usually has the good sense to keep them covered. But the widow Orford? Honestly, pet, that woman's so tight in her ways, I fear for your eventual progeny. She could take you in and snap you right—"

"Trixie," he interrupted quickly before his own grandmother could put him to the blush, "what the hell are you up to this time?"

He had to give her credit; she didn't attempt to dissemble, bat her kohl-darkened lashes and trill, "But whatever do you mean?" No. She simply smiled that smile that had her clear blue eyes sparkling.

"You mean Reggie, don't you? Max never could keep a secret. I gave the duke a good run, more than he deserved. But I can't simply let him die peacefully in his bed, now can I? Lilyann Smithers, late of Bath, Tunbridge Wells and the beds of whomever, soon to be the next Wickham duchess? Delicious! Just think, pet. Reggie condemned us Redgraves as not being fit for a peerage, and now his heirs will henceforth descend from a whore who's been sat in more than any village barber chair, if you take my meaning."

"I do. I'd go so far as to ask you to tell me where you heard that description, but then you'd tell me."

"Most probably. In any case, she's been instructed to tell Reggie of her great and most helpful friendship with me when her husband first introduces her on their return from Gretna. That's part of our bargain, and I paid dearly for it. Modistes, tutors. Why, I myself taught her the intricacies of proper behavior at table. Comely girl, biddable and really quite fetching, but shocking table manners. In any case, she's turned into a tolerable silk purse, thanks to my attention, but the sow's ear of her former, shall we say, *occupation?* That will soon come to light. I'll enjoy knowing Reggie will take that realization to hell with him."

"I can see you've put considerable planning into the duke's downfall. Who was it said it's women who most delight in revenge?"

"I have no idea, but I should have, because it's true. You men haven't the proper appreciation for a well thought-out revenge. I do know the source of my most favorite quote, if that helps you in any way. The dear Pierre Laclos, in his marvelously naughty *Les Liaisons dangereuses,* warned, 'Old ladies must never be crossed: in their hands lie the reputations of the young ones.' Something to keep in mind, pet, although I would protest I'm not yet old. I suppose I will be, someday, but in my mind and heart, I'm only a girl."

"You were as ancient as sin in your cradle," Gideon told her, earning himself a playful tap on the forearm as they sat down beside each other. "And if I recall correctly, it ended badly for the conspirators in that immoral tale."

"Ah, but they were all French. Give me credit for being smarter than any Frenchman, if you please. They chop off heads. How gauche! I'm much more subtle. Now, if you aren't going to cut up stiff with me about a paltry thing like the soon-to-be late duke—and trust me, his is a paltry thing indeed and sadly lacking in talent—why are you here?"

Gideon smiled sadly. "I'm not certain I remember. Perhaps it's been too long since I've felt dizzy, turned around and around by a crafty old woman who should be minding her knitting."

"Or her grandson's children, whom I've little hope of at the moment, sadly. Don't think the widow Orford will give you sons. Her womb has to have shriveled to nothing by now, as she's at least fifteen years your senior. Really, Gideon, what could you possibly have been thinking, to bed her?"

"Lucile and I aren't lovers, Trixie. You shouldn't put credence in every rumor."

"You're not tipping her? You greatly relieve my mind. But then, for God's sake, why *are* you seeing her? You've squired her around the Park at least twice in the past week, and you've stood up with her at balls three times. No, four, I nearly forgot Suffolk's flat affair this past Thursday. It can't be for her conversation, her wit. She possesses neither."

"Her late husband was one of my father's cronies. I was interested in the manner of the man's death last year. She's just out of mourning, remember? Cultivating her friendship and confidence seemed the easier way of learning the particulars that might not have become public knowledge."

"Particulars concerning the manner of his— How perfectly *morbid* of you. Gideon, why would you even care about a thing like that?"

She was so good at playacting. Nibbling around the corner of the subject would get him nowhere; she was too proficient in deception to be caught out so easily. Which left the direct approach. "My father's fellow members of that damn Society of his have been dying with alarming frequency of late, Trixie, all of them in a variety of accidents or other misfortunes. Orford, for one. Lady Malvern's uncle, Sir George Dunmore, for another. I know they were members because they all wore the rose. Are you killing them?"

Her response was swift. She slapped him hard across the face.

He lifted a hand to his burning cheek. "I believe I should be remiss if I didn't point out that's not an answer, madam," he told her coldly.

"Perhaps not, but it was most deserved. What's going on, Gideon? I'd decided not to ask about the stickpin, waiting for you to tell me, which you would have done eventually. Thank God you've stopped. I was not, however, expecting you to come to me today with an absurd inquiry more suited to a man possessing less of the strong intelligence for which I've always given you credit."

"Forgive me. I only learned of your plans for Wickham this morning and probably acted hastily. But twenty years, Trixie? It all happened so long ago. Why bring down the ax now?"

"Because he's going to die soon, of course. I settled the others immediately. And, lest you're confused on that head, I *killed* none of them. If I made it advantageous to them to destroy themselves, that was their decision. Save Perkins, who is still living in his disgrace in prison."

"Not prison, Trixie. You're losing your touch if you didn't hear he's slipped his mind entirely, and is now raving in some small cell in Bethlehem Hospital."

"Delicious! May he survive another two decades and sleep every night in his own filth. But we're speaking of Reggie now, aren't we? My mistake with the others was moving too quickly. They barely had time to realize their error in threatening me."

"Much more satisfying to destroy them an inch at a time?"

"Now you understand, and with all the inches reserved for the duke since the others were gone. Reggie's known nearly from the first he's on my string, and I'd tighten it one day. He simply never knew when, or how. You've never had anyone at your beck and call, have you, eager to do you any service—*any* service, Gideon. Able to pick that person up and then put that person down, time and time again. To listen to the pleas for your favors, the piteous weeping when made aware there are others to whom you're at times bestowing those favors. Imagine that person suffering, loving so deeply, desperately, yet living constantly in fear that one day the blade will fall. It's heady stuff. I may have grown a touch lazy over the years, as well, content to flaunt the jewels he gives me beneath his wife's nose as he watches in horror, fearing I'm about to tell her from whence they come."

She shrugged her slim shoulders eloquently, almost sadly. "Or perhaps I grew somewhat fond of the man over time. I'm not completely heartless. But in the end, Gideon, the bill always comes due, the piper has to be paid. It's Reggie's time to learn the full cost of his crime against the Redgraves, and most especially my grandchildren, who he would have stripped of lands and title. That is not a small thing, Gideon, and never forgivable. Although I suppose I may miss him. A little."

Gideon lowered his head, unable to look into Trixie's tear-bright eyes. "I beg your pardon. I had no right to suspect…to question you. My only excuse, lame as it is, is that I've lately been under some duress."

"I forgive you, pet. And I've indulged you this one time, but you must never again question me. You would rarely like the answers. I'll surely burn in hell one day along with Reggie and so many others, but that is my concern, not yours." The countess took his hand and lifted it to her lips. "You children are my weakness, you know, and always have been, from the day your father died and Maribel fled the country. Now, tell me more about these mysterious deaths. And why you took to wearing that damnable rose."

CHAPTER FIVE

JESSICA STOOD IN HER USUAL place, the one she'd long before decided provided the best vantage point from which to observe the gaming room. She smiled and nodded absently to the gentlemen from time to time, although never encouragingly, as it didn't take much for some of them to believe she'd offered a more intimate acquaintance.

They were rather thin of company this evening, and unless more guests arrived in the next hour she might consider eliminating the second supper and close the doors to newcomers at two. It had been a long time since they'd made an early night of it, and she was looking forward to her bed.

Doreen had already left her post at the door to help with the first supper, but Jessica didn't have to sit in at Richard's chair at the faro table so that he could take the maid's place. Not now that Seth was being taught by Doreen and Richard as to how to go on. His imposing size seemed to be enough to "go on" with so far. His open smile and boyish face, when put in contrast with his enormous frame, sent a clear signal: we're delighted to see you, but if you don't belong here or don't behave, I will cheerfully hold you up by your heels while I carry you outside to bounce your head on the cobblestones.

Richard had somehow procured a decent suit of

clothes for the boy, although the jacket did seem to strain at the shoulder seams, and Doreen had explained—undoubtedly in her usual excruciating detail—about the need to be careful as to who was admitted to the house. It would take him some time to become familiar with the usual faces, but he'd learn. Doreen, bless her wise Irish eye, could spot a constable at thirty paces.

Being hauled off to the guardhouse for operating an illegal gaming house was to be avoided at all costs! As far as her neighbors and most of the world was concerned, Jessica and her "Uncle Richard" held nightly soirees for those of an intellectual nature—the reading of self-composed bits of poetry and literary criticism, etc.

Richard had actually penned an "Ode to Dame Fortune;" he then had ordered the thing framed, personally hanging it in the ground-floor foyer. He thought it a fine joke.

After glancing at the mantel clock to see it lacked only fifteen minutes until eleven, Jessica surreptitiously rubbed at her right temple, hoping to ease the headache that had followed her back to Jermyn Street and still stubbornly refused to vacate the premises.

Her brother was a twit. A fool. An uncanny reflection of his brainless, flighty mother. Worried for his soul, Jessica had thought to rescue a nearly grown version of the sweet, shy, delightful Adam she remembered, only to come face-to-face with a simpering, posturing jackanapes rigged out like some Tatony pig, and displaying a similar intelligence.

Her only solace was the look of aggrieved pain on the earl's face when Adam had presented himself in the drawing room. She had thought her sweet brother was in imminent peril of being corrupted by those scandalous Redgraves. Instead, if anyone was in any danger in that new association, she would have to lay odds Gideon Redgrave would be the first to run screaming into the night, begging rescue.

Jessica covered her smile with her hand. Poor Gideon. She'd handed him an easy escape, and he'd gotten his back up about her demand and refused. By rights, when he showed up here tonight—if he dared—she'd have to ask him if he symbolically carried his nose with him in a small velvet bag...having sliced it off to spite his face.

Still, she felt dreadful at having so quickly deserted the sinking ship that was Adam. It had been the shock of it; that had to be the reason. It wasn't as if the boy was mean or evil. He had simply left the nursery and become a nincompoop. If there could be any pleasure in that knowledge, it had to be that their father must have been yanking his hair out by the roots each time he contemplated his fribble of a son.

But that's what happens when you wed a nincompoop nearly thirty years your junior for her looks and her fertile womb. You had then set yourself up for fifty-fifty odds of her giving birth to a nincompoop. Really, you'd think more men would consider this.

Of course, that also meant he'd gone into the union with fifty-fifty odds she would have produced a likeness and disposition that mirrored his own.

Either way, Jessica realized now, too late, whatever way Adam was to go, he'd already gone there in the five important, formative years she had been separated from him, and there was no going back.

And there really wasn't anything anyone could do to *undo* those five years. She'd be overweeningly ambitious to believe otherwise. *Which would likewise mean there could be nothing the Earl of Saltwood could do to corrupt or correct Adam,* she thought, and then mentally added to that thought: *something else that might have occurred to you considerably sooner.*

In short, if she'd been less of a sentimental goose and more hardheaded earlier, she would not have just passed through the most excruciatingly embarrassing twenty-four hours of her existence, or be standing here now in her same black hostess gown, attempting to look unconcerned that the clock had just begun chiming out the hour of eleven, and the exasperating man was nowhere to be seen.

And still she hadn't told him what he needed to know about Adam. What he must know, why she had been so willing to sacrifice herself…and ended making a total fool of herself.

She would have thought, if nothing else, the earl was a man of his word. But perhaps not. Dangling a word like *murder* and coupling that word with *your father* should not be done lightly, not if the person doing the dangling didn't mean to follow through with some explanation, for pity's sake. Had the man no notion of what was correct?

Jessica rolled her eyes. Of course he did. He was the earl. *She* was the one operating an illegal gaming house. Then again, being an earl only proved he knew what was correct. It didn't naturally follow that he'd do the correct thing.

Not that she cared. Except for the *murder* and the *your father* portions of the business. It wasn't as if she ever wanted to see Gideon Redgrave again. Because he was an annoying man. Extremely annoying. Unsettling. So cocksure of himself. Why, it put her teeth on edge, just thinking about him.

But he had apologized about the rose. Why had he done that? Why had he worn it in the first place? Who was this man?

If only she could stop thinking about him....

"Jess, he's here."

"Hmm?" she said as Richard's roughly whispered words penetrated the introspective fog that was now her mind. She mentally shook herself back to the moment and turned her gaze to the landing in time to see Gideon once more looking perfectly put together, as if he'd just stepped out of a bandbox. He really was remarkable—a dazzling mix of precision and nonchalance, his dark handsomeness vying with his studied reserve.

She wondered if all women felt as she did when she saw him: how delightful it would be to see him discommoded, disheveled, vulnerable.

At her mercy.

Oh, dear, where had that thought come from?

Jessica lifted a hand to her high-necked bodice, perhaps to still her rapidly beating heart, and pasted a welcoming smile on her face as she crossed the room to where Gideon still stood, clearly playing Master of the Domain. *Her* domain.

"I warned you not to wear armor," was his greeting, spoken quietly, yet reverberating inside her as if she'd suddenly grown harp strings inside her chest and he'd just plucked them.

The arrogance of the man! "And I did not, not this morning. Your ridiculous state of near undress to one side, I was nothing but presentable when I dared cross your threshold. Tonight, however, you are the guest, and what I wear is of my concern, not yours."

His smile, so unexpected, nearly had her rocking back on her heels. "Perhaps we should give your brother the dressing of both of us. He's convinced he's in the very first stare of sartorial perfection."

Jessica couldn't help herself; she returned his smile. "I fear even your immense consequence could but crumble beneath the addition of a puce waistcoat, my lord. As for me, I'd rather go na—"

Gideon leaned in as if to hear her better. "Pardon me, I didn't quite catch that? You'd rather what?"

"Could we possibly be serious, sir?" she asked, drawing herself up to her full height, which still made her feel small and insignificant in his presence. She wasn't used to that. Her stature had always been a blessing, she'd thought. Why, she was taller than at least a quarter of the men in this room, including Richard.

"I rather thought I was being serious. You do know it's inevitable, don't you? You and I, that is. I won't even point out it was you who began this intriguing dance of ours."

"I apologize for that," Jessica said quietly, shooting her eyes from side to side, praying no one could overhear them and this damning discussion. "Profoundly."

"Ah, but not profusely. Profusely would be nice."

"In that case, Gideon, I most *profusely* apologize for apparently goading you into the ridiculous display of ungentlemanly behavior I was so unfortunate as to witness this morning. You must feel so ashamed."

He tilted his head to one side as he contemplated her, seemed to be measuring her in some way. "You're not lacking in intelligence, are you? Or brass. There are few who would dare to speak to me so."

"Perhaps if more did, you wouldn't be so insufferably smug. I'm not afraid of you, Gideon. As to this absurd idea of anything between us being *inevitable,* I should point out that I have absolutely *no* interest in— Let go of me."

"Don't cause a scene," he said, his grip on her arm looking to the casual observer to be one of easy familiarity, when in fact she swore his fingertips were crushing her bones as they walked straight cross the room to the doorway leading to her apartments. "We don't want to rouse Richard's suspicions. He's got thirty years on me—it wouldn't be a fair fight. And I'll remind you, Seth is mine, not yours. Smile, Jessica. Let everyone know you're just fine."

"This is absurd. You…you're kidnapping me in my own house," Jessica whispered angrily, even as she saw the sense in not alarming Richard.

Richard paused in the act of drawing in the cards for a reshuffle. "You're going upstairs?" he asked worriedly.

"We've some business to discuss, yes. I shan't be long."

"Very good," Gideon complimented as she concentrated on inserting the key in the lock she'd earlier made sure was engaged this evening, which wasn't a simple matter considering he had hold of her right arm and her left hand was shaking with nerves.

Once the door was open and he was forced to release her arm in the narrow hallway, she lifted her skirts and ran up the stairs, thinking to slam the upper door in his face.

Which he appeared to realize, as he stayed so close behind her it was impossible to implement her admittedly less than hopeful plan.

Once inside the small sitting room he took hold of her arm again, swinging her about so that her body was fairly slammed against his, his face not two inches from hers.

"Now, you were saying?" he asked her smoothly.

She was? She'd been saying something? What had she been saying? Dear Lord, she couldn't remember! He was so close. His smile was so...intimate. Mocking. Inviting. Infuriating. Intriguing...

"Can't remember?" he asked her, his arms somehow having slid around to her back, holding her in place, one hand high, between her shoulders, the other lower... provocatively lower. "Let me refresh your memory. I had been saying what will happen between us is inevitable, and you were protesting that you disagree, you harbor absolutely no interest—in what, Jessica? In this?"

He swooped in like a bird of prey, capturing her mouth just as she opened it to say—what? What could she possibly say?

Oh, my. She could say that. If his tongue wasn't in

her mouth, she could say that. If his right hand wasn't so skillfully cupping her bottom, bringing her into intimate contact with the evidence of his arousal. If her eyes hadn't closed on all remnants of sanity left to her, if her heart weren't beating so wildly, if her arms hadn't entwined themselves about his neck…if the world hadn't suddenly gone mad.

She was left gasping for breath when his mouth left hers to traverse new ground, exploring her ear, the sensitive skin behind that ear, the length of her throat as she tilted her head to allow these further inroads on her sanity, let alone her common sense.

Never. She'd never experienced anything like this sudden fierce onset of desire, this curious tightening between her legs that had nothing to do with hoping to hold off an inevitable cruel invasion.

Gideon was cupping her breast now, rubbing his thumb across the stiff material of her gown. She gritted her teeth, wishing away the fabric, feeling her nipple straining for a more intimate touch. Perhaps his touch would be different. Perhaps his mouth more knowing, less harsh, taking this budding physical arousal her body seemed to understand and nurturing it, not turning it to pain and humiliation and tears.

There has to be something more, her mind promised her, *or else women like Mildred wouldn't be so eager to partake in it, time and time again. Perhaps it wasn't me but James who was the sad failure.*

Jessica felt herself being lifted off the floor and high against Gideon's chest. She buried her head in his shoulder as his long strides took them across the room. He turned to his left.

"That's…that's the stairs to the kitchens," she managed, and his short, pithy curse brought a tremulous smile to her lips as he turned abruptly and headed, this time, toward her small, spinsterish bedchamber. Now she noticed his breathing had become nearly as ragged as her own, and the first stirrings of fear dragged at her arousal, slowing it to a near stop.

She'd been selfishly thinking of herself, only herself. She'd forgotten the effect of passion on a man.

Hers had been a virginal bed for more than four years, since James's death, and she'd been glad of the respite, the sanctuary it held for her. How could she be doing this? Willingly doing this? What on earth did she think it could possibly prove? She was unnatural, James had told her so, time and time again. She wasn't a real woman.

Gideon would know, and he'd either turn away in disgust, or he'd slake himself, anyway, pounding hurtfully inside her until he was done.

Either way, she lost.

"I don't… I can't…" she said as he stood her on her feet beside the bed, turned her around and began expertly working open the line of buttons from her neck to her waist, as he had done the previous evening. Only tonight his mouth followed after his hands, his tongue licking at her skin, sending shivers of what had to be pleasure rippling through her.

It was as if he hadn't heard her. He took hold of her shoulders and turned her back to him. In the light of the small candelabra burning at her bedside, he locked his eyes with hers as he touched his hands to her long, unbound hair, smoothing it back over her shoulders.

She was naked to the waist now, her gown snagging at her hips. He lowered his head, taking her in his mouth, teasing her with his fingers, destroying her now silent warnings of his imminent disappointment, her ultimate disgrace. No matter how hopeful the beginning, when her own body tried to believe this time it might somehow be different, there was always that same bad ending.

Somehow, the coverlet had been stripped back, and she was on the cool sheet. Somehow, her gown was gone, her only undergarment was gone; she was lying there, eyes closed to reality, listening to the whisper of fabric as Gideon rid himself of his evening clothes.

She'd been here before, in this position, brought low by the mere fact of being female.

She had no maidenly shame about her naked body, experienced no wild urge to try to cover herself. James had stripped her of that years ago. She knew what her body was for—a man's pleasure. The man wanted what the man wanted, and now was as good a time as any to get it over with, so that they could move on. Resistance only brought pain. She'd simply have to pretend, go along. He'd soon learn the truth about her.

She didn't dare look at him. She'd seen a fully aroused male before and knew what that arousal meant. Jessica believed herself to be a strong woman in most things, even an independent woman—a hard-earned independence. But this had always defeated her; she couldn't physically best a man, and she couldn't shoot him. Struggle was useless, embarrassing and often countered with violence. She knew herself to be the weaker vessel. It wasn't rape if she let him take what he believed he wanted. It was simply easier.

The bed sagged slightly as he joined her, as he leaned over her, as he brought his head close to hers once more. Good. At least it would soon be over.

"You're even more perfect than I imagined," he told her as he slowly drew his hand down her body. "No flaw, anywhere. Perfect seduction. Last night was an uncomfortably long night for me. Was it for you?"

Was what uncomfortable for her? She couldn't think, couldn't concentrate on anything but the travels of his hand, knowing where he was heading, to the juncture of her thighs.

Would he please just finish it, this *inevitable* he spoke of, the inevitable she'd stupidly goaded him to. That would tell him more than she could ever hope to say. Then they could put all of this behind them and move on to the subject of her father's supposed murder, the golden rose he'd worn in his cravat.

His hand slid over her lower belly, and she sighed, opened her silk stocking-clad legs to him. Let him take what he believed he needed. This meant nothing to her. It was only her body. A few more minutes, that's all. Just, please, quickly.

His kiss surprised her; she hadn't expected any more coaxing now that he had her where he wanted her. Not that James hadn't tried this sort of arousal in the beginning, until he'd realized he was only wasting his time, delaying his pleasure. But, Lord, he had tried, each thing he'd attempted worse than the last. The bites, the pinching fingers, the supposedly arousing slaps, believing perhaps pain would turn to pleasure. And it had...for him.

Jessica felt tears burning behind her eyes and forced her mind to stop thinking about James. He was dead, he didn't control her any longer. She owed him nothing she hadn't paid back tenfold in the nearly eight long months of their bizarre marriage.

Now another man was touching her, taking what he wanted. What would he do if he knew what she'd been thinking? No, he couldn't know.

She raised her hips slightly, as she'd been taught.

Gideon's response was to continue his travels across the landscape of her lower body. His fingertips drew a route from her navel to within a heartbeat of her center, then moved on to skim the inside of her thighs. And still he kissed her, his tongue teasing, tasting, coaxing a response that surprised her; that curl of desire returned, deep inside her.

She moved her hips again, this time without first thinking about the action. Was he avoiding her? Did he have to be pointed in the correct direction?

Hardly. The man kept four mistresses.

Jessica swallowed hard, barely given time to draw in a fresh breath between kisses, barely wanting to waste time in doing so. Because Gideon's mouth was so provocatively enticing, she actually heard herself moan in loss when he broke the last kiss and began moving his head lower, beginning a new journey that led to her left breast and ended when he took the nipple into his mouth.

She braced herself for the pain, but it didn't come. He didn't take, he...*worshipped*. Yes, that was the word.

He tasted, he suckled, he drew the tip of his tongue around her, he *coaxed* rather than *commanded.*

She opened her eyes, raised her head as best she could and watched. Her arm seemed to rise, unbidden, so that she could run her fingers through his dark thatch of hair. She felt a closeness, a communion with the man, a feeling unexplainable yet perfectly understood. It was like nothing she'd ever felt before.

When he finally slid his fingers between her legs, curiosity overcame her fear, even though she held her breath, until the slow, nearly circular strokes set off a curious sort of pleasure that showed every sign of turning her limbs to water.

Oh, yes. The words came unbidden to her mind and repeated themselves. *Oh, yes. Yes. Yes, yes, yes...* "Do that," she moaned, not realizing she'd spoken. "Please... there. Do that..."

She drew up her feet, bending her knees, allowing them to fall open for him, lifting her hips as he seemed to somehow spread her and stroke her at the same time, finding some previous hidden center of her that had to be acknowledged, demanded some sort of satisfaction.

I'm real, she rejoiced inside her head. *This is real, this is happening, this is...* And then she didn't think at all. Her body simply reacted to Gideon's touch, flowering, quivering, pulsating, flinging her out over some abyss as pleasure held her aloft, in its thrall.

He filled her then, levering himself up and over her and then plunging into her in one swift movement.

From some distant place, out over the abyss, she saw herself wrap her limbs around him as if fearful he would leave her. She saw herself kissing his heated skin, biting into the straining muscles of his strong neck and shoulders, rocking with him, urging him on, almost grimly determined to give pleasure for pleasure.

Gideon pushed himself up and looked down at her, as if to gauge her response. "Now?" he asked, watching her closely. "Please God, woman, say *now*."

"Now," she responded, not quite certain what she'd just agreed to, because nothing could be better than what she'd already felt. That was impossible.

But it wasn't. Gideon didn't just move inside her now. He plunged, he took, he pumped. Ground himself against her and then took up the rhythmic movements again, each time faster, each time deeper, each time giving more, demanding more, and all while watching her, watching her, watching her.

"No," she said at last, fear finally finding its way back through the haze of passion. A new fear, one she'd never before had to face. This felt too good, she might shatter with it, disappear inside the pleasure. Her heart might burst, her mind explode. Too good. This was too dangerously good. *"Oh, God...no."*

"On the contrary. Oh, God...*yes,*" Gideon said, and then buried himself inside her one last time, their bodies fitting so tightly together they may have merged into one. She felt her own body clench and unclench again and again, even as his did the same, on and on, until at last he collapsed against her, chest to chest, and they both lay still, perhaps he as well as she in order to assess whether or not they'd just died.

A single tear escaped Jessica's eye and ran down the side of her head, into her ear. It tickled. All right, she was still alive.

Gideon finally stirred, and she moved her hands over his sweat-slick back, reluctant to let him go as he made to leave her.

"Insatiable, are you, madam? I'm devastated to admit I'm of no further use to you for at least an hour," he said in a joking voice as he turned onto his back, his forearm over his eyes. "I should have taken you up on your offer last night, although it's possible the anticipation increased the pleasure. Clearly you were born for this, Jessica Linden. And at least I know now how your late husband died. Undoubtedly in bed, and with a smile on his face."

As more tears threatened, Jessica quickly turned her head and surreptitiously wiped at her eyes with a corner of the sheet. "He wasn't smiling, no," she said, and then quickly shut her mouth so she could say no more. She wanted to rest her head on Gideon's shoulder, to curl her arm about his waist and simply…cuddle. "Could… would you please gather your clothing and give me my privacy? I'll join you in the sitting room. There's wine in the decanter."

"Suddenly I feel this strong urge toward leaving a purse on your bedside table," Gideon said, his tone having returned to the careless sarcasm he seemed so adept with most times. He left the bed, most probably to gather his clothing from the floor. "Very well. But ten minutes, no more. I'll help you with those bloody buttons, as it wouldn't do to return to the gaming floor in another ensemble."

"And not before you tell me more of what you hinted at earlier. You do remember that, don't you?"

If he noticed she was speaking to him with her back

turned to avoid seeing his nakedness, he didn't call her on it. "I've rethought the matter. I shouldn't have said anything. It's none of your concern."

Now Jessica did turn toward him, making certain the coverlet she'd reached for earlier covered her breasts. He'd already donned his breeches, thank the Lord. She didn't think she could continue this conversation if they both were naked. "None of my concern? You all but guaranteed me my father and stepmother were murdered. I have a right to know why you think that."

"Why would that be? You hated your father, fled from hearth and home many years ago. That was the way of it, you said."

"Oh, and that means I shouldn't care if he and his wife were murdered? Perhaps you think I should be doing a jig? No, don't answer that! Besides, you wanted to talk to me about the Society, remember? Your father's Society?"

"My mistresses don't plague me with talk. I prefer my pleasure without prattle."

"I'm not one of your mistresses and I'll speak when I wish," Jessica countered, at last far enough removed from the revelations of the past half hour that her mind had begun to function once more. "Must I add, Gideon, that you're not my lover? You said the word *inevitable*. Perhaps it was. But now we move on."

He looked at her blandly, as if what she'd said meant nothing. "Just get dressed," he said, and then— finally—quit the room.

Leaving Jessica to wonder what on earth had happened, why it had happened so easily with this infuriating, totally exasperating man, if it was the man or something else that had changed inside her to make what had happened possible.

And, having happened once, was it possible for it to happen again? Surely not with the insufferable Gideon Redgrave, but he wasn't the only man in the world. It very well could have been James who had been the aberration. Not that she was now about to go the route of Mildred or her ilk in order to satisfy her curiosity. She simply couldn't allow what had happened with Gideon to happen with Gideon again. He was an earl and thoroughly unlikable, and she was a widow running a gaming house. He was not for her, and she definitely was not for him.

Although she could, being at heart an honest person, feel some gratitude toward the man.

"Not that he can ever know what he did, or else he'd be more than insufferable. Much better to allow him to continue to think of me as nothing more than one of a probably endless list of casual liaisons. Yes, this all is going to take some concentrated thinking," she told herself as she held up her gown and frowned at the wrinkles, her hard-won practical nature finally coming to her aid. "And perhaps a pressing iron…"

CHAPTER SIX

THE WINE IN JESSICA'S SITTING room, again tonight, was of good quality, but there was an insufficient quantity of it for his needs. There might not be enough wine in all of London sufficient for his needs, as his need was to drown the disquieting feeling he'd taken some sort of fateful step into an unknown he did not recognize and had little chance of escaping unscathed.

"What in bloody hell just happened in there?" he muttered, directing a fierce glare toward the bedchamber door before downing a full measure of wine and filling his glass once more.

He'd set out to prove a point. He'd set out to taste the wares so blatantly put on offer the previous evening. He'd been out to convince himself that a night spent wakeful, consumed by thoughts of what he would like to do to Jessica Linden, had been an aberration, perhaps caused by some juvenile fit of pique over that ridiculous pistol, possibly brought on by simple curiosity: Could she live up to the intriguing expectations he'd felt as he'd helped her unbutton her gown?

He damn well hadn't expected what had happened. He felt half defiler of innocence, half possibly king of the world, as she'd been so genuinely passionate, so clearly astounded as he took her over the top with him. She'd seemed eager at first, then resigned, even detached from her surroundings, a whore who would endure, even attempt to feign interest, if only her client would take what he'd paid for, and then let her get back to work.

And then…*damn*. He'd nearly lost himself in her then, hadn't he? That never happened. There was always a part of himself he withheld, that part of him he shared with no one, tried to believe didn't even exist.

She'd seemed so vulnerable. He didn't want vulnerable, had no use for vulnerable. He wanted expertise, and he paid for it. Paid well for it and then walked away when it suited him to be gone.

She'd made him want to stay in the bed with her, she'd made him want to hold her, feel her heart beat against him, listen to her breathe as she drifted into sleep, her head on his shoulder. By God, he couldn't get out of that bed quickly enough!

Was that something she practiced? That intoxicating mix of reticence and passion? If so, she'd definitely perfected her technique, because he wanted more. He'd been satisfied, but certainly not satiated; she shouldn't still be in his mind, but she was.

He should leave. What was she going to do, chase him down Jermyn Street? Confront him again in Portman Square? No, of course she wouldn't do that. She hadn't been anywhere near Portman Square last night, yet he'd done nothing but think about her.

He'd simply have to get her out of his system, that's all. She'd hit him unawares, unprepared, the mistress of whatever game it was she played. She'd been married, she lived her life on the fringes, she'd probably had more lovers than many women had consumed hot dinners. She'd offered her body, clearly not for the first time. Her trick was in somehow making him feel she'd offered more.

A week, two, and he'd wonder what he'd ever seen in her that had attracted him in the first place.

Gideon nodded his head, as if in agreement with himself and his plan, and then settled down on the slightly shabby sofa, glass in hand, to await her exit from the bedchamber. She'd walk in, that chin of hers held high, so like how Trixie faced down the world, and he'd close up her buttons while he recited verses of *Paradise Lost* inside his head to keep his mind occupied, and then they would discuss his father's damnable Society.

Not that he'd tell her anything too specific...just enough to keep her interested until he lost interest in her. As for her assertion they weren't to become lovers? Let her lie to herself if she wished, let her repeat that lie each night as he left her warm and rosy from his lovemaking.

Yes, two weeks. Perhaps a month. No longer. Until he figured her out, until he figured out what had just happened.

Tonight, once he'd shared some small morsel of what he knew, he would escort her downstairs, he'd carefully lose five hundred pounds at the faro table in lieu of actually offering her payment for her services, and he'd return to Portman Square, lock himself in his study and drink until dawn.

It wasn't much of a strategy, and thank God both Valentine and Max were not in residence, but for the moment, the plan satisfied him.

He could hear her moving about in her bedchamber, and a very long ten minutes later the door opened. She was once again clad in that damn black gown, so at odds with the flowing mane of red hair that put the lie to the prudish ensemble.

Without speaking to him, she turned her back and employed both hands to lift her hair, giving him access to the long row of buttons…and her bare back. What woman shunned at least a chemise, wearing only a pair of those flimsy French drawers tied at her waist? What torment for a man to look at that high-necked gown, those modestly covered arms, knowing what lay beneath! Modesty and vice. No and yes. Prude and wanton. Oh, yes, the mistress of the game she played.

Gideon drew his finger down the length of her spine, and she shifted her shoulders slightly, either in delight or to warn him to stop. He couldn't know, and he doubted she would tell him unless he could goad her into an answer.

"Perhaps an hour was an insult to myself," he whispered beside her ear as, instead of putting his hands to the task of closing her buttons, he slid them inside the gaping fabric, to gently cup and squeeze her unbound, uplifted breasts, his thumbs circling her taut nipples. *Item three on the list of things he wanted to do to Jessica Linden he'd composed in his head during his near-sleepless night.*

For a moment, she seemed ready to melt against him. For a moment.

"Richard was correct in his assessment. You are your father's son, aren't you, Gideon? Does nothing save rutting occupy your mind for more than a minute?"

"You—" He withdrew his hands, closing his mouth on the word *bitch,* and buttoned her gown as impersonally as he'd pull on his own boots. He'd figure her out, there would come a day when he called the shots, when she would be rebuffed, left feeling like a pleading, bleating fool. *But clearly,* he told himself, *not yet.*

"Thank you," she said as she lowered her hands, and her luxurious curls tumbled free past her shoulders. She then immediately sat down and looked up at him, clear-eyed and composed, as if they'd just come upstairs, and nothing had happened between them. "How do you know my father and Clarissa were murdered?"

That she'd traded her body for information was clear now. She'd let him have her so that they could get down to business. A cold woman.

Gideon took up his wineglass once more. He could play the game as coolly as she did, better. He'd had considerable practice. "I don't know if your stepmother was deliberately killed. She may simply have had the misfortune to be in the coach. But Turner was definitely murdered. Their hired coach supposedly overturned at night, with the full, lit coach lanterns breaking, the oil spilling out and igniting. Trapped inside the coach, your father and his wife were burned to death."

By now, Jessica had her hand to her mouth, finally shaken out of her reserve. "My God. I always believed he was destined for hellfire. But not while he was still aboveground. Yet, clearly an accident. Why did you question it?"

Gideon set down his wineglass. "I was already

aware of other deaths, other members of the Society perishing in *accidents*. All, like your father, wearing the rose. Orford, last spring, shot by mistake by another hunter in his party—just whom, nobody could say, as they were all drunk, all shooting as fast as their bearers could load for them. Sir George Dunmore drowned six months ago after somehow toppling into the Channel from a friend's yacht in the middle of the night, the conclusion being that he must have slipped on the rain-wet deck and tumbled overboard."

"Both plausible conclusions," Jessica said. "But there was another one?"

"Yes, the one that finally aroused my suspicions. A few months later it was Baron Harden's turn to be careless. He took a tumble down a dark flight of stairs after leaving his mistress. When I heard of your father's accident just outside London, most especially the part about the coach lamps, I was already past believing all these accidents were a matter of coincidence. I immediately traveled to the estate, to view the bodies for myself before they were interred."

Jessica's brown eyes widened. "That's ghoulish. How could you even look at them?"

He was in no mood to tread softly. "The bodies were in no fit condition to be laid out in the house, thankfully. So the answer to your *how* is, with a fat bribe to the groom guarding the remains in the stables until the interment, my extremely discreet physician brought along for his expertise, my valet, Gibbons, holding up a lantern for us, handkerchiefs tied around all our faces and wearing riding gloves we immediately consigned to the waste bin."

She folded her hands in her lap. "I believe I was asking a rhetorical question. But thank you for that explanation. You are a determined man, aren't you?"

"When I want answers, yes, I go after them. They actually didn't die in the fire, Jessica. From what my physician could tell, admitting my own limited contact with dead bodies, they'd both sustained pistol shots to their skulls. Fire doesn't melt bones, most of all, the skull. With a little prodding at the remains, the holes were not that difficult to spot."

Jessica had gone rather pale. "Shot. Not an accident at all. At least they didn't burn, thank God."

"No, the fire was meant to obscure the wounds. The coachman, alas, was long gone, so I couldn't question him."

"Had he shot them? Perhaps set the coach on fire to cover what he was about. A robbery, I would suppose?"

Gideon shook his head, amazed at her sangfroid. She was shocked, but she showed no signs of subsiding into a swoon; her mind was ticking along in a rational fashion. "Anything's possible. Am I being too suspicious, Jessica?"

"No," she said quietly. "My father was always tight with his purse, so the fact he'd hired a coach rather than bring his own cattle and servants to London isn't surprising. Lord only knows *who* he hired. Their deaths could have been a result of a robbery, but when combined with the other supposed accidents? All of the men members of your father's Society?"

"They wore the rose. To me, that links them. Four accidents stretches coincidence a step too far."

"I only wonder why he and his wife were traveling to London at that time of year. No one can count on the roads being anything but snow-filled or quagmires. Did your sleuthing extend to finding an answer to that question?"

"No, but you're right, I should have thought of that. I was in London to settle some financial affairs for my former ward, turning them over to her bridegroom's man of business, or else I wouldn't have been in town myself."

"Lucky for you, I suppose, and your theories."

"Yes, I suppose so. Damn, why didn't I think to ask myself that question?"

"How lowering to discover one isn't omnipotent, Gideon," she said sweetly, so that he glared at her. She shrugged. "I was only thinking it would be interesting to know their reason for the journey. A fanciful mind might even consider the notion they were on their way to a meeting of the Society you're so certain was dissolved two decades ago."

This wasn't the first time she'd alluded to that possibility. He might as well tell her the rest.

"We've had some curious happenings at Redgrave Manor in the past year. Glimpses of lit lanterns moving through the estate at night, strange holes appearing inside the greenhouse which, when investigated, seem very much to have been caused by the cave-in of some sort of tunnel being dug beneath it. Oh, yes, and my father's crypt was broken into. His remains have gone missing."

"What?"

Well, at last! He had begun to wonder if the woman was completely unflappable.

"Yes, that was very much my reaction, as well. However, in the interests of full and honest disclosure, save for the rare sightings of curious lights at night this past month or more—possibly poachers—I can't for certain say when the tunnel was dug, but only when that portion of it collapsed. As for the theft of my father's body, that was only discovered when lightning struck a nearby tree and it fell, a large branch breaking one of the stained glass windows. We none of us enter the mausoleum unless it's to shelve another Redgrave— we've got enough of them in there that we stack them up like bolts of cloth in a Bond Street shop, you see, and then wall them in. The stone used to wall up Barry was on the floor of the crypt, broken in two, the body gone. But again, the theft could have occurred any time in the past twenty years."

Jessica was quiet for some time, her hands twisting in her lap, before she looked at Gideon again. "Do... do you think perhaps they took him—your father, that is—almost immediately? To, um, to perform their own ceremony? Oh, Lord, that's disgusting."

"And only one of several possibilities," Gideon said, just voicing his thoughts of the past few months aloud easing his mind somewhat. "To whit—propping him up on some throne to overlook their *activities?* To grind up his bones into powder, mix that in with sheep's blood or some such ridiculousness, and *drink* the man? To slice him up, as they did the saints of yore, with each member then blessed to carry a knucklebone as a memento, a holy relic? Don't answer yet—I've had time to consider more than that. There's one more. Did his followers, as my father was the acknowledged leader, believe the supposed treasure was interred with his bones, and come looking for it?"

Jessica held up her hand to stop him. "Not that last one, surely. A treasure? Why would your family do that? And why would anyone take the body with them, whether there was some sort of treasure to be found there or not?"

"I agree. It was only one of many possibilities, and a rather feeble one at that. However, I do believe, after years of not believing it, there may be some sort of treasure. Some precious gem perhaps, made a part of a larger golden rose, the symbol of the Society? Or something they prayed to—mayhap an enormous diamond stuck into the fat belly of a pagan idol?"

Jessica tucked her legs up on the couch, as if prepared to stay there all night, until she'd somehow solved the problem that so confounded him. "But wouldn't every member of the Society know the location of that sort of thing? They all gathered for their—I hate saying *ceremonies*. The word is too respectable for what they did."

"Drunken orgies?" Gideon offered. "Debaucheries? Deflowerings of whores paid handsomely to pretend they were intact innocents being offered up for some carefully orchestrated sacrifice? The open passing around of wives in some hope of alleviating the boredom of marital fidelity? Christ! Their own *wives*. Were they willing or unwilling, do you think?"

She shot him a dark glance that made him want to know more of what had happened to have her run off with James Linden. "I'm not convinced the members cared. All done in praise of the devil."

"Devil worship. Imitators of Sir Francis Dashwood and his ilk, but without any cursory bow to a pretense of an interest in the intellectual. We're back to that. I'd rather think them drunks and idiots. Otherwise I'd have to believe my father—my father!—discovered a way to make them all able to believe they were better than they were, acting in some higher purpose. Still, it's possible. I don't know how he'd have accomplished it, how any one person manages to twist minds to do his every bidding, no matter how vile, but he could have managed it."

"Until his wife shot him in the back when he was about to duel down her lover," Jessica said quietly. "I'm sorry. Was…the man one of the Society?"

"I can't say anything for certain. I was only nine years old at the time. I thought he was my new tutor, a Frenchman who'd fled France immediately after the fall of the Bastille. He'd only been at the Manor for a few weeks before both he and my mother were gone."

"Again, I'm sorry, Gideon. Not that your father was shot, I can't honestly say that, but that you lost your mother. I'm certain she didn't want to leave you. She must have felt she had no choice."

"I wonder if she would have made that choice if she could have known she and her lover would be swept up in the Terror two years later and sent to the guillotine. As someone reminded me just today, in the end the bill must always be paid."

For a moment, he could see his mother in his mind's eye. Beautiful, loving, but sad. Her eyes had always been so sad. There had been times he could coax a smile from her, but those times had been seldom. He treasured those few good memories. Strangely, he remembered his father only through the painting of him as a young man that hung in the portrait gallery.

Damn, but this woman was getting to him. He never thought about the boy he'd been twenty years ago. He'd never spoken of any of this. Not with his siblings, not with his grandmother. He'd shut it all down, all he'd felt at the time, all he'd so carefully avoided since he'd been awakened to the news of what had happened just before dawn that long-ago morning. Max and Val had been too young, and Katherine only an infant. He'd been the only one to really understand what *dead* meant, what *gone* meant.

Jessica got to her feet. "So what bill has come due for the members of the Society?"

Gideon snapped himself back to attention.

"I can think of one theory. It's not as if any of them could be proud of what they've done, and want it out in the world. The sins of relatively young men, trotted out for an airing twenty years later, could be more than embarrassing. Add even the whisper of devil worship to the mix, and the secret becomes dangerous. Your father sat in Parliament, remember. Someone may be blackmailing the others, or simply killing them off to silence them. I can't even be sure how many of them there are. There could be some who no longer wear the rose."

"Thirteen," Jessica said quietly. "The devil's dozen. At any time, there must be thirteen. James told me that much. One dies, two die, they must be replaced, or there can be no ceremonies. I promise you, they were still active five years ago. There could have been several new members since your father's time. The usual method was to draw from the blood relatives of the members. And, of course, a member's eldest son inherited his father's position by right."

Gideon looked at her curiously. One day they'd have to speak more of this James Linden. "No one has ever approached me."

"You were a child when your father...died. As an adult, I doubt anyone would have dared. You're a rather formidable man, Gideon."

He looked at her in sudden realization. "Adam."

"Yes, very good. Adam. Because the Society must still exist, I'm certain of that now more than ever. I'll grant you, I was appalled at what I saw this morning, but not so much so that I'm not relieved he's...he's... well, we both know what he is."

"A bacon-brained halfling who couldn't locate his own backside with both hands?"

Jessica smiled. "Thank you. Adam is, after all, my brother. I didn't want to say it myself."

"You're welcome. Still, until and unless you're proven wrong, I suppose I'm now doomed to keeping him close, explaining that particular part of his inheritance, and then watching over him?"

"Yes. I was going to tell you tonight, if I thought I could convince you to listen to reason. Because you're right, I can't protect him from the Society if they're desperate enough to go after him. But you can. My initial reaction was they wouldn't want him. But if they've run out of suitable candidates, they might make an exception."

"You say I can protect him, and I can. From the ones I know of, yes, but we can't know them all," Gideon said, the futility of what he was attempting to do all but smacking him in the face like a cold, wet cloth. He'd been curious, intrigued, and now he was beholden, damn it, the reluctant guardian of one Adam Collier, spotty-faced giggling twit who'd probably think dressing up in a mask and hooded cloak, playing at devil worship, to be the height of good fun.

But it was left to Jessica to really shock him.

"We might, soon. You've been seen sporting that horrible golden rose, remember? When I first saw it, I thought you were a member, something that should have occurred to me before I ever contacted you, I suppose. Still, I almost immediately realized you're not. I believe you on that head."

"I'd hoped wearing it would— I don't really know what I'd hoped. I'll not wear it again. And, again, I apologize."

"Yes, I know. As I apologize for the pistol. But who is to say, now that my father's dead, and considering Adam's clear unsuitability once anyone with two reasonably good eyes sees him, that rose might gain you an invitation to be the new thirteenth member. The eldest child of the founder, Gideon? You'd be a splendid catch."

CHAPTER SEVEN

THEY'D GONE BACK DOWNSTAIRS separately, Jessica suggesting it would be better that way. He could simply slip into the gaming room, hopefully crowded at this hour, and she would come down a few minutes later, going directly to the ground-floor supper room to mingle with the patrons stuffing their faces at her expense and hopefully guide them back to the tables.

After all, she still had her business to attend to, and Gideon had kept her from it long enough.

He'd agreed, and left her once they'd decided on an hour to meet the next day. He suggested she come to Portman Square. She'd politely declined, and they'd settled on his coming for her at noon, in his curricle, for a ride to Richmond Park.

"You're amenable to being seen in public with me?" she'd asked, thinking of his consequence.

"Your half brother is my ward. I see nothing unusual in the two of us becoming acquainted. You're a widow who earns her living with her uncle, hosting intellectual evenings, correct?"

"And the bloody blazes with anyone who knows better and who'd dare whisper otherwise?"

"I'm not known for concerning myself overmuch with whispers. We'll make one brief call before getting on our way, if you don't mind."

"You have someone you wish me to meet?" She was genuinely surprised at that.

His smile had curled her toes. "Someone I wish to shock would be more accurate. Although I doubt that's possible. Until tomorrow, Jessica."

And that had been that. He'd bowed in her direction, and taken his leave. Just as if they'd never been intimate. Just as if their conversation following that intimacy had centered on the state of the weather, or the fripperies of the latest fashions.

He was the most confounding man.

She had remained on the gaming floor until three, when the last of their patrons had finally toddled off, four young gentlemen slightly lighter in their pockets but vowing they'd had the best of good times and would return for a chance to recoup their losses. One of them had very pointedly winked at Mildred, who'd shot a quick, worried glance toward Jessica.

"Nothing more than a friendly round of slap and tickle behind the supper room," the girl had promised before heading for the kitchens, as her duties included helping Doreen and Seth clear away the remains of the food and dirtied dishes.

Jessica hadn't found it in her heart to remonstrate with the girl. Not now, considering she herself had gone far beyond a friendly round of slap and tickle. *And at last understood its appeal,* she'd reminded herself, avoiding Richard's curious look.

They quietly had gone about the business of gathering up cards and chips and covering the tables with cloths, Jessica still avoiding Richard's pointed glances until he'd at last directly asked her if perhaps it wasn't time to close up shop and move their enterprise to Bath, or even Tunbridge Wells.

"I'm fine, Richard," she'd assured him. "We're fine. Coming to London was your idea, remember? We'll soon be able to afford our inn. It would take another two or even three years to earn enough money anywhere but here."

"He could destroy you with a snap of his fingers." Richard had come around the faro table to cock his head and look into her eyes. "He may have already done so. You've got a new look about you, Jess, and I don't like it. Soft around the edges. You can't afford to think like a woman. I always felt that was your best defense—you don't think like a woman. James beat that softness out of you long ago. Your brother or no, this is not the time to discover you still have a heart."

"My *heart* is not involved, Richard," she'd told him. "What Gid—what the earl and I have between us is strictly business. He wants the Society destroyed, and so do I. For Adam's sake, for my sake. That's all it is."

"And now you're lying to me. Me, who knows the truth. Two days, undoing the trust of more than four years together." He'd sighed, shaken his gray head. "We're all we've got, Jess, you and me. At the end of the day, when he's done with you, that's all we'll still have. So you guard that heart you say isn't at risk, and I'll be here to pick up the pieces, as always."

Jessica had kissed him on the cheek, given him a fierce hug, and they'd gone back to work. As it was, she'd have only a few hours' sleep before Gideon returned to Jermyn Street. Then she'd crawled into her unmade bed to realize Gideon had left his scent behind, and even those few hours of oblivion had mostly alluded her. She didn't fall asleep until nearly dawn and woke shortly after ten, her eyes going immediately wide and shocked as she threw back the tangled covers, grabbed at James's banyan to cover her bare body and went in search of Mildred and the tub they kept in the kitchens.

"Doreen!" she called out as she ran barefoot down the stairs. "I need a tub, now. And fresh clothing. And something to eat. Doreen—oh, my God!"

She clasped the wrapper more tightly around her at breast and thigh as Seth looked up from the table, a piece of thickly slathered toast clamped between his jaws, his eyes gone round as saucers.

"Out!" she commanded, not daring to let go of the wrapper in order to point him toward the door.

Seth scraped back the chair and stood up, the toast still held in his teeth. He was looking at her bare feet, for pity's sake, as if he'd never before in his life seen a woman's toes. Strawberry jam slid off the slice of toast and plopped onto the floor, unnoticed.

"Come along, Seth," Richard said calmly, appearing from behind Jessica and walking over to take the boy's arm. "We'll leave your corruption to another time." He stopped in front of Jessica and pushed the boy ahead of him, through the doorway. "I consider it a blessing of our understanding that you do not cavil at prancing about this place in all manner of undress, but now we have the boy to consider."

"I know, I know. I didn't think. I overslept, and Gid—and the earl will be here at noon."

"Gideon. I can resign myself to hearing you call your lover by his name."

"He's not my— Oh, hang it, Richard. It's not as if I'm some vestal virgin, now, is it?"

"And he's a very pretty man. I don't fault you your attraction, even as it surprises me. But wounds heal, so that's probably a good thing. It's the avoidance of new wounds that worries me. Seth and I are just back from the stalls at Covent Garden," he went on, just as if he hadn't all but delivered a stern warning, at least stern for Richard. "Capons were too dear, so we settled on fish chowder for this evening's suppers."

"I loathe fish chowder," she said, smiling. "You're punishing me, aren't you?"

"With my usual subtlety, yes. Wear the yellow. It suits you. But put up your hair. It will drive him mad. He shouldn't be the only one to have slipped half her wits, should he?"

And then Richard was gone, and Doreen was pouring a mere two inches of heated water into the small tin tub.

Jessica was just putting the final pin in her slightly damp hair when Doreen knocked on the bedchamber door to tell her his lordship had sent in his tiger. His name was Thomas—the cutest little scrap, really, and all dressed in the finest livery—to beg Mrs. Linden didn't keep the earl's bays standing above five minutes, because that's what he said, and he said it quite nicely, and called her *ma'am* and everything, all so very prettylike.

"I'm ready," Jessica responded quickly to cut Doreen off, grabbing up her bonnet and shawl. "How do I look?"

"Like spring itself, Mrs. Linden," the maid of all work and front door sentry exclaimed, clapping her hands. "You ain't worn the yellow since last summer, now have you, and it's a shame the sun shines so little here, though thank the saints it's fine today, because the fog is yellow itself at times and dirties everything. Why, it took me *hours* to brush it all away last time you wore it. Now when was that? Oh, yes, last summer."

"Thank you," Jessica told her, chagrined that she'd so forgotten herself as to think Doreen could give a simple answer to a simple question. Still, if there were ever a person who could stall a constable on the ground floor whilst Jessica and Richard and their patrons hastily stowed the cards and markers and pulled out the tomes of poetry, it was Doreen.

The maid's prattle followed Jessica all the way down to the street and outside, where Doreen pointed to the young tiger and said, "See? Cutest little imp. Now you hold on tight once his lordship puts you to riding back there, young man," she called out, wagging a finger at him.

Jessica avoided Gideon's amused expression as the tiger helped her up onto the seat. He was, as usual, looking fine as nine pence as he lightly held the ribbons while his bays signaled their willingness to spring, his curly brimmed beaver at a jaunty angle on his head, his cravat a miracle of snow-white cloth. And no golden rose stuck in the center of it.

"And again, thank you, Doreen. I understand it's to

be the dreaded fish chowder tonight. You must have a considerable amount of chopping to do?"

"Oh, yes, Mrs. Linden. First the onions. They always make me cry, so I get them out of the way directly at the start. Then there's the pork fat, and that needs must be sliced thin, and all of the potatoes and the parsley and such. Mr. Borders brought us back some fine bunches of carrots, and I was thinking about putting in some of them while I was about it, seeing as how fish chowder takes most anything, doesn't it, and mayhap some—"

Jessica waved to Doreen as Gideon released the brake the moment the tiger was up behind them and then turned her face forward to hide her smile. "Doreen quite delights in detail," she said as they moved into the light noon traffic at the corner.

"The correct term is excruciating detail. I had a tutor rather like that. Max and I put a frog in his bed. Seven frogs, actually, and all at once. People always expect an even number. Although we think it was the fifth that had him hastily penning his resignation. Still, if you ever wish a comprehensive accounting of the major agricultural products of India, feel free to apply to me. You look exasperatingly pretty today, Mrs. Linden. Were the pins truly necessary?"

Jessica touched a hand to her bare nape, her bent elbow nicely concealing her triumphant smile. "Richard thought so. Exasperating was exactly what he'd hoped for."

"Your *uncle* doesn't care for me?"

"More correctly, he cares for me. He believes you may be out to destroy me."

Gideon didn't react by so much as a flicker of an

eyelid. "Really? Has he given any indication as to how I'm to go about this destruction?"

"He believes you've already begun. But I assured him I know what I'm doing."

"Good for you. And you're convinced of that?"

She turned to look at his profile, which could have been chiseled out of the finest marble by a master sculptor. Except that she knew his lips were warm and soft, not cold and hard like stone. A lie seemed in order. "Utterly."

"So you didn't dream of me last night?"

Jessica folded her hands in her lap. "No." As she'd barely slept at all and then it had been the deep sleep of exhaustion, that answer was mostly truthful.

He turned to look at her, his dark eyes alive with mischief. "Now there's a pity. I dreamed of you. Would you care to hear about my dream?"

"Again, no."

"Again, a pity. It all but had me flying to Jermyn Street at dawn, to knock down your door."

"I thought we'd agreed. That doesn't happen again."

He turned to face forward once more. "You pronounced, Jessica. I agreed to nothing. If we're to work together, we may as well continue to enjoy each other."

She very nearly opened her mouth to say she hadn't enjoyed him at all, but even she knew she couldn't tell that particular clunker with any hope of being believed. "I won't be your mistress. I'll keep the five hundred pounds you all but tossed away at the faro table because half of it is by rights Richard's, but don't insult me like that again. You're banned from the cards at

Jermyn Street. Besides, four women should be more than enough for any man."

He laughed. "Four? At one and the same time? Madam, I enjoy my pleasures, but that much pleasure would have me a bent and crippled man by now."

"Richard's never wrong."

"Richard should withdraw his nose from my business before he loses it. Who are these women?"

"I'm not going to continue this discussion," Jessica said, belatedly remembering the young tiger hanging on to the back of the curricle. *"Pas devant l'enfant."*

"Not in front of the child? Ah, you refer to Thomas. He's been in my employ for two years, and rendered impervious to shock long before, and if not then, long since." Without turning around, he raised his voice to ask, "Haven't you, Thomas?"

"Sir?"

"See, he isn't even listening, are you, Thomas?"

"Singing inside my head, my lord, like always. Would you like me to sing outside it for his lordship?"

"Perhaps another time. Go back to your inside singing."

Jessica shot a quick look behind her, to see the tiger had closed his eyes and was tipping his head from side to side as his lips moved, clearly singing "inside his head."

"He's really singing inside his head?"

"Yes, and much preferable to having him sing *outside* it, which he's only allowed to do around the horses, that unaccountably seem to enjoy the sound of Thomas's *joyful noise.* I think they're reminded of the goat we keep in the stables at Redgrave Manor to bear them company. Both *bray* with great enthusiasm."

Don't make me like you, Jessica warned him mentally…and perhaps herself. "The first is kept in Mount Street, the second is a Covent Garden warbler and the others are society ladies. The widow Orford and—oh."

"The widow and the niece of two of our murdered society members, yes, cultivated—but not in the literal sense—for any information they might have. But to be fair, the usually infallible Richard couldn't know that. As to Curzon Street and warbling, he is, sadly, behind the times. The warbler sings elsewhere, with my full approval and a fairly impressive strand of pearls around her slim neck. Do you like pearls?"

"More than I like you," Jessica grumbled half under her breath, but not because Mount Street had not been denied. Really. She didn't care. Not a whit! "I was merely making a point, Gideon. I don't care if you *cultivate* half of London. I just have no plans to have my name added to that lengthy list."

"'The best laid schemes o' mice an' men, gang aft agley…'" Gideon quoted, directing his cattle to the flagway.

"'And leave us nought but grief an' pain for promis'd joy,'" Jessica ended, probably giving away more of her fears about this man than she should have allowed.

"And a pretty piece of jewelry," Gideon quipped, setting the brake and tying the ribbons around it as Thomas leaped down and ran to the horse's heads. "But we'll argue this later, most likely in bed." Then, as she opened her mouth to protest, he winked and lightly jumped down from the seat, to come around the back of the curricle and offer her his hand.

She ignored it, preferring to look up at the facade of the imposing stone structure in front of her. "Where are we?"

"Cavendish Square. Old, respected, the town residences of some of the most stuffy and high in the instep members of the *ton*. And my grandmother, whose presence for some casts a blight on the entire neighborhood."

Jessica looked at the mansion again. "Your *grandmother?* I thought you meant you would be stopping at some shop for a moment. Why in heaven's name would you bring *me* to see your *grandmother?*" She was nearly squeaking, she was that shocked. And that confused. Even one of the scandalous Redgraves didn't bring his mistress...lover...whatever the devil he thought she was...to visit his *grandmother.* But he had!

"You're forgetting she was there during the heyday of my father's secret society. She was there the morning my father was shot. I've already told her about my suspicions as to the rash of accidental deaths, and about what's been happening at Redgrave Manor. I neglected to tell her about you, but now that I understand our possible predicament with Adam, I thought we should all three of us put our heads together."

"To come up with what? Other than possibly the most embarrassing quarter hour of my life?" She clasped her hands together, avoiding his outstretched hand. "I'm not going in there. Only a fool would go in there."

"Your parents were respected members of the *ton*.

You speak French. You can quote Robert Burns. I haven't had the pleasure of sharing a meal with you, but I'm tolerably certain you don't line up your peas on a knife blade and then attempt to slide them down your gullet—although your brother thinks that quite the height of hilarity."

"I run an illegal gaming establishment," Jessica whispered hoarsely.

"A minor impediment, not that Trixie would give a damn. I can name at least five titled ladies who discreetly encourage gaming in their Mayfair residences, three of whom who hold faro banks."

This information came as a shock to Jessica. "Then why did you turn up your nose—not that such a thing is physically possible, not with that beak of yours—when you realized you'd walked into *my* gaming room?"

"References to my nose to one side, I leaped to a mistaken conclusion. Mildred, you understand."

"Oh," Jessica said in a small voice, but then rallied. "But I'm still not going in there."

"Yes, you are," Gideon corrected her just before he reached up, put his hands on her waist and bodily lifted her down to the flagway as if she weighed no more than a feather. "I'd say my grandmother is harmless, but that would be a lie, so be on your toes. We need information, Jessica, and Trixie's the fastest way to it. She is, however, also a firm believer in *quid pro quo,* so she'll demand information in exchange."

"Have you ever stopped to wonder what it is you'd *do* if you had whatever information it is you think we need?"

"You mean other than returning my father's remains

to Redgrave Manor? I may not revere the man's memory, but I'll be damned if I'll simply shrug my shoulders and ignore what I now know. Other than that, no, not really. Although it might be charitable of me to find a way to put a stop to these accidents, don't you think?"

"No," she answered honestly. "I doubt any of them deserve saving. Except Adam. He will grow up someday, won't he?"

"I'd hoped to send him off to school and forget about him until he reached his majority. But I suppose I could take him in hand, if we are to assume the Society might soon show an interest in him. Would I be rewarded? I can think of several ways you could accomplish that."

"I'll have Doreen make you a large bowl of fish chowder," Jessica said as the front door of the mansion opened and a worried-looking older man in butler's black stuck his head into the breach.

"Excuse me, my lord, but her ladyship says you and the young miss are to come or go, but don't just stand out here with your fingers in your mouth or else people will wonder if your brain cracked. Sir."

"She said all that, did she, Soames? In just that way?" Gideon asked, extending his arm to Jessica, who saw no recourse now but to take it. His grandmother had been looking down at them from one of the windows? How embarrassing!

"She may have said a few more words I chose to either alter or discard rather than repeat them in front of the young miss, my lord, but I believe you can imagine them."

"Yes," Gideon said, handing over his hat and gloves to a liveried footman while Soames relieved Jessica of her shawl. "I believe I can. We'll find our own way upstairs."

"She's a tartar?" Jessica whispered the question as they mounted the wide, curving staircase, covertly examining the life-size marble statues set in niches along the wall. They were all male and curiously devoid of fig leaves.

"Hard and strict and abrasive? Hardly. She's sweetness itself, and her conversation is delightful. It's only when you go to move that you realize you've been sliced into ribbons. Give as good as you get, Jessica. She likes that."

"It would appear she likes others things, as well. Those statues are all naked," she mumbled as they gained the landing and another wide foyer. "Everything is so opulent, so beautiful, it took me a moment to believe I was seeing what I saw."

"Trixie has a curious notion of humor and never ordered them removed after my grandfather died. Imagine the *ton,* cooling their heels for a good half hour as they stand cheek by jowl on the stairs, waiting to be announced for one of Trixie's famous balls. The ladies never know where to look. The gentlemen vary in their reaction. Red ears. Quiet sniggers. Open admiration for some, which is rather disconcerting. It has been whispered that there's also an extensive collection of interesting paintings, etchings, even playing cards and a fascinatingly explicit set of china. If it exists, we grandchildren have not been allowed to inspect the collection, although I imagine we will be forced to do so at some point when Trixie dies, which she is not planning to do."

He didn't sound ashamed but only amused. "I've heard you Redgraves referred to as scandalous. I thought the reference referred only to the circumstances around your father's death. And whispers of his Society, of course. I had no idea—"

"No idea the taint goes beyond my father? It's said we Redgraves descend from a long line of satyrs. Trixie is our grandfather's third wife, the two others having died, the first in childbed, the second murdered by her lover. Trixie was barely sixteen when she was brought to the marriage bed by a man thirty years her senior. Truthfully, I think she was even younger than that. I once researched the subject and found the legal age for females to marry during that time was twelve."

"I doubt she'd want anyone to think she's four years older than assumed," Jessica said, inwardly cringing at the thought of a twelve-year-old bride. "Although perhaps not."

"It was another time, and definitely not a better one. In any case, my father merely resurrected what had been created by my grandfather years earlier. As I already told you, there were many such clubs back then. Most were tame imitations of Dashwood's, but not all. Some were worse, both here and in Ireland, other places. If we want to know the truth about the Society and its secrets, we need to talk to Trixie, and with the gloves off. Hers, and yours."

"We were never going to Richmond, were we?" Jessica asked, looking toward the closed double doors to what had to be the drawing room. A pair of small yellow pug dogs stood outside them with their heads turned hopefully toward Soames, who had followed up the stairs and now scooped up the dogs and carried them away.

"Not today, no. I know this will be embarrassing for you, and I apologize, Jessica, truly. But if you're at all worried the Society is still active, and they'll come after your brother at some point, we need to do this."

"You forgot to remind me that my father was murdered," Jessica said archly. "Or reiterate your own reasons."

"I'm Adam's guardian."

She rolled her eyes. "Oh, let's not go through that again, please. Let's simply get this over with so that I don't have to look at you anymore."

"Not even tonight in Portman Square? Adam is eager to meet his sister at the dinner table."

"You just made that up."

His grin made her want to slap him. "True. But he'll be there, if I have to tie him to the chair. I don't always play fair, but I'm most always effective when I want something. Now come on," he said, holding out his arm. "We stand out here any longer, Trixie will be forced to abandon her pose of lady-at-leisure and come hunting us."

And it was a lady-at-leisure Jessica saw when they entered the blue-and-white drawing room, a large chamber filled with sunlight and enormous vases and bowls stuffed with fresh flowers.

The Dowager Countess of Saltwood reclined on an intricately carved white-and-gilt one-armed lounge, her dainty feet encased in silver slippers tucked up beside her, her slim body draped in a high-waisted lace-edged burgundy silk gown cut for a much younger woman, colored for a dowdy matron. The effect was startlingly effective.

Her hair, a wondrous curled mass of white-gold ringlets woven through with several narrow silver ribbons, teased at her forehead, caressed her slim neck, touched on her right shoulder. She was painted, definitely, but with a subtle hand, so that the color in her cheeks and on her smiling mouth seemed natural.

If this was Beatrix Redgrave at—at Jessica's quick calculations—nearly seventy years of age, the Trixie of her youth must have been the most stunningly beautiful woman ever born.

Jessica immediately felt too tall, incredibly plain and decidedly gauche, as she imagined every woman ever in the same room with the dowager countess had felt from the time Trixie had reached her fifth birthday.

"Gideon, my pet!" the woman exclaimed now, her voice like the soft tinkling of delicate silver bells. She raised one small, heavily be-ringed hand for his kiss. "What dastardly thing have I done that merits me two visits from my eldest grandson in as many days? You must tell me, so that I can repeat the transgression again and again, as I see you far too seldom."

She looked past Gideon to smile at Jessica, who immediately curtsied. "And who is this gorgeous creature? She puts me in mind of dearest Juliette Rècamier, whom I so enjoyed when we met in Coppet while I was visiting Madame de Staël. Coppet is in Switzerland, pet," she said as an aside to Gideon. "Such a beauty that one is, if poor as a church mouse, dear thing, and married at fifteen to her own father, if rumor is to be believed. And then there's that unfortunate business about her inability to enjoy— Ah, but that's again, only rumor. Suffice it to say the woman has been painted time and time again as a virginal figure."

If the dowager countess was hoping to put Jessica to the blush, she had badly misjudged her by appearance: in point of fact, the butter-yellow gown with its modest neckline and her total lack of jewelry, such as a "fairly impressive strand of pearls."

Gideon quickly stepped in and made the introductions, so that Jessica found herself curtsying yet again before being invited to sit. Soames entered the room then, trailed by two maids who quickly arranged a magnificent tea tray on a low table in front of Jessica, who was then asked to pour.

A test, possibly? To see if this Jessica Linden woman who had shown up here unannounced with her grandson had any notion of how to properly serve tea? What a wicked woman!

"I would be delighted," Jessica said, inching forward on her chair. "Your ladyship will, I'm convinced, forgo sugar. In favor of cream."

"Teased one naughty puss to the other," her ladyship said, nodding her head in acknowledgement of the hit while delivering one of her own. "All right, Gideon, we've no simpering miss here. Who is she?"

"Jessica's the half sister of my new ward, Adam Collier. You remember him. You met last week in Bond Street."

"The cork-brained popinjay?" Trixie looked at Jessica again. "Clearly his mother was the imbecile in that union, although I never put much store by Turner

Collier's ability to think much beyond his— No, don't frown so, Gideon, I'll be good."

Jessica bit back a smile. The dowager countess was so petite, so beautiful, the very picture of a sweet and gracious lady. When she spoke as she did now, it was rather like the surprise one felt when a child uttered a naughty word. You really weren't sure at first you'd heard correctly. A line from an old nursery rhyme flitted through Jessica's head: *And when she was good she was very, very good...and when she was bad...*

Trixie's expression took on the attitude of interested listener. "Now explain why this cheeky child is here. I'm not such a slow-top that I don't realize it has something to do with what we discussed yesterday."

It didn't take long for Gideon to relate Jessica's concerns that the Society might approach Adam to take his father's place in the devil's dozen, but the dowager countess quickly pooh-poohed any notion the Society was still active.

"I won't say it ended with Barry's death, not immediately, but it couldn't have gone on for more than another year before straggling to a halt, or I would have known."

"Your grandson is of the opinion you know everything, your ladyship, up to snuff on all suits, as it were," Jessica said as she offered the woman a small plate of iced cakes. Gideon had warned she'd have to give in order to get, and she would do so now. "As I was promised as the guest of honor at one of their ceremonies five years ago, I can only conclude he's incorrect, and you don't know everything." She raised her chin a fraction. "Or you're lying."

Trixie's kohl-darkened eyes assessed Jessica again and then slid to her grandson. "Linden, you said?"

"Yes, James Linden. Jessica's late husband."

The dowager countess swung her feet to the floor and sat up, again skewering Jessica with a look. "By-blow of a baron who shall remain nameless, invested with all the myriad vices of his father and the cunning of his blowsy strumpet of a mother—perished of the clap, I believe, the pair of them, and the baron's innocent wife, as well, poor thing. Jamie Linden. Now there's a name I'd hoped never to hear again. Dead now? Wonderful. If you were smart, you buried him upside down, so he couldn't dig himself out, but only closer to hell."

"Actually, ma'am, we left him in the bed where he died, only careful to first empty his pockets," Jessica said, feeling more vindicated for what she'd done then she'd ever had until this moment. "I have no idea what the innkeeper did with the body."

"*We?* You said 'we'? No, don't answer that yet, we'll get to it. Gideon, clear away this insipid tea and pour us all some wine. Begin at the beginning, Jessica, if you please."

"I'd rather not if you don't mind, ma'am."

"I *do* mind, most especially that you insist upon calling me ma'am, as if I've one foot hovering over an open grave. Perhaps it would help if you called me Trixie, as I believe we're going to be discussing things that could only be hindered by formality. Lord knows it would help me. Ma'am?" She gave a delicate shudder of her slim shoulders.

Jessica bowed her head, concentrating on her hands,

folded in her lap. "Thank you…Trixie. But I'd still rather not."

Gideon pressed a wineglass into her hands. "She'll have it from you one way or another, you know. Trixie? Who was Jamie Linden, other than some anonymous baron's bastard?"

"When I knew him? Thank you, pet." She took the wineglass and quickly downed half its contents. "No, the foul taste is still in my mouth, just from saying his name. Who was Jamie Linden? I suppose that would depend on the day of the week. Card shark, schemer, purveyor of pipe dreams too numerous to enumerate and always with airs above his station. When riding high, he was accepted on the fringes of society, as he always knew the location of the best cockfights, the jockey who could be bribed to lace his mount with pepper to get a good run—there was this one time he managed to have a live river eel shoved up a stallion's rump just before the race. Ran like the wind, pet, that horse did, and if it hadn't managed to expel the thing before the bets were settled, your father would have pocketed a tidy purse."

Jessica felt herself blushing. She had been the man's wife. How could she look at Gideon again and not see condemnation or, worse, pity in his eyes?

"So Linden was one of my father's contemporaries?"

Jessica could feel Gideon's gaze on her, imagine him adding figures in his head.

"Yes, but not a friend. Jamie Linden was your father's man of all work, Gideon," Trixie said. "He would make arrangements, ease his way whenever necessary. Provide the entertainment for their gatherings, as it were. If the ceremonies did go on, I would imagine he continued to offer his services as procurer."

Jessica took a swallow of wine, as her mouth had gone quite dry.

"You would *imagine,* Trixie?" Gideon asked, his voice low and hard. "You're still telling us you didn't know? I think Jessica's right. Either you've lost your touch, knowing everything there is to know, or you're lying."

"And you're impertinent," the dowager duchess told him sharply. "All right. I may have...heard things. Five years, you said, dear? I suppose that could be true. As I remember it, old Walter stuck his spoon in the wall five years ago, so they would have needed to hunt up a replacement. Explaining the investiture ceremony Jessica spoke of, you understand. Oh, don't glare, Gideon, I didn't make up the rules!"

"What else do you expect me to do?" he asked angrily, and Jessica bowed her head, attempted to make herself invisible if possible.

"I agree. It was all...terrible. And yes, I'll admit I suspected it was still going on five years ago, in its own haphazard way, not nearly as efficient as when Barry was in charge. He had a true talent for leadership, your father, much of it sadly wasted on feeding his myriad vices as he eventually caught himself up in his own trap. Not all of them continued to wear that damnable rose your father concocted, so you wouldn't know their names. If they still meet, they're much more covert now, more of the members from a generation not as familiar to me."

"But perhaps with the requisite number still replenished with eldest offspring, as Jessica suggests? And yet I was never approached."

Jessica raised her head to look at Trixie when she didn't immediately answer Gideon's question.

"They knew better than to dare come anywhere near you," she said at last, for a fleeting moment looking every day of her years. "I would have destroyed them."

"And Adam?" Jessica asked, her heart pounding.

Trixie retook her reclined position. "Yes, please, back to the twit. He'd be the perfect candidate, actually. Devoted to his own pleasures, not too sharp in his wits, although clearly with a high opinion of himself even if everyone else refuses to see his brilliance. Easily coddled into most any stupidity, led by his most intimate appendage, as it were, introduced to the delights of the flesh as his birthright, told he was better than anyone, privileged, untouchable. Heady stuff, especially for a twit. He'd do as a lesser member—everyone can find a good use for a biddable idiot."

Gideon sat down beside Jessica; she resisted the urge to reach out, take his hand. What his grandmother was saying couldn't be easy for him to hear; it certainly wasn't easy for her. "Lesser member? There are— were—degrees of membership, even inside the devil's dozen?"

"Everything has tiers, pet. And leaders. There were their other interests to consider—our way of government being uppermost. Barry was very much impressed by the French and their third state, the *tiers état,* and I'm sure, had he lived, would have applauded them for having the good sense to eventually separate their monarchs' heads from their shoulders."

"There was a dislike for kings?" Gideon asked, sounding somewhat surprised. Jessica decided he had a flair for playacting, and that Trixie was only now getting to the part of her tale that interested him most.

"Hatred would be a better term. Disgust, for another. Hanoverian upstarts, beginning with the first George, who brought his odiferous *sauerkraut* and guttural language to the Crown, followed by his forgettable son. And then Farmer George, our current mad king, who lost us the American colonies. Barry didn't live to see the posturing buffoon who is destined to be the fourth George come into his full flower of idiocy, but I can imagine his displeasure with the man. And for all government save the one he and his acolytes would have erected in its place. Remember, pet, your father died in 1789. The Bastille had just fallen. Passions were running quite high throughout England, both in support of the French and in fear of the same thing happening here. But that's enough of that, and I'm sure it all died with Barry."

"They were planning their own revolution?"

"You'll badger me until you get it all, won't you? You're a lot like me in that regard. Very well. But then we will never speak of this again. I mean that, Gideon, never again. Even two decades in the past, what your father planned could come back to destroy the Redgraves. Sedition? Regicide? No, we don't speak of it."

She held out her wineglass to be refilled, waiting until Gideon had replenished it and handed it to her before speaking again. "Your father and his cohorts were not the only ones to dream such dreams. Again, remember the times. *Liberté, égalité, fraternité!* Pretty words for the masses, opportunities for the ambitious. There were many hot-blooded young men who looked to France and saw what they believed were great opportunities if repeated here in England. Your father planned a lot of things. He was young, yes, but as with Caesar's Cassius, he was *ambitious*. He took what your grandfather began in the pursuit of pleasure, and saw the possibilities for so much more."

"But there were only the thirteen," Jessica pointed out, immediately wishing she hadn't spoken. The dowager duchess was clearly unhappy with this conversation.

"Yes, thirteen. But providing carefully selected invited guests—there were so many guests, safe they believed, in their masks and cloaks—with free and unbridled access to their every vice, their every twisted appetite? Gathering those of weak moral fiber and yet with entry into every corner of society, every door in government from the House of Commons to the King's Privy Council, corrupting them, thereby *owning* them? Think about that. Stupidly, unwittingly, they gave Barry power over them all. It was a brilliant if distasteful strategy, I suppose, as far it went. If I told you some of the names, which I will not, you would be appalled. Sadly, these two decades later, some of them still occupy positions of power."

She took another sip of wine. "Barry saw in the French unrest what Napoleon Bonaparte must have recognized several years later, knowing *someone* eventually had to rise from the ashes and take the reins. Although the victories that would bring your father and his handpicked minions into power would not be on the battlefield, but covert—and more than faintly disgusting. I never wanted you to know any of this, Gideon. But he was quite mad, your father. Brilliant, but quite mad. Could he have succeeded? I sincerely doubt that, his appetite for opium would have brought him down, eventually. But it became increasingly clear even to me, his own mother, that he must soon be stopped, one way or another. We would have been ruined if he failed, ruined if he succeeded. I both mourned and rejoiced the day he died, almost welcoming the scandal that followed, as we had been saved from the most damning scandal of them all."

Jessica turned away as the dowager blinked back tears before taking refuge in her wineglass once more.

The room was silent for a time, a long, uncomfortable time, before Gideon spoke. "How many other members from my father's time are still alive?"

"One," she said quietly. "With Turner gone now, too, just the one."

"Yes, but you're forgetting those who took their places," Jessica said, her mind racing. "The eldest offspring. Why couldn't one of them be our killer, to protect his father's memory, or to protect his own reputation if word were ever to get out? And what about those guests Trixie spoke of—one or more of them might also feel vulnerable. Your father's Society was plotting the overthrow of the monarchy, Gideon, for pity's sake. The Society was still active five years ago in some ways, I promise you that, although I can't say it functioned as it once had. It may still go on today, in one form or another. But to be a member today would make it logical for anyone to believe there are still plots against the government, and all while Bonaparte threatens to invade us. That's reason enough for a dozen murders."

"Now you're simply speculating, my dears, and rather wildly at that. Without Barry, their leader was gone," Trixie reminded them. "The ceremonies, the masks, the orgies, the opium eating, I'm sure they went on. It was that side of things that most attracted many of the members, as Barry well knew. So, yes, I *know* they went on. But I was assured by Ranald Orford himself, the rest of it quickly shriveled to nothingness. Barry made them believe they were capable of anything. Without him, they had to convince themselves, and that wasn't possible. If they still meet, it's only to be naughty little boys, nothing more."

"Naughty?" Jessica was instantly incensed. "My father was going to turn me over to be used in some horrible ceremony."

Trixie shrugged yet again. "He may have been attempting to impress someone with his loyalty. It has been done before."

She turned her attention back to Gideon. "That would be unsettling, however. It would mean there's a clear new leader, perhaps even as strong as Barry. You force me to do some investigating. Go away now, Gideon. Thank God you've left off wearing that damnable golden rose. You can't allow anyone to speculate that you've stumbled onto them. Your best strategy is to do nothing else until you hear from me."

"I don't know that I want you involved, Trixie," Gideon said, getting to his feet and holding out his hand to Jessica. "If we're anywhere close to correct with our speculations, you might be putting yourself in danger."

"Danger? You forget, I have weapons of my own, so don't worry your head about me. As to the boy? If you truly believe the ceremonies continue, in any way or form, I'd suggest locking him up somewhere. When the world goes mad, you can't take too many precautions."

CHAPTER EIGHT

THE DRIVE BACK TO JERMYN Street was accomplished in tense silence, but when Gideon tossed the reins to Thomas and followed Jessica inside, she didn't object.

"We'll be upstairs, Richard," he called over his shoulder at her business partner. "See to it we're not disturbed."

"Yes, but—" the man protested before Jessica motioned him to silence.

"Take the knocker from the door, please, Richard. I'm sorry, but we won't be entertaining for a while. I'll explain later."

"We won't— Jess? What's going on? You look as if you've seen a ghost."

"Go on up," Gideon told her, touching his hand to her back. "I'll join you shortly."

She looked as if she might wish to argue the point. She looked at him for a long time, actually, as if memorizing him or some such thing, but then nodded and headed for the stairs.

"Richard? If you'd kindly put down that thing you're waving about, I believe we need to have a conversation."

The older man looked at the feather duster he'd been wielding and then laid it on one of the sheet-covered tables. "I wasn't planning to employ it as a weapon," he said. He reached beneath the sheet and came up with a nasty-looking wooden club. "This has served me well enough over the years. Do I need it now, my lord?"

"I most sincerely hope not," Gideon said wryly as he pulled two chairs out from one of the card tables and pushed one toward Richard, choosing to turn his own around and straddle it. "Tell me about Jamie Linden."

Richard eyed the chair as if considering other uses for it but then sat down. "A fellow of much my own age, but much better set up, I should think people would say. A winning smile, a clever tongue. You could almost like him, I suppose, although not quite so much when he was in his cups. But I barely knew the man."

"Really? And are you quite sure you want to go on with that? I've already had to wade through evasions and outright lies once today. I don't have the patience for a second round. I know what he was before he and Jessica ran off to escape her father's plans for her. Now I want to know about the time between then and the day he died."

"No, my lord, you don't." Richard extracted a large handkerchief from his pocket and wiped at his suddenly damp brow. "It was another time, another lifetime. The past is long behind her now, dead and gone."

Gideon felt his muscles tensing. "He hurt her?"

"He hurt her," Richard answered simply.

There was no easy way to ask his next question. "Only him?"

"Did he pass her around? Sell her body? Is that what you're asking? Not after the first time, no. He couldn't afford to lose his only asset."

"Explain that." Gideon felt physically ill and nearly

on the sharp edge of madness. Everything Jessica had suffered, endured, could be led straight back to his father, the man who had begun it all.

"Look at her wrists." Richard stood up. "I've got to get back to work, customers tonight or not. Damn, and what are we supposed to do with all that fish chowder?"

"Sit down. I'm not finished. How did you meet her? How did you end up here, together?"

"Most all of that's not my story to tell, my lord."

"Richard, you can tell me the whole, or I can choke it out of you. In my current mood, I'm amenable either way."

"Yes, I can see that. You care, don't you? Thank you. Very well." Richard took up the chair once more and then fell silent, as if attempting to line up his facts in good order. "He took her up as he was ordered—I suppose when you say you know what happened, you know what I mean, and who gave him the order."

"Her father, yes?"

Richard nodded his head. "But who ordered *him,* my lord? That's a question I can't answer, nor can Jess. Jamie Linden took that knowledge to his grave with him. The only thing she knew was he was terrified of someone and itching to get himself free of the country."

Damn. One speculation put to rest, unfortunately. As of at least five years ago, there was a new leader. A strong leader, a dangerous leader. Another Barry Redgrave. One, if Trixie was to be believed, Turner Collier was prepared to hand over his own daughter to as a way of showing his loyalty to the man.

"So Linden had himself a problem," Gideon said, just to keep Richard talking.

"He did that, sir, certainly. He'd seen someone that day he shouldn't have seen. He was in a wild state. It would be his death he could be facing if anyone knew, but he had no money to flee with until they paid him for bringing her to the ceremony, so he had to risk it."

"Money more important than his life? That's quite the gamble. None too intelligent, was he?"

"No, my lord. He wanted to help her, he swore he did, but the way he saw it, there was no choice but to do as her father had told him. That part of the story never fit so well for me, to tell you the truth, but, again, Jess said Linden wanted to help her, he simply couldn't. She believed him, my lord, not having much choice, I'd say. And damn if she didn't up and tell him she knew where her stepmother kept her jewels, offered them to him if he'd take her with him. Eighteen, just a girl, tied up hand and foot and half out of her mind with fear, I'm sure, but she found a way to survive. I think Linden put a value on Jess, just like he did on the jewels, and saw himself a safer man, a richer man. Yes, that's how I see the thing."

Gideon wrapped his hand across his forehead, rubbing hard at his temples with fingers and thumb. His head felt ready to explode. *Bound hand and foot.* Turner Collier was so very lucky he was dead. "Go on."

"Jess never told me too much, except about that time he'd— Well, we already spoke of that. They married in Brussels, with Linden knowing a wife is chattel, my lord, and anything he did with her was above the law, as it were. If she ran, he'd be within his rights to haul her back, punish her without fear of consequences. Again, at least that's how I see the thing, why he insisted they marry. She was young, sir, in a strange land, alone. There was no going home, not to a man like her father. There was nothing else she could do."

Gideon wanted a drink. Needed a drink. "I agree. She had no choice."

"There's nothing stronger than the will to stay alive, no matter how terrible the living may be, poor mite. They traveled the continent, Jess and Linden. He always kept them moving, always looking over his shoulder as if fearful some would find him. He avoided cities, where he might be recognized, plying his talents in villages and small towns."

"And what talent was that?"

"The cards. He gambled every night, sometimes winning, sometimes losing—more often losing. And always with Jess forced to stand just behind his chair the whole night long, dressed in one of those thin, dampened gauze gowns Empress Josephine and her sisters so favored back then, tricked up beyond all modesty and common decency, her face painted, her hair piled high like Josephine's, her body meant to distract the bumpkins at the table. She stood quite still, hour after hour, her hand always on Linden's shoulder. A living statue."

Richard closed his eyes, shook his head. "She never reacted, not by so much as a blink, keeping her attention on the cards. That's how I first saw her. I'd stopped at the same inn just outside Lyons, for I made my own blunt at the gaming tables. We were fairly stranded at the inn, as spring storms had made the roads a mass of mud. In any event, I looked at her, disbelieving what I was seeing. That sweet, beautiful girl, amid all the ugliness. Then, when I asked to join the players, she looked at me for a moment. There was something in her eyes...."

Gideon nodded. Yes, he agreed. There was something in Jessica's eyes. Some vulnerability she couldn't hide. Some nebulous, unexplainable something that made a man want to slay dragons for her. "I wondered why she dresses herself the way she does. I referred to her black gown as armor."

"And well it is, your lordship. It was either one nasty outfit or the other, each night. She'd had enough of dampened gowns, or cruel corsets laced so tight she could barely breathe. Enough of rough louts and gape-mouthed farmers in taprooms leering at her, thinking she was there for their amusement. Each evening, when she'd appear with Linden, I wanted to strip off my jacket and cover her, take her out of there."

Richard sat back in his chair and sighed. "Three nights later, when the roads were all but dry again and fit for travel, I did."

"She did say *we,* yes. You emptied his pockets and left him on the bed he died in."

Richard shifted his eyes to the floor. "The bed he died in, yes. We've been together ever since, Jess and me. She didn't waste the months she spent with Jamie Linden, not once she'd got her spirit back, but had been biding her time, learning what she had to learn in order to be free of him. She plays a splendid hand of cards, your lordship, and can all but tell you what cards you're holding before you've taken a good look at them yourself. She'd been planning on how to escape him, thinking to gamble her way back to England with the money she'd been lifting bit by bit from Linden's purse when he was lost in his drunkenness. Brave, brave girl. It was a daring scheme, but she wouldn't have fared well, bless her. She can read the cards better than most, but all but a blind man can read *her*. I have her wear an eye shade when she fills in at the tables, elsewise we'd be living in a gutter."

At last Gideon smiled, albeit ruefully. "She couldn't bluff her way out of a wet sack, I agree, at least not to a discerning eye. So you're saying you're a father to her, Richard? Is that it?"

"Yes, that's just what I'm saying. Father and friend. Is that what you wanted to hear, your lordship? Or is all this concern about who might be bedding her? You're no better than that? Knowing what I know, I wouldn't dream to touch her. She was a child, she's still a child, and innocent, for all her three and twenty years. And she's older than time itself. She's who she is, what her father and Jamie Linden and the world made her, and what she's made of herself since. Leave her be."

"I can't do that, Richard, no more than you could. I have my reasons. How did James Linden die?"

"How do you think he died, your lordship?"

Gideon stood up and returned the chair to its place at the table. "Why, Richard, I think you looked, you saw, you understood and then you did the only thing an honorable man could do in your situation. I think you bided your time until you believed you could safely get her away, and then you bloody well killed him."

Richard's bushy white eyebrows rose, but he said nothing.

Gideon waited him out for some moments and then asked, "Did he suffer?"

"Not enough, no," Richard said as he also stood up, his knees faintly creaking at the exertion. "By that third night, I was nearly made mad with the waiting, listening to him rage at her. He'd lost that night and clearly blamed her. I could only imagine what was going on in that attic chamber next to mine, and my thoughts made me ill. When I finally heard his drunken snores, I knew it was time. I'm not a strong man, your lordship, or a young one, but a well-placed pillow and a man too drunk to put up a proper fight was well within my ability."

"Dead in his sleep. Plausible. You couldn't have employed the club, as the wounds would have been too obvious."

"That's how I saw the thing, yes," Richard said quietly. "It pained me deeper than you can know, to wait until I was certain he was finally asleep. I had to keep telling myself it was the last time he'd hit her, I'd see to that. I'm not sorry for killing the man. I'd do it again."

Gideon held out his right hand and shook the other man's hand warmly. "Thank you, Richard. I believe I can manage from here, although you could wish me luck."

"Sir?"

Gideon had made his decision. He'd come to it in a flash of understanding halfway through Richard's recitation. How brave she'd been to offer herself up to gain her brother, when all she knew of men was pain and humiliation. Why she had reacted as she had when he'd taken her to bed…the hesitation, the moments when he'd felt she'd gone away from him to someplace in her mind…and then the surprised passion, the reluctant and then, finally, eager giving. It could all have ended in disaster, but it hadn't. It had been the most memorable, soul-shaking night of his life. More so now than ever.

"Go pack your belongings, *Uncle* Richard. You and your widowed niece and whomever else you choose to bring with you are to be situated in Portman Square yet today. I'll have my town coach sent round at five. The tongues will wag mightily once the betrothal is posted in the newspapers, sure I've some dastardly plan to wrest the nincompoop's inheritance from him by wedding his half sister, but I think we can withstand that. After all, it's nothing more than most of them would expect from a Redgrave."

"You're going to…to *marry* her, your lordship?" Then Richard's eyes narrowed. "Why?"

"If I had the answer to that question, my dear fellow, I would sleep much better tonight. Or never sleep again. I only know you're a fine man, but from this day forward, Jessica is in my care, and God help the man who would try to hurt her. Now, if you'll excuse me?"

"Yes. Yes, of course!" Richard grabbed Gideon's hand this time, in both of his, pumping it up and down in some agitation. "Not many men would do the honorable thing, sir, knowing what happened to her."

"I'm not many men, Richard. In point of fact, I may just now be discovering exactly who I am."

He extracted his hand from Richard's hearty grip, not without effort, and headed for the stairs. Now to tell Jessica what he'd decided. He doubted her reaction would mirror that of her *uncle*.

When he entered the small sitting room, it was to see her tucked into a corner of the couch, her head bent low, her knees tucked up almost to her chin. She'd taken the pins from her glorious red hair, so that it hung down, nearly obscuring her face. Her hands were clasped together around her shins, her bare feet poking out from beneath the hem of the simple yellow gown. It was as if she was trying to make herself small, trying to disappear inside herself. A…defensive position. Habit, he supposed, adopted during her time with James Linden. One he could only hope to break.

At the sound of the door closing behind him, she pushed back her hair and tilted her head to watch him as he crossed the room and sat down beside her. "I assumed you would have thought better of it and gone on your way," she said before turning her face forward once more, to continue staring at whatever it was she saw in front of her…either the fireplace, or her past. He felt fairly certain it was the latter.

Gideon extracted a white linen square from his pocket and held it up in front of her. "Blow your nose."

"I don't need to—" She snatched the handkerchief and did what he asked. And not very daintily.

Stupidly, he felt himself smiling. *Young and innocent…older than time itself.* Yes, Richard had that one correctly, didn't he?

"Thank you," she said after wiping at her tear-wet face and just before nearly handing him back the handkerchief before pocketing it. "I'll see that Doreen washes and presses it for you."

"I think my grandmother likes you," he said after they'd both stared at the fireplace for some time.

"I don't care."

"Not many people would dare to speak to her the way you did."

"Perhaps more should. She's the worst sort of tyrant. She's likable."

"She's also quite intelligent," Gideon said, lifting his legs and crossing them one ankle over the other on the low table in front of the couch. He was, after all, a man who enjoyed his comforts. "Or don't you think so?"

"Intelligent? Yes, definitely. And devious. She wasn't going to tell us anything until I'd told her things I've never said to anyone save Richard."

"*Quid pro quo.* I did warn you."

Jessica sighed and made use of the handkerchief once again. "And Richard? You were downstairs for a long time. What did he tell you, and what did you tell him in return? Or did you simply bully an old man?"

Gideon picked a bit of lint off the knee of his fawn breeches. "I know now how James Linden died, and Richard now knows you and I are to be married. He didn't say it outright, but from the way he pumped my hand until I thought it might fall off, I believe we have his blessing."

And then he waited for the explosion, outwardly calm and relaxed, inwardly tense and taut as the string on a cocked crossbow.

The explosion never came.

"Yes, I thought that might be the case. Either you left, which most men would have done, or you'd concoct some ridiculous notion that your father was indirectly responsible for what happened to me and you see yourself as doing penance for his sin."

"Is that what I'm doing? Really? I've never seen myself as the penitent sort."

"I doubt many would disagree with you," she said quietly. "But I saw your face as the dowager countess was speaking, telling us things I already knew but you couldn't know. My father is responsible for what happened to me. My father, and...and my husband. They're both dead. It's over, Gideon, and I simply want to get on with my life. I've seen more of the world than most people will and enjoyed many of my travels. Richard and I have managed to save a considerable sum toward the inn we're going to own one day. I'm content as I am, and you are not responsible for me. To think otherwise would be ludicrous."

"Penitent and ludicrous. Not the usual words to follow a marriage proposal, not that you haven't already turned down what you've not allowed me to yet offer."

"Don't be agreeable," she said, lowering her head to her knees. "It doesn't come naturally to you."

No, it didn't; Gideon rather liked the idea of being the oldest son, the earl. He enjoyed getting his own way. Clearly Jessica hadn't just learned to read the cards during her time standing behind Linden's shoulder. She'd also learned to read people. That she'd even allowed him to sit down next to her was a wonder. "All right. Then let's at least be honest. Give me your hand. I mean that in the literal sense. Let me see your hand. Both of them, actually. Then I'll go."

She lifted her head, her eyes dark with tears. "Richard gossips like an old woman," she said, sighing. "And you're lying, just like your grandmother."

"Probably. It would appear to be one of a myriad

of unflattering family traits. In all honesty, there are more. Now show me. Please."

She lowered her legs and shifted her position toward him, turning over her hands to expose her wrists. He saw the scars, a thin line running just below the base of each palm.

"Sweet Jesus."

Jessica retracted her hands, folding them neatly in her lap. "And now you want the story, don't you?"

Gideon shook his head. "Not if you don't want to tell it, no."

She shrugged, as if it didn't matter to her one way or the other. "My stepmother's jewelry, most of it, wasn't where I'd supposed, so what with hiring coaches and booking passage for two of us, the pittance James was forced to take wasn't going to last long at all. It would seem nobody believed he hadn't stolen the pieces, and the prices he was offered weren't nearly as wonderful as he'd hoped."

"He could have simply left you and gone on off on his own."

"I suppose. But James had another answer. He was always the one for coming up with new schemes. I was in our room at a small hotel in Brussels. It was early days, the evening of our wedding. He'd explained that he'd compromised me by taking me with him, and he was doing the only honorable thing by marrying me. No, I didn't know him well, but I'd seen him on the estate several times, and he'd always been polite. At the very least, he was clean. And he had saved me, no matter that he was mostly saving himself."

Jessica smiled. "I was so young, so stupid. Even

grateful. What he said seemed logical. I certainly couldn't go home to what my father planned for me, could I? Marriage seemed the only answer. James ordered a tub for me after the ceremony, and then a lovely meal brought up to our bridal chamber. I dressed in the new gown he'd bought for me. I was nervous, very much so, but I had made my bed, as my old nurse had been prone to tell me when I'd done something to displease her, and now I was resigned to lie in it. And… and then there was a knock at the door. I opened it, thinking it was James…."

Gideon suddenly knew where this calmly told story was heading. "That son of a bitch."

"Yes. That son of a bitch. He entered behind the man and told me what he'd done, what I was supposed to do. He'd sold my virginity, our wedding night. When I understood, I snatched up one of the knives from the table and…I didn't do it very well. The cuts were fairly shallow, but the blood was enough to send the man scurrying away. At least he never tried to sell me again, for fear I'd succeed in killing myself the next time. He found another use for me."

"Distracting his fellow gamblers," Gideon said, "all while you watched the cards, plotting your escape."

She wiped at her damp cheeks and smiled. She actually smiled. "While pilfering small sums of money from James when he was too drunk to remember how much was in his pockets, and then sitting quietly on the hearth as he slept, using the light from the fire to see while I sewed coins into the hem of my cloak. For too long, I did nothing but cry, and feel sorry for myself and my terrible plight. But I didn't stay stupid forever, Gideon. I couldn't afford to, could I? Two hundred and twelve days, that's how long I was with James. Each one of them an eternity, but each one bringing me closer to freedom. I was all but ready to make my escape, biding my time until we visited a port city again, when Richard came along. My *real* knight in shining armor."

"I'm going to settle twenty thousand pounds on him tomorrow. It isn't enough. There could never be enough."

Jessica's smile disappeared as if it had never been, as if the light had never come back into her eyes. "Now you want Richard to sell me?"

"Oh, God. Damn! That wasn't what I intended. Marry me, Jessica, don't marry me. Richard still gets the settlement, the two of you get your damn inn or whatever you want. But we want answers, or at least I do, and you want to protect your brother. Become my countess, and you can go into society with me, we can do our own investigating. Trixie is…I don't know how much she knows, how much she didn't tell us."

Jessica got to her feet, smoothed down her gown. "You sensed it, too? For all she said, I think she may have been holding something back. I can understand that. He was her son, after all, and he was a monster."

"A monster, yes. Playing a very dangerous game." Gideon rose, as well. "So she seemed frightened to you, as well, handing out her warnings about your brother? Trixie isn't the sort to be frightened."

"It wouldn't be natural if she wasn't frightened. People are dying, Gideon, people who knew the sort of things she knows. She says no one would dare touch her—but can she be sure?"

"Can any of us be sure of anything? We also have to consider Adam. You'd be with him, residing under the same strong, well-guarded roof. He's young, Jessica, just as you were young. But not nearly so strong as his sister. If they're keeping to the devil's thirteen, your father's vacant seat needs to be filled. Adam could be approached, you said so yourself."

"I know what I said, you needn't keep beating me over the head with my own words, you know." She seemed to search his face with her eyes, as if hunting some escape route. "There's no other way to go about it?"

He had her on the ropes now, he could see it. He was a Redgrave, so he would push his advantage. And, yes, please God, he would sleep nights.

"I'm the Earl of Saltwood. I have a reputation, God help me, but at times it serves me well. My countess will be accepted everywhere. Nobody would dare to deny you. If our murderer is in society, we need to be there, as well. I haven't stepped inside Almacks in years, nor do I usually attend every damn ball and rout and picnic that litters the Season. But with a fiancée, a new bride on my arm? I'd be expected to make all the rounds. Invitations from the curious will pile up on my mantelpiece like snow. Perhaps several from members of the Society, anxious to see Linden's widow. We won't have to search them out, Jessica, they'll come to us. I pride myself on being observant, but you've the better of me there, I'm convinced of that. And then there are the widows, the wives. It should be easier going for you to gain their confidence than me. It's all logical."

"Logical. I suppose so. But I don't want to marry you. I vowed never to marry again. A woman has no power beyond the will of her husband."

"No power?" He touched a hand to her cheek and kept it there. When he spoke again, his tone was soft, perhaps even tender. "You sincerely don't know, do you? How beautiful you are, how desirable, what an extraordinarily strong, brave and special woman you've made of yourself against all odds. You have no idea how you can figuratively take me to the floor just by looking at me. I'm not going to go down on one knee to profess some undying love for you. You're too intelligent to swallow such a bag of moonshine. In part I'm attempting to pay a debt my family owes you, thanks indirectly to the actions of my father and grandfather. I'm attempting to soothe my own conscience for what happened here the other night. I admit that freely also. But know this, as well, Jessica soon-never-again-to-be-Linden, I would never, *never* intentionally hurt you."

A single tear ran down her cheek, burning his skin.

"You're a fool, Gideon Redgrave, and arrogant into the bargain. Nobody can save the world, you know, not even you. Yes, all right, I see the wisdom in marrying you."

Gideon covered his relief with a chuckle. "My sister has said the Redgraves are the least romantical people in all of England. You'll fit in very well. Now, to seal the betrothal?"

He leaned in and kissed her. On the cheek. Bloody hell, on the *cheek*.

But that was now. He could scarcely have heard what she and Richard had told him this past hour and dare to attempt anything more. The ancient Greek was right: *timing is in all things the most important factor.* He'd had her beneath him, he'd felt her first stirrings of fire; he could awaken her even more, teach her pleasure she could still not possibly imagine. He knew what awaited him, awaited them both, if he was patient, and he was very good at being patient.

He left her where she stood and strode into her bedchamber, returning moments later with James Linden's wadded-up banyan clutched in one angry fist. "*This* doesn't come to Portman Square with you," he said, holding it aloft as he headed for the stairs.

He didn't look back, but he hoped she was smiling....

CHAPTER NINE

"I SUPPOSE IT WILL DO," Adam Collier said, sighing disappointedly as he made his way around Jessica, taking a full circuit in his red-heeled shoes, quizzing glass stuck to his eye. "But perhaps too crushingly ordinary? I mean, really—lavender? *Must* we?" He waved the glass at the hovering modiste. "Bows. That's what's needed. At the hem, on those capped sleeves. Yes, that's the very thing. I'm never wrong. See to it, woman."

Jessica rolled her eyes as she looked into the mirror at her reflection. "Bows, Adam? We're in mourning, remember? By rights, I shouldn't be going into society at all. You may escape with that ridiculous black band, but I can hardly pretend Papa and Clarissa aren't barely in their graves. Even if he did publicly disown me for eloping with James."

"I had that wrong, didn't I? You didn't eat bad fish, you *married* it." Adam shrugged eloquently in his tightly fitted swan tailcoat. "I was young, and not told much of anything. Your name simply wasn't to be mentioned again. Mama explained that, though."

"Oh? And how did that explanation go, precisely?"

"It pained Papa to think of you, of course." Adam snatched up one of the hastily constructed bows made up of the same lavender silk and held it to the center of Jessica's bodice. "No, not there. Yes, just as I first thought, on the sleeves, and then a dozen more, dancing about the hem. And perhaps dusted with something sparkling? I do adore sparkles. A pity we men can't embellish ourselves with brilliance. Although Papa used to sprinkle glittering dust in with the powder for his wig on special occasions, as I recall it. Vain man, our father, and he would persist in clinging to his periwig even after the fashion so clearly changed. He should have seen himself after the fire. No amount of glitter could have been any help to him then, hmm?"

"Adam!" Jessica pulled him closer, ignoring his near shriek of alarm as she wrinkled his neck cloth in her fist. "Take a moment to think where we are," she whispered in warning. "Someone could overhear you. Imagine Gideon's reaction."

Adam carefully disengaged himself from her grip, then anxiously fluffed at the lacy cravat. "I'd rather not, thank you. I'd rather not think about him at all. Are you quite sure you want to bracket yourself to my brute of a guardian? He won't let either one of us take two steps in any direction on our own. His dogs *drool,* and he dresses with no imagination whatsoever. Black and white. Blue and tan. Black and white again. I imagine he will expire of *ennui* within the year. No sense of style. None. Did I mention his dogs *drool?* And leave their hair everywhere, to be caught up on my rig-outs? I don't know how I put up with it, truly I don't. As it is, my valet must follow me around with a brush…and a sponge."

"If you're quite finished, Adam?" Jessica said as the modiste pinned the last bow to her hem. "Thank you,

Marie, that's much better. My brother may have a future in designing women's gowns."

Adam brightened at this suggestion. "One can only hope so. Only those with a keen eye for such things are invited to witness a woman's *toilette,* you know. And once in the proximity of the bedchamber, a clever fellow can make further inroads."

"More clever than attempting to *inroad* Mildred in a cupboard, I would hope."

Adam gave a wave of his hand, the lace-edged handkerchief perpetually clutched in his paw giving off a whiff of rather cloying scent. "I should ask the woman just who was the instigator of that aborted tryst, were I you. She offered to further my education. I knew what that meant, let me tell you! Demmed inconvenient of you to discover us just as she was being so clever about unbuttoning my breeches. Strong teeth, the woman has. We did, however, reconvene later, and it would appear Mildred is a creature of her word, for it *was* an education I received. Oh, my, yes."

"Adam, for the love of God…"

"Yes, yes, for the love of somebody, I'm sure," he said offhandedly. "For Mildred, however, it was a half crown and my most sincere thanks. I'll turn my back again now, so that the lavender disappears, which may not please God but will thrill me beyond measure. What else were you so silly as to order without first consulting me?"

"*I* only ordered a few things," she told him. "Gideon insisted upon taking care of the rest after I was measured, while I had tea and cakes in a small guest parlor.

It's his money, so that seemed only proper. Besides, I don't know the current fashions."

"Does that explain the lavender, or was it his choice?"

"Mine, if you must know," she admitted, feeling rather put upon.

"And again we give thanks, and good on Gideon," Adam said. "If I were to have to witness the unveiling of an entire wardrobe of the incredible *dullness* you consider proper, sister mine, I would wonder what terrible sin I've committed to be punished so. But good old Gideon has had the dressing and undressing of literally *dozens* of women, I would suppose, so he may have developed an eye for what best flatters the female form."

"You say the most delightful things, Adam," Jessica told him as Marie looked at her in some compassion before bustling out of the room.

"I do? Oh, that wasn't a compliment, was it? How gauche of me. My apologies, I'm sure. But think on it, Jessica, the man's dead old, so he has to have had his share. I'm just eighteen, and I've already bedded eight—no, Mildred wasn't an actual bedding, now that I think on it, but more of a footnote—so, seven different females already this year. A dozen last year, and the year before, ten, I believe. I keep a journal, you see, so I can check if you should want me to total them up for you. All my conquests are captured there in detail, names, dates, number and level of *encounters* and the form each took. In the event I decide to one day pen my memoirs, you understand. Papa suggested it and reviewed it every year, making suggestions as to how I could improve. But to continue, the year before that—"

Jessica looked to the curtained doorway, relieved to see Marie wasn't already heading back into the fitting room with another gown. "The year before that you were *fifteen!*"

He shot her a look over his shoulder. "Yes, I was. For my birthday, Papa took me to the Duck and Grapes and sent me upstairs with two of the barmaids, to make a man of me, he said. *Two,* Jessica! Conquest is what a man is all about, and he would be sure to make me a man. Each birthday, a new delight was in store for me. The passions of the flesh feed the passions of the mind, so that it's imperative for a man with aspirations of greatness to dine, as it were, with regularity, et cetera, *ad nauseam.* It's our duty to fornicate with as many women as possible. That's what Papa told me, all but drummed into my head."

He laughed. Perhaps giggled. "I just wanted the women, you understand, so I humored him. Mama, bless her, encouraged me, as well. I was surrounded by comely housemaids, handpicked by her. Adventuresome sorts, and eager to please. Isn't it grand to live in such a free and open society?"

Halfway through these astounding revelations, Jessica's mouth had dropped open, and she stared at her brother's back, unable to tell him to stop. This was what she'd wanted to hear, although had dreaded the hearing, had still not found a way to broach the subject with him. But now he was volunteering it all, and without shame, even without pride, thank God. But did he have to pick this place, this moment?

"Although I didn't much care for the lessons."

"Lessons?" Jessica squeaked, horrified.

"Yes, I had Papa as a tutor, over and above my schooling. Why did I need to read all these treatises on history and politics and such? That Machiavelli chap? Now there was a queer duck, let me tell you! And others. Lets see. There was Marat, Robespierre, Thomas Becket. Caligula—now *he* was interesting! More, but I forget them. All assassinated, you know, for the good of others who wanted to take their places or rid themselves of an opponent. I forget most of it, how each one died. But I do know how many times Julius Caesar was stabbed by his small swarm of enemies, if you'd care to learn? Twenty-three! The trick to it was that no one could actually say for certain which thrust of which blade did the actual deed. Clever, don't you think?"

Jessica's heart was pounding as she tried desperately not to sound shocked and repulsed to her toes. Wait until she told Gideon about *this!* "I suppose so. We'll talk more about this later, Adam, if you don't mind."

He shrugged, still with his back to her. "Certainly. Time and place, Jessica, time and place. I have no idea why you wanted to talk about it now."

"Why *I*— Adam, you're a noodle, do you know that? An absolute *noodle.*" And then she said a silent *thank you* to God that he was.

"Now you sound like Papa. If I had a penny piece for each time he despaired of me as useless…" he complained without much heat. He extracted a snuffbox from his waistcoat and proceeded to take a dip, and then sneezed several times into his handkerchief with some enthusiasm.

Marie bustled back into the room as the last sneeze faded and Jessica bent at the knees so that the modiste could lift the lavender gown up and over her head, leaving her in her new undergarments.

At Gideon's express orders, each and every piece had been lined with silk, and the corset she wore at the moment, cut low straight across her breasts, was such a beautiful confection of white lace and pink lacing ribbons that secured in front, so that she had control over how tightly they were tugged, that she felt enhanced rather than trapped inside the thing. Beneath it were her wonderful French drawers, and the petticoat tied at her waist assured her she could move freely in sunlight or candlelight without fear her body would be immodestly outlined.

She lifted her hands to cup the undersides of her breasts, thinking she looked rather wonderful in these glorious new garments. It seemed almost a pity to cover them.

"And another thing— Ah, I shouldn't have turned around, should I?" Adam said. "I suppose I'll wait somewhere else until you call me back?" He pointed to the curtained doorway leading out into the shop.

"Yes, that seems a good idea," Jessica told him as she quickly crossed her arms over her bosom, happy to see that at least her brother had enough sense to finally be put to the blush. Honestly, was there anything he wouldn't say?

Marie indicated she should remove her corset, and, while still thinking about everything Adam had told her, she complied, before Marie helped her out of the slip. She shivered slightly in her near nakedness, hoping Adam didn't decide to poke his head back into the fitting room to tell her something else she wished she didn't need to know.

Getting to know her half brother this past week and more as he was, rather than to continue imagining him as the shy child she remembered, had been an education for her. He really was quite adorable. Rather like a puppy, she'd remarked to Gideon, who'd agreed, saying you were sometimes tempted to scratch him behind the ears, but all while keeping aware that in his excitement he may at any moment piddle on the carpet.

Gideon. Jessica tried very hard not to think about him at all. Since that was impossible, she'd done her best to avoid him as he went about doing whatever it is earls do, the two of them meeting most often at the dinner table, as she breakfasted in her rooms and he was rarely in Portman Square in time for luncheon.

Having Adam and Richard at table with them every night was not conducive to anything more than polite conversation. Gideon would then take himself off again, making the rounds of several parties, paving the way, he said, for their appearance as an affianced couple or, better yet, husband and wife, if he could convince the archbishop to issue a Special License before the necessary three weeks to call the banns.

As he was clearly chafing against waiting out the days, he'd teased just yesterday that he was tempted to soon sic Trixie on the man, who wasn't immune to her charms. Jessica had asked him how he would know that, but then had tactfully withdrawn the question.

He did accompany her to Bond Street on three separate occasions, but then he was so busy autocratically ordering gloves and footwear and bonnets and gowns that she had found herself retreating into a more comfortable place in her mind, where she could pretend she wasn't being dressed up for a reason that had less to do with a fiancé gifting his betrothed with wedding clothes than it did with tricking her out for show, just as James had done.

She didn't believe Gideon saw it that way, but she couldn't quite help herself sometimes, when the past seemed to intrude on the present.

In any event, what with one thing or the other, they had seemed to communicate for the most part by way of notes.

The announcement will appear in all the morning newspapers tomorrow. Richard is explained as a maternal uncle. Too late now for second thoughts, my dear, for either of us. G.

The dowager countess sends her blessing, pointing out her grandson neglected to petition for it, and alluding to the possibility you may have been raised by wild wolves. I don't believe she has considered how this reflects on her. Or perhaps she has, and this was a warning. When it comes to your grandmother, I may overthink matters. J.

I've attempted to speak to your brother, but gave it up as a bad job before I could be tempted to throttle him. Suffice it to say Seth will be attached to his hip whenever he leaves the house. Thorny tells me you took the air in the Square this morning. With the brisk breeze, I look forward to some flattering color in your cheeks tonight at table. Are you quite certain Adam wouldn't care for Jamaica? G.

I will assume you are being polite in your distance, but would appreciate some direction as to how to deal with these invitations written to my name. J.

Redgraves don't respond on command. We either grace curious hostesses with our presence, or we don't. Burn them. We aren't ready. Don't forget your fitting at two, on Thursday. I shan't be available. Take the puppy, but beware scratching behind his ears. G.

I was told you do not care for green beans. I was then careful to order them for tonight's dinner. J.

Ha! Prepare for fish chowder at tomorrow's luncheon table. A pity I will be busy with my tailor. G.

The fish chowder was well received in the servant dining hall. Do you ever plan to spend an evening in Portman Square? J.

You are sometimes even more beautiful in sleep. I look forward to the day I'm blessed to observe you in slumber at my leisure, and then kiss you awake. G.

THAT NOTE HAD APPEARED just this morning, on her pillow, after she had so let down her guard as to show she missed him. What a sly one he was. The less she saw him, the more she wanted to see him. The more politely he treated her, the more she wanted him to be the man she remembered, the man who had fisted his hand in her hair and brought his mouth down hard against hers, the man who had lifted her in his arms and carried her to her bed.

"*Madame?* You approve?"

Jessica shook herself back to attention. She held out her arms, to see that they were encased in silken cobwebs of ivory lace, long cuffs dripping halfway to her fingertips. Goodness, she had been dressed without her conscious participation. How had that happened?

"If *madame* were to turn about, so, to see this grand creation in the mirror?"

What Jessica saw stole her breath.

She was wearing a thin silken shift, the bodice all lace to just below her breasts, the simple skirt falling from there to the six or more inches of lace edging her ankles. The dressing gown was composed completely of this same lace, the most exquisite lace she'd ever seen, tying just below her breasts, covering her so very modestly, yet still the most enticing and, yes, inviting creation.

She supposed she looked virginal. She supposed she looked like a woman looking forward to ridding herself of that virginity. All in one—innocence in the cut of the cloth, subtle decadence in the materials.

"His lordship pressed us most firmly in the design,

madame. Each bolt of material, each ribbon and button, each gown, each *ensemble,* all to his specifications. All *très magnifique!* We have been closed to everyone save him these past nearly ten days. Every day he has been here, reducing my girls to tears, pressing us to rush, to change, to alter, to make everything perfect. So demanding, yet so generous! He brings them sweet cakes, and combs for their hair, and every day the flowers, so many fragrant bouquets my Giselle, she sneezes all day long, and must do her sewing in the attics. He knows them all by name and they are all half in love with him, silly girls that they are. But he is a genius, no? He must love you very much, *madame,* to see you so well."

Jessica didn't know how to respond to that. Gideon Redgrave always had his reasons for anything he did, she felt certain of that. He planned for her to make her *entrée* into society on his arm, and he wanted attention called to her, to the both of them. "Yes…a genius. It's, uh, it's…do I really look like this, Marie?"

The petite Frenchwoman squeezed Jessica's hand. "She who sews the seams can only do so much, *madame.* The rest lies with you. Shall we see more?"

"Oh. Oh, yes. We'll see more. We'll see all of it," Jessica said, smiling even as she blinked back tears. No matter what the reason for Gideon's close involvement in her wardrobe, she had never felt so wonderfully, gloriously *pretty.* "Do you suppose we could do something with the lavender?"

"I have just the matron who would adore it, *oui.* But not for you, no, no, no, not for you. I was to put it on you first, so you could, as his lordship said, see the error of your ways. Ah, such a man! Do you wish the silly fribble to return, *madame?*"

"The silly— Oh. No, thank you. Perhaps some tea and cakes for Mr. Collier are in order. Are there many gowns? How long do you think we'll be?"

The modiste began counting on her fingertips. By the time she'd begun her second round on her fingers, Jessica could see Adam would be cooling his heels in Marie's small sitting room for a considerable length of time.

She bent her arm to stroke the soft lace. If this was the beginning, what else was she about to see? More importantly, was this how Gideon saw her?

Adam could wait for her. If he wanted to be up to the mark in all things pleasing to women, as he said he did, he should learn early on that the virtue women most admired in a man was his ability to display patient forbearance when being forced to cool his heels whilst she was shopping.

GIDEON WAS PACING THE drawing room when the dowager countess floated into the room, still stripping off her long kid gloves, then tossing them over her head one after the other, so that Soames, trailing behind her, could snare them out of the air.

"Goodness, pet, you're looking harassed. When you vow not to bed a woman until she's properly wed, in the interim it would behoove you to not have her sleeping under your own roof. At least, were you at Redgrave Manor, I could suggest you cool your ardor by immersing yourself in the pond. I don't think many would understand you leaping into the Serpentine in the Park, however."

Soames, neatly snagging the second glove, couldn't restrain his chuckle.

"I'm just so gratified to amuse you both," Gideon said, looking at Trixie's reticule, a silly thing of beads and ribbons, and judging it too small to hold what he'd hoped to see. "You failed?"

Trixie walked up to him and raised a hand to pat his cheek. "Let's be clear about this, Gideon. I tease you. You do not insult me. Soames? Give the boy what he wants before he expires of anticipation."

"Yes, my lady," the butler said, tucking the gloves into his pocket and then reaching inside his waistcoat to withdraw a rolled sheet of thick vellum and handing it to Gideon.

The Special License. She'd done it. It had been his blunt that helped ease the way, granted, but it was Trixie's way with persuasion that had turned the trick with the speed of the thing. He unrolled the document and quickly scanned it. The archbishop could sign, of course, but so could any number of other high church officials. "Whose signature is this? I can't make it out."

"You aren't supposed to, pet. Suffice it to say the license is completely legitimate and aboveboard." The dowager countess subsided onto her one-armed couch, drawing her dainty feet up beside her. "Did you ever wonder what *below* board could be?"

Gideon was still working on deciphering the signature and answered absently. "To be aboveboard, as I know the term, means keeping your hands above the gaming table at all times. So to be below board, you'd have to keep your hands—"

"Precisely where I had them as our mostly eminent church official was signing the license. Interesting."

Soames turned on his heels and left the room, his ears positively burning red.

"I have to keep reminding myself not to walk into your little traps," Gideon said. "Did you enjoy that?"

"Soames's embarrassed reaction, or my ability to bring things to attention? I would have to answer yes to both. Oh, don't scowl, pet. Next you'll be telling me you're putting in an application to warble in some choir. You knew what I was going to do when you applied to me for help. If I learned nothing else from my unlamented husband, it is the power of sex. We females hold most of that power, by the way, and can enjoy its rewards longer. By the time you're my age, Gideon, you'll be happy most evenings with a roaring fire, your dogs at your feet and a snifter of brandy at your elbow, while I consider myself, modesty aside, to remain near the top of my form. After all, most times all it takes is a strong *hand*. Ah, finally I've managed to raise a blush from you."

"You're right, I shouldn't have asked for your help. I tried to tell myself you would apply to some bonds of friendship with whomever you visited today. I should have remembered you don't have friends, do you, Trixie?"

"No, I don't. I have family. And, if the gods are kind,

and you're truly as hot to bed this woman as it would seem, soon I will have more of it."

"And here I was earlier, wondering why I don't visit as often as I should. I don't wish you dead, Trixie, but I do selfishly wish you older."

"And cuddlesome, perhaps even quaintly dotty?" she asked as he dangled a slim diamond bracelet in front of her eyes. "Ah, now isn't that pretty? Your thanks would have been enough."

"Then I'll have it back?"

"Give it to your wife once I'm planted," she said, holding up her arm to him so that he could close the bracelet about her wrist. She turned her hand this way and that once the clasp was secured, admiring the way the diamonds, formed into an endless circle of petite flowers, caught the sunlight streaming in through the windows. "Quite lovely. You've exquisite taste, pet. Do you have any news for me?"

"No, nothing. I've stopped wearing the rose, you'll notice. I'm keeping a close eye on the nincompoop, but nobody's approached him. Frankly, I've reached a dead end."

"A temporary setback only, I'm sure. Now a kiss, please, and then you may go. I've an engagement this evening, and to shine at night, it is sometimes necessary to nap during the day."

Gideon bent to kiss her cheek. "You're admitting to age, Trixie?"

"One must sometimes make allowances, yes. I've invited Guy Bedworth here for a midnight supper, and it wouldn't do to not be awake on all suits with that one."

"Bedworth? The Marquis of Mellis? That doddering old fool? What do you want with him?"

"That doddering old fool, pet, was at one time the youngest member of your grandfather's original *coterie* of scoundrels. Before you count on your fingers, yes, your grandfather died roughly forty-eight years ago. The marquis won't see seventy again, or even seventy-five, but was still, shall we say, amorously active when your father decided to resurrect what he may have thought a family tradition. Naturally, Guy, risen to the title by that time, was invited to participate, and to lend his expertise in the finer points of ceremonial rites, I would imagine. As a sort of mentor."

"And to continue in that role after my father died? Perhaps even as long as five years ago?"

"Who's to say, one way or the other? Well, in point of fact, Guy is to say, which I sincerely intend to have him do tonight."

A sudden thought struck Gideon. "How would my father have known the marquis was a member of Grandfather's...coterie?"

"Through the journals, I suppose," Trixie said, shrugging. Then her eyes went wide. "I did tell you about those blasted journals, didn't I? Dear God, maybe I *am* growing dotty."

Gideon sat down on a corner of the low table. "Grandfather wrote things down? About...about his group?"

"No name, pet. Simply the Society. He thought it

safer that way. Your father wasn't quite so brilliant and devised those ridiculous golden roses. Although they have made your search for members that much easier, which proves your grandfather's point, doesn't it?"

Trixie began turning her new bracelet over and over again around her wrist. "But, yes, he very carefully catalogued their actions, year by year. They all did. In excruciating detail. Dear God, there were drawings, charts, codes. They called them testaments, of all things. Truthfully, I burned the ones I found in your grandfather's study. What went on during the blessedly few years of our marriage was not, I felt, anything to preserve for the ages. I was young and powerless, and he... But that was a long time ago. Unfortunately, I couldn't locate all of them. The rest were hidden somewhere."

"At Redgrave Manor?"

"In the Manor, or somewhere on the grounds. I never found them, but clearly your father did. And they all kept journals, each member, before annually handing them over to your grandfather like the fools they were, as it was up to the Keeper to review them, check them for veracity and then assemble all the information into their *bible*. I never found that, either, although I had seen it a time or two. Some of the etchings were very nearly true art, if disgusting. The things I read, however, the things I could tell you about people the world admires? Ah, but most of them are dead now, so what does it matter?"

"Was my grandfather a Jacobite? Were he and his devil's dozen plotting treason?"

Trixie smiled. "No. His motives were even less

laudable, I'm afraid. He did what he did, they all did, merely for the pleasure of it. Half-hearted Satanists, reckless libertines, naughty little boys obsessed with their drunken preoccupation with sex. It was left to your father to see the opportunities for something more. When I realized..."

"That couldn't have been an easy time for you," Gideon said softly.

"No, it wasn't," Trixie agreed, turning her head toward the windows, clearly looking to the past. "I'd lost him by then, that much was clear. My own son, my only child. It was all so long ago. Barry had always been wild, impetuous, even as a young boy. When he found the journals..."

"Do they still exist? The ones my father found?"

She shrugged, turning back to him, her eyes lively once more. "Yes, back to the present, please. I never saw them, so I can't say they still do or don't exist. But as I said, Guy well might. He only returned to town a few days ago after taking the waters in Bath, or some such hopeful nonsense."

"You can't make him suspicious."

"I know what I'm about, pet. Lord knows I've been doing it long enough. We'll speak of past times, reminisce about ancient glories and conquests, friends still aboveground and those now looking at the grass from the wrong side, as it were. I'll tease and pet and pat him as if my memories of those days are fond, as he mostly likely needs to believe. I'll flatter the toothless old roué, pretend he is still capable of rising to what he most patently is not. If he doesn't fall asleep in his pudding, I'll have some information for you tomorrow."

"And you'll be careful?" Gideon knew he couldn't dissuade her from what she planned.

Trixie tipped her head and smiled. "Really, pet, there's no need for concern. What could possibly go wrong?"

CHAPTER TEN

JESSICA DRESSED FOR DINNER in one of her new gowns, with both Mildred and Doreen fussing over her the entire time, admiring her undergarments, squealing in delight when she at last chose the dusky-rose over the sky-blue, saying one couldn't possibly be better than the other but wasn't it a marvel how the rose went so well with Jessica's red locks. "And who would have thought any such thing?"

Gideon would, Jessica answered silently as she sat in front of the dressing table while Mildred, who was proving a marvel (although not in the sense Adam would have meant), handled the curling stick with flair, and not once did Jessica have to remind her that pins were to be put into hair and not her scalp.

Her mind traveled back in time for a moment, recalling Alice, her maid and friend of a lifetime ago. Jessica knew she had been a petted and pampered child, lacking in nothing, at least in a material way. She'd had a lovely roof over her head, had never known what it was like to worry about where her next meal or bed would come from. She had missed her mother, loathed her stepmother, enjoyed spoiling her half brother, could say she barely knew her father...but she had been content. Indeed, she'd been looking forward to her first Season, sure she'd be at least a moderate success. Fear had no place in her life.

That she'd been through what she'd been forced to endure these past five years and survived it all might be considered something of a miracle, and to once again be sitting in the lap of luxury very nearly erased those sad memories from her mind. Truly, it was amazing how adaptable a person could be. Although it was much easier, she knew, to accustom oneself to luxury than to the catch-as-catch-can existence of those five long years between her girlhood and the woman she had been forced to become.

As Mildred fussed with the trio of curls she was arranging to fall just so on Jessica's left shoulder, Doreen gathered up mountains of tissue and paper and string now that all of the new clothing had been carefully put away in drawers and cupboards and armoires. Jessica's own wardrobe, from shifts to shoes to shawls, had been playfully argued over, with the shoes going to Mildred, who said she could stuff tissue in the toes while Doreen couldn't stuff her toes into the toes. Doreen laid claim to the night rails, Mildred the bonnets, and nobody begged to please be given the black gowns Jessica had worn in the gaming room.

"His lordship asked to be informed as to your choice for the evening, ma'am," Doreen told her when she'd returned to the bedchamber after disposing of the wrappings. "I was just running down that footman with the Adam's apple big as a lemon, to get him to help me carry everything down to the kitchen fire, when one of that pair of blasted mongrels started jumping up at me, trying to get a bit of trailing string, and I said to stop, and it wouldn't, and the lemon boy—"

"His name is Vernon," Mildred interrupted. "And wouldn't a person with a hulking great Adam's apple have one the size of an apple, not a lemon?"

"Don't interrupt her, Mildred," Jessica warned, smiling. "She might decide to start again at the beginning."

Fortunately, the Irishwoman did not. "All right, then, *Vernon.* My goodness, Mildred, but you're a stickler. At any rate, as Mr. Borders says I should keep things from getting so long they grow whiskers, I scolded that dog something terrible, but it still would persist, and did so until his lordship himself called it to heel. *That's* when he saw me and asked what it was that you were thinking of wearing tonight, and I told him you were going back and forth with the rose and the blue for the longest time, but in the end decided on the rose, and he said to follow him, so I did. I followed him all the way to the back of the house without once taking a turn or a back stair, and then he put out his hand so graciouslike and had me *precede* him into his study. That's what he said. He said, 'Doreen, please precede me into the study whilst I fetch something.'"

"Now that's a lie. Lordships don't say fetch," Mildred protested as she stood behind her mistress, so that Jessica gave her a sharp elbow in the thigh as the last curls were set in place.

Doreen sighed in exasperation. "They shouldn't say *precede,* either, to my mind, because I didn't know what it meant for the life of me, but once he told me I did, so I *preceded* him into the study and then cooled me heels, not touching a thing, I swear it, and not even so much as looking at anything too hard, all those lovely things, until he came back with this."

At last, finally, and not a moment too soon for the consideration of Mildred's and Jessica's nerves, the maid produced a blue velvet-covered oblong box from her apron pocket, all but tapping Jessica on the nose with it. "I didn't look. I wanted to, but I didn't. I just curtsied, twice over, and ran hotfoot back up here. Using the back stairs, as I knows my place, even if his lordship don't. Lemon boy, that is, *Vernon,* he'd already taken away the wrappings. And the dog. His name is Brutus, which isn't a very kindly name for a dog, is it? Call a thing a brute, and it will be, just to make you happy. You mark my words on that one!"

Jessica had stopped listening. She took the box from Doreen and eyed it for some moments before daring to press on the round button clasp. The lid sprang open to reveal a choker made up of four strands of perfectly matched pearls, their ivory luster faintly shaded with pink. In the center of those pearls was a circlet of much smaller pearls surrounding—

"Well, now, would you look at that," Mildred said, leaning in close. "It's a lady's face."

"It's a cameo, Mildred. Carved out of some sort of shell, I believe, so that the lady's profile is much lighter than the background. Many of them are made in Italy. Isn't it beautiful?"

"Yes, ma'am, it is that. She looks like an angel, even if we can only see half her face. But seeing as it looks like it cost the earth and more, you'd think they'd carve the whole face."

"She's in profile, and I'm convinced that was done

on purpose," Jessica said, handing the necklace to Mildred. Thank goodness the two women were here; Jessica couldn't dare to cry, or else they'd both fuss and wonder.

He'd chosen the perfect piece of jewelry to match a perfect gown, one of nearly two dozen perfect gowns and riding habits and capes and shawls and— Was there anything the man couldn't do?

Mildred carefully aligned the necklace against the exact center of Jessica's throat and then squinted over the small clasp. "There! Now let's go see what all we've done."

Jessica dutifully stood up, needlessly smoothing down the folds of her gown, because it didn't bunch when creased, as her black had done, but simply flowed, as if a part of her.

Her reflection looked back at her from the pier glass, showing her a wonderfully set-up looking young woman, complete to a shade, or at least she was once Doreen unearthed the long, narrow rose-and-silver paisley shawl and threaded it through Jessica's elbows so that its fringed ends reached nearly to the floor.

"That was the second gong that just went, ma'am," Mildred said, opening the door to the hallway as if she hoped to hear an echo confirming her conclusion. "Ah, and here comes Mr. Borders down the hallway to fetch you."

"You said *fetch*," Doreen pointed out, handing Jessica a small reticule fashioned of the same paisley, its slim chain silver, its clasp fashioned of pink pearls. Was there no detail too small for the man? When he made love to a woman, was he equally as interested in detail? "See? Other people do so say it, not just me."

"Just not earls, you fool," Mildred muttered, pulling Doreen back and signaling they were to drop into curtsies. They were both eager learners, and with the gaming room now a thing of the past, they were bound and determined to once again make themselves indispensable to their mistress. "We'll wait up, ma'am, to help you into bed."

Jessica felt hot color run into her cheeks, probably clashing badly with both her hair and her gown. The note on her pillow this morning, when combined with the gown and the necklace, had her hopes rising that Gideon would not be going out after dinner. Not tonight. "Oh. Oh, I don't think you need to… That is, I may be quite late. I'll manage."

"But—" Doreen began.

"She says she'll manage," Mildred cut in quickly. "Honestly, Doreen, you're thick as a plank sometimes." The hostess-cum-lady's maid curtsied yet again. "I'll just go lay out your night rail and dressing gown and turn down the bed. Good night, ma'am."

"Good night, Mildred. Doreen. And thank you. I don't know what I'd do without either one of you."

Still keeping her head slightly averted, Jessica escaped to the hallway and called out to Richard, who seemed to be pacing near the head of the staircase. Gideon had seen to it Richard be outfitted with new clothes, and she had been thrilled to see the older man's pleasure in his wardrobe. He looked distinguished now in some unexplainable way, and actually rather comfortable, as if more used to fine things and lavish surroundings than she would have imagined. Someday perhaps he'd tell her who he had been before he'd taken to gaming. To date, he'd told her he was a bastard prince, a defrocked priest, a pirate and a schoolteacher, which was as good as to say she should not ask him again or else be prepared for another tall tale.

He turned about and smiled before he bowed in her direction, his knees creaking audibly. "And who might you be, lovely lady?" he asked. "I don't believe we've been introduced."

Jessica held out her arms and turned about in a full circle. "I'm magnificent, aren't I? And all accomplished without sparkles. Adam will be dumbfounded."

"Your brother hasn't the brains to be dumbfounded," Richard said, holding out his arm to her. "He'd rather believe he knows everything worth knowing. You're looking happy as well as beautiful this evening, Jess. Is that because of the new gown, or the fact that his lordship awaits you downstairs?"

"He awaits me downstairs each evening," Jessica pointed out as she lifted her hem slightly, to help her navigate the marble steps.

"Not with a pink rosebud pinned to his lapel. I wondered about that earlier, when I went down. I only came back up to fetch my handkerchief."

"Uncles don't say *fetch,* Richard. I have it on good authority." Her heart then heard what Richard had said and decided to skip a beat. "A pink rosebud?"

"Yes, it shocked me, as well. He dresses fine as nine pence, but no geegaws for the man, not in the usual run of things. So I didn't comment on it. And, we have a visitor."

Jessica didn't take that bit of information in immediately, either. She was too busy wondering how Gideon would have managed to produce a blue rose, if she had chosen the blue. Knowing the man, he'd probably have just dipped its stem in an inkpot until he'd achieved the proper shade. "Oh?" she said belatedly. "Who is he?"

"Not he, but she. And it's Lady Katherine, his lordship's sister, come into town for new boots or some such thing, and if I were thirty years younger, I'd be wearing rosebuds myself. Oops, nearly tripped there, didn't you? You have to be careful where you step, Jess."

He was trying to tell her something but without really telling her. "Yes, I suppose I do. In every way."

They reached the first-floor foyer. Richard turned toward the closed doors to the drawing room, but Jessica held him back. "What is she doing here?" she whispered fiercely.

"I told you, something about new boots. Now come along."

Jessica looked closely into her friend's face. Saw the slight twitch of his left eyelid. "What's going on, Richard? What's *really* going on?"

"Now why would you be asking that?"

"I'm asking that because you never forget your handkerchief. I'm asking because Gideon doesn't wear posies. I'm asking because nobody told me Lady Katherine was expected. I'm asking because the doors to the drawing room are closed. And I'm asking most of all because your eyelid is twitching."

"It is not," he said, and it twitched again, just as a small bead of perspiration made its way down his temple.

"It does when you're lying. You may bluff with impunity at cards, but never with me. Something is awaiting me on the other side of those doors, and that something is more than Gideon's sister."

"I told him to send somebody else upstairs to get you," Richard said, sighing, making use of his handkerchief to wipe at his brow. "Adam, for one. I still don't think he realizes what's going on, he's so busy making a total ass of himself, running around tables and chairs in those bloody stupid red heels of his, trying to avoid the dogs. I have to ask the cook for a marrowbone for Brutus. He won't let the fool alone. Just come along, Jess, won't you? You knew this was inevitable, in any case."

"I knew what was—"

The double doors were flung open, and Brutus, closely followed by Cleo, was escorted into the foyer by Thorndyke, who was holding some sort of raw meat chop aloft with two fingers, his expression one of extreme distaste. Jessica quickly bit her bottom lip until the butler and his tongue-lolling admirers had disappeared behind the baize door at the end of the hallway, and then released her delight in peals of laughter.

"Oh, good, she's not a stickler. We can't have one of those."

The voice was female, and it had come from inside the drawing room.

"Lady Katherine?" Jessica whispered the question, as they were still near the stairs and could not see into the drawing room.

Richard nodded. "Beautiful. One might say exotic. But without a single air or touch of starch about her.

Had me shake her hand rather than bow over it. And she's wearing riding clothes, says there's time enough later to change if she has a mind to, which she doesn't."

Jessica considered this for a moment. "But you think I'll like her."

It was Richard's turn to consider. "It's like with the earl, Jess. I don't think you have a choice."

"And since they heard me laugh, no choice about going in there," Jessica agreed. "Richard, do you sometimes think it was easier when it was just the two of us?"

"No," he said, grinning. "I like the gravy boat I've somehow been dropped into too much to say that. And so do you."

Jessica was still smiling as she entered the drawing room, still hanging onto Richard's arm, that smile only fading when she began taking inventory of its other occupants.

There was Adam, dressed this evening in shamrock-green jacket and fawn pantaloons, bent over one of the many couches, snapping at the seat with his handkerchief, probably to dislodge any dog hair.

There was Lady Katherine Redgrave, exotic as Richard had said, in her deep burgundy riding habit as she all but sprawled on another couch, both arms stretched out along its carved wooden back, one long booted leg crossed over the other in a highly unladylike way that flattered her all hollow.

One thing Jessica could say about the Redgraves, at least the three she'd met; they certainly knew how to relax and didn't appear to much care where they were when they did it. And, oddly, the more they relaxed, the more on guard you felt you needed to be.

Her ladyship's darkest brown hair, glinted with golden highlights, was piled haphazardly atop her head, several softly curling tendrils escaping the pins in a way many would suffer hours of curling sticks and poked pins to achieve. Her eyes were huge and dark and slightly tip-tilted, her mouth wide and pink and lush, her nose rivaled the perfection of the profile on Jessica's new cameo, as did her creamy complexion.

She tilted her head in Jessica's direction. And winked.

Jessica smiled in return, hoping she looked pleased rather than terrified.

And there was Gideon, standing at the mantel at the far side of the room, dressed in his usual impeccable black and white, the rose visible on his lapel, seemingly deep in conversation with…who was that man, and why was he wearing—

"Oh, my God. Now? Tonight? Is he out of his— Richard, why didn't you tell me about— *Now?*"

She must have spoken that last word above her strangled whisper, because Gideon and the man wearing the starched white collar of the church turned to look at her.

And that's when the world stopped.

He left the clergyman where he stood and crossed the wide expanse of the drawing room in his coolly determined way, making a dead-set at her, his dark eyes never leaving her face. Smoldering. Yes, that was the word. He was smoldering. All sophistication, all his devilishly handsome dark good looks, all his fine clothes and finer physique enough to cause her to forget to breathe.

"Damme," Richard breathed quietly, in some awe. "If there was ever a man who wanted a woman…"

Jessica quickly lowered her eyes, praying they hadn't revealed what Richard had seen in Gideon's. Because if there was ever a woman who wanted a man…

She dropped into a curtsy and held out her gloved hand, some bit of her brain remembering what she'd been taught a lifetime ago, as a young girl preparing for her Come Out. Gideon bowed over it, turning her hand at the last moment in order to press his kiss just below the pearl button fastening the soft kid against her wrist. The tip of his tongue touched her heated flesh and was gone, leaving her branded.

Richard melted away, physically removing himself. The rest of the world simply disappeared, as they, the room they gathered in, the entire city of London, were no longer important.

"Tonight?" she asked when she could finally locate her tongue.

"God, yes. Tonight," he answered quietly, his tone all fierce seduction as he drew her arm through his and walked her back into the foyer, just out of sight of the others. "You flatter the gown just as I knew you would. I know what lies beneath it, and what lies beneath that. The silk of your stockings, the laces that lift and mold your breasts. The fiery center of you, the memories that have driven me mad these past endless days. I'll be undressing you with my eyes for the eternity of time we have to yet get through until I can turn thought into deed. You must be gentle with me, Jessica, for I'm a man who has touched the silks that now touch you, imagining how I will rid you of them with reverent hands and delicate kisses, a man who is now rapidly approaching the end of his tether."

She opened her mouth, and the silliest words in all the world popped out. Perhaps because she had wondered and then hated herself for wondering. Men had needs. She knew that, certainly. She hadn't realized women could share those needs, but she did, now, thanks to him. That he would wait for her, however, astounded her. "You've been celibate these ten days?"

"Gives you pause, doesn't it, knowing my reputation?" he asked, at last gifting her with a half smile, one that made him look younger, even vulnerable. "But I made myself a promise, and I keep my promises, although if I hadn't been able to secure the Special License this afternoon, God only knows how I would have made it through another night without breaking down your door."

"I've thought much the same," she admitted, feeling heat flow into her cheeks…and other parts of her body. "I have this new…curiosity."

"You'll have to tell me about this curiosity. In some detail, please, and I will attempt to satisfy it all…also in some detail."

The small bud of pleasure between her thighs, which he'd awakened from its lifetime of innocent slumber, contracted and released, sending a ripple of sensation throughout her body. Her skin tingled. Her nipples strained against the silk lining of her corset. Her knees could barely support her. If this was what his mere words could do to her…?

He touched the back of his hand to her cheek. "You're thinking about it, aren't you? I can see it in your eyes, your pupils gone all dark and wide. There's heaven and there's hell in what we humans desire, Jessica. But the past is the past, and now we start fresh. From now on, for us, and only between us, we reach for the stars."

"You're...you're a remarkable man. Arrogant, always bound and determined to get your own way... but remarkable." She watched his own eyes go dark and felt herself leaning toward him, angling up her chin for his kiss.

"Haven't you finished *yet,* Gideon? Should I help? Jessica, please marry the man, which he's assured me you want to do, although I can't see the attraction, frankly, and let's go in to dinner. I've been on horseback nearly all day, and I'm famished."

Jessica lowered her head, the spell between Gideon and her broken.

He took her arm once more and turned her about to see his sister standing a few feet away, one hand on her hip, her left boot tapping against the marble floor. Her grin was very nearly unholy. "Oops," she said cheekily, clearly a young woman devoid of fear. "Are you going to growl now, Gideon?"

"Not tonight. Jessica, allow me, please, to introduce you to my sister, the incorrigible but kind Lady Katherine Redgrave. Kate, my bride, Jessica."

Jessica dropped into a curtsy, realizing Gideon had not added *Linden* to that introduction. But as he'd said, the past was the past. "My lady."

"Kate. My name is Kate, and since you're about to

become my sister, I think we can also dispense with curtsies, considering it would be I curtsying to you if Gideon ever gets this ceremony behind us. Gideon, the man is quoting sermons in there, and the fool is attempting to make *limericks* of them. Oh, that wasn't nice of me, was it, Jessica? Your brother is a very… That is, he's a well set-up young—" She hesitated, flashed a smile that could bring down kings, and ended, "He's a bit of an adorable twit, isn't he?"

"Of the first water, although only a woman would include *adorable* in that description," Gideon agreed, laughing. "I could have had Brutus and Cleo fully trained by now, if I put my mind to it. But I'm enjoying Adam's discomfort too much. Jessica, I asked Kate to come to town to bear witness at the ceremony, along with Richard. As I left the invitation rather late, Kate chose to travel the final leg via horseback, her groom in tow and her carriage containing her luggage lagging behind. But she is obedient," he ended, grinning at his sister.

"Dying of curiosity, more like," Lady Katherine admitted. "And, not that I don't appreciate having you include me, brother mine, why didn't you just have Trixie fly on over here on her gilded broom to bear witness? Oh, wait, I believe I've just answered my own question."

"Not really. She has other plans this evening in any case." He looked toward the doorway. "I suppose we should get this over with."

"How could any woman refuse such a romantic proposal?" Jessica smiled at Kate, who winked at her yet again, and the three of them at last entered the drawing room, Gideon guiding them directly toward the fireplace and a clearly uncomfortable clergyman.

"Jessica, there you are! Quickly, what rhymes with leper? All I can come up with is pepper, and that won't fadge."

"Adorable," Kate said again, in some amusement. "And much preferable to the way he's been attempting to impress me with his clearly irresistible charms. Whoever let him off his leading strings this soon was overconfident in his hopes."

"Yes, about that," Jessica said to Gideon as the clergyman hastily arranged everyone in the proper order in front of him. "Adam told me a few things this afternoon. Shocking things. We should talk about them."

"Tomorrow," Gideon promised as the clergyman pointedly cleared his throat and opened his prayer book.

In the next few minutes, much more quickly and even prosaically than she could have imagined, Jessica became the Countess of Saltwood. She hadn't really given much thought to that particular result of marrying Gideon, even after Lady Katherine had earlier joked about curtsying to her. Many people would now curtsy to her, address her as my lady, or your ladyship. Just the sort of thing she had once daydreamed about a lifetime ago, back in the days of her innocence.

Now Gideon, by wedding her, had given her back what he so clearly thought was the life she deserved. He'd married her because he felt the Redgraves owed her something, that was clear. But he also desired her. She hadn't thought about *desire* as a young girl awaiting her first Season. She certainly hadn't thought about it during her months with James, except to think men were no better than animals in the forest.

Yet when Gideon looked at her with desire in his eyes, she knew the trappings of society meant nothing. The titles, the curtsies, the balls, the nights at the theater, all of it.

How strange that her father and stepmother had clearly been preparing Adam for what was to come, but had not attempted any such education with her. Considering her father's plans for her, that did seem odd. Unless that was to be her appeal…her ignorance. Her *innocence.*

Unless…unless her father had never planned any such thing for his daughter and had only been obeying someone else, who'd demanded her from him, demanded his obedience. James had been afraid of someone. Had her father been equally terrified? Cowed enough or frightened enough to allow his own daughter to be sacrificed? Yes, that seemed the more logical explanation, not that she could ever forgive her father, no matter how deep his fears.

Jessica looked down the length of the dining table to see Gideon watching her, and realized her wandering mind had been taking her to a place that had no *place* tonight.

He raised his wineglass to her in a sort of salute, and immediately Lady Katherine took up her own, rising to her feet. "Since my brothers are not here to do the thing properly, I suppose it is up to me to propose a toast to the Earl and Countess of Saltwood. Which I hereby do." She raised her glass higher. "To a long and happy life, Jessica, even if that means having Gideon in it. Cheers!"

"Oh, hear, hear!" Adam agreed, also on his feet, glass raised high. "To a long and happy life, Gideon, even if that means having *me* in it!"

Everyone laughed, as they were hopefully meant to do, and Jessica gazed at her brother in real affection. He'd be all right, he truly would. They'd all be all right, in time. Because Gideon would see to it. She truly believed that.

CHAPTER ELEVEN

WITH KATE YAWNING into her hand and Adam thoroughly in his cups and half-asleep in his chair, Gideon exchanged a meaningful glance with Richard, who immediately stood up, stretching and yawning and then quickly apologizing for his lapse.

"Quite a day for an old man like me, quite a day," he said, smiling at Lady Katherine. "Would you do me the extreme favor of allowing me to escort you upstairs to your chamber, my lady?"

"What was that?" Adam stumbled to his feet, blinking. "I can do that. I've always wanted to escort a lady to her bedchamber, damned if I haven't."

"Adam!" Jessica exclaimed from her seat beside Gideon. "You really must learn to not say everything you think!"

"He thinks?" Gideon asked quietly, eying the curls at Jessica's shoulders, the ones he'd been manfully resisting wrapping around his finger this past hour or more. But it hadn't been easy goings. "It is rather late, Richard, isn't it?"

"Oh, yes, my lord. After a long day," he added helpfully, and then winced as the mantel clock struck ten. Many carriages were just now leaving Portman Square, for an evening round of parties. "All things considered, that is."

"You're all as subtle as a sharp jab to the ribs," Lady Katherine said, but then held out her hand to Richard, to allow him to help her to rise. "I held out as long as I could, as I'd like to think part of my mission in life is harassing you and Max and Val, Gideon, but I will admit I'm more than ready for my bed." She looked to Richard and Adam. "And I would greatly appreciate both you fine gentlemen accompanying me upstairs. To my *door*," she added, shooting Adam an amused look.

"We'll all go up," Gideon said, holding out his hand to Jessica. He wouldn't look at her, because she might smile at him, and if she gave him one more ounce of encouragement he might just take her here and now, on the couch.

The way she looked at him from beneath her lush lashes, the way she held her spoon as she sipped her soup, her endearing habit of touching her hand to the middle of her breasts as she leaned forward to listen to the conversation. He'd even envied her serviette as she'd dabbed the fine linen against her lips.

It hadn't been her fault. He knew that. She'd done nothing out of the ordinary. She hadn't purposely teased him. She had only to breathe to make him want her.

Ten days. Who knew ten days could be so long a time? He'd given Gwen her *congé,* even introduced her to Freddie Banks, who much to Gwen's delight immediately offered her his protection. He'd harassed a modiste and her dozen seamstresses like a man possessed. He'd petitioned the church for a Special License, pretended not to know his grandmother's favored way to secure, well, favors. He'd paced the floor each night, he'd counted the hours each day. He'd stared at the

locked door between his and Jessica's bedchambers
and suffered the torments of the damned.

And all for a woman he barely knew. A woman who
was now his wife.

He'd wanted her. In the beginning, it had been that
simple. Because what he wanted, he took. Had always
taken. He'd never seen any reason to deny himself anything.

But he'd never wanted anything the way he wanted
Jessica.

And now he had her.

They entered her bedchamber together, his hand at
the back of her waist. He turned and closed the door.
Turned the key.

They moved farther into the large chamber, to see it
was subtly lit with candles and the light from a small
fire, the curtains on the four-poster bed tied back on
one side, draping the other three. The coverlet was
turned down, a confection of ivory lace rather artfully
arranged atop it.

He couldn't believe he wasn't seeing a scene well-
laid for seduction.

He placed his hands on her shoulders. "Where are
your women?"

"I dismissed them for the night."

He cocked his head to one side. "You did? And why
was that?"

"I don't know. The note I found this morning. The
new clothing, the necklace…all of it. I had…hopes,"
she said, and then stepped closer, raising her hands to
his neck cloth, deftly beginning to undo it. He decided

to help, quickly dealing with the buttons on his waist-coat and shirt.

His smile brought a hint of color to her cheeks. "You had two eyes in your head when you saw yourself in this gown, and knew I couldn't see you tonight and then simply walk away."

"So now you know how I feel, every time I look at you. It was only the once…but I can't forget it. How you made me feel. I hadn't felt anything, Gideon, not in a very long time. But this was new, what you made me feel. I wanted… I want to know if it was real, what I felt. I want to know if there's even more. Is that wrong? Please tell me it's not wrong."

He was already straining almost painfully against the fabric of his pantaloons. "I want to be inside you so badly." His hands went to her back, seeking out the row of buttons, dispatching them quickly. "I want to make you mine. But I don't want to rush you…."

"I may already be ahead of you," she told him breathlessly, tugging his shirt free of his waistband as she began backing toward the bed. "Let's don't talk anymore, Gideon, please?"

He picked her up at the waist, her arms going around his neck, and continued on toward the bed, smiling as he saw the pink rose petals strewn across the sheets. He hadn't been overly enthusiastic about Jessica's request Mildred and Doreen act as her ladies' maids, but now he believed they were both wildly underpaid.

He put Jessica down and quickly finished the job of ridding her of the dusky-rose gown, leaving her clad in an ivory lace corset laced in front with pink satin ribbons. The corset was purely ornamental, not fashioned for any other purpose than the joy he'd find once he'd slid open the laces to touch the treasure beneath.

For now, however, it could stay where it was, softly molding and raising her perfect breasts. The French drawers, however, had to go.

They went.

The silk stockings stayed. The necklace stayed. The golden circlet of diamonds remained on her left hand. The pins, and there were blessedly few of them, submitted to his search, and her glorious red hair was free, tumbling, enticing.

There was no time for his evening coat; it was too well fitted, for one thing. Jessica, bless her, had already managed to undo the buttons of his pantaloons. He was so ready to explode, no more than a few deep hard strokes from bursting. Reciting lines from *Paradise Lost* in his head wouldn't help him now. He couldn't even remember the damn words.

He hadn't felt this way since... No. He'd never felt this way. Never.

She slipped her hands inside his opened shirt, and his skin felt scalded by her touch. With a low groan of need, he lifted her onto the edge of the bed and spread her thighs, pulling her legs around his back even as he plunged into her, knowing she was ready for him.

"Yes! Gideon—yes!"

Yes, his mind echoed as he drove into her. *Yes, yes, yes!*

And then it was over. But it wasn't over. The long days and nights of unbearable *need* had been addressed, but not the *want*. Because he would want her for the rest of his life.

He laid her back on the rose petal-strewn sheets, lifting her legs onto the coverlet, and smiled down at her. She looked unfocused, lost in a dream, her limbs loose, her hair spread out on the pillows like a living thing. He'd done that. *Him.* He would banish her past. He'd chase away every last shadow. He felt all-powerful. She *made* him all-powerful.

Gideon stripped off the rest of his clothes and joined her in the bed, placed a kiss on her mouth with a gentleness he didn't know he could feel. "At least we're still breathing," he said as she smiled up at him. "We could have killed each other, you know."

Jessica caressed his cheek. "But now you're no use to me for at least an hour," she said, her tone teasing. Unafraid. Even daring.

Leaning over her, supporting himself on one elbow, Gideon located one end of the bow securing her corset, began slowly pulling on it to release it. "Not entirely."

He began kissing her just at the top edge of the corset, and then inched his way down even as the laces were undone. He kissed her breasts, licked at them, paid special attention to her taut nipples until she moaned quietly and raised her hips.

He kneaded her breasts, trailed kisses along the soft flesh inside her arms, down the length of her rib cage. His tongue found and teased at her navel, and she made a small, shocked sound of pleasure. He pressed his palm against her lower belly, bringing her heat that seemed to melt her…and then slowly turned his hand so that he was inching his way closer to her center even as she opened herself for him.

But not yet.

He cupped her, but then brought his mouth to her inner thighs, the sweet skin behind her knees. He worshipped, he teased, her every soft whimper of pleasure and frustration enflaming him.

But not yet.

He was in control now, he could wait her out; he needed to see what she'd do when he'd driven her beyond her limits.

She moved her hands down to the vee of her thighs, pressed his hand more firmly against her, shifted on the bed so that she could dig her heels into the mattress. She tugged upward on the skin of her belly, as if she could bring him in better contact with the parts of her that had to be aching to be touched, stroked into bloom.

He obliged.

He slid two fingers inside her, brought his mouth down to her and kept it there until she began to convulse around him, a living pulse of pleasure, taken over the edge in a new way, a different way. Ah, and there were so many ways....

Jessica attempted to sit up, blindly holding her arms out to him, clearly wanting to be held, needing to be held. He'd never understood that in a woman, why indeed anyone would have that need. Until now.

Gideon gathered her to him, her arms and legs once more locked behind his back as he buried himself, and perhaps his own past, deep inside her, clinging to her as she clung to him, the two of them riding out the storm, together.

When they collapsed against the pillows, Jessica didn't comment that he would be of "no use to her" for a while. Which was probably a good thing, as Gideon couldn't do much more than lie there as she picked crushed rose petals from his sweat-slick body before curling into him, resting her head on his shoulder.

He was going to have to learn to pace himself. If Trixie had been right and in another thirty years he would be happy most nights with his dogs, some brandy and a warm fire, at least he'd have that thirty years. He could only hope to tire out Jessica by that time, which he rather doubted would happen. But they'd work something out....

He pressed a kiss against her hair and then closed his eyes, more than ready for sleep, and drifted away....

"Your lordship?" There was a knock on the door. "Your lordship?"

Gideon raised his head a fraction. "Go. Away."

"Yes, sir, your lordship," Thorndyke answered. "I would do that, surely. But I can't."

Jessica stirred slightly but then only sighed and continued to sleep.

"Yes, Thorny, you can. You simply have to apply yourself. You managed to propel yourself here, now manage to get yourself gone."

Jessica yawned and stretched. Rather like a cat, rubbing her body against him. Part of Gideon took notice and became interested. The other part wished his butler on the far side of the moon.

"What's going on?" Jessica asked, the grace of a cat deserting her as she tried to prop herself up by pushing on her elbow, which then jabbed into his chest. "Who are you bullying?"

Gideon gave it up. "My butler. But don't worry, I bully him all the time. Go back to sleep."

She pushed her tangled hair away from her face, grumbling something about never sleeping without first braiding her hair or it turned into a rats' nest. "What does he want? Is it morning? It can't be morning, it's too dark."

The knock came again. "Your lordship? It's the dowager duchess, sir. She's sent a note."

Now Gideon was awake. "Trixie?"

"Yes, sir. You're to read it at once, sir."

Gideon pushed back the covers and left the bed, using the near-to-guttering light from a few of the remaining lit candles to locate his breeches. "Slide it under the door. What bloody time is it?"

"Gone three, my lord. I'm so sorry, but the footman who brought it was most insistent. I'll have the coach brought round."

"The— Damn it!" He watched as a folded note was pushed beneath the door and bent to pick it up. "This couldn't wait until morning, Thorndyke?" he asked as he broke the seal and opened the single page.

Get here. Now! The word *now* was underlined three times.

"Well, that's succinct." He raked his fingers through his hair. "I'll be down directly."

"We both will," Jessica said from behind him, and he turned to see she was standing beside the bed, unashamedly naked, crushed rose petals in her hair. And several other places. He looked down at himself, momentarily amazed at his powers of recovery in the face of distraction, and then silently cursed his grandmother's pathetic command of proper timing.

Gideon tore his gaze from the trio of rose petals fortunate enough to be in such intimate contact with Jessica's left hip, and then manfully squinted into the near darkness, looking for his shirt. "No, you stay here."

"We'll both be down directly, Thorndyke," she called out, and then began foraging for her underclothes, her bare bottom enticing as she bent over to retrieve the French drawers. Ah, more rose petals....

"I never before realized my own grandmother hates me," Gideon muttered, once again turning his eyes away from temptation.

It was closer to a quarter hour before he and Jessica were heading down the curved staircase, thanks to Jessica's "rats' nest," but they were nearly to the door before Kate hailed them from the top of the stairs.

"What's she done this time?" Lady Katherine asked as she bounded down the stairs with an energetic lack of caution that could have brought anyone else to grief. But not Kate. She never made a misstep, never gave a thought to decorum or, God help them all, her own safety. It was what he loved about her and why he worried so much about her. She was too damn much of a man for a woman. Somehow she'd lost any soft feminine side she'd ever had, preferring to act and be treated as if she was fourth and youngest Redgrave son.

He gave a moment's thought to his sister's question, and the fact that his grandmother had been *entertaining* the Marquis of Mellis. What if she wasn't as deft as she believed herself to be? What if she'd slipped, or become angry with something he'd revealed to her? What if— "You're not going with us, Kate."

She ignored him as if he'd said nothing, brushing past him and through the open doorway to the foggy, damp street beyond. She'd climbed into the coach, taking the rear-facing seat, and was buttoning the last few buttons of the jacket to her riding habit as Gideon and Jessica entered and the coach jolted forward.

"Trixie's her grandmother, too, Gideon," Jessica said, as if he'd forgotten. "Stop glaring at her."

"He's glaring? Just think, all these years I thought that was his usual face."

Jessica laughed but then slipped her hand into his as the coach turned out of the Square. "Trixie always lands on her feet, Gideon. I don't know her well, but I'm certain of that much."

He squeezed her hand in return. "I never should have started this."

"Never should have started what?" Kate asked him. "And before you open your mouth, remember, I'm not a child."

"Another time," he said evasively, grabbing the strap as the coachman made the last turn into Cavendish Square. They'd accomplished the drive in a quarter of the time it would have taken them during the day, with only a few drays and delivery wagons sharing the streets with them. "Let's just see what we're facing."

"All right. But you might want to do something about that rose petal clinging to your left cheek, brother mine."

Gideon raised his hand to brush away the petal. "There's nothing there."

"No. But Jessica's women spoke with my Sally, so I know there could have been. You've just confirmed that for me. Thank you."

"Pernicious brat," Gideon commented as Jessica

bent her head, hiding her face and, most probably, her flaming cheeks.

The door to the dowager countess's mansion was opened the moment the coach came to a halt, a wedge of yellowed light cutting through the fog. Gideon bustled the two women out of the coach and quickly hurried them into the foyer.

"Soames?"

The butler inclined his head. "Your lordship, Lady Katherine. Mrs. Linden."

"No, my countess," Gideon corrected, looking at the large standing clock in one corner of the foyer, "for the past nearly nine hours. But never mind that now. Where is she?"

"In her boudoir, my lord," Soames said, his ears going crimson as he shot glances at Jessica and Kate. Really, you'd think the man had passed beyond blushing decades ago. "As is his lordship. You're to go right up, sir."

"Remain here," Gideon ordered the ladies. "Soames, make them some tea or something."

"Oh, I don't think so," Kate announced. "Jessica? Do you think so?"

"I think you and I are going to be very good friends, Kate. And, no, I don't plan to remain down here."

When had he lost control of his life, his air of consequence, his ability to command? Gideon looked down at his clothing, as Soames was looking at him rather strangely, to see that he may have buttoned his waistcoat, but one of his shirttails was hanging loose beneath it. "Bloody hell. All right. But if I tell you to leave, you leave. Understood?"

"Oh, definitely understood," Jessica said…and then she did the oddest thing. She *winked* at Kate.

"You're wasting time, brother mine," Kate reminded him. "I saw the note. She wrote *now*."

And so it was that the trio, all of them now Redgraves, mounted the staircase together, turned and climbed another flight, following Soames, who then pointed them toward the closed double doors to what had to be Trixie's bedchamber.

He then bowed and said, "Whatever it is we're to do, it will be done, sir. I've ordered the staff to remain in their quarters. I'll be right here, anticipating your orders."

"Well, that was ominous," Jessica whispered as the butler backed away from the doors. "Go on, Gideon. Open it."

The chamber, one he'd never before visited, was quite large and fronted by an antechamber hung with red velvet draperies. Beyond it, the room opened up considerably, which seemed a pity to him, as none of its furnishings or colors appealed to him. Red, everywhere, red with touches of gold. Move the chamber to Piccadilly, and it would, other than in its sheer size and the cost of the fabrics and furnishings, become quite an inviting bordello. To see such a room here, in the most straitlaced area of Mayfair, was something of a shock.

There was a movement near the fireplace, and Trixie's barefoot legs appeared, searching for the floor as she uncurled herself from one of the large upholstered chairs positioned there. "There you are," she said, getting to her feet, her midnight-blue velvet dressing gown tightly tied at her waist, a glass of wine in her hand.

"My goodness, are we having a party?" she asked, appearing not at all upset that Gideon had not come here on his own. "Kate, Jessica, how good to see you both. More heads to consult, I suppose."

She employed the hand clutching the wineglass to gesture toward the large, curtained bed. "Now, what do you propose we should do with *that*?"

CHAPTER TWELVE

"SON OF A BITCH. Bloody damn son of a bitch…"

Jessica shot a look to Trixie, who was pointedly inspecting the perfectly buffed nails on her left hand, and approached the bed. She didn't want to look, but Gideon was looking, so she supposed she should be a supporting prop for her husband to lean on, or some such thing.

After all, it was bad enough Kate had plunked herself down in the facing chair halfway through her grandmother's explanation, laughing so hard she'd been forced to clutch her arms about her waist as she rocked back and forth in the chair, fighting a bout of hiccups. *Shy* and *missish* were not words one could ever think to use to describe Lady Katherine Redgrave.

They'd been talking, the marquis and Trixie, nattering of this and that over the late supper Soames had set out, the remains of which were still in evidence. Speaking of this and that, she'd said again, adding as she looked pointedly to Gideon, "And perhaps a few other things."

She'd thought to tease, flattering the man by kicking off one small slipper and running her silk-clad toes up and down his leg and…well, there was travel involved, and that would be all she'd say. That distraction had done wonders at loosening the man's tongue.

There came a moment, however, only a moment,

when she may have asked too pointed a question, or perhaps given too much away by dint of one of her comments. In any event, the marquis made to leave, which of course he could not do, not in his current mood, one that bordered on suspicion, of all silly things. It was only practical that she…distract him.

The distraction had ended happily, albeit, for the marquis, also permanently.

"He's really dead?" Jessica asked, looking down at the sheet-covered mound that had until recently been the Marquis of Mellis.

"Oh, yes, he's dead," Gideon grumbled. "There's probably a lot to be said for dogs and fires and snifters of brandy. At least after seventy. Although, as exits go, I suppose it wouldn't be all that terrible."

"Excuse me?"

He looked at her and then blinked. "I'm sorry. I'm afraid my mind was wandering. It's not every day I see a naked nobleman in my grandmother's bed, alive or dead. In fact, I try not to think about Trixie's bed in any way or form."

"I should certainly hope so." Jessica leaned her head against his upper arm. "He's rather large, isn't he? What are we going to do with him?"

Kate, apparently at last recovered from her fit of giggles, was beside them now, also looking down at the mounded sheet. "He can't stay here. At least not *precisely* here." She reached for the edge of the sheet. "Come on, you two, we'll have to get him dressed."

Gideon's hand shot out, his fingers clamping around his sister's wrist. "There are times, Katherine, when

I could cheerfully throttle you. Downstairs. Now. All three of you. And send Soames in here."

Jessica led the grinning Kate away, and, along with the dowager duchess, they descended to the drawing room where, as they'd been informed by Soames, tea and cakes awaited them.

Jessica was too concerned for Gideon to sit down, but once Trixie had taken up her usual half-reclining position on the one-armed couch, Kate dropped to the floor beside her, to ask, "What happened, Trixie? I mean, what *really* happened? What first did you do when you realized he'd cocked up his toes?"

Jessica was a matron now, a wife. She should be scolding her sister-in-law for her questions, and searching out some spirits of hartshorn for the dowager countess, as Trixie should by rights be having a fit of the vapors. Since neither action appeared to be required, or indeed looked for, she decided to take up one of the facing chairs and simply listen.

"Naughty puss," Trixie said, patting Kate's cheek. "I should be terrified that you're so like me, were I not so flattered. Now, as to your last question? I didn't notice. Not at first. I was much too occupied with wondering if drinking those horrid Bath waters truly has some sort of medicinal or restorative effect. I mean, the man was—well, not the man he used to be, surely, but certainly no sluggard."

Jessica looked down at her toes. There was nowhere else to look, not really.

"He always roared like some great bear when he was— I really shouldn't be saying this, not to you two innocent girls. I must be more overset than I imagined."

"Gideon and Jessica married tonight, Trixie," Kate supplied helpfully. "From the way they were looking at each other when they went up to bed at ten o'clock, I don't think Jessica's innocence should be a worry to you."

The dowager countess smiled in Jessica's direction. "No grass growing under my grandson's feet, is there? I should have realized he wouldn't wait so much as another day. I'll expect a grandchild within the year." Then she turned her attention back to Kate. "However, if you tell me you're no innocent, I'll have the man's name tonight and his ears on my mantel tomorrow."

"I didn't mean I'm not innocent, Trixie," Kate protested. "I'm simply not, well, *innocent.* Or do you forget who raised me? Remember when I was ten, and I asked you about those statues lining the staircase out there, and what those funny *things* were?"

Trixie shook her head. "Oh, I have so many sins to account for…" But then she rallied, as if eager to be on with it. "Very well, where was I?"

"There you go, Trixie. You'll feel better for the telling, I'm sure, you poor dear. Now, he was roaring…" Kate prompted, grinning at Jessica.

"No, that wasn't what I was saying. He was in the *habit* of roaring once brought to the, shall we say, summit. Tonight it was rather more of a surprised *oh* and then nothing. He simply collapsed on top of me. So I noticed only when I pointed out that, proud of himself as he might be, he was now crushing me and would he please move—which, sadly, he did not do. I nearly exhausted my strength until I could manage to extract myself from beneath him. I scribbled a note to Gideon and have been imbibing this lovely wine ever since, which is the only reason I'm running my tongue, which I shouldn't be doing, although, after the first time, you'd think I'd be less prone to hysterics."

Jessica sat up very straight. "This has happened to you *before* tonight?"

"Oh, yes, this makes it twice now. But other than to shamelessly trot after younger men, I see no escape from the possibility of a third time. Save celibacy, of course, which is out of the question."

"Of course," Jessica agreed weakly. It occurred to her it was a very good thing she wasn't some sheltered debutante suddenly thrust into this scandalous nest of Redgraves.

Kate rested her chin in her hand and looked adoringly up at her grandmother. "I want to be like you. I never want to grow old."

"We all grow old, pet," Trixie told Kate, patting her cheek. "Why else do you think I try so desperately to tell myself I'm still young? Being old terrifies me, because each day brings me closer to the moment I have to face my sins before my God. You don't want that sort of terrible moment for yourself, and I most certainly don't wish it on you." She took a steadying breath. "And now I believe I'd very much like another glass of wine, to aid me in maintaining my accustomed sangfroid."

"I'll see to it," Jessica said when Kate looked at her, her full bottom lip caught between her teeth, tears standing in her dark eyes.

A minute later there was some slight commotion on the other side of the closed doors, and all three women looked in that direction. There were a series of muffled bumps capped by a string of barely contained curses, followed by the sound of footsteps, perhaps even the sounds of something being dragged across the floor and, finally, the closing of a door.

"'Good night, sweet prince; and flights of angels sing thee to thy rest.' As long as you're no longer *resting* under my roof." Trixie raised her refilled glass in a salute, and then downed its contents in one long, smooth glide. "I wonder what Gideon decided to do with him? Oh, well, whatever it is, it won't kill him. The marquis, I mean."

An hour later, with Trixie now slumbering while almost politely snoring beneath a cashmere shawl on the couch, Jessica and Kate had that answer from Gideon.

"He'll be discovered in his usual chair at his favorite club. His coachman was most willing to accommodate my request for both his help and the club's direction, as he could see the inherent problems in explaining what his master was doing in Cavendish Square."

"So you told the coachie what the man was doing?" Kate asked, yawning, as if the subject interested her still, but not enough to keep her awake for much longer.

"Yes," Gideon said, rubbing at the back of his neck. "He was rather proud to hear it. They'll keep the marquis in a small storeroom until the club closes, and then trot him out to his chair, where he'll be found in the morning. Kept saying *good on him, the randy old bugger, good on him*—the coachman kept saying that, I mean. I haven't been able to muster the same enthusiasm about Trixie. Are we going to leave her here?"

Jessica got to her feet, pushing her hands against the small of her back. One way or another, it had been a long night. Something to tell her grandchildren, she supposed, although she doubted she ever would. "She says she's not going to sleep in that bed again, not until the entire thing has been stripped away, mattress, hangings, everything. She's also quite drunk, Gideon. I imagine I would be, too."

"Then we'll learn nothing more here tonight, or should I say this morning. It will soon be dawn. Ladies?"

"Oh, yes," Kate said, jumping up. "I'm more than ready to get back to Portman Square. Tomorrow is soon enough for you all to tell me more about whatever the devil is going on here."

"There's nothing going on here."

"So you say, Gideon. Silly me simply doesn't believe that," Kate announced as she headed for the foyer.

Gideon and Jessica exchanged looks as they followed her.

"Just before she nodded off, your grandmother asked me to lean down close so she could whisper in my ear. She said to tell you she's learned a few things, and that you'll soon have your murderer."

Gideon waited for Kate to be handed into the coach. "And Kate overheard. The girl's got ears like a bat. Wonderful. Now we'll never be rid of her."

"I heard that," Kate warned from inside the coach. "But you're probably right."

"Damn it, Kate—"

"Not now, Gideon," Jessica begged. "We're all exhausted."

He nodded his agreement, and helped her into the coach. They were halfway back to Portman Square when Kate asked about the commotion they'd heard outside the drawing room. "What happened?"

"Nothing," Gideon answered shortly. And then, a few moments later, his shoulders began to shake. "We dropped him."

Jessica looked at him in the dim light of the false dawn. He was smiling. "You *dropped* him?"

"It wasn't all that terrible. We'd tied him up in a sheet, and partway down the stairs Soames lost his grip on his end."

"Oh, Gideon," Jessica said, her own lips twitching in amusement. "How...um, how horrible."

Gideon shrugged as if unconcerned, but the devil had crept into his eyes. "I suppose we could have apologized, but the marquis didn't seem to mind."

They were all three of them still laughing as the footman set down the coach steps in Portman Square, Jessica going off into new peals of exhausted mirth when she saw the clearly apprehensive look on the young man's face. "My goodness, Waters," she managed to choke out, "you look as if you've just seen a dead man."

At that, she felt herself being swept up into Gideon's arms as he climbed the steps to the mansion and headed for the stairs. "Bed now, for all of us," he said, including Kate in this order.

"When do we go back to Cavendish Square?" Kate asked as she actually pulled on the railing to help propel herself up the stairs.

"We don't. You're returning to Redgrave Manor."

"Giddy," she said, very nearly whined, "don't make me badger you. You know you'll give in."

"Not this time. Good night, Kate."

Jessica gave the girl a quick wave as Gideon kicked open the door to their bedchamber. Once the door was closed again—and locked again—they both made short work of ridding themselves of their clothes and tumbling into the unmade bed. He kissed her, thanked her and then turned onto his stomach, clearly intending to sleep away what little remained of their wedding night.

Goodness! They were behaving like a long-married couple. Or at least like a long-married couple that had just disposed of a dead marquis.

She lay on her back while he lay on his belly. She lifted her hand and idly began stroking his bare back, more content than she could even imagine. Which, if she were to think about the entirety of her current situation, wouldn't be very sensible of her. But it seemed sensible enough for now.

"*Giddy?* Really?" she asked him after a bit.

He mumbled something she probably shouldn't have heard, and then sighed. "Good night, Jessica."

She smiled up at the draperies. "Good night. Giddy."

GIDEON LAID DOWN HIS FORK with extreme precision. Indeed, he'd kept his entire posture under careful control throughout the length of Jessica's embarrassed recitation of the conversation she and Adam had shared in the modiste's dressing room. He'd asked no questions. Until now, with her final admission.

"A journal? He was told to keep a journal?"

Jessica nodded, not meeting his eyes. "Or a diary, I suppose. In any event, he called it a journal, yes. But weren't you listening? Adam's…keeping a *tally*. As if the whole thing were some sort of twisted game. Even worse, if that's possible, our father had been giving him lessons in assassination. You have to talk to him, Gideon. I certainly can't. As it is, I can barely look at you, just telling you about it."

"I need to see this journal."

Jessica put the lie to her last statement as her eyelids flew up, and she stared at him. "Must you? I'd like to see it burnt. The point is, my father was training Adam to be just like him."

"No, Jessica. The point is, we now know without a doubt the Society remains active. You confirmed it existed five years ago. Adam's journal tells us it's still going on. You see, we know they all kept journals, all the way back to the beginning, with my grandfather. Trixie told me about him, about the journals, just yesterday."

Jessica put a fist to her mouth, closed her eyes. "I thought it was just something my father thought of, rather like keeping score of his kills at the hunt. They... they *all* wrote down what they did?"

"In great detail," Gideon said, and then told her what Trixie had seen in his grandfather's journals.

"Drawings? Charts? Are they all insane?"

Gideon pushed away his plate, his appetite gone. "One would think so. Either that, or terminally naive, considering the members all turned their yearly journals over to my grandfather for this business of verification, so their exalted leader or whatever they called him could verify the information and make the additions to their blasphemous bible. Once they'd done it, turned over a single journal, they were bound to him for life. There was no choice but to continue the practice, year after year."

"Didn't they realize what they were doing?"

"You mean, turning over their lives to their leader, their futures? They had to, surely. With those journals, the leader held them hostage to whatever demands he might make on them. And don't forget, Jessica, there were *guests* at these so-called ceremonies. One person's word might not inflict too much damage, but to be able to produce a dozen different journals, all naming the guest, all cataloguing the same depravities? If knowledge translates to power, and it always has, my grandfather, and my father after him, held the reputations of perhaps dozens of important men and, at least in my grandfather's time, even some women in his hands."

"And after them, whoever carries on with the Society even now. You think the journals are the reason the members are being killed?"

"I'm not certain if it's the journals themselves, although I'd certainly want them destroyed if I had written any of them, or had I attended one of their ceremonies and then found out they existed. To have some stupidity I'd engaged in at twenty—"

"Or eighteen," Jessica interrupted, sighing.

Gideon pushed back his chair and got to his feet. "Or at eighteen, yes. To have that act of idiocy brought back years later, when I was about to marry, or enter Parliament or some other government service? If I were to put my sights on becoming Prime Minister, or take the floor in the House of Lords to argue a position someone else might not care to have brought to a vote. On and on, Jessica. My life wouldn't be my own. I could be forced to support causes that disgust me, vote against laws I felt proper. I could be forced to hand over copious amounts of money—even kill someone on command. The list of trouble those journals could cause a man is limitless."

"But what about the leader? Your grandfather, your father, whoever else has served as the leader? The members could just as easily have controlled him, couldn't they?"

"Try to control the one man who held all the evidence, on all of them? To threaten him, to expose him, would destroy them all. Who threatens the man who holds so many lives in his hand? But we have to consider the other side of this coin, as well. To belong to the Society, to be one of the chosen few—perhaps that prize was worth the rest."

"And the...ceremonies. They may not want to give those up, either."

"Your every vice indulged, your every perversion encouraged. Wine, women, opium. A new world order perhaps, with the Society in charge. All powerful persuasions. We'll talk more about this when we know more."

"Yes, but where are you going? It's only eleven o'clock, Gideon. Adam's still asleep."

"Then it's more than time he was awake." He came around the breakfast table and put his hand on her shoulder. "We're in this together, aren't we?"

She looked up at him quizzically. "We are," she said carefully. "Now why do I feel as if I'm not going to care for whatever you say next?"

He smiled and dropped a kiss on her hair. "Probably

because, as I'm going to confront Adam, that leaves you to tell Kate what's going on. I don't think of myself as a coward, but the idea of Kate's possible questions bids fair to make me consider a lengthy sojourn on the other side of the world."

"I understand. I'd rather have a tooth drawn than have to listen to Adam say anything else on the subject. And then we'll go to Cavendish Square, to hear what Trixie has to tell us?"

"Yes. But just the two of us. Adam stays under the guard of his keeper, but I want Kate back at Redgrave Manor, preferably on her way yet this afternoon."

"Oh, and I'm supposed to accomplish that particular part of the miracle, am I? Do you have any suggestions as to how I'm to do that?"

"Put her to searching the estate for journals and this supposed bible," Gideon suggested, having already given the matter some thought during his morning bath. "Trixie burned the journals she found after my grandfather died, and searched for the volumes my father had without any success. Kate won't find anything if Trixie didn't, but it will keep her busy, or at least too busy to come riding back to town."

"But what if she does find something? You know she won't just send them to us. She'll bring them. After reading them."

Gideon grimaced. Yes, he could imagine Kate paging through the journals. "I'll send Max and Val to help her, as soon as either one or both of them show up again. That keeps all three of them out of the way, and if any journals are found, at least my brothers will have the sense to keep them from her. And before you say there's any number of flaws in this plan, remember, I should by rights be sending you to Redgrave Manor along with Kate. I am looking for a murderer."

She covered his hand with her own as she looked up at him. "And that's still all you're looking for, Gideon?"

"No," he admitted, "it's not. Trixie called my father a monster and, before him, my grandfather. Now, all these years later, it's up to this generation of Redgraves to learn what those monsters may have spawned. The scandalous Redgraves, Jessica. We all rather enjoy that reputation at times. Reckless, daring, impulsive, laughing in the face of society's rules. That was the reputation we foolishly enjoyed. We had no idea how deep the scandal might run, where and why it had its beginnings. If the Redgraves started all of this, it's up to the Redgraves to finish it."

"Thank you, Gideon. Thank you for including me, for not sending me away."

He leaned in and kissed her on the mouth as he ran his hand down over her breast. "No, don't thank me. I could tell you any number of lies about why it would be best all around for you to be here. I could say you deserve a chance at some revenge for what happened to you. I could weave any number of tales meant to ease my conscience. But the truth is, I'm being entirely selfish. I'm not ready to let you go."

The moment he said those last words, he knew he had made a mistake.

"And when you are? Ready to let me go, that is. What then, Gideon?"

He stood back, looked down at her, her question repeating itself inside his head. "I don't know. I haven't thought that far. I've never had to…"

Her smile came as a surprise to him, just as had her question. "No, I didn't think you had. You're one of those reckless, impulsive Redgraves, you admit it out of your own mouth. You see what you want, and you go after it with everything that's in you until it's yours, and the devil take the hindmost. But when the chase is over, once you've won? Once you've solved all the mysteries of the Society, perhaps even found your father's remains and returned them to the mausoleum? Once you and I have nothing more in common than a need to explore each other's bodies, a need I see no reason to deny? What then? What of this ring I wear? What of a future beyond tomorrow?"

He didn't answer her. He couldn't answer her. He'd done what he'd done because it was the right thing to do. The Redgraves owed her for all the heartache she'd suffered in her life. That he desired her had been some fortuitous coincidence. But beyond that? Beyond tomorrow? Physical intimacy aside, clearly it was still too early for her to believe they might find love together, something deeper than the passion.

"I thought as much. Are all men little boys, Gideon? Even you? Not thinking beyond the end of your noses—although I'm sure your grandmother would say that differently? Oh, dear. What to do about Jessica, once you've found what you're looking for, once you've tired of her, as you've tired of every one of the women you've bedded, hmm? This could prove interesting in the end, couldn't it?"

"We're married," he said at last, knowing his answer

wasn't an answer at all, not to the real question Jessica had put before him. "That *is* the end of it."

"Of course," she said, turning her attention back to her plate. She picked up her fork. "I'll see to Kate. You go rouse Adam, as you said, and tell him some home truths. As it is, he's too eager to slip his leash. Let's hope you can make him understand why that isn't a good idea. My worry is he's had a myriad of strange ideas drummed into his head, so he may think otherwise."

"Jessica, I—" Gideon shut his mouth, because he'd nearly said something they'd both regret. Him, because he wasn't sure if he knew what the word meant, and Jessica, because she'd know it would be too pat to be believable. He doubted he believed it himself. They enjoyed each other; they both admitted that; they even liked each other. But as to more? "I do care for you, Jessica. Beyond what we shared last night."

"Thank you," she said, and then took a bite of what had to be cold eggs.

Thank you? He'd said he cared for her, and she'd said *thank you?* What sort of answer was that? She may as well have thrown a bucket of cold pump water in his face.

"You're… Yes. I leave Kate in your capable hands, hoping I can do even half so well with the journal-keeping nodcock. I should like to leave for Cavendish Square by one o'clock." He quit the room then, knowing he should have said more, or less, or anything other than the words he'd chosen.

And then, halfway up the stairs, he realized he was angry, and not just with himself. They were adults, he and Jessica. They knew what they wanted, and they'd wanted each other. They still wanted each other, unless she had been attempting to tell him that last night—at least the parts before Trixie's note had arrived—had been enough for her; she hadn't needed the ring, the vows.

But *he* had, damn it!

It was just understanding *why* he'd felt he needed them, that was the question, because paying a debt seemed a pitifully lame explanation, even to him....

CHAPTER THIRTEEN

THE DOWAGER COUNTESS turned another page in Turner Collier's journal and looked at Gideon over the top of a pair of simple half-spectacles. Collier's name and the year 1809, and beneath that, *The Society,* were all embossed on the leather cover in gold script. She handled each page with only the tips of her slightly trembling fingers, as if the contact could prove poisonous. "Does the fool even know what this is?" she asked at last.

Jessica also looked to Gideon, who had been standing at the fireplace, his face an expressionless mask. It was two o'clock, Adam was safely in Portman Square with Seth, his new keeper, and Lady Katherine was already on her way to Redgrave Manor, a young woman on a mission. Jessica could only wish her new sister-in-law hadn't seemed so eager to begin the hunt.

"He tells me he never paid all that much attention to it, as he couldn't understand most of what's there. He's only interested in his own conquests, of which I believe half exist purely in his imagination. He only handed over his father's journal as some sort of afterthought. He'd had it in his room at school, with orders to study it, when word came about his parents' fatal *accident.* When he was packed up to come to me in London, it came along with him. Otherwise, we'd never have known it existed."

"All these years gone by since I've seen one of these, and yet still not enough time to lessen the pain. I believe I've succeeded in banishing the memory of those days, gotten past the shame, the horror of it, and then…this. But I suppose it has to be said." Trixie turned another page and sighed.

"What is it?" Jessica asked nervously, wondering if she really wanted an answer. The dowager countess's cheeks were so pale, she feared for her. "Did you recognize a name?"

"I've recognized several. Have you shown this to your wife, Gideon?"

"No," he answered and took another sip from his wineglass. "I thought we'd let you tell us what you see."

Trixie slipped off the half-spectacles and laid them in her lap. "I see history repeating itself," she said sadly. "The codes remain the same. For instance, V, of course, stands for virgin, although they saw damn few of them. Playacting, most of it, with willing, highly paid prostitutes. Naughty little boys, drinking, whoring, one trying to outdo the next in manufactured, carefully orchestrated depravities. That's all most of the hellfire clubs were, back then, Dashwood's included, from all I've heard of the thing. There was a surfeit of deviltry, but little actual devil worship."

"Yes, I'd assumed that," Gideon said tightly, joining Jessica on the couch facing Trixie's one-armed reclining couch. "And the double V?"

"You do need to know, unfortunately. This is where your grandfather's Society differed, pet, and first grew ugly. The letters refer to vestal virgins, the true virgin sacrifices. Jessica, dear, I would rather you left the room until we call you back."

"No. If Gideon needs to know, then so do I."

Trixie's mouth worked for a moment, as if she was searching for the least offensive words concerning a subject that had few to offer. "Very well. Vestal virgins. They're reserved for the highest rite, when a new member is welcomed into the thirteen which, thankfully, isn't often. The Society takes everything and stands it on its head. Evil for good, wanton for chaste. In ancient Rome, vestal virgins were kept safe from the priests. In the Society, they are for the empowerment of the priests, and become the living altar for the induction rite. The more elevated the vestal virgin, by way of birth and social status, the more power flows to her initiator, who is first, but definitely not last, to approach the *altar*. I won't say more than that."

Jessica laced her fingers together in her lap, her knuckles white with strain. Gideon covered her hands with his own and murmured something he must have supposed to be comforting. She couldn't make out the words for the buzzing in her ears. Her father had turned her over for such a *rite?*

"Jessica, I'm sorry, but we need to know all of this," Gideon apologized. "What you're saying, Trixie, is that five years ago, a new member was to be installed?"

"And Jessica was chosen for the honor of gifting him with her virginal power. One thing has bothered me since first you told me about what nearly happened to you, Jessica. Turner Collier was an ass, but I find it difficult to believe he *volunteered* his own daughter."

"I find everything in that journal difficult to believe," Gideon said, his tone bitter. "Explain the other code letters, if you please. There's nearly an entire alphabet of them listed inside the rear cover."

Trixie slipped her spectacles on again and reopened the book to the page she'd marked with her finger. "Must we? R stands for *restrained*. F-W for *free will*. The rest denote the acts themselves. I believe you can figure out those without my help. Find a coded name and then read the strings of letters that follow, one set per line for each encounter, all neatly dated as to time, place and other participants. Monsters all, but quite orderly, and with steadfast attention to detail. Your grandfather was always quite particular about detail."

"And these names denote guests?"

"Yes. And wives, of course, to be schooled in the arts of submission and arousal. That also was your grandfather's idea, as it neatly circumvented the tiresome necessity of constantly hunting up enough prostitutes and training them as to their roles, you understand. No damp caves or sneaking about, not for the Society. Simply gather the members and their wives together at one of their estates, slip into their masks and hooded cloaks, feast, drink, partake of their indulgences and then go out shooting or fishing the next day as the wives went back to their embroidery and water colors. Very neat, very orderly, remarkably civilized. We are speaking of men who enjoyed their comforts. Some of the women took to it quite well, even enthusiastically." Her voice went very faint. "Most didn't. But there was no choice. What else could we do…?"

"All right, Trixie," Gideon said gently, forced to think about his grandmother and mother living with such monsters, which he did not wish to do. "I think we've had enough of that, and I can only apologize for the necessity of any of this."

"Apologize? Why?" Trixie lifted her chin in a way Jessica had begun to admire very much. "I haven't been a faint-at-heart miss for a half-century and certainly lay no claims to innocence. Or did you think this journal would be as innocuous as a book of fairy tales? Ah, and now you're frowning. Don't ever worry about me, pet, I'm a practical woman, or haven't you noticed?"

"I'm still sorry, Grandmother," Gideon said. "I know that doesn't help."

"Actually, pet, it does. I'm sorry, as well, for so many things. But what's done is done, and sad to say, I would do it again. Now, back to business. The journals are divided into parts. The first is the diary, kept in as much detail as the member chooses. Turner was crude, but blessedly brief. His wife, you'll note if you care to check, is notated as F-W. As I said, some took to it with remarkable enthusiasm. The second section is the real meat of the volume, denoting what I've already told you. I can see by the dates listed that, blessedly, they don't meet for ceremonies nearly as often as in your grandfather's or father's time—only four meetings in the entire year—although there could be other gatherings, for other purposes."

"Such as planning sedition," Gideon grumbled. "For my father the Society, the rites, were the means to an end. Isn't that what you said?"

"One problem at a time, pet. But, yes, these rutting fools are also powerful fools. Remember, my late houseguest occupied quite a high office in the Royal

War Office until only a few months ago when his health began to fail, and if that doesn't give you pause, also bear in mind Jessica's father had the Prince of Wales's ear concerning more than fashion. What confuses me is I see no high rites at all last year, even though several members died. It hardly seems possible, but they may have made some alteration into the usual way of inducting members?"

"No more vestal virgins?" Jessica asked, praying it was true.

"Even sex can become tiresome, difficult as that may be to believe. Then there's the problem of abducting suitably high-born virgins. Six in the space of a year? That would have to raise an alarm," Trixie said, her forehead wrinkling as she considered her own words. "There could be a wholesale shifting of purpose we're seeing here, Gideon."

"Again, sedition."

"I wish you'd stop saying that. With Bonaparte still running amok through the world, the thought is unnerving. He has too many admirers, even here in England. Worse, your search for members now borders on the impossible. Remember, pet, that body you carried out of here last night belonged to the last of the members from your father's time, the last name I know for certain. Who knows, he may have been the next one to suffer a fatal accident. He should be grateful to me, if I saved him from that."

"Yes," Gideon said flatly, "a lucky man."

Trixie laughed softly. "I know you're being facetious, but he did seem happy…at least up until the end. Now, stop scowling at me and listen carefully. This last section is the most valuable, the list of member names. Once a code name is assigned, it becomes permanent, whether it be the original member, or handed down to the next generation, which is why family names are used, as titles can change. The *bible* would have all the details, everything spelled out. Find the bible, Gideon, and you've solved it all, as that's the single volume that traces the history all the way to your grandfather's time. Names, events, purposes, triumphs. All of it dutifully recorded every year. It's quite the magnificently fashioned tome, huge, ridiculously ornate, wrapped all about with gold chains, the lock in the shape of a devil's head. Highly melodramatic."

"That..." Jessica had to clear her throat, finding it difficult to speak. "That journal is for last year. Wouldn't my... Shouldn't it have been turned over to somebody, to have the information recorded in the bible?"

"Yes, that is puzzling," Trixie said, turning the journal over to look at its cover. "Gideon? Do you suppose the Keeper of the bible has died, or was one of the *accidents?* Could the society be in the midst of choosing a new leader, so that all the members still hold their journals from last year? Could this be what all the deaths are about—a weeding out of competition, bringing in a whole new order?"

"Or Cotsworth didn't much care for the new leader, and had decided to leave the Society," Gideon suggested.

"Pet, no member ever *leaves* the Society. Not alive. The accidents you've uncovered fairly well prove that point. But what an interesting theory, killing off the competition within the Society. Death certainly has made quite a run at the devil's thirteen." The dowager duchess opened the journal once again and adjusted her spectacles, that had slipped down her nose. "Let's have a good look at the list as it was last year, shall we? All right, here's the first. *Either.* That's Ranald *Or*ford."

"The first death I know of," Gideon said. "Hunting accident."

"Yes, I remember. And then this one. *Less.* That could only be George Dun*more,* eldest son of Walter, who was one of your grandfather's original devil's thirteen. He's the one who drowned? And, if you're beginning to understand this silliness, Gideon, *Soft* would be…?"

"Baron *Hard*en, who died in that fall down the stairs. My God, it's that simple?"

"The journals were only for the members. They aren't all so simple as mere opposites, but they're not all that difficult. *Either, less, soft.* If you didn't already know the names, you would have no idea what this list of words refers to, now would you?"

"And my father?" Jessica asked, leaning forward on the couch.

Trixie ran a fingertip down the list of names. "Ah, here we are. *Miner.* Because colliers are miners, correct? Now let me see…" She squinted at the page. "Yes, here are the two I can add to our list of deceased members. The Right Honorable Noddy Sel*kirk,* another second generation member, has to be *Church.* He fell afoul of a rock slide while hiking in the Lake District this past autumn, and Cecil Appleby would have to be *Pear.* Lord knows he was shaped like one. He supposedly succumbed to some sudden stomach ailment a few months past, although I now have it on the highest authority his tongue had turned black."

"Who is this highest authority?" Gideon asked.

Trixie rolled her eyes. "You're questioning me? Cecil's valet is brother to my glover's assistant, if you must know. It can take positively *hours* to fit a new glove properly, and there's plenty of time for gossip. It took an entire afternoon last Thursday, and an order for six new pairs of gloves, but I'm assured my information is correct. I had the bill sent to you."

"I suppose I can't quibble with that," he said, smiling.

"As well you shouldn't. And now poor Guy has cocked up his toes. Here he is. *Cot,* which of course stands for Bedworth." She ran her finger down the list of names. "Strange. I don't recognize any of these. If they were still passing father to eldest son, I should know these names. Perhaps one of you should be writing them down?"

Jessica got to her feet and walked over to the writing desk, where paper and pen were already assembled for just such a purpose. She only hoped her hands wouldn't shake so much her words wouldn't be legible. She felt as if she was trapped in some sort of nightmare. How else could they be speaking so calmly about murder and other atrocities?

She had soon assembled a list, as dictated by Trixie. Hammer. Weaver. City. Bird. Post. Burn.

By now, Gideon was standing behind her, leaning over her shoulder to look at the list of words. "You're right, Trixie. Simple words, but if you don't already know the answers, all I see here are questions."

Jessica looked at Trixie, who was still paging through the journal. "But you said you had more information for us. Did Cot give you any other names?"

"A question you should have asked, Gideon. I may have had them all, if Guy hadn't gotten so belatedly suspicious and then so inconveniently dead. Why women don't rule the world has always been a conundrum to me. Greater physical strength has led you all to believe your minds are stronger, as well, which is poppycock. At any rate, we women couldn't do worse—you men just keep bollixing it all up. But yes, two others, although I can't say I know them personally, although I know their families. Lord Charles Mailer, and Archie Urban."

"Post and City," Gideon said quickly, almost triumphantly, as if they were solving puzzles in some game. Perhaps that was the only way to deal with any of it without going mad?

"Leaving us with Hammer, Weaver, Bird and Burn. Four more members."

It was wrong. So wrong. Jessica felt so ashamed of herself, even as she opened her mouth and heard the words come tumbling out: "Three French hens, two turtledoves and a partridge in a…"

And then Gideon was catching at her as she felt herself slipping sideways on the chair, darkness closing all around her….

THE KING IS DEAD, long live the king.

Those words kept repeating themselves inside

Gideon's head as he sat in his study, trying to make sense of all they'd learned.

With the Marquis of Mellis sticking his spoon in the wall at the same time he was sticking his—no, he wouldn't go there—the last of the members active during Barry Redgrave's time had died.

Gideon realized he might now never know what had happened to his father's body, why it had been taken.

But there was still the matter of the tunnels at Redgrave Manor, the lights seen moving through the trees, both easily explained when set apart from everything else, but damned unnerving when put together with everything else. He'd already discarded the idea of some sort of treasure; whatever was going on was much more malignant than a mere treasure hunt.

After returning Jessica to Portman Square with orders she lie down for a nap, he'd gone back to his grandmother with more questions. Trixie had completed his education in the ways of the Society as it had been in his father's time. But she wouldn't speak about his mother or what had happened that last morning, only to say her son's death had been for the best, for the sake of the country he would betray, for the sake of the family his growing madness could destroy.

Gideon hadn't pushed her for more. He could readily see the toll these past days had taken on her. He left her with her damn pug dogs, a glass of wine and Soames, who had actually sat down on the one-armed lounge just as if this familiarity was nothing out of the ordinary. He'd drawn Trixie's legs up onto his lap and had begun massaging her lady's bare feet and slim calves with fragrant oil. This didn't shock Gideon. He'd passed beyond being shocked, he'd supposed, and his grandmother was entitled to anything that pleased her, damn it!

But now he had to concentrate, using the information Trixie had given him. In the past year, six men had been murdered. The Marquis of Mellis probably would have been the seventh, just as Trixie had supposed. The Society had killed off its remaining original members or their descendants from Barry Redgrave's time, but the Society itself was not dead. No, what his grandfather had begun, what his father had resurrected and enlarged, had fallen victim to some sort of coup. That was the only sensible answer.

But for what reason, to what purpose? To be rid of old, dead wood more interested in brandy, a comfortable chair by the fire, a dog napping nearby, than they were in the debauchery the Society had been formed for in the first place? To remove those who disagreed, silence dissent? To make room for members who could be of more use?

There was one thing about the deaths of those members to cheer Gideon: they were the last to know of Trixie's intimate knowledge of the Society. Otherwise, he couldn't feel certain of her safety, her immunity to becoming another "sad accident."

His grandfather had been a strong leader. With his death, the Society had fragmented. His father had been a strong leader. With his death the Society had lost its purpose over and above its base obsessions. The rites had continued, however, including the induction of a new member five years ago, when Jessica was nearly made a part of the ceremony.

But Trixie had seemed certain Turner Collier would not have voluntarily offered his daughter. Had he been intimidated in some way, threatened?

James Linden had seen or heard something on the day of the proposed ceremony that had frightened him enough to take Jessica and run.

The king is dead, long live the king.

That was the answer, the only logical answer.

There was a new leader of the Society. Perhaps it was that leader who had demanded a well-born vestal virgin be brought to him five years ago, just to demonstrate his power. A strong leader, someone like Barry Redgrave, someone who looked at the Society and saw an opportunity for personal greatness, just as Barry had done.

Gideon was back to the same question: opportunity for what? What in bloody hell had he stumbled onto?

At least he had two names.

Lord Charles Mailer, second son of the Earl of Vyrnwy.

Archie Urban, no title, but a family name that stretched back to William the Conqueror.

Both men were in their primes, although Urban at least had to be nearly fifty. Neither was a society fribble; both were considered to be smart, patriotic servants of the Crown during this time of war. Lord Charles volunteered his services to the Admiralty. Urban was one of the many undersecretaries to the Prime Minister. Both were members of the Society, two of the devil's thirteen.

Trixie had explained how it all worked during his father's time, this matter of *guests:* members of the

Society would invite carefully selected persons to join them in their fun; to prance about in robes and masks, chanting satanic nonsense as they indulged their most base desires and depravities with willing or even not-so-willing women...or whatever pleasure they craved. All quite sophisticated and civilized.

Oh, there'll be a foxhunt in the morning, with a lovely dinner to follow. Do bring your lady wife if you wish, I'm sure we'd all enjoy having her.

And then would come the day when the demands for favors in exchange for not telling the world of those depravities would be issued, blackmailing them to gain their cooperation. Over and over and over again.

Both the other members and any guests controlled by a strong leader, one who knew everything and could exploit their weaknesses. *In time of war.*

"My God," Gideon moaned, slicing his fingers through his hair. "Madness. Just...madness."

It was imperative he learn the other names.

Hammer. What could that mean? Would it be something that rhymed with hammer? Was it the opposite of hammer? In the same general family as a hammer? Sharp, compared to the dull, blunt face of a hammer?

Weaver. Could that be literal? No, too easy.

Bird. Too many species to narrow that down.

Burn. Fire? Its opposite—what was the opposite of fire?

No, it was impossible to guess.

There was no choice but to go after the known, Lord Charles and Archie Urban. But first he would check on Jessica and tell her what he and Trixie had decided.

It was time for some sort of good news. He pushed

himself away from the desk, not bothering to don the jacket he'd hung on the back of his chair earlier, along with the neck cloth he'd stripped off at the same time, and headed upstairs in his shirtsleeves.

He passed Mildred in the upstairs hallway. "Is she still asleep?" he asked the maid.

"No, my lord," Mildred answered, attempting to curtsy while holding a silver tray cluttered with crockery. "Her ladyship's up and fed and telling us she's fine to go downstairs if she wants to. Doreen and me, we told her she didn't want to. Never saw anyone quite so pale and wobbly on her pins as her ladyship was when you brought her home, sir."

"Yes, thank you, Mildred. See to it we're not disturbed."

The maid rolled her eyes. "Well, if you think it might put some color back in her cheeks, I suppose it's—"

"I'm not asking your permission, Mildred," Gideon said, trying to look imperious, which was more difficult than he would have imagined only a few short weeks ago.

"No, your lordship," Mildred agreed, a hint of color entering her own cheeks. "I suppose you think you know best. Well, then, sir, I'll just leave you to it. Doreen's downstairs, so you're safe enough there."

"And ain't I just the fortunate one," Gideon mumbled under his breath as he watched the maid as she scurried off toward the back of the house and the servant staircase. The entire household would know within moments that his lordship had taken his ladyship to bed, and in the middle of the afternoon, no less, but then, that was the quality for you. He wondered if there'd be cheering. He supposed this was what happened when a doxy turned lady's maid, but it would take some getting used to, even if he'd been grateful for the candles and the rose petals.

He knocked lightly at the door and then depressed the latch, not waiting to be invited to enter his bride's bedchamber. It didn't occur to him that she might not wish his company, but if it had, her smile of greeting would have calmed those fears.

"Have you come to free me?" she asked him from her seated position on the high tester bed, her ivory lace dressing gown barely covering her most delectable bits, her legs crisscrossed in front of her, a plate of iced cakes balanced on one knee. She looked wonderfully recovered; in fact, she looked radiant. "I'm being held prisoner by my maids, you know. Doreen put forth the possibility I'm carrying your heir, but Mildred assured her, even if that's the case, it's much too early for me to be swooning. Or casting up my accounts every morning, which doesn't sound all that lovely a prospect to be looking forward to, does it? Thank you again for catching me."

Gideon sat down on the edge of the bed, one leg on the floor, for balance. "You're welcome. I've always harbored a secret desire to be of assistance to a damsel in distress." The possibility of a pregnancy he would allow to pass without comment. But it certainly was something to be considered. He believed he'd enjoy considering it, perhaps as much as he'd enjoy being a necessary part of the process. "Those look delicious," he said, eying the cakes, not to mention her barely covered breasts.

"Oh, they are. Almost as good as sugared figs, I'm sure. Here, take a bite." Jessica held out one of the cakes, a two-inch square iced in pink on all sides and with a small sugar flower decorating the top of the thing.

Gideon dutifully leaned forward and opened his mouth, allowing himself to be fed—and to get a better look at her breasts, because he was, at heart, an evil man. He bit off half of the small square and watched as Jessica popped the remainder into her own mouth, then licked at her fingers. "Another?" she asked, sucking lightly on her middle finger.

Her innocent action raised a whole new hunger inside him.

"I think I have a different delicacy in mind."

She looked at him, her mouth open slightly, her tongue still lightly touching the pad of her finger. And then she smiled. "Is that so?"

"Yes, that's so." He took the plate and placed it on the bedside table, unbuttoned and tossed aside his waistcoat and shirt, slipped off his shoes and then joined her on the bed. "Not only that, I have permission."

Jessica cocked her head to one side, to look at him quizzically. "I beg your pardon?"

"Mildred believes I might be able to put some color in your cheeks." His fingers went to the sash holding her dressing gown closed. He found one end of the sash and gave it a slight tug. And then another.

"Oh, she does, does she?"

Gideon was concentrating on other things. "Um-hmm," he said, and then added, "You don't care for the matching gown? Not that I'm lodging any sort of complaint," he added as the bow came free and the dressing gown fell completely open.

"I, um, I just slipped this on after my bath, and then Doreen brought up these cakes, so I…I decided to eat them now. I'll soon be getting dressed."

"No, you won't," he said, easing back the concealing lace, slipping his hand between her crossed legs, unerringly finding her center. He spread her slightly, eased a finger inside her, applying pressure forward, against the wall of her tight sheath, then insinuated the pad of his thumb between her soft folds to stroke the small, exquisitely sensitive bud exposed now to his touch.

"Gideon!"

"I know. I'm depraved," he said, rubbing his thumb over her. "Should I go away?"

She looked down at her body, closed her eyes for a moment as he slid a second finger inside her. "I…I'll reserve judgment on that. You…ah…you're very adept at this, aren't you?"

"Modesty precludes me from answering that, but I do harbor hopes. Do you have any idea how good you feel?"

"I'm…I'm beginning to," Jessica said, leaning back slightly, bracing her hands against the mattress. "Oh… that feels wonderful."

"Yes. The purpose of the exercise. You don't mind?"

She made a small noise, rather close to a purr. He took it for a *no*.

He moved his fingers again, slippery now with the liquid silk of her quick arousal. Her breathing had gone swift and shallow, and he increased the rhythm of his movements even as he moved his mouth along her body, licking at her breasts, taking her nipple into his mouth.

She was all response, all heat and glory and freedom, at ease with her body and how he made her feel. But she was far from passive.

Just when he thought he was about to take her over the edge, she pulled away from him, only to push him down on his back and begin unbuttoning his pantaloons. Her glorious hair fell loose around her face as she looked at him. "I already know how I like it best, and that's with you inside me. Do you mind?"

Did he mind? Such an intelligent woman, such a silly question.

The speed with which he divested himself of his pantaloons, then lifted her up and over him, lowering her until their bodies meshed, became one, was probably as good an answer as any.

"AND YOU'RE CERTAIN you locked the door?" Jessica asked him as they lay there, bodies still delightfully entangled, attempting to recover their breaths. Really, she was turning into quite the wanton after only a single day of marriage. She rather liked it.

"I did. And warned Mildred we weren't to be disturbed."

"Good. Because I really don't want to move. Not for days."

"That's convenient, because I don't think I can move, perhaps not for entire days, but at least not in the near future. You didn't tell me you ride," he said, nipping at her earlobe. "You're quite...accomplished."

She didn't pretend not to understand what he meant.

What would be the sense in that? "Thank you, naughty as that statement was. It's been years, but I've always loved to ride. Is that how you see the thing? As riding?"

"How do you see it?"

She snuggled closer. "As much more satisfying than the sidesaddle, that's for certain. Is that why men ride astride and condemn women to the sidesaddle?"

"Fearful you might gain pleasure from it, you mean? I hadn't considered it, but you may be right. Shame on us."

She slid off him, her expression once again pinched, her cheeks pale. "Yes, shame on men. Not all of you, but certainly enough of you. Where did men first get the idea women are here for their pleasure but are to be denied any of their own? Really, denied much in the way of any sort of freedom. As if our minds are feeble, and we're not to be trusted with our own bodies. I'm sure Trixie has opinions on that."

"Yes, and she's been taking her own peculiar brand of revenge for most of her life."

Jessica laid her head on Gideon's shoulder and absently stroked her hand over his bare chest. "I hadn't thought of that. But she is, isn't she? I remember teasing Richard about women always being the downfall of men, in one way or another. Is that it, Gideon? Are you men afraid of us?"

He kissed her hair. "Terrified."

"Well, you probably should be. We seem to know your weaknesses."

"You've certainly found mine," he agreed, lifting her hand to his lips. "As for the rest of it, on behalf of all mankind, I most abjectly and humbly apologize."

"Thank you. But it's not enough." She gathered the sheet about her and sat up, looking down at him. "I don't mean you, not precisely you. I mean men. In general. Apologies are not enough. Especially since most of them wouldn't mean a word they said in any event."

"Probably not."

Jessica ignored him, for she'd gotten the bit between her teeth now, her mind whirling with various bits of information that seemed to be parts of a puzzle she'd carried with her for a long time, its pieces suddenly falling into place.

"Men are stronger, physically. You can't be afraid of a woman's inferior strength. So it has to be our minds you fear. After all, you can take our bodies—because we're not as physically strong—but that doesn't mean you can control our minds." She looked at him again as he pushed himself up against the pillows. "You think we're smarter than you, don't you?"

"It's not that simple, Jessica."

"Oh? Then you admit we're smarter?"

"And there's your answer, just in the way you so neatly turned my words to your advantage," he said, pulling her against his shoulder.

She laughed. "I rather did, didn't I?"

"Yes, you did. And we men have yet to learn how to defend ourselves from that particular little trick. You're smarter, softer, definitely prettier, with the ability to think with your hearts as well as your minds—while we men have just to look at you to lose our control over both. You possess the ability to have us make total fools of ourselves, madam, and we resent the hell out of that. We'd much rather think of you as weaker, in body and mind and morals, devious and manipulative by turn, needing our guidance and protection—and we reserve the right to blame you for anything stupid we do, as well as any evil anywhere in the world."

Jessica considered all of this for a minute. "Oh," she said at last. "That actually makes sense. You're afraid of us, but since you're physically larger and stronger than we are, you've been able to create laws and all sorts of rules meant to keep us firmly under your thumbs, and make false declarations of how better fashioned you are to take care of us, not in order to protect us, but in order to protect yourselves from us."

"And since you're smaller and softer and so much smarter than we are, you continually find ways around the barriers we've so carefully built around our supposed superiority."

"And then you condemn us as devious, when it's you who force us to employ those superior weapons, because otherwise we'd be nothing. Chattel."

"Sex is a woman's game, Jessica, even if men believe they invented it. It's the lever, when placed in the right spot, which has always been able to move the world. We men can't give you any more weapons than you already hold—a place in government, or commerce, or even on the battlefield. We know you'd be too good at all of it. Why else do we insist on calling the great Elizabeth Tudor our *virgin* queen, made her, in our minds, not really a woman at all, but more of an aberration. We can't risk seeing you as equal to men, treating you as our equals, not when we know you're vastly superior."

She looked at him assessingly. "And you really believe that? I mean, that women pose so much danger, and have to be kept under the thumbs of men?"

"Me? Absolutely not."

"Yes, but if you *did* subscribe to this supposed theory, would you admit it?"

His grin was wicked. "Absolutely not."

"Why, you—" She launched herself at him half-playfully, and he snagged her wrists, all but flipping her onto her back, his body lying across hers. "Oh, so now you're out to prove your superior strength?"

"On the contrary. I'm about to prove yours. Do you remember the first day you came to Portman Square?"

She wriggled her body beneath his, rather enjoying the feelings he was arousing in her. "I do. But what does that have to do with—"

Her wrists still trapped, he brought his head down to within inches of hers, his eyes clearly contemplating the sight of her slightly parted lips. "Do you remember our wager that day?"

"The dogs," she said. And then, beginning to understand, she wet her lips with the tip of her tongue.

"You're not playing fair, Jessica. Some would say *just like a woman.* But yes, the dogs. You wagered me Brutus wouldn't be able to withstand temptation for ten seconds, but that Cleo could and would."

Sex is a woman's game. He'd said it, and she was beginning to believe him.

"I believe he didn't make it past four." She moved again, lifting her leg and curling it around his. "Cleo could have managed twice that and possibly more. Just as I could outlast you with ease."

Gideon raised one expressive eyebrow. "Really?

Would you care to wager the five pounds I lost on that assumption?"

She noticed his breathing had become rather shallow. "Oh, yes, I'd wager twice that. Who is *really* the stronger, that's the wager, who can better resist temptation. I'll put my blunt on myself, naturally."

"Naturally. With one caveat, if you don't mind."

"And what would that be?"

"That you stop moving your hips against me."

She looked at him in feigned surprise. "Was I doing that? And that…upsets you? I'm so sorry. We'll neither of us move, all right? I'll call the count, shall I? One…"

She lowered her eyelids so that she could watch him through her lashes.

"Two…"

She drew in a breath that raised her breasts slightly, released her breath on a sigh.

"Three… Is it warm in here, Gideon? Your skin feels slightly *slick* against my breasts. But it's nice."

She watched his throat move as he swallowed.

"Four… I could do this all afternoon, you know, as I'm quite comfortable. Are you comfortable, Gideon? Five… And it was *your* idea. It's difficult to believe you could possibly lose, being so much *larger* and *stronger* than—"

Thank goodness, Jessica thought as Gideon ground his mouth against hers. *I never would have made it past six….*

CHAPTER FOURTEEN

"AND YOU'RE POSITIVE you and Trixie are correct? All because of my father's journal?"

Gideon finished fastening the diamond circlet around Jessica's throat before turning her about so that she could look into his eyes when he answered her, see that he was sincere.

She looked beautiful tonight, a certain glow about her, the sort that signaled to the knowing that she had spent the afternoon in bed. And not alone.

"As certain as we can be, yes. With the last of the original members from my father's time now dead, and with Trixie admitting she doesn't recognize the other code names, I believe it's safe to assume that...well, that you're safe. You, Trixie, Adam."

"Because the Society is no longer seeking out the eldest son to take his deceased father's place, and that's why Trixie doesn't recognize all those other code names."

"Yes, and because those who knew James Linden are those same now-deceased members. No one will look at you and wonder what you might know, what he may have told you. And, lastly, there's no one remaining aboveground who would realize Trixie knows anything at all. Thank God."

Jessica stepped away from him, to check her reflection in the pier glass. She looked beautiful in ivory lace, just as he'd known she would, and he was well satisfied with the demi-train he'd added to its design. "Whoever ordered my father to…to hand me over? Are you certain that person wouldn't look at me now and, well, and wonder? Because we did decide the Society has a new leader, didn't we? A strong leader? He could have been the one who ordered—"

"Here again I defer to Trixie. There are two things the members of the Society lend no credence to—women and hirelings. As far as the Society is concerned, you managed to convince Linden to run off with you. Or do you really think you would have made it even halfway to Dover if there was any concern either of you could prove a danger to them?"

"I never really thought about that." Jessica walked over to her dressing table to pick up her reticule. "There were storms in the Channel. We had to wait in Dover for three days before we could set sail. James was terrified. He wouldn't leave the rooms he'd hired at the inn once he'd finally managed to sell the jewelry. But I suppose we would have been easy enough to find."

"And that answers the question, doesn't it? Nobody came, because nobody felt the need. You're safe, Trixie's safe, Adam is not going to be issued an invitation to join the Society."

"And the rose? You haven't worn it again, but certainly it was noticed."

"By whom? The Marquis of Mellis was in Bath, and the other members from my father's time were already dead. There are thirteen members, correct? Yet nobody else ever wore the rose. Jessica, there's nothing tying any of us to anything that's going on within that damn Society. Nothing. If we want, it's over. We can walk away."

"If we want," Jessica repeated as he held out his arm to her, to escort her downstairs. "Not even the search for your father's body?"

She had him there. "That still bothers me, yes. But with Mellis gone, there's no one else left to question. The tunnel beneath the greenhouse collapsed thanks to an unusually wet spring and the ravages of age, and the lights in the woods were most probably cast by lanterns carried by poachers. Not everything is a mystery. Not when taken separately."

"Six men have been murdered," she reminded him as they approached the drawing room. "Including my father."

"You want to avenge him?"

She sighed. "I should say yes, shouldn't I?"

"I wouldn't. Somebody carried off my father's body, and I see that only as a personal insult to the Redgrave name, a name already carrying enough dirt on it. Trixie could have ordered him buried in a bog for all I ever cared about the man. I don't relish telling her that her son's body was taken, no. She deserves the right to one day rest beside her only child for eternity." He stopped her as they were about to enter the drawing room. "I like this, Jessica."

She looked at him in confusion. "Pardon me?"

"Being honest. Open. Being able to talk with you this way. I don't know why you make it so easy, but you do. I've never been honest with anyone about what it means to be a Redgrave, what it means to be the eldest son of a man so depraved and twisted his own wife shot him in the back, the eldest son of a mother so desperate to be free of her husband that she'd desert her own children. You sometimes don't realize the weight of the things you carry through life with you, until you put them down. I'm feeling considerably…lighter."

She bowed her head for a moment, and when she raised it again he could see tears standing in her eyes. "I feel much the same. Lighter. *Cleaner,* if that makes any sense at all. But I still need to tell you—"

"Tell me we can neither of us walk away from what we suspect," he ended for her. "I know. There's a reason those six men were killed. We have two of the names of current members, thanks to Trixie. We know the code names for four more, thanks to your father's journal. Yes, the journal is out of date. And, lastly, no, we don't have the rest of the names. But we've enough to go on with. We know the Society still exists."

"With a purpose larger than what Trixie called naughty little boys playing at games. I agree with you on that head."

"And how do I take any of this to the Crown? For one, I have no real proof, and secondly, I might be reporting what I believe to one of the new thirteen or one of their blackmailed *guests.* No, it's us, or it's nobody. I said we could walk away, but I can't turn my back on this, Jessica. Not knowing it was my family who one way or another laid the foundation for it all."

"I didn't think you were applying to me for permission, either way. But I would like to think you still want my help. That was the plan in the beginning, wasn't it, because we thought it would help us protect Adam?"

He leaned in and kissed her. "It was a part of the plan, certainly. But not above and beyond my overwhelming need to have you in my bed and easing my conscience by telling myself my offer of marriage provided a way to compensate for what happened to you."

"I don't know if you need to be *that* honest, Gideon. Not that I'm not…flattered."

He smiled. "Not that I'm not grateful. But to get back to our now slightly altered plan? I'm counting on your discerning eye and your powers of observation as we learn more about our friends Lord Charles and Mr. Urban, yes. I want you to read them, assess them, as you would players at the card table. And more than that, I believe I want you to cultivate their wives. If there's a weakness in the Society, I think it would have to be the wives."

"Because they're weaker?"

"No, I think we settled that earlier."

"Yes, and you still owe me five pounds. But I know what you mean. There can't be many women who would be happy with the sort of arrangement Trixie spoke of, being passed about to the other men in the Society. It's sickening, to think such a thing is happening in this day and age. I don't know how I'd broach the subject, but I think I will be able to tell if these two women are unhappy."

"All right, play the game any way you like. Just promise me you won't try to *bluff* anyone."

She rolled her eyes. "Really, you and Richard—"

They both turned toward the stairs and the sound of the knocker being banged on with considerable enthusiasm, followed closely by a cheery voice exclaiming,

"Thorny, you old dog, if you're going to scowl every time I bring a little rainwater inside with me, I may go into a sad decline. M'brothers here? One or both? I like being prepared before I face Gideon's scowl or Max's— Well, what does Max do, anyway, other than find new ways to grow his hair? Damme, it's wet out there tonight! What did you say? Speak up, man. No! Say that again. Where is he? Is he upstairs? That *dog!*"

"Valentine," Gideon said, breaking into a grin. "Prepare yourself, Jessica, you're about to be bowled down by my youngest brother."

CHAPTER FIFTEEN

THE SOUND OF RIDING boots hitting the marble stairs was closely followed by the appearance of Lord Valentine Redgrave's smiling face and tall, lithe body.

"Gideon!" he exclaimed, throwing his arms wide as he approached, but then lowering them again as he espied Jessica. He tipped his head to one side and grinned. "This is the bride? Thorny told me just now, but I didn't believe him. My lady," he said, sweeping Jessica an elegant bow. "Whatever lies did my brother tell you to get you to agree to join your life to such a sorry specimen?"

Jessica laughed, as she really had no choice in the thing, and held out her hand to be bowed over. Except Lord Valentine Redgrave clearly was having none of that, because he grabbed her up in his arms and soundly kissed both her cheeks. "My God, you're gorgeous. Are you sure you want Gideon? I'm clearly the better choice."

"Put her down, you fool," Gideon said, laughing. "Jessica, may I present my youngest brother, Lord Valentine Redgrave, connoisseur of all things frivolous, carefree *bon vivant,* generous by nature, soft of heart and yet somehow still managing to be an all-round menace to society. Val, my lady wife, Jessica—and no, you can't kiss her again."

"It's a pleasure to meet you, Lord Valentine," Jessica said, dropping into a curtsy.

"Please, call me Val," Valentine said, "and I'll call you Jess? Jessica? Sister? Gideon, you've given me a new sister. Do you have any suggestions as to what we should do with the old one? She will persist in hanging about, won't she? Or have the both of you found romance in my short absence? I won't ask about Max, as there's nobody who'd want him."

Gideon motioned for Jessica and Valentine to precede him into the drawing room, at which point Cleo and Brutus made a dead set at Valentine, tongues lolling, tails wagging. He went to his knees and allowed them to lick his face.

His incredibly handsome face. Jessica could see hints of both Lady Katherine and Gideon in Lord Valentine, but there was something else there besides the attractively mussed dark hair, faintly bronzed skin and magnificent bone sculpture. She decided it was Valentine's eyes. They were light amber in color, quite startling in fact, ringed with long dark lashes beneath sweeping black brows...and they were full of life and mischief. And kindness.

How strange to look at such a well set-up gentleman and think first and foremost: this is a kind man.

"Kate's at Redgrave Manor after a brief visit here in town, and Max is still off North somewhere, aiding Trixie in one of her stunts, so the two—no, the three of them, remain heartfree. Unless you've somehow been struck by one of Cupid's arrows, only two things have changed since you left. I've married, and these two miscreants have finally learned to perform their only party trick outdoors, rather than on the carpet in my study."

"Wonderful! Thank you for keeping them, Gideon."

Jessica looked to Gideon. She hadn't known Cleo and Brutus weren't his dogs.

"I didn't have much choice, did I? You simply left them here and rode off."

"Yes, but Freddie said he couldn't afford them, not now his father's taken that bad turn. What else was I to do?"

"Nothing, I suppose. But now that you're back, I think it's time they adjourned to the country. Clearly these are animals who belong out-of-doors, or at least at Redgrave Manor, where we've got the dog gates to keep them from running through the entire house as if there may be a rabbit behind every door."

"Only if Kate remembers to latch the gates," Valentine said, getting to his feet again. "My leg still aches when the weather turns damp."

Gideon sat down next to Jessica and explained that last statement. A few months earlier, Kate had left open the gate at the bottom of the staircase, allowing three of the family dogs free to race upstairs to see Valentine, only to knock him head over teacup down the stairs to the first landing, his brother suffering a broken leg in the fall.

"Oh, I'm so sorry," Jessica said, looking at Valentine.

Gideon laid his arm behind her on the back of the couch. "Don't be. My brother was simply being rewarded by the fates for stepping in and doing a good deed, or what he thought was a good deed. It wasn't, and the leg was probably a suitable punishment. Not that you learn, do you, Val? You missed my nuptials thanks to your latest act of charity, escorting Freddie home to his recently impoverished father. Kate was here."

"Kate was here. Yes, you said that," Valentine repeated, pulling a face. "But not Max? Are you planning to ring a peal over his head, as well, when he returns?"

"I'm not ringing a peal over yours, brother. I'm merely pointing out, as does our sister when she's anywhere close, that one day you're going to do one favor too many and end up missing more than a wedding. Kate worries about you."

"But you don't," Valentine said, sipping from the glass of wine he'd poured for himself. He was resting nearly on the bottom of his spine as he slouched in the facing couch, his booted legs crossed at the ankle and propped on the low table between them. Jessica had seen the same pose from Gideon and from Kate, and now had no doubt when she met Max she would know him first by his extraordinary ability to *relax*.

"I don't stay up nights, pacing the floor, no," Gideon admitted. "Now that you've returned the coach, when do you head to Redgrave Manor?"

"When do I deliver Cleo and Brutus to Redgrave Manor, you mean. Why? And don't say it's because you want me to stay in town for the remainder of the Season because you know I won't do that, much as I love you. One Redgrave gone to the Marriage Mart a season is enough, no insult intended, Jessica."

"None taken," Jessica said, still fascinated by this youngest Redgrave. "You'd rather be in the country?"

"I'd rather be in Paris, but since Bonaparte grows more frisky by the moment, I'm stuck in London, a sorry substitute I'm sad to say. I've already visited two of my clubs this afternoon and found them thin of company and fairly flat, thanks to a boxing mill taking place this week in some faraway village in the back of beyond, so there's really nothing keeping me here. I'd like to leave in the morning, actually," he said, looking to Gideon. "And yes, I'll take the reformed piddlers with me."

"More than the dogs, Val. I was hoping you or Max would be back in town soon. As it's you, consider my request to be in the nature of performing a good deed."

"And if it had been Max?" Valentine asked.

Gideon shrugged. "I suppose I would have attempted to convince him he was about to go on some adventure. In any event, since you're the one who arrived first, I'd like you to take Jessica's brother with you as, well. You remember my ward, don't you?"

Valentine pushed his boots against the edge of the table as he sat up straight. "The twit? He's Jessica's brother? Really? Well, now, that explains how you two met. And you want me to haul him off to— No, that won't work, Kate will lock him in the cellars. *After* she murders him."

"No, she won't. She's met him and thinks he's highly entertaining."

Valentine grinned at his brother. "Oh, she does not. Not unless she's fallen on her head. Or he has, perhaps knocking his brain into something less resembling a block of cheese."

Jessica bit her lip to keep from laughing.

Gideon helped her to her feet as Thorndyke announced he'd ordered another setting at table, and dinner was now served. "Adam's not here this evening, as I've given him permission to attend the theater with his keeper. It's my fondest hope he can restrain himself from throwing oranges into the pit from our family box, but I wouldn't be surprised if he does, as he informed me that's what all the fashionable young idiots do. I need you to take him under your wing, Val. Make a man of him. You can do that, surely."

"I've seen him, remember, and if he manages to clunk anyone on the head with an orange I'll be mightily surprised, and that's with the pit directly below our box, for God's sake. Make a man of him? I'd first have to strip him to the buff and start over— Again, Jessica, no insult intended."

"Again, none taken. Adam is very young and silly," she answered as they entered the dining room. "Would that mean Cleo and Brutus would be riding inside the coach with them? All the way to Redgrave Manor?" she asked Gideon, carefully keeping her expression neutral.

Her husband smiled, and Jessica learned something new: husbands and wives could speak volumes without actually saying a word. Wasn't that nice. For instance, right now Gideon's smile was saying, "Yes, I'm as amused by that prospect as you are."

"Jessica and I are promised to something this evening, Val," he said as he helped Jessica into her chair, "so we'll be leaving you directly after dinner. There's things you need to know before you head off tomorrow, however, so I'm afraid we'll be having a fairly unusual mealtime conversation." He seated himself at the head of the table. "I'll begin with Trixie."

"Trixie?" Valentine placed his serviette on his lap. "And you announce her name in nearly the same breath as you say *unusual?* That raises a question. Am I going to be amused or terrified?"

THEY DIDN'T LEAVE Portman Square until nearly eleven. Gideon purposely left their departure late, so that he and Jessica wouldn't become part of the masses herded onto a curving flight of stairs and forced to stand there for an hour or more, slowly inching their way, step by step, up to the receiving line outside the ballroom.

The Earl of Saltwood much preferred to make an entrance, especially with his bride on his arm.

The hours in between sitting down to dinner and their departure had been busy ones, but now Valentine had been brought abreast of what was going on, what Gideon suspected, what Trixie had confirmed. Val had agreed Kate was probably even now ripping Redgrave Manor apart, from attics to cellars to chicken coops, hot on the hunt for the journals their father had found more than two decades previously and added to every year since then, until his murder.

The journals and the bible, although Gideon and Trixie now both believed the bible, at the very least, had been turned over to the new leader and was still in use. After all, hadn't Burke, Barry Redgrave's loyal valet, disappeared the day after the small, private funeral? Burke, his wife and their daughter.

Val also agreed having Kate find so much as a single journal could prove disastrous, unless he and even

Max were there to physically wrest the thing from her hands before she so much as opened it.

Or, to quote him exactly, and Gideon knew he wouldn't soon forget his brother's words, "You put a job in front of Kate, she does it. If she finds something, she won't simply hand it over, you know. No, she'll demand complete inclusion in whatever the hell it is we may end up having to do—which would be your fault, Gideon. And if she thinks she's been put to hunting mares' nests just so you have her out of the way, well, then, brother mine, it will be more than your fault, it will be your *head.* Either way, I don't know that you thought this plan of yours through very well, did you?"

Which he hadn't. Gideon knew that. Having his youngest brother point that fact out to him, however, brought home to Gideon how little he *had* been thinking these past weeks, perhaps even months. He should have brought his brothers in on his suspicions long ago. Why hadn't he?

But he knew the answer to that question. He was the oldest brother. He was the head of the Redgrave family. The burdens belonged on his shoulders. He hadn't wanted his brothers involved, hadn't wanted Max or Val and definitely not Kate to learn how much of a monster their father had been, how much of a victim their mother had been. And Trixie? Well, there was no stopping them from learning about Trixie, as the woman lived her life quite openly, didn't she?

There was one other thing. He could have been wrong. The deaths he'd begun to notice could all have been accidents and coincidental. Just as the cave-in of a tunnel beneath the greenhouse could have been a natural event, the lanterns in the forest carried by poachers.

Of course, finding out their father's body had been taken might have been a good time to bring at least his brothers into his confidence.

Still, he could have been wrong about the rest, at least until the night he'd dragged his physician to that stable and they'd found the hole in Turner Collier's skull.

He should have brought them in then. Except then he'd met Jessica. Val may have heard most of what Gideon had learned, what Trixie had confirmed, but Gideon had told him only that Jessica was Adam's half sister, estranged from the family after making an unfortunate marriage. He'd seen no reason to go into more detail than that. The past was the past, Jessica's past her own. It was the uncertain future that had to concern them all now.

He'd had so many very good reasons to not do what he had all along known he should.

He was so used to being a man who kept his secrets to himself, the worst of his family's sordid past carefully hidden behind closed doors. It was Jessica who'd changed that, with her openness and honesty, even when the facts proved painful.

And the burden of his family shame, shared now with Jessica, was lighter just as he'd told her. Speaking with Val had made it lighter still.

No, it wasn't the past Gideon carried with him now, it was the future that lay heavily on his shoulders, and the responsibility to correct whatever may have been set on a dangerous course so many years ago.

"I like your brother," Jessica said as she and Gideon settled against the velvet squabs of the Redgrave town coach for a ride of merely blocks. "He's serious when he has to be, and quick enough to understand what to say and what not to say. He didn't ask a single question that would have made me uncomfortable, although I'm sure his head was buzzing with them. Do you really think he'll leave?"

"Yes, I do. It was putting him in charge of Kate that turned the corner for us. The thought she might actually discover the journals was all the incentive he needed. Plus, he understands now why I want Adam away from London. We're certain he's safe from the Society, but I'd rather be more than certain. You know, you didn't tell me how you convinced Kate to leave."

"Oh, that was easy enough. I told her you wanted her to stay in London, fearful that she'd try hunting out the journals if she went back to Redgrave Manor."

"And she believed you?"

"Probably not. But I know she wants to help, and finding the journals might be a help. So it worked out."

"Once again proving women are smarter than men. She and I would have all but come to blows before I would have been able to boost her out of town. My congratulations." He lifted the curtain and peered through the window. "Good. We've just turned in to the Square. Sally Jersey's a good friend, so don't be intimidated when she looks you up and down as if you're a race horse she's considering purchasing. Just remember you're the most beautiful woman in the room. Any room."

"I'm not nervous. I've been looked up and down

before, Gideon, and in surroundings far less civilized than a London mansion," she told him. "Besides, I'm with you, so there's nobody who would dare say or do anything to upset me. Because, as I recall the comment, you Redgraves spit bigger than most people."

He threw back his head and laughed. "I should have our crest reworked to include that somehow, shouldn't I? Would it sound better in Latin, do you think?"

"Probably not even in Greek. Now, tell me again about Lord Charles and Mr. Urban. You can recognize them both on sight?"

"Yes, although I can't say we're friends. Urban is also a member of the Four-in-Hand Club, although I rarely ride with them anymore. Lord Charles is on his second wife, the first having died a few years ago. A fall down the stairs, or from a cliff that gave way while she was out walking, something like that." He heard what he'd just said and looked quizzically at Jessica. "You don't suppose…"

Jessica wrapped her shawl more tightly about her. "It's easy to become fanciful, isn't it? Is Mr. Urban married?"

"I don't know. We can't even be certain either one of them will be here tonight, save for the fact that nobody turns down an invitation from Sally Jersey, not if they're at all concerned with being seen as the very crème of the *ton*. I'm only sorry your first evening of the Season is going to be spent playing at spy, but we have no time to waste."

"I understand. I'd also like to get it over with as quickly as possible. There will be whispers, with my father's death only a month behind us. Should I prepare to be cut by some of the other guests—over and above your immense consequence as Saltwood, that is?"

"My consequence has little to do with it. You simply never know what a Redgrave might dare if provoked, you understand. They'd be more afraid I'd toss somebody off a balcony or bloody their elevated noses for them. You can't trust a Redgrave, you know. Kate proved that again just last Season. Poor society. It can't avoid us, it can't ignore us, and it can't turn away from us because we fascinate them so. At least that's what Trixie believes."

"I imagine gaining a Special License to wed the sister of your new ward, the woman you announced as your fiancée not even two weeks ago, and then bringing her to a ball within twenty-four hours of your hasty marriage is just the sort of thing society expects from you?"

Gideon considered this for a moment, as the groom let down the steps of the town carriage. "You know, Jessica, I just may have topped myself. But no matter what, from now on it's up to Max and Val to hold up the family's reputation for scandal. I can't possibly think of anything to cap the stir the two of us are going to cause in the next few minutes."

"You don't have to sound so pleased," she pointed out as he helped her onto the flagway and into the light cast by the large flambeaux flanking the front door of the mansion. "Anyone would think we're on our way to a fair. Should I be prepared to watch as you balance a ball on your nose?"

"No, but I may kiss my wife on the nose while on the dance floor, just to remind everyone that I am husband to the most beautiful, desirable woman in the room. Listen closely, and you'll hear the gnashing of envious teeth, not because of the kiss, but because they will all know what's going to happen once I take you home. Poor devils. I have never been accused of being a particularly nice man."

"Or particularly modest, either, I'd imagine. What makes you believe anything at all will happen once you *take me home?*"

Gideon extended his arm to her, and she slipped hers around his elbow as they entered the mansion and crossed to the now empty staircase. "Two things, really. One, I'm a hopeful man by nature. And two, I am fully prepared to grovel."

Jessica's delightful peal of laughter had just the effect Gideon had been striving for, as everyone at the top of the stairs turned to look down at the approaching couple. What they saw, he knew, was a beautiful, flame-haired creature dressed in the first stare of fashion, her exquisitely designed ivory gown alight with spangles, the Redgrave diamonds at her throat, wrist and fingers catching every bit of light thrown by the huge chandelier above their heads—all put in the shade by the genuine, open smile of a woman totally at ease with herself and her world.

His wife. His countess. Not his penance, not his love, yet not simply his possession. Just *his.* And Gideon Redgrave protected what was his.

"Gideon, you monster, I thought you were going to snub me!" Sally Jersey called down from the receiving line. "Instead, you've brought me a present—the *coup* of the Season thus far, and most probably forever."

Gideon bowed over Lady Jersey's hand even as Jessica dropped into a graceful curtsy.

"And now you owe me a favor, Silence, my dear," he said quietly. "I wish a waltz to immediately follow the announcement of my arrival. Now, now, don't open your pretty mouth to tell me that's impossible. You may not yet condone the thing at your dreary Almacks, but does society really dictate to Sally Jersey in her own home?"

"You court scandal as others crave their daily bread," the countess whispered back, but then summoned a liveried footman, to send him scurrying off to inform the small orchestra of her demand. "Here, as I was just about to leave my post, anyway, I'll walk between you as you enter the ballroom, to lend you my consequence, not that you need it. By the way, the dowager countess is here, titillating us all as usual, and holding court over a veritable coterie of young admirers, all rigged out in their regimental colors. She arrived on Selsby's arm, and he's been virtually sitting at her feet all the evening long, like some hopeful puppy. The man is barely out of leading strings when compared to Trixie, Gideon. You don't suppose the two of them are— No, I won't even say the words."

"Please don't or I might blush, and that wouldn't do wonders for my consequence." He stopped just at the entrance to the ballroom and lifted his quizzing glass to his eye. "You've got the entire world here, haven't you, all cheek by jowl? My congratulations, not that I'm surprised. Tell me, did you deign to invite Lord Charles Mailer or the Right Honorable Archibald Urban?"

The countess looked at him out of the corners of her

eyes. "Why? What did they do? Is it delicious? Are you going to cause a scene?"

"Not at all. Are they here?"

"I shouldn't answer, not when you're going to drive me wild with speculation. But, yes, they're both here. Lord Charles and his little mouse of a bride, Archie Urban and his patently unhappy spouse. But I'll let you find them on your own." She turned and nodded to a servant on her right, who immediately puffed himself up and announced the arrival of the Earl of Saltwood and his lady countess in a suitably stentorian tone.

The reaction was all Gideon could have hoped for. Conversations cut off. Heads turned. He bowed over Sally's hand and then extended his left arm to Jessica a heartbeat before the orchestra struck up the scandalous waltz.

"Take my hand."

"Should I point out I've only waltzed with my dancing master, a less formal country waltz at that, and it was over five years ago, sans musical accompaniment?" Jessica asked as she put her hand in his and he drew her out onto the floor. "Something you might have considered before pulling me along after you like some tricked-out pony expected to perform."

But she was smiling as she said it, so that Gideon's heart, which admittedly skipped a beat at this news, calmed once more. "I'm not putting you on show, although it occurs to me now you might think so. Sally, who owes me more than a single favor, has just bestowed her stamp of approval, and we are going to, pardon my crudity, milk that teat for all it's worth." He took her hand in his. "Are you ready?"

Jessica stepped back, dropping into a curtsy even as she seemingly effortlessly found the silken ring of fabric on her gown and slipped her finger through it, raising the right side of her overskirt so that it would float through every dip and turn of the dance. "I'll want to hear more about this promised groveling, my lord, I believe," she said as his hand went to her waist, her arm lifted to his shoulder. "In detail."

Now it was Gideon's laughter that drew the attention of anyone who had not already noticed the stunningly handsome couple standing together on the otherwise deserted dance floor. "You're a wicked woman, Jessica Redgrave."

"Agreed. But first, we dance our waltz. I'm confident it's much like riding a horse. It shouldn't take me more than a few moments to recall the movements."

"You do ride well," he agreed, tongue-in-cheek as he eased her into the first turn of the waltz. "I'd have to term your *movements* exemplary."

"Although doubtless capable of improvement, with repetition." And then she winked at him. His mind flashed a quick, taunting image of her above him, her breasts bare, her head thrown back as he gripped her hips, as their bodies melded. He very nearly trod on her toes.

Oh, good, she's not a stickler, Kate had said. *We've no simpering miss here,* Trixie had declared.

And they'd both been correct.

Because what they *had here,* what Gideon had found—and he knew he could take no credit for the discovery—was the most magnificent creature in the world, a rare combination of beauty and bravery, intelligence and humor, goodness and fire.

Together, Jessica as light as any feather in his arms, they whirled about the dance floor as, two-by-two, other couples dared to join in the scandalous waltz. Their eyes remained locked on each other, their smiles hinting of things that put onlookers to the blush, breaking every rule, and wonderfully so, spending perhaps their first true moments together, their most personal moment of discovery here, in Sally Jersey's candlelit ballroom, in the midst of all of the *ton*.

It was above all things amazing. And wonderful. And humbling.

His wife. His countess. And yes, quite possibly, one day soon, his *love*.

THEY MADE THE ROUNDS OF the ballroom for over an hour, Jessica's head positively spinning from all the introductions, all the names and faces that seemed to swim in front of her eyes as she clung to Gideon's arm.

There were a few whose greetings were rather strained, as if they were being polite only under duress, and more than one or two of the highest sticklers quickly found their way to the supper room in order to avoid the couple completely without being forced to give them the cut direct. But that was of no matter.

Jessica had only one awkward moment, when introduced to Lord and Lady Kettering, whose estate bordered on that of her late father. They gushed over her, saying how they'd always thought she was the most splendid girl and they hadn't believed the half of what they'd heard from her stepmother.

"You mistake the matter. You heard nothing," Gideon had told them in that way he had about him, smooth, polite, and yet all of it wound around a rock any fool knew they did not wish to see unwrapped. The couple hastened to agree and then excused themselves.

"Bully," Jessica told him.

"Yes, a large part of my charm, don't you think? But a lesson here, if I might. You swiftly and firmly deal with what must be dealt with, and ignore the rest. There is nothing quite so unsettling to people who wish to upset you than for you to ignore their efforts. Of course, there are exceptions, those you can't ignore. And there she is."

And then, as if he'd avoided the encounter for as long as possible, Jessica found herself curtsying to the Dowager Countess of Saltwood, who looked much at her ease as she half reclined on a gilt-backed couch, her tiny slippered feel resting on the thighs of the young soldier who'd positioned himself on the floor as if his main goal in life had always been to be a living footstool. Behind her, another young swain waved an ivory stick fan to help ward off the heat of the ballroom.

The dowager countess could not be mistaken for forty, or even fifty. She was not a young woman. But the traces of a once great beauty were there, the eyes were as bright and mischievous as any *Incomparable*. She was petite, almost doll-like, her smile dazzling, her every gesture as graceful as a prima ballerina trodding her own special stage. Beatrix Redgrave would be beautiful to the world if she lived into her nineties. And fascinating, always and forever, fascinating.

"I adore her, you know, but if one of those young

idiots produces a peeled grape for her, I don't know that I'll be able to keep from giggling like a loon. Is she always this outrageous?"

"Sometimes it's worse. I'm rather worried she's celebrating something tonight, something I probably don't want to know," Gideon whispered back, raising his quizzing glass and skewering each young exquisite in turn, until they all found reasons to take themselves off elsewhere. "Trixie? What new delights are you selling tonight?"

"The same old delights, pet, those fuzzy-faced darlings are simply a new audience. I've been reciting several of the sillier bits of John Wilkes's and Thomas Potter's *An Essay on Women,* which as we know, turned poor Alexander Pope's *An Essay on Men* very much on its head. 'The gasp divine, th'emphatic, thrilling squeeze, the throbbing panting—'"

"I believe we've heard enough, thank you. You promised you wouldn't again go beyond *The Life and Adventures of Miss Fanny Hill.* That's *education* enough for those young randy goats. Why do you persist on doing this?"

Trixie shrugged her slim shoulders. "It amuses me? Or perhaps to educate? You know how tedious it is to attempt to procure a copy of either work, thanks to our prudish government. Darling, think of it. Half of those young gentlemen soon will be off to the continent if Bonaparte's ambitions can't be contained. When they're cold and starving and wetting themselves with fear in their trenches, let them think back to tonight and smile, remember what they are really fighting and dying for. Or do you think it's for green fields and white cliffs, hmm?"

Jessica bit her bottom lip and looked down at her shoe tops.

"Sally thinks you're bedding them," Gideon said gruffly.

"I always warned Silence is an idiot. I'm their *grand-mother,* pet." She shrugged again, and smiled. "Albeit their *naughty* grandmother. You're much in looks to-night, Jessica. Good to know my grandson is no slow-top in the bridal chamber. I recognize the glow, you understand."

Jessica didn't want to say thank you, she really didn't. But what else was there to say? "Thank you, Trixie."

"Yes, and now down to business," the dowager duch-ess said, raising a lorgnette and scanning the perim-eter of the ballroom. "Ah, still there, where they were put. The obedience born of fear, I recognize that, as well. I've been watching them for you. Gideon, be-hind you and to the left are the pair of shrinking wall-flowers you needs must introduce to your lady. And there's an empty seat beside them, which is perfect. The blonde dressed in yellow—such an unfortunate choice, with her sallow coloring—is Lady Caro, Lord Charles's bride of less than a year, and beside her sits Felicity Urban, who always looks as if she's sucking a lemon. Their husbands put them there an hour ago and then deserted them for the card room, which is where you should be heading, pet, rather than standing there scowling at your naughty but brilliant grandmother. Now go, shoo, and let me get back to my boys. I believe we left poor Fanny lying on a couch, goggling at something quite new to her experience."

"I should lock you up in the dower house and throw the key in the well, not to punish you, but to protect my fellow man."

"Yes, yes, now go. Oh, but first, I believe I have some sad news to impart. It would seem Wickham's only son cocked up his toes early this morning. Not that it wasn't expected—that spotty liver, you'll recall. Poor old Reggie's all in a dither, of course, most especially at being unable to locate his grandson and now the heir to the dukedom. But I expect he'll show up in a day or two, don't you? Perhaps even with a lovely surprise in tow?"

"I told Jessica you might be celebrating something tonight. You're a hard woman, Trixie," Gideon said, shaking his head.

"Nonsense. I've already sent round a note of most sincere condolence to the duke and duchess. Oh, and I shall be traveling to Wickham Court for the interment, so if I don't see you two again for space, try not to behave yourselves."

"You'll attend the funeral? You really want to be on hand when the duke learns about his *surprise?*"

"How could I not? I've already paid for the pleasure."

"And now, so will the duke pay for his long-ago attack on the Redgraves. I suppose some might call it justice," Gideon said as he bowed over Trixie's hand once more and then offered his arm to Jessica. "Shall we?"

"We shall," Jessica agreed, doing her best to pretend she hadn't seen the two women even as she and Gideon made a dead set toward them. "May I ask what all that was about? Someone died?"

"Yes, someone certainly did, and Trixie is totally innocent of that death, I'm happy to say. The next one? That one, at least indirectly, will be her kill."

Jessica looked back over her shoulder to see the flock of regimental birds had come back to roost, gathering around the dowager duchess once more, to Trixie's laughing delight. "You'll tell me about this someday?"

"Someday. But for now, I'm putting you to work. I promise to return within the quarter hour." He drew her forward and bowed to the pair of lonely-looking ladies, introducing his bride and begging they welcome her whilst he adjourned to the card room to search out a few friends.

The ladies smiled and agreed, informed him that their own husbands had already adjourned to the same place, and Jessica sat down beside Felicity Urban, the older of the two by at least ten years.

A quarter hour wasn't much time, not if she had to deal with the usual inane pleasantries and comments on the sad crush of people, the heat of the ballroom. She decided to go straight for the jugular.

"It's vastly kind of you ladies to allow me to join you. I know so few people in town, but my husband swears to me I'm not allowed in the card room. I'm also forbidden to dance once the orchestra returns, as he's quite the jealous bridegroom. He can take umbrage if any other man so much as looks in my general direction, for goodness' sakes— Oh, should I have said that? Really, it's rather flattering, don't you think? I wouldn't want you ladies to believe him oppressively possessive."

"Better than the alternative," Felicity Urban said, a trace of bitterness—more than a trace, really—in her tone. "So you are newly married, my lady."

Mrs. Urban's eyes seemed slightly unfocused, and her breath smelled of laudanum overlaid with some sort of pungent spice. Jessica felt a pang of pity for the woman.

"Very newly, yes. It's all been such a mad rush. His lordship went so far as to secure a Special License."

Lady Caro leaned forward slightly, the better to see Jessica. "We watched you on the dance floor. I nearly swooned to see the look in his eyes, I will admit. He seems quite besotted."

"That fades soon enough," Mrs. Urban declared. "Enjoy it while you might, my lady."

"Yes, that's true," Lady Caro agreed, and then sighed.

Jessica summoned a smile. Lady Jersey had been quite correct in her assessment of the two women. Lady Caro, the new bride, was definitely a little mouse, and Mrs. Urban couldn't be more sour. That the two women could be friends seemed incongruous; they were as unalike as chalk and cheese. "Your husbands are friends?" she asked before she could stop herself, or at the least, find some smoother way into this leap in the conversation.

But Lady Caro didn't seem to notice anything strange about the question. "Oh, yes. We go everywhere together."

"Everywhere," Mrs. Urban repeated dully. "To balls,

to the theater, to country parties. Everywhere. Delightful times."

Lady Caro flinched visibly, almost as if she'd been slapped. "Do…do you enjoy the theater, my lady?"

"The earl tells me we have a box, but I've not attended a performance as yet, I'm sorry to say. My life, as I've said, has been a whirlwind of late. If you are soon to remove to the country, I do envy you. I'm sure country parties are much more relaxing."

Lady Caro's smile was weak and rather trembling. "Yes, I suppose so."

Really, this was hard going. "Do you agree, Mrs. Urban?"

Felicity Urban appeared to be attempting to raise her eyebrows but couldn't seem to manage the act. "Do I agree with what, my lady?"

"Um…that country parties are relaxing."

The woman turned hard brown eyes on Jessica, as if something inside her just woke up and took notice. When she next spoke, her words couldn't be more affable. "Oh, yes, I very much agree. In fact, my husband and I are even now planning a small get-together at our estate near Isleworth, quite a pleasant day's journey from London, I assure you. Please do give it your consideration. It would be a lovely break from the hustle and bustle of the Season."

"Felicity," Lady Caro whispered hastily, "do you think…?"

Mrs. Urban's voice had knives in it. "Yes, I do. You should attempt the exercise."

"I will, of course, be delighted to forward your kind invitation to his lordship, Mrs. Urban," Jessica said quickly, pretending not to notice the new tension between the women. "How exceedingly kind of you. Other than my husband, I have no real acquaintance, I'm afraid, having lived out of the country for several years."

"Ladies, your servant."

At the sound of the man's voice, Jessica saw Lady Caro reach out her hand to clutch at that of Felicity Urban, as if seeking protection.

"My lord," Mrs. Urban said, her previously strong voice quavering slightly. "How condescending of you to notice us languishing here amidst the potted palms. You know Lady Caro, of course, but please allow me to introduce you to our new acquaintance, the Countess of Saltwood. My lady, may I present Simon Ravenbill, Marquis of Singleton."

Disappointed by the interruption, Jessica summoned a smile and raised her head to see a magnificently constructed man, surely as tall as Gideon, but light to her husband's dark. His eyes, startlingly blue, his longish hair nearly guinea gold. "My lord, it is an honor," she said, quickly lowering her eyes once more even as she offered her hand, prudently recalling Gideon's warning not to attempt to *bluff* anyone. Because her mind had heard Ravenbill and immediately thought *Bird,* one of the names listed in her father's journal.

But dear and merciful God, that had only been the half of it!

"The honor is completely mine, my lady, I assure you. I arrived only a few moments ago and have been punished ever since for my tardiness, as the ballroom is abuzz at the news Saltwood has taken a wife. My further punishment is that he saw you first, or else I would have stolen a march on him, most definitely."

Jessica smiled, as she knew she ought, even as she worried her heart might leap out of her chest. "I don't think my husband would have allowed that, my lord. He's quite the determined man."

"Yes, we all know the stories of the infamous Redgraves. Such a fortunate thing that dueling has been outlawed. Not that Redgraves concerned themselves overmuch with the rules of the thing."

Jessica felt her cheeks growing hot with indignation, her own fears forgotten. "You're no longer amusing, my lord."

"Oh, no, my lady, don't say that," Lady Caro interrupted, nearly pleaded. "I'm certain his lordship most certainly didn't mean—"

"Ah, yet his lordship most certainly did," the marquis interrupted. "But I will take myself off now, mumbling insincere apologies as I go. Ladies, my best to your husbands. Do tell them I will be seeing them at some other time, as I'm always about somewhere, aren't I?"

Jessica watched as the marquis bowed with much grace and some insolence and then turned away, moving unerringly across the ballroom now cluttered with couples taking up positions for the next dance, and heading straight for the staircase. He didn't look back. He didn't have to. He had to know her eyes had followed him.

"Well, whatever was all that about?" she asked the ladies, struggling to compose herself. "He seemed so pleasant and then…well, and then not quite so much."

"The marquis is not known for his polite manner," Felicity Urban said. "He was a naval officer you know, a mere second son until his brother's death, and not at all suited to ascend to the title."

"He *exudes* power, don't you think?" Lady Caro asked nervously, as if to counter Felicity's complaint.

"I think you've been sneaking wine from the servant trays again, and your brain has disconnected from your mouth," Felicity Urban said, turning her back to the woman, blocking Lady Caro from Jessica's sight. Suddenly, inexplicably, her eyes were alight with intelligence and perhaps some desperation. "So you'll consider joining us in Isleworth, my lady? I'll send round an invitation in the morning. Please do give it your attention. Your immediate attention."

"Yes, thank you, I'll be certain to do that," Jessica said, her heart leaping as she saw Gideon striding toward her. She stood up to greet him as would a stranded sailor at the sight of an approaching ship.

CHAPTER SIXTEEN

"Is she always like this?"

Richard Borders took another sip from his teacup and replaced it on the tray in front of him. "You mean the pacing? Yes, I'm afraid so. Jess, sweetheart, you'll soon wear a rut in his lordship's pretty carpet."

It was after two, and Gideon was more than ready to say goodnight so that he and Jessica could adjourn to his bedchamber. They had only made love in hers, and it was time he introduced her to his, where she would spend the majority of her nights in any case. He'd made a mistake, plunking her down with the wives before he knew more about Lord Charles and Archie Urban. He wanted to make amends, or at least divert her from her fears.

But Richard had still been awake when they'd returned to Portman Square, and once she'd seen him she'd gone rushing toward him, to tell him what had happened at Lady Jersey's ball.

"Yes, Jessica, sit down," Gideon said, not for the first time. She was still the most beautiful woman in the universe, but she looked exhausted, drained of her usual liveliness. "You can't know he recognized you any more than you can be certain it was him in the first place."

She stopped her pacing at last and plopped herself

down rather inelegantly beside Richard, rather like a rag doll that had lost half its stuffing. She took the man's hand in hers. "But only because I'm exhausted. No, Richard, I can't be certain. And I kept my eyes down as much as possible. And it was more than four years ago in any event. Still, those eyes—"

"And the man you speak of was wearing a French uniform when we saw him," Richard pointed out, again not for the first time. "Speaking flawless French as he asked his questions."

Gideon rubbed the brandy snifter between his hands. If Jessica was correct, they may have just made a large leap forward. But at what cost? She was obviously terrified; all the way home from the ball she'd been working her hands together in her lap, clearly trying to hold on to her composure. Did he need to remove Jessica and Richard from London before this Ravenbill fellow's mind could be jogged into remembering them? It seemed a prudent move. "Tell me again if you please, Richard. From the beginning."

Richard ran his fingers through his shock of white hair, as if that might help put his thoughts in order.

"We'd traveled no more than a few miles' distance from the inn just outside Augsburg where we'd left Jamie, when we were stopped. This man, this marquis, or so thinks Jess, was at the head of a small troop of Bonaparte's soldiers. They were everywhere in Bavaria, roaming quite freely, popping up in city after city with rarely anyone attempting to stop them."

"I looked so guilty," Jessica said on a sigh, her head fallen back against the cushions, her eyes closed. "I know I did. He wanted to know why we were abroad so late at night, and with only the one horse. But Richard was magnificent, he really was, and had an answer for every question. I was his niece, our last name was Anderson, my horse had tripped and broken a foreleg so that it had to be put down. We were actors on our way to rejoin our troupe in the next village. On and on, just as calm as can be."

"I wasn't quite that brilliant," Richard said, smiling. "I really did think we'd come a cropper, but at last he let us go, advising we consider the advantages to be had in emoting on the other side of the Channel during such dangerous times, as the winds of change could otherwise blow with some menace toward even the most honest of English citizens. We took his advice and none too quickly, considering Bonaparte's advances that came soon after." He turned toward Jessica. "Are you positive it was the same man?"

Jessica kept her eyes closed, clearly seeing something, or someone, out of her past. "I told you. Those eyes. Even with only the moonlight to see him by, a person could never look into those eyes and forget them."

"Ravenbill," Gideon said consideringly. "I vaguely remember the brother, the late marquis, but not this Simon fellow. Ravenbill. Bird. And you said Lady Caro was in awe?"

Jessica sat forward, tucking her legs up beneath her gown. "What she actually said was that he exudes power. What struck me most was the way she grabbed onto Mrs. Urban's hand, as if afraid. Felicity Urban was so here-and-there, so obviously dosed with laudanum, I'm not certain *what* she thought of the man, or of me. At one point she seemed to be measuring me, as if attempting to calculate my worth to her. Believe me, I've seen *that* look before, as well."

"And I apologize that you were forced to confront it tonight. But again, her ladyship seemed frightened by the man?"

"Yes, I would have to say that's true. Neither of them was delighted to see him. He was…insolent. And he made a point of telling them to remind their husbands that he's always about somewhere. Perhaps he meant for me to remind you, as well. I can't say that for certain, however. Honestly, Gideon, I'm not prone to hysterics, but I had to fight to remain in my chair. Especially when he insulted your family."

"But not to my face," he reminded her. "At least our brash marquis shows some intelligence. Or he may have left the insult as a form of calling card. At any rate, if we Redgraves were thought to be harmless, upstanding pillars of the *ton,* we'd be even more insulted. Not to mention bored."

Richard chuckled into his teacup.

"I'm so happy you're amused, Richard," Jessica said testily. "And don't encourage him, he's arrogant enough as it is. You have no idea what it was like tonight. A London ball is much like being tossed into a nest of vipers. Every word seems to contain two meanings."

Richard patted her hand. "Well, I'm sure you did just fine, Jess. Now, if you don't mind, I'm for my bed."

Gideon lifted his hand to signal his agreement with Richard's departure and then took up the seat he'd just vacated. "I had an interesting conversation tonight myself, with the husband of one of your new bosom chums."

"Those two women are not my bosom chums," Jessica protested. "Lady Caro is such a poor, whipped creature, and Felicity Urban, if I'm not being too fanciful, invited us to be guests at one of their horrible gatherings."

"The cheek of the woman, to think I'd share you," Gideon said, and then held up his hands in case Jessica decided to attack him.

But Jessica only sighed. "She ran so hot and cold. One moment as if in a daze, the next all cheery and friendly. And then, just at the end, there was a moment…"

Gideon lifted her hand to his mouth and pressed a kiss against her heated skin. "Yes?"

"She's sending round an invitation tomorrow. I am to read it *immediately*. Really, it was as if she were giving me an order." Jessica laid her head against his shoulder, her entire body sagging in fatigue. "I felt horribly sorry for them, they're both so clearly unhappy. Did you learn anything from their husbands? You haven't said."

"I haven't been given the chance to say anything," he pointed out as he gathered her into his arms and stood up, having decided to adjourn to his bedchamber before she fell asleep against his shoulder. "However, I did manage to corral Archie Urban for five minutes. He said something interesting."

Jessica wound her arms around his neck. "I'd say I'm too heavy for you and you should put me down, but I'm too selfish. I can't even remember when last I slept, thanks to you. But tell me, what did he say?"

"I interrupted a conversation he was having with a few other gentlemen as they waited for an opening at one of the tables. Urban was offering the opinion Emperor Napoleon is a genius. Tactically, politically. His recent marriage to Austria's Marie Louise a stroke of brilliance, et cetera. I raised my quizzing glass—an affectation, I know, but often quite effective—and asked if surely he meant *evil* genius, which he immediately agreed he did. However, I was left with the impression he was soliciting opinions, and one or two actually had agreed with him before I stepped in."

"Are you saying Mr. Urban was sniffing the air, looking for like minds?"

"Oh, very good, Jessica. You're better at this than you supposed."

"Thank you." Jessica turned her face into his chest to cover her yawn. "And that was all?"

"There was a little more. A few discreet inquiries inform me Urban's responsibility is to see our troops quietly massing on the Peninsula are supplied adequately and in a timely fashion. Weapons, ammunition, foodstuffs, blankets, all funneled into Portugal, most especially into Lisbon. We're preparing to go back at it with Bonaparte in full force once we're assured of Spanish cooperation, that's clear enough. An army is nothing without supplies. Knowing what we think we may know about the man, I find that unsettling."

He put her down once they reached his bedchamber, and he began the pleasurable job of acting as lady's maid for his bride.

"I find it unsettling that you were able to learn so much so quickly and easily. Why on earth would anyone tell you about—what was it you said?—a massing of troops on the Peninsula?"

"What? I'm not a man who inspires trust?"

She turned to face him, holding up her now un-buttoned gown, her nearly bared breasts distracting him mightily. "I believe you could coolly bluff your way into forcing your opponent to foolishly declare he can win the *Misère Ouverte,* and then make certain he doesn't take more than three tricks. I would never play whist against you, or any other card game. Or any game at all, for that matter. Now tell me how you learned what you learned."

"Spencer Perceval is a friend," Gideon told her, guiding her to a chair so that he could help her off with her shoes and stockings.

"The Prime Minister? Really? Well, now I am impressed."

"You're weren't before?" he asked, grinning up at her. "But much as I'd like to take the credit, it's Max we have to thank for Perceval. He's worked with him a time or two, on other matters. We all know how it is, Jessica. Even when we're not formally at war with Napoleon, we're at war with Napoleon, truces be damned."

Jessica stood up and allowed Gideon to help her step out of her gown. She wasn't being immodest, or coy, or anything that would give Gideon any reason for hope. She was simply a woman anxious for her bed. He may as well have been Mildred, he realized with some chagrin.

"You've called Max an adventurer, and now you tell me he's performed services for our Prime Minister. Are you next going to tell me that Val is secretly working for the War Office or some such thing?"

He turned her about and headed her toward his

turned-down bed, clad now only in her silk French drawers, following behind her to take the pins from her hair. "Valentine? I'd as much attempt to tell you I'm one of Liverpool's advisers."

It wasn't an answer, but he hadn't wished to give her an answer.

He watched, in some admiration, as Jessica crawled onto the bed and pulled the covers over her. "I'm not that silly. You don't take orders from anyone." She turned her back to him and sighed. "Don't think I haven't noticed you didn't answer my question about Valentine. But I'm too exhausted right now to care. Good night."

So much for his supposed genius....

Gideon stripped off his clothing and joined her, pressing himself up against her back, curving his body to mimic her bent-knee position. "You do realize you're in my bed, madam?"

He felt her body stiffen slightly, imagined her eyes going wide as she belatedly took in her surroundings. "Oh, God, I am, aren't I?"

"Yes," he spoke against her hair. "And I promised you some detailed groveling, I believe."

"Gideon, you could recite lines from this *Fanny Hill* Trixie spoke of while hanging from one of the bedposts with a rose clamped in your jaws, and I will still be asleep in the next two minutes."

He slid his arm around her, to cup her breast, rub the pad of his thumb lightly across her nipple. "Are you quite certain?" he asked, smiling in the near dark.

She turned onto her back and looked up into his

eyes. "Oh, good, you're not being serious." Then she turned onto her side once more. "Good night, Gideon."

Gideon had never shared a bed with a woman unless he was, well, bedding her. Now here he was, in bed with his brand-new bride, and he hadn't so much as been offered a kiss good night. He'd been rather cavalierly dismissed, actually.

He thought about this for a while and then realized he was listening to the sound of Jessica's soft, even breathing. He liked the sound. He liked listening to it. He liked being where he was, with her, even if that only meant they were together. He didn't need more than that. Even in the midst of all he supposed, all that may pose danger to them, to England itself if he was right, he was content. Just to be here. Just to listen to his wife breathe.

How strange...

"HE KNOWS WHAT HE'S ABOUT under the blankets, don't he, my lady? And that's fine, it is, for you. But he doesn't know much about what it takes to press the wrinkles out of a fancy gown, oh, no, he doesn't. Will you have a talk with his lordship about that, ma'am? Doreen fair to cried when she saw your gown this morning."

Jessica was caught between pointing out to Mildred that she didn't wish to discuss her husband's prowess *under the blankets* and the fact that poor Doreen seemed to be paying the price for that prowess. "I'll see what I can do," she said as the maid ran the sea sponge over her shoulders. "And I apologize again that the two

of you waited up until three for me last night. It was
highly inconsiderate of me."

"That's all right, my lady. We've all of us got to learn
our way here, and that's what I tell Doreen. Now, if you
were to stand up, I'll fetch you that bath sheet I've got
warming by the fire."

A few minutes later, Jessica was sitting at her dressing table and Mildred was standing behind her, muttering over the tangled hair she was doing her best to
tame and suggesting mayhap his lordship might wish
to consider learning how to weave a fine braid if he
wasn't going to let her lady's maids within ten feet of
her at night.

"Mildred?" Jessica asked, watching the woman in
the mirror. "Is this all real, do you suppose? I mean…
that is to say…it all seems like a dream, doesn't it?
And…and perhaps too wonderful to last?"

"Ah, and now you're staring into the mouth of a gift
horse, is that what you're doing? That's dangerous, my
lady, and courting trouble. His lordship is bosky over
you, any fool can see that. And it's not a bubble soon
to burst, I don't think."

"But how would a person know that?" Jessica asked,
taking the brush from the maid's hand, needing to do
something more than just sit there; she had a long way
to go before she could simply be waited on, she'd lived
too many years on her own. "I met a pair of ladies last
evening at the ball. Married ladies. Neither seemed
very happy. They hinted husbands become disen-
chanted sooner or later. And when all you have is…
How do I say this?"

"When all you have is that hot burning to be in each

other's drawers and then mayhap just as sudden there you are, stuck looking at each other across the mutton and trying to remember what all the fuss was about?"

Jessica turned about to goggle at the maid. "Mildred. How did you know? That's exactly it, exactly what I meant to say. I mean, perhaps not in that way...."

"Make it as pretty as you want, my lady, but it comes down to the same in the end, that's what I've learned. One minute it's, oh, laws, come here and let me have that, and the next it's for the love of all that's decent, keep that nasty thing away from me."

"Mildred!" Jessica felt her cheeks go hot. *It hadn't been like that. She'd simply been tired. Exhausted. She hadn't actually told him to go away.* "I don't think we should—"

The maid went about folding up the bathing sheet and continued as if Jessica hadn't spoken. "It's the same for the men, you know, but even worse. They want you till they get you, and use you every which way while they have you, but then it's not a game anymore, you see. They won, and now it's time to move on to the next one. That's what they want most, the winning."

Jessica didn't protest this time. "I see."

"I suppose so! And then there's the worst of all of them. The lying buggers who swear they love you. Ha! We all know what it is they love, and it's not our pretty smiles or pleasant ways."

The maid's voice had taken on a fierceness now, and Jessica bit her lips together and simply listened, turning about to see pain on the woman's face.

"I love you, Millie, is what he told me," she said, her eyes squeezed shut. "I surely do love you, so why don't you lie down right here and let me do what I want. Nothing splits wide a girl's knees like hearing some handsome liar swearing he loves her. Oh, they're the worst, ma'am, those what swear they love you. Then they run off like their breeches is on fire when you say, oh, yes, Johnny Hopkins, and I love you straight back, I love you quite truly. Run like the wind, they do, when they hear that, and the next thing you know your sister Bettyann tells your Da what you've been doing at the spinney and he tosses you out, and now you're doing what you have to do to feed your belly, and figuring out what you should have figured out long ago, and that's that love has nothing to do with lying down and letting them do what they want, even when you like what they're doing."

And then Mildred stopped, clapped her hands to her cheeks as if finally realizing what she'd been saying. "Oh, but not his lordship, ma'am! I wasn't meaning him, no, I was not. Like I said, he's bosky for you, we all say so. Chased you till he caught you, didn't he, and here we are, and here we're going to stay. We've a fine life now, all of us. Those society ladies you talked to, well I'll wager they're just jealous of that handsome man you've got trailing along at your shoestrings. Yes, I do! Would you want me to lay out your clothes for you now, my lady? Doreen's still off muttering over the pressing iron."

"Yes, thank you, Mildred. I'd appreciate that."

"The blue sprigged muslin, my lady?"

Jessica nodded her agreement, her mind traveling back to a morning that seemed so long ago now and yet far from in the past.

She'd thanked him for not sending her away, she remembered that. But mostly she remembered what he'd said in return: *I'm not ready to let you go.*

God, she'd accused him then, hadn't she? Accused him of being just what Mildred had described, a man who had *won,* had gotten what he wanted. He'd even gone so far as to marry her, to get what he wanted. With never a word of love. Perhaps she should be thankful for that.

Because if Gideon had told her he loved her, she would have told him she loved him, too, *I love you quite truly.*

And that, at least according to Mildred, would be the worst thing she could do.

CHAPTER SEVENTEEN

GIDEON WATCHED JESSICA as she kept her head bent slightly, as if she needed to keep all her concentration on the luncheon plate in front of her. Perhaps she was remembering how their evening had ended and wondered if she believed she'd reneged on some sort of marital *agreement* they'd made. *My protection in exchange for your body.* That was a lowering thought and didn't make him feel particularly proud.

Then again, was what they had really a marriage, except in the legal sense of the word? He had a quick, fleeting thought of Jessica and him lounging on the grass at Yearlings, one of his smaller estates, located in prime horse country. Just the two of them, alone—talking, laughing, getting to know each other far from London and any thoughts about a possible lethal legacy of his father's damn Society.

It seemed so unfair that they couldn't have that. Or could they?

He hadn't seen her since he'd pressed a kiss against her hair that morning and left her to snuggle deeper beneath the covers. He'd rather prided himself on the fact he hadn't attempted to kiss her awake, hadn't attempted a lot more. Perhaps he was learning restraint. It was a new experience for a man who had never really questioned his belief that he could take what he wanted because… No, he had no ending for that thought. At least none that wouldn't make him uncomfortable.

In any event, he'd hurried his valet through the chores of bathing and dressing, and ordered his mount brought around front before the clock had struck nine, an ungodly hour for any gentleman of the *ton* to be out and about in Mayfair unless he was finding his way home after a long night.

A discreet enquiry at one of his clubs—meaning, a gold coin slipped into the gloved hand of the major-domo—had given him the direction of one Marquis of Singleton, for all the good that had done him. It was hours too early to leave his card, but at least now he knew where the man lived, in case he decided to pay him a visit.

From there, he had gone to Cavendish Square, brushing past a disapproving Soames and heading straight for his grandmother's bedchamber. After all, thanks to the recently deceased Marquis of Mellis, he now knew the way.

He learned three things during that very brief visit.

One, Trixie had no recollection of a Ravenbill ever being mentioned as a member of the society.

Secondly, there was a reason no one saw his grandmother before two in the afternoon. Gideon's conclusion was nobody would want to, not if they'd sleep nights! He'd found Trixie still abed, lying on her back in the very center of the large mattress as if she'd been laid out for a viewing, her hands and arms wrapped in thick, greasy-looking cotton gauze, her hair dark with some sort of pomade, and her face, neck and chest slathered with a lavishly applied cream the color of spring leaves. The room was hot, and smelled of at least six different scents; some medicinal, some flowery, none of them particularly appealing.

And, lastly, he'd learned that, petite as she was, old as she was, Beatrix Redgrave could launch a silver candlestick more than twenty-five feet with deadly accuracy.

Absently rubbing at his left shoulder—he'd been too shocked to duck quite fast enough—he finally broke the not completely companionable silence of the luncheon table. "I saw Trixie this morning. She sees no connection between the Marquis of Singleton and the society."

Jessica laid down her fork. "But Ravenbill? Bird?"

He shrugged. "Coincidence? Or it proves we were right to conclude they're no longer confining membership to eldest sons, which seems eminently logical. In other words, I don't think we can dismiss Simon Ravenbill as yet. I'm much more concerned with your belief you saw him several years ago."

"Wearing a French uniform," Jessica pointed out, and now she was turning the fork over and over on the tabletop. "I know it was him. I just don't know what it means."

Gideon felt the impulse to go around the table and take her in his arms, swear to her that no one would ever hurt her, not while he lived. He wouldn't allow it. But fear was fear, and he wasn't immune to the feeling; he had to protect her.

"It could mean two things," he told her. "If the Society is somehow aligned with the enemy, he could have been there to help further their cause with Bonaparte.

Either that, or he's working for our government. The former worries me, the latter possibly more so, as we wouldn't want to do anything that might jeopardize whatever role he's playing and put him in danger."

Jessica blinked at him. "I hadn't thought of that possibility. It would make what he said to Lady Caro and Mrs. Urban last night take on an entire new meaning. It would have been a threat, or even a dare, wouldn't it?"

"It would, yes. The man may be playing his own game. No matter which scenario we could choose, I believe we need to stay out of Singleton's way until we know more. Hell, Jessica, at the moment, seeing you with those women, he may believe *I'm* a part of the Society."

"If he's even aware of the Society," Jessica pointed out correctly. "Perhaps he's been watching them because of what they're doing, perhaps he has suspicions of his own or the government has suspicions for some reason. But perhaps only Lord Charles and Mr. Urban are suspects. They may have no idea of the scope of the conspiracy, that there's a devil's dozen of them plus anyone they might be blackmailing into cooperating with them. There are so many possibilities, far too many of them. We were chasing murderers, that's how this began for you, and I was attempting to protect Adam. We're out of our depth now, Gideon."

And now they'd come to the heart of the matter.

"I agree. We'll soon have a different theory for every day of the week, won't we? It's the deaths of the more longtime members that started it all, just as you said. That, and a tree branch poking a hole in the Redgrave mausoleum. I certainly didn't go into this with any

thoughts of stumbling into anything quite so dangerous. My father has a lot to answer for, doesn't he, even
twenty years dead?"

"Your father, and mine. But there's something else
to consider. If my father hadn't died, you and I would
never have met, would we? I wouldn't have approached
you about Adam, you wouldn't have learned what happened five years ago, you wouldn't have confronted
Trixie—none of it. Those murders may have been the
worst mistake the Society could make. Gideon, we
know so much, but clearly not enough."

That wasn't precisely true, but Gideon knew this
wasn't the moment to tell her he did know one thing,
one very important thing: it was time for Jessica to be
as far from London as possible. He'd have to ease his
way into the subject, however; he'd already ducked one
candlestick today.

"For the moment, let's concentrate on the marquis.
I won't ask you again if you're positive you recognized
him, but I will ask you to once more consider if he may
have recognized you."

She shook her head. "No, I don't think so. I had the
hood of my cloak raised, and I stayed behind Richard
for the most part. But I suppose it's possible he might
recognize Richard, and then remember me."

"Yes. Richard. We'll have to do something about
that, won't we?"

Jessica lowered her head into her hands. "Yes, I
know. Poor Richard, he loves London so. You'll send
him off?"

"Only as far as Redgrave Manor." He took his
chance. "And you with him."

Her head shot up, her eyes gone wide. "What? But why?"

"Because, either way, Jessica, patriot or traitor, if Singleton recognized you last night or his memory is jogged when next he sees you, you are now a problem to the man."

He could tell she hadn't considered that possibility. "I was thinking only of how he could be a problem to us. But I see your point. We could confront him, ask him if he's working for the Crown and— No, that wouldn't work, would it? If he is, he'd lie to us, and if he isn't, he'd lie to us. And if he's neither, and I've mistaken him for somebody else, well, that would be even worse, wouldn't it?"

Gideon smiled. He enjoyed listening to Jessica think out loud. "Immensely, yes. So we're agreed?"

"Agreed to what? What are you agreeing to, Gideon? I've agreed to nothing."

"I noticed that. Are we about to have our first argument? Yes, what is it, Thorndyke?"

The butler bowed and held out a small silver salver with a folded note on it. "Excuse me, my lord. This just arrived by messenger. I was informed it's imperative her ladyship reads it immediately."

"Then why are you handing it to his lordship, or have I been somehow rendered invisible?" Jessica asked, snatching the missive from the tray even as Gideon reached for it.

"And now we've both been put in our place, haven't we, Thorny?" Gideon remarked, laughing.

"Firmly, my lord," Thorndyke agreed and quickly bowed himself out of the room.

"I'm sorry. I'll apologize later."

"To Thorny or to me?"

"Not you, certainly. Thorndyke hasn't gotten used to having me about as yet, but you should know better," she explained absently, eyeing the missive as if it could possibly turn into a writhing snake at any moment. She slid her fingernail beneath the wax seal and unfolded the sheet, her eyes going immediately to the bottom of the page. "It's from Felicity Urban."

"Our invitation?" Gideon asked, rising from his chair, in order to stand behind her as she read. "Hmm, obviously not the invitation we were told to expect."

Jessica read the note aloud. "'I know what you and the earl are about. Help me and I'll help you. Four o'clock today, *Le Bon Modiste,* Bond Street. Ask for Fontine. I will need five thousand pounds, and safe transport.'" She tilted her head back to look up at Gideon. "So much for my belief I was subtle last evening, I suppose. I told you she was looking at me curiously, as if measuring me or some such thing. She says she can help us? Honestly, I thought I'd be much better at this than I am."

"You got results, and that's what's most important. But if it's any comfort to you, I didn't do much better at subtlety. She knows what I'm about? It has to be that damn rose. I only wore it for a few days, but obviously Felicity Urban took notice."

Jessica was looking at the note again. "But didn't mention it to her husband?"

"Yes, I'll have to ask her about that when I meet with her, won't I?"

Gideon Redgrave—and Thorndyke, for that matter—had a lot to learn about what it meant to be married to Jessica, but there wasn't much he didn't know about women in general. Or at least he prided himself on learning quickly.

"When *we* meet with her," he corrected almost before Jessica could take in a breath in order to disabuse him of his former statement.

After all, Trixie may have thrown a candlestick, but there were knives on the dining table, for God's sake....

LE BON MODISTE WAS A small shop in a tall, narrow building. Gideon had insisted they make a business of visiting several shops as they strolled along the block and even convinced Jessica to purchase a new bonnet in one of them. They walked arm-in-arm, stopping to peer into store windows. They nodded to passersby, even stopped so that Gideon could chat with a rather florid-faced matron who begged permission to be introduced to the new countess and invited them both to a delightful musical evening the following Thursday.

Gideon had promised he would do his best, but it was possible they would be adjourning to the country prior to that date.

"I never said I'd go," Jessica had pointed out once the lady had taken her leave and they were walking on once more.

"You never mentioned a burning desire to submit to a session with the thumbscrews, either, but that would be an almost enjoyable experience when compared to listening to Hetty Frampton's offspring—and there are an even half dozen of them—as they attack your ears with song and defile every musical instrument known to man."

"Oh," Jessica said quietly. "I mistook your motive. I'm sorry."

His smile melted her knees, which he had to know. "I'm sure you'll be able to find some way to make it up to me. Now, are you ready? I believe, rank amateurs that we are, we've been suitably clandestine about our approach to *Le Bon Modiste*."

"In case anyone is following us? Who would be following us?"

"Other than Richard, who is prudently keeping out of sight as he watches for the Marquis of Singleton, you mean? I believe that would be Max, who returned to London late last evening."

"Your brother? Really?" Jessica made to turn around, but a short, sharp tug on her arm reminded her that spies, or whatever it was they were playing at, didn't stop dead on the flagway and turn about to peer into the distance, now did they?

"I begin to see the logic in banishing me to the country," she admitted on a sigh as they turned in to the narrow shop.

"That argument sounds familiar. However, I believe it was my brother saying something of that nature concerning me. I would have taken umbrage, but he's probably correct."

"He actually said you're not up to the task? That wasn't very nice of him."

Gideon's smile took her by surprise. "But probably true. He reminded me I am a newly married man, and my concentration perhaps isn't as focused as it might otherwise be."

"Oh? So he's blaming not you, but me?"

"He blames the marital state in general, actually. According to Max, a man who goes into battle with a woman on his mind is a danger to himself and everyone around him."

Jessica fought a sudden urge to preen. "And you've a woman on your mind?"

"And plans for that woman and myself for later tonight, yes, which probably proves Max's point. Now why don't you go admire the pretty ribbons on that table to your left, please, while I seek out this Fontine person, all right? Discreetly, of course, and I assign that description to us both."

Jessica looked at the displayed ribbons without really seeing them while Gideon spoke to a young blond clerk behind the counter. Her heart was pounding in a most disconcerting way as she wondered if they had just walked into some sort of trap. Villains laid traps, didn't they? It was basically their stock in trade.

She kept her back turned, said back feeling quite vulnerable, while the blond-haired clerk came out from behind the counter and crossed to the door, lowering the shade and then turning a key in the lock.

Which, Jessica realized with a start, effectively put Richard and Gideon's brother Max firmly on the other side of that door.

"This way, *madame*," the woman said as she walked back to where Gideon was now holding wide a beaded curtain that led to the rear of the shop.

Jessica slid her hand into Gideon's, and they followed the clerk up a narrow flight of stairs that opened into a small sitting room, the shades of both front windows pulled down, the only light coming through the dirty panes of a window to the rear.

Felicity Urban was seated on a shabby couch, a bandbox at her feet. She was so nervous her knees were visibly shaking. Gone was the hard woman from last night. In her place, a clearly terrified creature. She did not rise to greet her invited guests.

"Mrs. Urban," Gideon said, bowing.

"My Lord Saltwood," she replied tightly. "You have the money? And the transport? I say nothing until I've seen both."

Gideon turned to Jessica. "So much for any offer of refreshments, hmm?" He directed her to a straight-backed chair and then walked over to the couch and pulled a thick envelope from a pocket inside his coat. He slid the packet back inside his coat. "Five thousand pounds. You may count it later, as to insist on doing it now would quite injure my sensibilities," he said affably. "If you would care to look out that window behind us, you would see a plain black traveling coach and a coachman awaiting orders. Fair enough?"

"Fair enough," the woman said as she extracted a small dark brown bottle from her reticule, uncorked it with trembling fingers and lifted it to her lips. She then recorked the bottle but did not replace it in her reticule. "Opiates, the true refuge of cowards. Yet all that keeps me sane, you understand. Ah, yes, that's better. It was Archie's idea. He keeps me generously supplied, but that won't be for much longer. I'm very careful, you see. I drink half, and hide the rest away, watering what is left. He wants me insensible, but I've fooled him there. I don't *need* this," she said, holding up the bottle. "But I know I'm needing it more. I heard him speak of Ringmer last week, with his valet. You know of the place?"

Jessica looked to Gideon.

"A discreet asylum for those of weak minds, yes."

"You're too kind, my lord. A discreet dumping ground for those with enough money to rid themselves of their problems," Felicity countered, seeming to gain courage. "Problems such as wives who no longer suit their needs. I suppose I should be grateful he didn't follow his good friend Lord Charles's lead. But, then, there are no soggy cliffs on our property to break away whilst I'm out for a solitary stroll."

Again, Jessica snapped her head round to look to Gideon, who merely shook his slightly, as if warning her to remain silent.

Felicity shrugged and slipped the bottle back into her reticule. "You were wearing the rose. Was I wrong to believe it was because you wanted to make contact with the Society?"

"No, you were correct."

She nodded. "I thought as much. I wasn't the only one who noticed. You've been discussed, my lord, and let that be a warning to you. They're watching. And then you sent your wife to us last night. You really should be more careful, my lord. You and your bride both, her being who she is. What did you think to gain? You wanted, perhaps, to learn more about your father? I can tell you all you need to know, for I've heard the stories. Your father was a terrible man, a monster. Your mother was right to shoot him, put him down for the animal he was." She shook her head. "But he wasn't a patch on what's happening now. Oh, no. Not a patch. None of them were."

"Is that why they're dead? The members who date from my father's time, or soon after? In order to make room for members more in agreement with whatever in hell they're doing now?"

The woman looked up at Gideon, her mouth gone hard. "That's not why they're dead, and you somehow know it, or else your wife here wouldn't have come to us last night, asking such obvious questions, and we wouldn't be here now, talking. But, yes, that is what happened. I'm afraid we began something without considering the possibility we were aiding the Society, giving them a chance to finish building a thirteen more suited to their purpose. We thought we were so clever, just as your mother was so smart, so wise to see there was only the one answer for her, and damn anything else."

Only the one answer for her. Jessica felt a shiver climbing her spine. How often had she sat at night, watching James Linden sleep, and thought *there's only one way I can be truly free of him.* What was this woman saying, really saying? Could it be…?

Gideon sat down on the edge of the low table in front of the couch. "I'm sorry. I'm don't understand. What does my mother have to do with any of this?"

"You understand. You just want me to keep talking, don't you? But I've seen the packet, I believe the coach, so you might as well hear it all, the both of you."

Felicity sat back against the thin cushions. "They

use only prostitutes now for the most part. None of the newer members include their wives, save for Lord Charles, who finds it amusing. For their games, you understand. Wives were more convenient over the years, less prone to carry tales. But wives grow long in the tooth, or they cry, or they kill themselves. The thirteen never cared. They have their games, just as I have my little brown bottle. But they can't give them up, they don't want to give them up. Devil worship. Ha! It's all a hum, you know, an excuse."

"Go on," Gideon urged, when the woman seemed to get lost inside her own mind.

"They're filthy, dirty bastards, every one of them, and they *like* it. They feel *powerful,* and *important,* and show off in front of each other like little boys. Look at me, look at what I can do, listen to her beg for more. No, not that one. I had her last time, and it's like falling cock first into a hole. By Beelzebub, pass me one who's still tight. One by one, we were pushed to the side, barred from the ceremonies. We were only whisked to the ceremonies and then banished back to our homes, never to see anyone not wearing a mask. After that, one by one, we were gone. Oh, yes, I know. It's Ringmer for me, and very soon."

The brown bottle appeared once more.

Jessica realized she had laced her hands together, squeezing so hard her knuckles had gone white.

"Ha! Look at your bride, Saltwood. I've put her to the blush. Now that's a talent I lost long ago. Should I tell you about their toys? The spanking horse, the stocks? Oh, and the whips, the paddles. Sometimes for us, sometimes for them, or else they couldn't—"

Gideon repositioned himself slightly, blocking Jessica from the woman's sight. "I believe we understand, Mrs. Urban, and you have our complete sympathy. But your husband, all of the members, also used these so-called ceremonies of devil worship as a way to lure guests who could be used to further their true purpose."

The bottle was recorked once more. "Their true purpose, my lord? They had no true purpose beyond their filthy desires. Not since your father was killed, him and his supposed plan for England to rise in its own revolution the way the Froggies did. I heard it said he'd already ordered a guillotine built, but that may be only rumor. No, there was just the opiates, the costumes and chanting, the *rutting*. Not until *he* showed up. Oh, he's sly, he is. Playing one against the other, bringing up all this nonsense about the rights of the most gifted and the freedom of man. How the French had it right as far as it went, but Napoleon has it better, and will reward those who help him gain the greatest prize, wretched England itself. He has promises from the French, he has a plan, and we'll all share in the glory. The thirteen, the *deserving*. Who needs an invading army if England can be rotted from the inside?"

Jessica listened carefully as the woman explained in more detail.

The few surviving members since Barry Redgrave's time and several of those who had been "invested" soon after had objected, saying treason was a dangerous game to play and would lead to exposure and disaster. But they'd been overruled by Orford and the others. The Society began to change. Proofs of loyalty were demanded.

"Like you," Felicity Urban said, leaning to her side so that she could look past Gideon to Jessica. "That was certainly a debacle, wasn't it? Your father barely escaped with his life over that one. But he'd made the gesture, hadn't he? He'd agreed to turn you over to the new Leader the night the man was to be formally invested in his role. Of course, your father couldn't have known the man's true plan."

"Him," Gideon said, snapping his fingers twice to draw the woman's attention back to himself and to the moment. "I'm assuming you mean the current leader of the devil's thirteen?"

Felicity sighed. "Yes, yes, who else would I mean? And now you're going to ask me his name, and I have no answer for you. The Society is the Society, and the Leader is the Leader. Orford introduced him, first brought him as a guest, and none of us women ever saw him in anything but a full-face mask and a hooded cloak. I can tell you his eyes are dark, like the depths of hell, but that's all I can tell you, except to say he never did more than sit on his throne and watch. He never participated…except the once, when he sacrificed the vestal virgin. Nobody dared cross him after that. Nobody."

Jessica got to her feet, trying not to notice that her knees had gone rather wobbly. "Are you saying…?"

The bottle appeared yet again, and this time Felicity took much more than a sip of the watered laudanum. "Now we were held together by murder, yes, even if we didn't hold the knife. He knew us, but we didn't know him. Only Orford knew him. We probably should have thought of that before we…" She frowned at the bottle.

It was empty. She reached into her reticule and pulled out another, but Gideon snatched it from her hand.

"Before you what, Mrs. Urban? Before you all agreed to become traitors to our country?"

"We're not traitors." She eyed the bottle. "Give it back."

Gideon pulled out the cork and tipped the bottle slightly, so that a few drops hit the floor. "Before you did what, Mrs. Urban?"

"Don't spill that! For the love of God, be careful!" she shouted, making a wild grab for the bottle. "Stop! You already know! Before we killed them!"

And then she put her head in her hands and sobbed.

Jessica sat down again with a thump, the realization of what the woman had just admitted hitting her like a physical blow. They'd done it. Dear God, they'd actually done it! And she understood. She understood....

Gideon was still pressing the woman. "Here, take it back. But don't drink any more, not until we're finished here. You said, before we killed them. I need you to be more clear. Who is *we*, Mrs. Urban, and whom did you kill?"

"The ones who were left, of course." She grabbed the bottle, replacing the cork with shaking fingers. "I told you. One by one, they put us out to pasture. Barring some of us from participating in the ceremonies, that was the start. Keeping the rest of us from speaking to each other, whisking us away after the ceremonies. We knew what could come next, once we'd outlived our usefulness."

"And perhaps because you knew the identities of the

other members, those you'd seen without their masks," Gideon suggested quietly.

"Yes, we knew that was also true. Lady Dunmore was the first, poor old thing. They said her horse threw her. But we knew better. She'd told us she didn't ride anymore, so what was she doing on a horse, hmm? Baron Harden's wife? He shipped her off to Ringmer, just as Archie is planning to do with me."

"So you killed them. Their own wives killed them." Gideon seemed to be trying to keep the incredulity out of his voice, but Jessica could hear his shock. But no man could fully understand the sort of helplessness and desperation those women must have endured for so long.

Felicity nodded her head. "Lady Orford wrote to us, since we were now barred from the *parties*. She suggested the answer for us had been there all along. We would take a page from your mother's book, that's what she said, and we agreed. We should have done it years earlier, but that only would have meant the eldest son replaced the father. Once that rule was put aside with the advent of the new Leader, we were free to act. Our letters to each other are carried by trusted servants, but we live daily with the threat of discovery. It took us some time to consider plans before we settled on *accidents*. Of course, then we had to find the money to engage individuals who would actually do the deeds."

"So my brother is safe?" Jessica asked. "We thought so, but we couldn't be sure."

"He's safe. So is my son, and several others. And several refused, to the point where the Leader's suggestion made perfect sense. The best and the brightest only, with no longer a birthright to gain anyone entry."

"The best and the brightest. And the most strategically placed and influential, I would imagine," Gideon commented. "Please, go on."

"I should think it would be obvious what happened after we'd decided what we had to do. We drew up a list. Noddy Selkirk was the first, and then Cecil Appleby—they seemed the safest to use as our tests before we could chance anything more bold. When no one suspected, we moved on. Orford, Sir George Dunmore, Baron Harden. Dead because they'd begun killing us, dead before they could rid themselves of the rest of us. We took revenge for those who had been destroyed, and vengeance on the rest."

"And the Marquis of Mellis?" Gideon asked, and Jessica realized he was testing the woman with that question.

"No, not him. The marquis died before we could reach him. He would have been right after Archie and poor Caro's Lord Charles, although she swears she still loves him and won't yet agree. But he and Archie would have been the last for us. All the members now wear full masks, just like the Leader, added one by one over the last five years. It was like being spitted by a thing, and not a person at all. It's horrible."

She looked up at Gideon, her complexion gone deadly pale, her pupils suddenly two small dots in a sea of watery blue. "You…you didn't know it was us who killed them? I thought— But you sent your wife to us. I was so sure— Oh, God, what have I done? Isn't this what this is all about? You figured it out somehow?

You wanted to know what I know about the Society or else you'd turn all of us over to the Crown to be hanged? But we have an agreement, my lord. Please. I beg you."

Jessica heard herself springing to the women's defense. "Gideon, they really had no other choice." She was terrified he wouldn't understand that the true victims were the wives. He had to see that. He had to!

"It's all right, Jessica," he said quickly. "And, yes, of course we knew, Mrs. Urban, we simply needed to hear you say the words. I'll help you, just as I said I would. But there are a few more questions, if you can manage them."

"Yes! Yes, anything I can tell you. Anything at all. Because we had no choice. You see that, my lady, don't you? You said that. We had no choice."

Jessica got up, went to sit beside Felicity Urban on the couch. She took the woman's shaking hands in her own. She'd had Richard. These women had no one but themselves and with their children to consider. "No choice, and every reason. We understand, truly we do. But I must ask about my father and his wife. Why them?"

Felicity looked from Jessica to Gideon, and then back again. "We didn't... *No!* We had nothing to do with that. It was a coaching accident. A true accident, a horrible accident. Wasn't it? Clarissa was different from the rest of us. She...she *liked* it. We would never have approached her with our plans. Turner could never say no to his young wife and her...appetites. But he hadn't been the same since the murder. The vestal virgin sacrifice, you understand. He hated the new Leader, the new members, all of them, even as he was terrified of them, the way all of us were terrified of them. But you don't leave the Society, especially when your wife has been named the High Priestess of Hymen. Oh, how she gloried in that role! She would have learned, in time, when her body began to sag, when even her talents weren't enough."

The woman smiled weakly at Jessica. "We women, we always thought your father hired Jamie Linden to spirit you away that night. Clarissa was so angry with him, you understand, when word came you and Linden couldn't be found. And here you are, landed on your feet."

Could it have been possible? Could her father have paid James to take her away that night, hide her somewhere? Had everything James told her been a lie? Had he been paid to escort her somewhere safe and then realized he'd been foolish to cross the new Leader, and it would be best if he disappeared, as well? Had her frantic offer of her stepmother's jewelry given him the idea? Had he always been looking over his shoulder for the pursuing Society or for Turner Collier, a man searching for his daughter? Oh, how Jessica wanted to believe that. But she would never know....

"All right," Gideon said reassuringly. "We believe you. You had no reason to kill Collier and his wife, just as you say. But who did?"

The brown bottle was uncorked yet again. "Nobody. It had to have been an accident. Turner was the Keeper. That's a very high honor."

Jessica closed her hand over the bottle. Felicity Urban's words had begun to slur, and her breathing had become rapid and shallow, as if she might soon pass out. It was important to keep her talking. "No more laudanum, Mrs. Urban, and only a few more questions, please. You said my father was the Keeper. Did that mean he kept the journals? The bible?"

Felicity nodded. "Yes. That's what the Keeper does. In the tabernacle." She looked up at Gideon. "We don't go there. We never go there. It's the most unholy of unholies, you see. Unholy ground, as they call it in their twisted way. Only Turner knew its location, and he wouldn't tell anyone. Since the days of his lordship's father, Turner was the Entrusted One. Those are the rules."

Gideon leaned forward, his elbows on his knees. "Are you saying even the leader of the Society doesn't know where the journals and bible are kept?"

Again Felicity nodded her head. "Turner told him that was the rule. Wasn't it?"

"Yes, of course. I simply supposed incorrectly. But what about the rites, the ceremonies? Weren't they held in this tabernacle?"

"With the women, you mean? No, never. The tabernacle was where they conducted their meetings. Only the men were allowed, but not since your father died, when it was ceremonially unblessed and then sealed by the Keeper. Archie and I weren't as yet married, so I was never at Redgrave Manor. Lady Orford told us, when we were still allowed to meet. Nobody ever went back there, not since your father died. Only the Keeper, and only then to store the journals and add to the bible. But even that stopped on orders from the Leader, although some of the members still kept to their journals because they liked to write down their exploits." She shivered. "Pigs. Animals."

"Meaning the journals are no longer mandatory?" Gideon asked.

"I mean they are no longer *allowed*. But the Keeper still secretly updated the bible. Lady Orford told me that, as well. She said he wasn't supposed to do that, the Leader had commanded it stop, but he continued. Turner Collier, she said, had an orderly mind and believed in the old ways." Mrs. Urban blinked a single time and then said, "Oh. Do...do you suppose that's why he's dead?"

Jessica and Gideon exchanged glances. She knew what he was thinking because she was thinking the same thing. Whether because of a love of rules or as a result of the leader's demand Turner Collier hand over his daughter to be sacrificed, thanks to her father, the bible still existed. All the old names were there, all the newer names were there. Wherever *there* was...

"What else do you want to know? We meet...the Society meets at designated spots located on the country estates of the members. I was there with the others, waiting, the night Jamie Linden ran off with you, my lady. There had to be a new ceremony, the next full moon. We all suffered for that, we women. But we were glad for you."

"Yes...um...thank you." Jessica had nearly said *I'm sorry,* nearly apologized. There was also the fact that someone eventually had died in her place. *Been sacrificed in her place.* She longed to scream but knew it would serve no purpose. "Gideon? Are we done now?"

"I'm sorry but not quite, no. Mrs. Urban...Felicity...

I know we can never truly understand the horrors that brought you and the others to do what you did. But are you certain you know no other names?"

"We don't. Really, we don't. I told you. The guests didn't bring wives anymore, and they always wore masks, even before the new Leader arrived and took charge. We only knew the ones we...we only knew each other. We only had each other. These last few years have been terrible, the worst of any of them. We couldn't concern ourselves with their wild plans. It was our husbands we needed dead, so that we'd finally be free, out of it. You can understand that. You were so lucky, my lady, that Jamie Linden died. Our husbands seemed to go on forever."

Jessica could only nod her head, unable to meet the woman's eyes. *Too many memories, all rushing back at once. Memories she'd pushed to the back of her mind, as Richard had told her to do, as she'd needed to do.*

Gideon got to his feet. "Very well, Felicity. You've been a tremendous help to us. Now allow me to keep my end of the bargain."

"There is the one other thing," she said as she leaned over, picked up the bandbox and handed it to him. "Archie had a locked cabinet in his study. I was able to locate the key and open it and bring you its contents, in the chance I needed to bargain. But now you can simply have it all."

Gideon took the bandbox and set it down on the table. "Thank you. This may be helpful. But we'd better get you moving now, clear of the city before your husband realizes you've taken this and mounts a pursuit."

Felicity Urban replaced the brown bottle in her reticule and rose unsteadily to her feet. She attempted a wobbly smile. "That's very kind of you, my lord, but don't worry. That's already been taken care of. With the Marquis of Mellis so conveniently dying without it costing us a penny, it was Alfie's turn, you understand. His turn…"

CHAPTER EIGHTEEN

"Pin money," Gideon said, staring into his wineglass once they were back in Portman Square, he and Max sitting together in the study. "The wives hired killers with their pooled allowances. No wonder the *accidents* always seemed to occur at the beginning of each new quarter. My God, it's almost funny."

"So where is the lethal Mrs. Urban off to?" Max asked as he lounged on one of the leather couches, his long legs stretched out in front of him.

"Ireland, although she wouldn't say exactly where," Gideon told him. "She has a cousin who will take her in. Her children were in another room at the shop. A boy and a girl. They took charge of her and led her down to the traveling coach. The boy is perhaps fourteen, and I don't think it's too fanciful of me to say he's the near mirror image of the late Noddy Selkirk. You'd think they would have considered that sort of possibility."

Max merely shrugged. "No one can say the four of us can't claim Maribel as our mother, but can any of us be certain who sired us? It's a question I've considered a time or two while looking at Barry's portrait in the Long Gallery at Redgrave Manor. Haven't you?"

"Not really, no, and I don't think any of us should

consider it again. Now, are you ready to see what's in this bandbox?"

Max got to his feet and wandered over to the desk. "On tenterhooks, actually. But first, tell me more about the bible. You believe his own Society killed Turner Collier and his wife?"

"Jessica and I discussed that on our way back here. Yes, we both think so. The Leader—damn, how I hate saying that word—probably found out Collier was still visiting the tabernacle, still updating the bible, and demanded to learn its location. I saw the bullet holes in their heads, Max, but God only knows what all it took to get Collier to reveal the location before the murderers finally ended it for them. I think we have to assume the tabernacle, wherever it is on Redgrave property, is now empty."

"Unless Collier lied to them about the location," Max pointed out. "A man so dedicated to our father's bizarre rules over the course of two decades may have protected him to the end."

Or cursed the Leader until the end for having made him turn Jessica over to him, Gideon thought, but prudently did not say. "Meaning we still have to locate the tabernacle. I agree."

"Do you think that's where they took Barry? Perhaps propped him up with a glass of wine amid row upon row of journals before they bade him their last farewells? You said there was some sort of ceremony."

"At this point, Max? After hearing what Felicity Urban told us? Yes, I could believe that. I could believe most anything."

"Then it's a good thing Val is with Kate. We wouldn't

want her stumbling over that sort of sight. How's Jessica? She was politeness itself when you introduced us but clearly under some duress. I did warn you about that. I can tell you've only half a mind for what we're about to do, the other half already upstairs with her. It's time you were out of this, brother, and let Val and me take over."

"I agree, as does Richard. I'd apply to Thorny for his opinion, but I believe it's already clear enough that Jessica and I have good reasons to remove ourselves from London for a space," Gideon said, taking out his penknife and cutting the ribbon holding the bandbox shut. "It's leaving things undone that's difficult to come to terms with, as you can imagine. I suppose we could join Kate and Val at Redgrave Manor, on the hunt for our father's bones in the most unholy of unholies, now that we're certain it exists."

"No, not far enough. You have to appear as if you've given up the hunt you started by wearing that damned rose. You're so very good at arrogance, Gideon, but subtlety isn't your strongest suit. Happily, you're also known for going after what you want and then, once you have it, losing interest and moving on to something else you'll acquire just as easily. You're the envy of many men, you rascal. Our enemies, if we can call them that, must be convinced you've tired of this particular game now that you've *acquired* Jessica, and have retired from the field. I suggest Yearlings, for a monthlong idyll with your lovely bride."

Gideon paused in the act of opening the lid of the bandbox. "Really? Yearlings? Have you got a crystal ball hidden somewhere on your person, Max?"

"So you've thought of it, as well? The most minor and most unlikely to be known of the Saltwood holdings and nicely secluded. Yes, it's perfect. We'll see what's in this damn box and then we proceed from there. Whether it's to turn everything, including your suspicions, over to the War Office, or for Val and I to continue what you began— With more finesse, of course."

"Of course," Gideon said, smiling. But the smile soon faded. "Bloody hell. Max, look at this."

He pulled out a black silk hood that would conceal the wearer, fitting closely over face and hair. There were openings for the eyes, nose and mouth. The design, fashioned of pieces of flame red silk sewn to the hood, was simple: a skull on a black background. A grinning skull, at that.

"The stuff of nightmares. With everything you've told me," Max said, reaching into the bandbox to draw out a long black cloak, "this still serves as a shock, doesn't it? We should probably take this to Trixie. I want to know if our dearest father wore one of these ridiculous things."

"Then you'd best do it yet today. She leaves for an interment in the country in the morning. But first, let's see what else is in here. All right, now this is interesting." He lifted out a journal similar to the one belonging to Turner Collier, save for the fact that it was embossed with the current year. "It would seem Archie Urban also preferred to continue keeping a journal of his exploits. Take this with you, as well."

"Bedtime reading?" Max asked, quickly leafing through it, stopping when he came to a rather detailed ink drawing. "No, I suppose not. I believe the man sketched his *endowments* with more of an eye toward optimism than accuracy. Do you really think he's dead?"

Gideon shrugged. "She said she wasn't worried about pursuit, that it had already been taken care of. So, yes, I'm fairly certain Archie Urban has been just lately introduced to the real hellfire club via some sort of fatal accident. You do realize the true beauty of the thing is all of these men supposedly were the victims of accidents. We have to hope the Society hasn't realized it's been under siege. There's Turner Collier's murder, but that had to be the Society. But unless Archie Urban is found with Felicity Urban's sewing scissors stuck in his back, he'll be just another unfortunate accident. We'll know for certain when the morning newspapers arrive, at any rate."

"Leaving Lord Charles as *der käse steht allein*," Max said. "That's part of a German nursery rhyme, brother, taught to me by one of the many tutors Trixie had parading through our childhoods. The cheese stands alone. Lord Charles, our last known link to the Society. You and I might want to pay Lord Cheese a visit tomorrow."

"Hmm? Oh, yes. We could do that. Max, you're the one who'd best understand what I'm seeing here, although I have a sinking feeling I already know. But look at this, tell me what you see." Gideon handed over several sheets of vellum, one of which had an official wax seal affixed to it.

Max spread out the sheets on the desktop, pushing his blue-lens glasses up onto his head and then leaning on his hands as he moved his eyes from one to the other, his expression becoming increasingly hard. When Gideon added several blank sheets of vellum, a metal sealing device meant to impress an image into wax and even a thick stick of red sealing wax and a few lengths of striped grosgrain ribbon, Max swore under his breath.

"Everything necessary to pen official orders. Why would Urban have all of this?"

"I've done some research on that. He acts—acted—as one of Perceval's many undersecretaries. I suppose either he was in charge of them or he pilfered them. Lord Charles, before you ask, volunteers his noble service at the Admiralty. Slacker that I am, I only take up my seat in the House of Lords, run six estates and ride herd on my siblings. We won't even discuss Trixie, because nobody controls her. In any event, you're better suited to tell me what you think is going on here, unless you want to keep up the charade you put on for Kate, that both you and Val are nothing more than feckless dilettantes who could give a damn about anything but your own pleasures while the rest of the nation is at war."

"We'll leave that last little bit for another time," Max told him, lifting the most official-looking of the pages. "This, I'm convinced, is real. A directive, to be distributed with accompanying documents concerning supply ships, their cargos, their destinations up and down the Peninsula." He put down the sheet and piled three more closely written pages on top of it. "The details meant to accompany the command. All right?"

"Yes, I agree. Because, much as we say we're not,

we're about to stop nibbling at the fringes and fully engage Bonaparte once again, that Spain is now committed and we won't have any more debacles as we did with the Convention of Cintra. Wellington is ready to move. Go on."

Max smiled at his brother. "Not as uninformed as many, are you? While Bonaparte plays to the East, the French are being quite helpful, splitting commands between Massena and Soult, who cheerfully loathe each other in the true French manner, so that they refuse to act in concert and should be easily overcome. From the looks of this, I'd say Wellington should be in the field by early July."

"By the looks of it?" Gideon asked, watching his brother closely.

"You don't give up, do you? All right, yes, I've already received my orders and will be taking up my post as part of his staff. Sadly, I don't think he'll allow me my lovely new glasses once I don the uniform."

Gideon was surprised. "I knew you wouldn't be content to do nothing, but I'd supposed you'd go back to the Royal Navy."

"Nothing much to do there anymore, thank God. No, the action will occur on land from now on. Lieutenant-Colonel Lord Maximillien Redgrave. It has a certain ring to it, don't you think? Besides, it's a damned pretty uniform. I've been dutifully studying Julius Caesar's campaigns—brilliant tactician, that man, although yet another proof that men at war should beware beautiful women. Val prefers Sun Tzu and his *Art of War*— I have no idea of that man's pursuit or lack of romantic entanglements. Now for the problem we've got here."

But Gideon wasn't ready to give up. His brothers were going to war. "It was all a hum, wasn't it? Val didn't escort an impecunious friend home to his financially embarrassed father, did he?"

"No. And before you ask, I have no damn idea where he got the dogs. You know Val, he likes to play any part to the hilt. I suppose he felt the dogs fit nicely into his lie."

Gideon managed a smile, but he wasn't amused. "You've never been in a ground battle, at least not to my knowledge. Study is one thing, action is another. You'll be careful?"

"I'll even have my valet pack my galoshes, if that will help ease your mind," Max said, still frowning over the papers spread out on the desktop. "And before you ask, because I know you will, our dear brother, Valentine, will for the most part retain his well-earned reputation as a useless bit of fashion and frivolity, right here on good English soil. Other than that, he probably wouldn't want you to question him. Younger sons, Gideon, it's either the army or the church. Neither of us is suited for the church, now, are we?"

"I wish I could go with you."

"The curse of being the earl, hmm? But I think you've had your fun. Truthfully, I think you've been bloody damn brilliant." He finished separating the piles of paper.

The official documents said one thing, about ships, sailing times, types of supplies, destinations for the delivery of same as per Wellington's hopeful progression along the Peninsula. Notes, most likely written in Urban's hand, did not match. Not at all. The ports of call had been shifted in their order, in some cases the supplies halved.

"So, Gideon, if I'm holding the official documents— dated three weeks ago, as you've surely seen—what do you think the Admiralty is not only holding but distributing down the chain of command? Oh, and didn't you tell me Lord Charles is at the Admiralty? Do you suppose he has anything at all to do with notifying ships' captains, purveyors? Never mind, we're both sure of that, aren't we?"

Gideon slammed his fist down on the desk, incensed. "Those sons of bitches! This isn't some sick game with capes and masks and orgies. This is treason. Wellington won't be resupplied once he begins his campaign. They'll run out of food, munitions, blankets, medicines, everything, while it all sits in the wrong ports or travels inland in the opposite direction of the troops. We're looking at disaster. Hell, *you're* looking at disaster, because you'll be there. My own brother."

"Along with a lot of good men, many of them dying for no reason. That's my conclusion, as well." Max gathered up the papers and the rest of it, and replaced them in the bandbox. "You complained about leaving things undone, but if you hadn't stumbled over those supposed accidents and gone out investigating, we'd know none of this. You and Jessica are bloody well heroes. My compliments. Go tell her that, brother, before getting the two of you somewhere safe, because without her, you'd still just be wearing that damned rose and maybe getting your head bashed in for your efforts to find Barry and have him properly replanted. I'm off to get this mess taken care of before it becomes a debacle."

"Wait. How will you know you aren't taking this information to one of the Society, or someone the Society controls?"

"Please, brother, give me some credit. I did sail with the sainted Nelson at Trafalger, if you'll recall."

"As a wet-behind-the-ears coxswain, not an admiral," Gideon retorted, grinning, as the brothers had never been above teasing one another.

"True. But as our own Royal Duke of Clarence has been known to say, especially when deep in his cups, 'There is no place superior to the quarterdeck of a British man-of-war for the education of a gentleman.'"

His brother had never lacked audacity. "You're taking this directly to the duke?"

Max slipped his blue-lens glasses down onto his nose once more. "He was a sailor with Nelson, too, in his time, and he's third in line to the throne the Little Corporal is after. Can you think of anyone less prone to be a traitor?"

JESSICA SAT AT THE VERY head of the bed, her knees drawn up tight, her arms wrapped around her shins. Making herself smaller, wishing she could disappear. She'd taken the pins from her hair, and it now fell around her face like a living curtain, helping to hide her.

She knew what she was doing. She was eighteen again, locked in an attic room at some foreign inn, hoping James would forget her existence, at least for the night.

Or she was shivering, huddled on the floor in some dark corner, holding the torn fabric of her night rail close against her, still feeling the sting of his hand even as he snored drunkenly, sprawled naked across the width of the only bed in the room, thinking of the many ways she could kill him.

Women were smarter. Sex was a woman's ultimate weapon. Men feared women because they knew females were the stronger sex.

It all sounded so wonderful, in theory. Gideon had been very kind and understanding.

But Jessica knew the reality, as did Felicity Urban and Lady Orford and all those other women.

All the laws were against them. The way their bodies were formed was against them. Their lesser physical strength was against them. There was no help, not anywhere.

There was only one way to defeat the monsters, only one way to be completely free of them.

They had to die.

"Jessica?"

She kept her head down, saying nothing. She couldn't face him now, not right now. Perhaps never. Not with what she had to tell him. *Had* to tell him. Keeping the secret was no longer possible.

"Jessica," Gideon said again, even as she felt the weight of his body as he sat on the side of the bed. "What is it? What's wrong?"

"They killed them," she said quietly, and she could feel Gideon moving closer, the better to hear her. "They did it because they had to. There was no other way."

"I know," he said softly.

She lifted her head, looked at him through her hair. "Do you? Can you, really? Or should they have asked for help, or found a way to disappear? Did they really have to kill them? Is there any way to justify what they did?"

"The law wouldn't help, even if the women could get anyone to believe what they were told. The same for their families, I'm afraid. The truth is too bizarre. If they tried to run off, they could be found, dragged back, and God only knows what would have happened to them then. They watched other women die, others perhaps take their own lives, others locked up. There comes a point, Jessica, when the only alternative is no longer unthinkable."

Tendrils of hair clung to her damp cheeks, and she used the palms of her hands to push them aside. "Do you know what it's like to have no power over your own life, your own body? You become a *thing*. You can cry, and despair, and feel so much anger inside you, so much hate…until one day you don't feel anything anymore. Nothing. That's the worst, feeling nothing, most especially not hope. You even begin to blame yourself, believe what he's telling you, that you're worthless, that something's *wrong* with you. Your father gave you away, was going to turn you over to monsters, nobody was ever going to save you and you couldn't save yourself. There was nothing. Just…nothing. Mrs. Urban said my father may have been trying to save me. *Save* me? But I couldn't know that, could I? I'll never know if that was true. He was a terrible man, I know that, but if he had tried to save me…? It would mean so much."

Gideon sat beside her and pulled her close, his arm around her shoulders. "No more, Jessica. It's over now. You've come so far, and you accomplished it all on your own." He pressed a kiss against her hair. "You're remarkable. I knew it from the first moment I saw you, and I believe it more every day."

She wasn't ready to listen. "I've tried so hard to forget, to put it behind me. Like some bad dream. Pretend it never happened. Now it's all come back. The worst of it…"

"I shouldn't have taken you along today," he said, stroking her arm as if to comfort her. "I had no idea Felicity Urban was going to say what she said. I'd assumed from the first the Society was killing its own members. You didn't need to hear that."

"But perhaps I did." Jessica pushed herself away from him, needing to see his face when she said what she had to say. "I know Richard didn't tell you the entire truth about the night James…died. I've tried to tell myself it didn't matter, that you didn't need to know."

"And I don't," Gideon told her. "Jessica, there's a future out there for us now, if we want it. I know I want it, just as I know I rushed you into bed, into marriage. I'm an arrogant bastard, God knows I am, and when I see something I want, I go after it, often without considering the consequences. You know that. You pointed it out to me quite well. I don't own you. I don't want to own you. I want you with me, I want to be with you. You, sweetheart. Not your past, and not mine. What we have, what I hope we have, begins now."

Jessica was crying in earnest now, her tears running down her face, blurring her vision. He hadn't said the words, but he'd said everything but the words. *I truly do love you.*

She couldn't allow him to say those words until she told him what she had to tell him. Needed to tell him.

"The...the night James died. It was one of the worst. He'd lost, badly, and he blamed me. We were stranded at the inn for several days because of the weather. After three nights, the other players were used to seeing me, and were ignoring me. That's why he lost. He didn't even have enough money to pay for our lodging. He said...he said there were men who liked their women... reluctant. He'd already arranged for someone to come to our room that same night."

"Jessica, don't..."

She held up her hand to stop him. "I told him, no, begged him. No, please, no. I'm your wife, you can't do this, you promised. He hit me, and then he threw me down on the bed and straddled me. He...he had lengths of cloth, and he was going to tie my arms and legs to the bedposts. First...first he shoved one of the cloths into my mouth, so I couldn't scream. I wanted to die. I just wanted to die. Except I couldn't. You don't die just because you want to. So I fought him. One moment I was struggling to keep him from grabbing my wrist, and the next he was this heavy weight on top of me."

"Richard."

Jessica nodded. "He'd hit him with something. I managed to wriggle out from beneath James, and then suddenly he was turned on his back, and now it was this man I recognized from the nights at the card table, straddling my husband. He grabbed a pillow and pressed it down over James's face."

"It's all right. I already know that, Jessica. Richard did tell me."

She began shaking her head. "Not all of it. I knew what was happening. The stranger was going to smother my husband, rid me of my problem. And all I could think was, good, good, *do it*. I didn't know who this stranger was, but he'd seemed kind, and anyone was better than James, what I'd already endured, what James had planned for me now. I wanted him *dead*. But then...then James began to struggle. I was terrified! It wasn't going to work. My rescuer couldn't hold him down on his own, it was all going to be for nothing, and James would punish me. It would be even worse than before. I couldn't face that, I couldn't. When the man told me to help him, told me to sit on James's legs..."

"Oh, sweetheart..."

Jessica looked at Gideon through her tears. "I didn't want to tell you. I never wanted to tell you. I told myself I could forget, that it was long ago and...and I had no choice. Like those women. I'm not who you think I am. I'm a murderess. I helped kill my own husband. There should have been another way, shouldn't there? For those women, for me? Was there really no other choice?"

He gathered her to him, pulling her half across his lap. She grabbed on to him, holding on fiercely, needing him close. "It's all right, it's all right," he crooned over and over again, rocking her as he would a child. "It was his life or yours, sweetheart. That's all there is to it. No, there was no other choice. I just thank God for Richard, and that you had the courage to help save yourself. It's all right, all right...you did what was right..."

And still she held on, seeking his comfort, needing his reassurance, some sort of absolution. Until the pictures in her mind began to fade. Until it was Gideon she felt all around her, strong and sure, and not the struggles of her dying husband. Until her body began to relax, her mind begin to drift. Until she was free, until the past at last faded and only the future remained. Until she sighed and closed her eyes, and finally drifted into sleep.

It was dark beyond the windows when she awoke and eased herself into a more comfortable position.

"Jessica?"

She snuggled closer to the warmth of Gideon's body. *Don't let go, don't let go.*

"Sweetheart? Open your eyes, please. I saw them open a moment ago. Come on, do it again. I want to tell you something."

"You don't have to, Gideon. I know what I did was wrong. I've always known. But I'd do it again, I really would. I only wish I'd done it before Richard had to share my sin."

"I see. And those women? Were they wrong, too? You told me they had no other choice. But you, alone, barely more than a girl, trapped into marriage with a man of no conscience, adrift in a strange country— you could have done it differently? You absolve those women, but you can't absolve yourself?"

"Don't—"

"Don't what, Jessica? Don't confuse you with facts? The sin isn't yours, nor is it Richard's. The sin belongs to James Linden. The sin belongs to all, men and women alike, who take advantage of the weak and helpless just because they can. And their mistake is in believing their victims are incapable of defending themselves."

"Richard said it was war, and James was the enemy."

"Richard's a very wise man. And in war, when it's kill or be killed, you can't hesitate, you can't hold back when you get the chance to strike the final blow."

"I know," she said, sighing. "Inside my head, I know. I didn't know if *you* knew. I wanted to tell you. From the beginning, Gideon, I wanted to tell you."

"And now you have," he said, cupping her cheek in his hand. "And the world hasn't ended, has it? In fact, nothing has changed, except, I sincerely hope, your heart is lighter. Your secret was a burden you shouldn't have carried this long. You didn't *cause* any of this. God, it began with my own grandfather."

"No," she said, pressing her fingers against his mouth. "It began when time began. There's always been opportunities for evil in the world, just as there's always been opportunities for good. I met a priest a few years ago, when Richard and I were in Belgium. He told me God gives a choice between the two, but it's up to us which one we choose. I didn't understand him then, but I think I do now. I'm so glad I met you, Gideon. Thank you."

He put his hand on top of hers, kissed her fingers. "You're classing me with the good, sweetheart? I'm flattered. No, I'm humbled. I could point out all the possible flaws in your assessment of me, but I'd like to believe I'm not an idiot."

She gave his chest a playful push. "I didn't say you're perfect, *Giddy*," she told him, laughing, her heart feeling light and free and fairly *giddy* itself. The storm was finally over, her personal storm, her last demon laid to rest, even if so much else remained unsettled and uncertain. "You're arrogant, not above pushing your advantage, rather enjoy intimidating people. You have a tendency, I believe, to think you're always right. Oh, and when you stick that quizzing glass to your eye you look positively—"

She giggled as he put her down on her back, bringing his face close to hers. "I look positively what?" he asked her.

"Positively wonderful," she told him as he brought his mouth down on hers, and her eyes fluttered closed, the better to experience the sensation his touch sent shimmering along her body.

"I have so much to tell you," he whispered against her ear. "So very many things. Important things. But none so important as this. I love you, Jessica Redgrave. I want to spend my lifetime loving you. Beginning now."

He took her mouth again, and her surrender was swift and total. There had always been passion, from the first moment he'd touched her. No, from the first moment she'd seen him standing just inside the door on Jermyn Street, looking for all the world as if he owned the room and everyone in it.

She'd believed her months with James Linden had damaged something within her, had destroyed whatever womanly feelings she could ever have. Any desire she might otherwise have had.

But that one look, that one touch…Gideon had changed her life even if he had gone away that night and she'd never seen him again. That had been the true reason behind the dare, the challenge she had set him. Over and above her worry for Adam. She couldn't let this man out of her life, not until she knew if there was still hope for her, that she still had a heart, even if she might be risking breaking it.

Now the last barrier that could have stood between them was gone. He knew her secrets, all of them, and he hadn't turned away. She'd been right to trust him, right to love him. Love him *quite truly*.

His kisses, his touch, were slow, not devoid of passion, but willing that passion to build slowly, following on the heels of what seemed to be wonderment, a joint voyage of discovery, new to them both even as they already had shared so much physical intimacy.

Jessica felt tears on her cheeks, but this time they were tears of happiness. Her body was a gift freely given, his every touch a blessing, a benediction. She returned his kisses, smoothed her hands along his firm body, gloried in his soft words of love.

When he came to her, when at last they were one, he raised his head to look down into her face. "Do you feel it, Jessica?" he asked, his voice low and intense. "It's the first time, for both of us. Clean and fresh and new… The very first time."

"I love you, Gideon Redgrave," she told him. "I love you quite truly."

He smiled, perhaps a bit bemused by her words, but then he kissed her again, sinking more deeply inside her, and took them both flying high above the world to a place where it was only the two of them.

Which was the way it should be.

He was hers, and she was his, and they were building a lifetime of love….

EPILOGUE

"WELL, WOULD YOU LOOK who's finally remembered a world still exists outside the door to their bedchamber," Max said as Gideon and Jessica entered the morning room the following day, hand-in-hand.

Gideon personally pulled back a chair and assisted his bride into it. "Be nice, Max, or we'll leave again. And weren't you the one who advised me it was time to depart the field in favor of an expert like yourself? An expert, I might point out, who wouldn't have known a damn thing, save for the efforts of two amateurs whom only one short day ago you declared heroes."

"Gideon," Jessica scolded, and he delighted in the way her cheeks flushed and she made herself busy spreading her serviette in her lap.

"No, Jessica, he's right. Not that I suggested he then immediately lock you up here for twenty-four hours. I believe I mentioned Yearlings."

"We leave for Yearlings tomorrow. In the meantime, I would suppose you have news for us?"

"That I do. Firstly, I'm sad to say one Archibald Urban had the unfortunate bad luck to somehow be launched out into the street just as a runaway dray wagon filled with beer barrels seemed to—according to witnesses quoted in the *Morning Post*—all but aim itself at him, to disastrous and quite fatal results. I'm sad to say it because he would have been more useful to us alive. As it is, we've decided to content ourselves keeping a close watch on Lord Charles, in the hopes he'll lead us to some of his cronies. To that end, I'll be leaving tomorrow for Urban's interment in Yorkshire, observing from a distance, of course. It will be interesting to see who else is in attendance. We already know his wife and children will not be present. They are, again according to the newspapers, visiting relatives in Edinburgh."

"Interesting. And, speaking of internments, I'm supposing Trixie has left town?"

"She has. All but danced out the door like a young girl, if you can believe that, as if she's on her way to a party. As to the rest of it, no, she won't look at the journal until she returns to London, if then. As to the question you urged me not to think of again, our dearest grandmother reminded me she's always harbored the notion I may be an idiot."

"I don't understand," Jessica said, looking at the two men.

"Another time, sweetheart," Gideon told her as he lifted her hand to press a kiss against her fingertips, and then quickly searched his mind for another question. "So everything went well with the royal duke?"

"Splendidly, yes. Once on the Peninsula, I will salute the pair of you every time I lift a forkful of stringy mutton to my lips."

"So nothing has changed there?" Gideon asked as Jessica laid her hand on his forearm, knowing his concern for his brother. "You're not to be reassigned to watching Lord Charles, for instance?"

"No, that's for someone more subtle than I am, and before you volunteer, I meant it when I said you and Jessica need to be clear of here for a while."

"And we agree." Gideon sighed. "It's to be Valentine, isn't it?"

Max adjusted his blue-lens eyeglasses, most probably to cover the concern in his own eyes. "Partially, when he's not hunting in hopes of locating the bible. It would be strange to have outsiders making themselves at home at Redgrave Manor, you understand. Although he won't be alone in that mission. Kate, you see, is about to acquire a suitor."

Gideon and Jessica exchanged startled glances. "Kate? Is she aware of this?"

"Hardly. Val will be welcoming his friend for a visit on the estate. Although I've already waged our brother a monkey it won't take her above three days to figure out the truth, at which point I believe I'll be a very happy man. I'll be aboard ship and heading for Lisbon. I've already advised Val by post he'd be wiser to disregard his orders and tell Kate outright, although I doubt he'll listen. But I'm told he's a good man, and that he expressly requested the assignment. He knows somebody with the power to make those decisions, although how he heard of the Society at all still eludes me."

"Max, you're certain he's trustworthy—this person who vouches for the man?"

"I would think so, Jessica, yes. The *somebody* is Spencer Perceval himself."

"Gideon?" Jessica asked. "Are you thinking what I'm thinking? A man who *exudes* power?"

"The Marquis of Singleton, yes."

Max laid down his fork and stared across the table at them. "How in bloody blazes did you know that?"

Jessica smiled at her husband. "And he dismisses us as *amateurs*," she said, and then damn if she didn't wink at him. God, how he loved this woman.

"We'll speak again later, Max. But for now, please excuse us," Gideon said, grabbing up the fully-loaded plate Thorndyke had just set in front of him with one hand and taking Jessica's hand in his as he urged her to rise.

"What? Where are you two going?"

Gideon grinned as he looked at his goggle-eyed brother. "Why, I think that should be obvious, to an *expert* like you. My wife and I are going to breakfast in bed."

* * * * *

Author's Note

History and writings from the time show us that while England fought valiantly to defeat Napoleon, there was a segment of the general population who looked to the man as their possible savior, and his form of governing a welcome change from that of the House of Hanover. Further reading on the subject is available in Senior Lecturer Stuart Semmel's Yale University Press book, *Napoleon and the British*.

As to hellfire clubs, although Sir Francis Dashwood's may be the best known, their number was quite high, not only in England but in Ireland, as well. They ranged from the ridiculous to the truly macabre, could be politically neutral or fiercely partisan, even seditious. Members for the most part preferred to think of themselves as witty intellectuals and, indeed, memberships could include high-ranking nobles as well as those in government and the arts and sciences. No matter what, the emphasis was on devil worship, real or feigned, and the primary occupations debauchery and the pursuit of sexual pleasure.

Although the supposed heyday of hellfire clubs ranged from as early as 1719 and seemed to drop out of popularity in the 1780s, for the purpose of this series, the tradition is carried on with the Society.

After all, there are those who believe hellfire clubs continue until this day. Which, knowing their reasons for existing, is enough to give anyone pause, isn't it?

Join *New York Times* bestselling authors

FERN MICHAELS

and Jill Marie Landis, with Dorsey Kelley
and Chelley Kitzmiller,
for four timeless love stories set on one
very special California ranch.

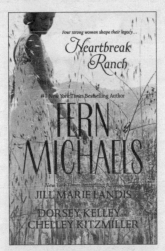

Heartbreak Ranch

Available now!

**His past has haunted him for a lifetime...
but one woman could be his salvation**

A sensual and provocative new historical tale from
New York Times bestselling author

SARAH McCARTY

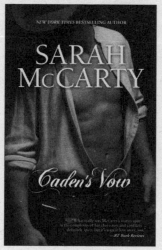

Caden's Vow

Pick it up today!

www.Harlequin.com

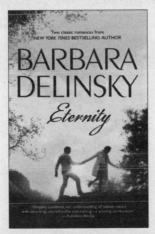

A grand old English estate where no one cares
overmuch for propriety....

Top historical romance authors

CAROLE MORTIMER
and HELEN DICKSON

welcome you to Castonbury Park, where all's fair in love,
whether in the lord's drawing room or in the servants' quarters!

Scandalous
Whispers

Pick up your copy today!

REQUEST YOUR FREE BOOKS!

2 FREE NOVELS
FROM THE ROMANCE COLLECTION
PLUS 2 FREE GIFTS!

YES! Please send me 2 FREE novels from the Romance Collection and my 2 FREE gifts (gifts are worth about $10). After receiving them, if I don't wish to receive any more books, I can return the shipping statement marked "cancel." If I don't cancel, I will receive 4 brand-new novels every month and be billed just $5.99 per book in the U.S. or $6.49 per book in Canada. That's a saving of at least 25% off the cover price. It's quite a bargain! Shipping and handling is just 50¢ per book in the U.S. and 75¢ per book in Canada.* I understand that accepting the 2 free books and gifts places me under no obligation to buy anything. I can always return a shipment and cancel at any time. Even if I never buy another book, the two free books and gifts are mine to keep forever.

194/394 MDN FELQ

Name _____ (PLEASE PRINT) _____

Address _____ Apt. # _____

City _____ State/Prov. _____ Zip/Postal Code _____

Signature (if under 18, a parent or guardian must sign) _____

Mail to the **Reader Service:**
IN U.S.A.: P.O. Box 1867, Buffalo, NY 14240-1867
IN CANADA: P.O. Box 609, Fort Erie, Ontario L2A 5X3

Not valid for current subscribers to the Romance Collection
or the Romance/Suspense Collection.

Want to try two free books from another line?
Call 1-800-873-8635 or visit www.ReaderService.com.

* Terms and prices subject to change without notice. Prices do not include applicable taxes. Sales tax applicable in N.Y. Canadian residents will be charged applicable taxes. Offer not valid in Quebec. This offer is limited to one order per household. All orders subject to credit approval. Credit or debit balances in a customer's account(s) may be offset by any other outstanding balance owed by or to the customer. Please allow 4 to 6 weeks for delivery. Offer available while quantities last.

Your Privacy—The Reader Service is committed to protecting your privacy. Our Privacy Policy is available online at www.ReaderService.com or upon request from the Reader Service.

We make a portion of our mailing list available to reputable third parties that offer products we believe may interest you. If you prefer that we not exchange your name with third parties, or if you wish to clarify or modify your communication preferences, please visit us at www.ReaderService.com/consumerchoice or write to us at Reader Service Preference Service, P.O. Box 9062, Buffalo, NY 14269. Include your complete name and address.

Two timeless stories of love and intrigue
from *New York Times* bestselling author

Catherine Anderson

endless night

Available now!

KASEY MICHAELS

77639	MUCH ADO ABOUT ROGUES	___ $7.99 U.S.	___ $9.99 CAN.
77610	A MIDSUMMER NIGHT'S SIN	___ $7.99 U.S.	___ $9.99 CAN.
77591	THE TAMING OF THE RAKE	___ $7.99 U.S.	___ $9.99 CAN.
77463	HOW TO WED A BARON	___ $7.99 U.S.	___ $9.99 CAN.
77433	HOW TO BEGUILE A BEAUTY	___ $7.99 U.S.	___ $9.99 CAN.
77376	HOW TO TAME A LADY	___ $7.99 U.S.	___ $8.99 CAN.
77371	HOW TO TEMPT A DUKE	___ $7.99 U.S.	___ $8.99 CAN.
77191	A MOST UNSUITABLE GROOM	___ $6.99 U.S.	___ $8.50 CAN.

(limited quantities available)

TOTAL AMOUNT	$ _____
POSTAGE & HANDLING	$ _____
($1.00 FOR 1 BOOK, 50¢ for each additional)	
APPLICABLE TAXES*	$ _____
TOTAL PAYABLE	$ _____

(check or money order—please do not send cash)

To order, complete this form and send it, along with a check or money order for the total above, payable to Harlequin HQN, to: **In the U.S.:** 3010 Walden Avenue, P.O. Box 9077, Buffalo, NY 14269-9077; **In Canada:** P.O. Box 636, Fort Erie, Ontario, L2A 5X3.

Name: _____

Address: _____ City: _____

State/Prov.: _____ Zip/Postal Code: _____

Account Number (if applicable): _____

075 CSAS

*New York residents remit applicable sales taxes.
*Canadian residents remit applicable GST and provincial taxes.

HARLEQUIN® HQN™
™ www.Harlequin.com

PHKM1212BL